NORA ROBERTS

Catherine and Amanda
THE Calhoun Women

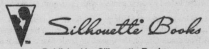

Published by Silhouette Books
America's Publisher of Contemporary Romance

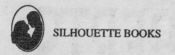 SILHOUETTE BOOKS

THE CALHOUN WOMEN
CATHERINE AND AMANDA

Copyright © 1998 by Harlequin Books S.A.

ISBN 0-373-48354-6

The publisher acknowledges the copyright holders of the individual works as follows:

COURTING CATHERINE
Copyright © 1991 by Nora Roberts

A MAN FOR AMANDA
Copyright © 1991 by Nora Roberts

**Praise for *New York Times*
bestselling author**

NORA ROBERTS

"There's no mystery about why Roberts is a bestselling author of romances and mainstream novels: she delivers the goods with panache and wit."

—*Publishers Weekly*

"Move over, Sidney Sheldon: the world has a new master of romantic suspense, and her name is Nora Roberts."

—*Rex Reed*

"Roberts is indeed a word artist, painting her story and her characters with vitality and verve."

—*Los Angeles Daily News*

"Nora Roberts is the very best there is—she's superb in everything she does."

—*Romantic Times*

"Characters that touch the heart, stories that intrigue, romance that sizzles—Nora Roberts has mastered it all."

—*Rendezvous*

"Ms. Roberts is an enormously gifted writer whose incredible range and intensity guarantee the very best of reading. So move over, bestsellers. The new 'top gun' of contemporary fiction has arrived."

—*Rave Reviews*

"A consistently entertaining writer."   —*USA Today*

Books by Nora Roberts

CONTENTS

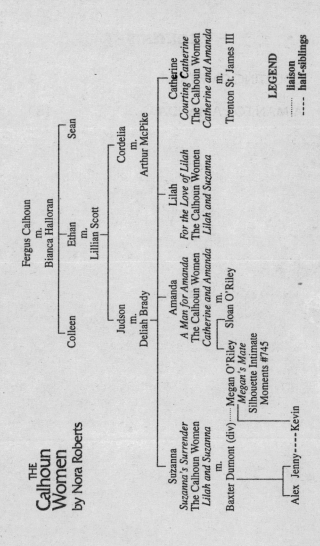

THE
Calhoun Women
by Nora Roberts

Fergus Calhoun
m.
Bianca Halloran

Colleen   Ethan   Sean
          m.
          Lillian Scott

Judson   Amanda   Lilah   Cordelia   Catherine
m.   A Man for Amanda   For the Love of Lilah   m.   Courting Catherine
Deliah Brady   The Calhoun Women   The Calhoun Women   Arthur McPike   The Calhoun Women
                         Catherine and Amanda   Lilah and Suzanna   Catherine and Amanda
                              m.   m.
                          Sloan O'Riley   Trenton St. James III

Suzanna
Suzanna's Surrender
The Calhoun Women
Lilah and Suzanna
m.
Baxter Dumont (div) .... Megan O'Riley
                              Megan's Mate
                              Silhouette Intimate
                              Moments #745

Alex   Jenny ---- Kevin

LEGEND
.... liaison
- - - - half-siblings

COURTING CATHERINE

Prologue

Bar Harbor, Maine
June 12, 1912

I saw him on the cliffs overlooking Frenchman Bay. He was tall and dark and young. Even from a distance, as I walked with little Ethan's hand in mine, I could see the defiant set of his shoulders. He held the brush as though it were a saber, his palette like a shield. Indeed it seemed to me that he was dueling with his canvas rather than painting on it. So deep was his concentration, so fast and fierce the flicks of his wrist, one would have thought his life depended on what he created there.

Perhaps it did.

I thought it odd, even amusing. My image of artists had always been one of gentle souls who see things we mortals cannot, and suffer in their quest to create them for us.

Yet I knew, before he turned and looked at me, that I would not see a gentle face.

It seemed that he was the product of an artist himself. A rough sculptor who had shorn away at an oak slab, carving out a high brow, dark hooded eyes, a long straight nose and full sensual mouth. Even the sweep of his hair might have been hewn from some ebony wood.

How he stared at me! Even now I can feel the heat rise to my face and the dampness spring to my palms. The wind was in his hair, sweet and moist from the sea, and ruffled the loose shirt he wore that was splattered and streaked from his paint. With the rocks and sky at his back, he looked very proud, very angry, as if he owned this jut of land—or the entire island— and I was the intruder.

He stood in silence for what seemed like forever, his eyes so intense, so fierce somehow that my tongue cleaved to the roof of my mouth. Then little Ethan began to babble and tug at my hand. The angry glare in his eyes softened. He smiled. I know a heart does not stop at such moments. And yet...

I found myself stammering, apologizing for the intrusion, lifting Ethan into my arms before my bright and curious little boy could rush forward toward the rocks.

He said, "Wait."

And taking up pad and pencil began to sketch as I stood immobile and trembling for reasons I cannot fathom. Ethan stilled and smiled, somehow as mesmerized by the man as I. I could feel the sun on my back and the wind on my face, could smell the water and the wild roses.

"Your hair should be loose," he said, and, putting

the pencil aside, walked toward me. "I've painted sunsets that were less dramatic." He reached out and touched Ethan's bright red hair. "You share the color with your young brother."

"My son." Why was my voice so breathless? "He is my son. I'm Mrs. Fergus Calhoun," I said while his eyes seemed to devour my face.

"Ah, The Towers." He looked beyond me then to where the peaks and turrets of our summer home could be seen on the higher cliff above. "I've admired your house, Mrs. Calhoun."

Before I could reply, Ethan was reaching out, laughing, and the man scooped him up. I could only stare as he stood with his back to the wind, holding my child, jiggling him easily on his hip.

"A fine boy."

"And an energetic one. I thought to take him for a walk to give his nanny a bit of a rest. She has less trouble with my two other children combined than with young Ethan."

"You have other children?"

"Yes, a girl, a year older than Ethan, and a baby, not quite one. We only arrived for the season yesterday. Do you live on the island?"

"For now. Will you pose for me, Mrs. Calhoun?"

I blushed. But beneath the embarrassment was a deep and dreamy pleasure. Still, I knew the impropriety and Fergus's temper. So I refused, politely, I hoped. He did not persist, and I am ashamed to say that I felt a keen disappointment. When he gave Ethan back to me, his eyes were on mine—a deep slate gray that seemed to see more than my face. Perhaps more than anyone had seen before. He bid me good day, so I turned to walk with my child back to The Towers, my home and my duties.

I knew as surely as if I had turned to look, that he watched me until I was hidden by the cliff. My heart thundered.

Chapter One

Bar Harbor
1991

Trenton St. James III was in a foul mood. He was the kind of man who expected doors to open when he knocked, phones to be answered when he dialed. What he did not expect, and hated to tolerate, was having his car break down on a narrow two-lane road ten miles from his destination. At least the car phone had allowed him to track down the closest mechanic. He hadn't been overly thrilled about riding into Bar Harbor in the cab of the tow truck while strident rock had bellowed from the speakers and his rescuer had sung along, off-key, in between bites of an enormous ham sandwich.

"Hank, you just call me Hank, ayah," the driver had told him then took a long pull from a bottle of soda. "C.C.'ll fix you up all right and tight. Best damn mechanic in Maine, you ask anybody."

Trent decided, under the circumstances, he'd have to take just-call-me-Hank's word for it. To save time and trouble, he'd had the driver drop him off in the village with directions to the garage and a grimy business card Trent studied while holding it gingerly at the corners.

But as with any situation Trent found himself in, he decided to make it work for him. While his car was being dealt with, he made half a dozen calls to his office back in Boston—putting the fear of God into a flurry of secretaries, assistants and junior vice-presidents. It put him in a slightly better frame of mind.

He lunched on the terrace of a small restaurant, paying more attention to the paperwork he took from his briefcase than the excellent lobster salad or balmy spring breeze. He checked his watch often, drank too much coffee and, with impatient brown eyes, studied the traffic that streamed up and down the street.

Two of the waitresses on lunch shift discussed him at some length. It was early April, several weeks before the height of the season, so the restaurant wasn't exactly hopping with customers.

They agreed that this one was a beaut, from the top of his dark blond head to the tips of his highly polished Italian shoes. They agreed that he was a businessman, and an *important* one, because of the leather briefcase and spiffy gray suit and tie. Plus, he wore cuff links. Gold ones.

They decided, as they rolled flatware into napkins for the next shift, that he was young for it, no more than thirty. Outrageously handsome was their unanimous vote while they took turns refilling his coffee cup and getting closer looks. Nice clean features, they agreed, with a kind of polished air that would have been just a tad slick if it hadn't been for the eyes.

They were dark and broody and impatient, making the waitresses speculate as to whether he'd been stood up by a woman. Though they couldn't imagine any female in her right mind doing so.

Trent paid no more attention to them than he would have to anyone who performed a paid service. That disappointed them. The whopping tip he left made up for it nicely. It would have surprised him that the tip would have meant more to the waitresses if he had offered a smile with it.

He relocked his briefcase and prepared to take the brisk walk to the mechanic at the end of town. He wasn't a cold man and wouldn't have considered himself aloof. As a St. James he had grown up with servants who had quietly and efficiently gone about the business of making his life simpler. He paid well, even generously. If he didn't show any overt appreciation or personal interest, it was simply because it never occurred to him.

At the moment, his mind was on the deal he hoped to close by the end of the week. Hotels were his business, with the emphasis on luxury and resorts. The summer before, Trent's father had located a particular property while he and his fourth wife had been yachting in Frenchman Bay. While Trenton St. James II's instincts as to women were notoriously skewed, his business instincts were always on target.

He'd begun negotiations almost immediately for the buy of the enormous stone house overlooking Frenchman Bay. His appetite had been whetted by the reluctance of the owners to sell what had to be a white elephant as a private home. As expected, the senior Trenton had been turning things his way, and the deal was on the way to being set.

Then Trent had found the whole business dumped into his lap as his father was once again tangled in a complicated divorce.

Wife number four had lasted almost eighteen months, Trent mused. Which was two months longer than wife number three. Trent accepted, fatalistically, that there was bound to be a number five around the corner. The old man was as addicted to marriage as he was to real estate.

Trent was determined to close the deal on The Towers before the ink had dried on this last divorce decree. As soon as he got his car out of the garage, he would drive up and take a firsthand look at the place.

Because of the time of year, many of the shops were closed as he walked through town, but he could see the possibilities. He knew that during the season the streets of Bar Harbor were crammed with tourists with credit cards and travelers' checks at the ready. And tourists needed hotels. He had the statistics in his briefcase. With solid planning, he figured The Towers would cull a hefty percentage of that tourist trade within fifteen months.

All he had to do was convince four sentimental women and their aunt to take the money and run.

He checked his watch again as he turned the corner toward the mechanic's. Trent had given him precisely two hours to deal with whatever malfunction the BMW had suffered. That, he was convinced, was enough.

Of course he could have taken the company plane up from Boston. It would have been more practical, and Trent was nothing if not a practical man. But he'd wanted to drive. Needed to, he admitted. He'd needed those few hours of quiet and solitude.

Business was booming, but his personal life was going to hell.

Who would have thought that Marla would suddenly shove an ultimatum down his throat? Marriage or nothing. It still baffled him. She had known since the beginning of their relationship that marriage had never been an option. He had no intention of taking a ride on the roller coaster his father seemed to thrive on.

Not that he wasn't—hadn't been—fond of her. She was lovely and well-bred, intelligent and successful in her field of fashion design. With Marla, there was never a hair out of place, and Trent appreciated that kind of meticulousness in a woman. Just as he had appreciated her practical attitude toward their relationship.

She had claimed not to want marriage or children or pledges of undying love. Trent considered it a personal betrayal that she suddenly changed her tune and demanded it all.

He hadn't been able to give it to her.

They had parted, stiff as strangers, only two weeks before. She was already engaged to a golf pro.

It stung. But even as it stung, it convinced him he had been right all along. Women were unstable, fickle creatures, and marriage was a bloodless kind of suicide.

She hadn't even loved him. Thank God. She had simply wanted "commitment and stability," as she had put it. Trent felt, smugly, that she would soon find out marriage was the last place to find either.

Because he knew it was unproductive to dwell on mistakes, he allowed thoughts of Marla to pass out of his mind. He would take a vacation from females, he decided.

Trent paused outside the white cinder-block building with its scatter of cars in the lot. The sign over the open garage doors read C.C.'s Automovation. Just beneath the title, which Trent found ostentatious, was an offer of twenty-four-hour towing, complete auto repairs and refinishing—foreign and domestic—and free estimates.

Through the doors, he could hear rock music. Trent let out a sigh as he went in.

The hood was up on his BMW, and a pair of dirty boots peeked out from beneath the car. The mechanic was tapping the toes of the boots together in time to the din of music. Frowning, Trent glanced around the garage area. It smelled of grease and honeysuckle— a ridiculous combination. The place itself was a disorganized and grimy mess of tools and auto parts, something that looked as though it might have been a fender, and a coffee maker that was boiling whatever was inside it down to black sludge.

There was a sign on the wall that stated No Checks Cashed, Not Even For You.

Several others listed services provided by the shop and their rates. Trent supposed they were reasonable, but he had no yardstick. There were two vending machines against a wall, one offering soft drinks, the other junk food. A coffee can held change that customers were free to contribute to or take from. An interesting concept, Trent thought.

"Excuse me," he said. The boots kept right on tapping. "Excuse me," he repeated, louder. The music upped its tempo and so did the boots. Trent nudged one with his shoe.

"What?" The answer from under the car was muffled and annoyed.

"I'd like to ask you about my car."

"Get in line." There was the clatter of a tool and a muttered curse.

Trent's eyebrows lifted then drew together in a manner that made his subordinates quake. "Apparently I'm the first in line already."

"Right now you're behind this idiot's oil pan. Save me from rich yuppies who buy a car like this then don't bother to find out the difference between a carburetor and a tire iron. Hold on a minute, buddy, or talk to Hank. He's around somewhere."

Trent was still several sentences back at "idiot." "Where's the proprietor?"

"Busy. Hank!" The mechanic's voice lifted to a roar. "Damn it. Hank! Where the devil did he take off to?"

"I couldn't say." Trent marched over to the radio and flicked off the music. "Would it be too much to ask you to come out from under there and tell me the status of my car?"

"Yeah." From the vantage point under the BMW, C.C. studied the Italian loafers and took an immediate dislike to them. "I got my hands full at the moment. You can come down here and lend one of yours if you're in such a hurry, or drive over to McDermit's in Northeast Harbor."

"I can hardly drive when you're under my car." Though the idea held a certain appeal.

"This yours?" C.C. sniffed and tightened bolts. The guy had a fancy Boston accent to go with the fancy shoes. "When's the last time you had this thing tuned? Changed the points and plugs, the oil?"

"I don't—"

"I'm sure you don't." There was a clipped satisfaction in the husky voice that had Trent's jaw tightening. "You know, you don't just buy a car, but a responsibility. A lot of people don't pull down an annual salary as rich as the sticker price on a machine like this. With reasonable care and maintenance, this baby would run for your grandchildren. Cars aren't disposable commodities, you know. People make them that way because they're too lazy or too stupid to take care of the basics. You needed a lube job six months ago."

Trent's fingers drummed on the side of his briefcase. "Young man, you're being paid to service my car, not to lecture me on my responsibilities to it." In a habit as ingrained as breathing, he checked his watch. "Now, I'd like to know when my car will be ready, as I have a number of appointments."

"Lecture's free." C.C. gave a push and sent the creeper scooting out from under the car. "And I'm not your young man."

That much was quite obvious. Though the face was grimy and the dark hair cropped boyishly short, the body clad in greasy coveralls was decidely feminine. Every curvy inch of it. Trent wasn't often thrown for a loss, but now he simply stood, staring as C.C. rose from the creeper and faced him, tapping a wrench against her palm.

Looking beyond the smears of black on her face, Trent could see she had very white skin in contrast with her ebony hair. Beneath the fringe of bangs, her forest-green eyes were narrowed. Her full, unpainted lips were pursed in what, under different circumstances, would have been a very sexy pout. She was tall for a woman and built like a goddess. It was she, Trent realized, who smelled of motor oil and honeysuckle.

"Got a problem?" she asked him. C.C. was well aware that his gaze had drifted down from the neck of her coveralls to the cuffs and back again. She was used to it. But she didn't have to like it.

The voice had an entirely different effect when a man realized those dark, husky tones belonged to a woman. "You're the mechanic!"

"No, I'm the interior decorator."

Trent glanced around the garage with its oil-splattered floor and cluttered worktables. He couldn't resist. "You do very interesting work."

Letting the breath out between her teeth, she tossed the wrench onto a workbench. "Your oil and air filter needed to be changed. The timing was off and the carburetor needed some adjusting. You still need a lube job and your radiator should be flushed."

"Will it run?"

"Yeah, it'll run." C.C. took a rag out of her pocket and began to wipe her hands. She judged him as the kind of man who took better care of his ties than he did of his car. With a shrug, she stuck the rag back into her pocket. It was no concern of hers. "Come through to the office and we can settle up."

She led the way through the door at the rear of the garage, into a narrow hallway that angled into a glass-walled office. It was cramped with a cluttered desk, thick parts catalogues, a half-full gum ball machine

and two wide swivel chairs. C.C. sat and, in the uncanny way of people who heap papers on their desk,
put her hand unerringly on her invoices.

"Cash or charge?" she asked him.

"Charge." Absently he pulled out his wallet. He
wasn't sexist. Trent assured himself he was not. He
had meticulously made certain that women were
given the same pay and opportunity for promotion in
his company as any male on his staff. It never occurred to him to be concerned whether employees
were males or females, as long as they were efficient,
loyal and dependable. But the longer he looked at the
woman who sat busily filling out the invoice, the
more he was certain she didn't fit his or anyone's
image of an auto mechanic.

"How long have you worked here?" It surprised
him to hear himself ask. Personal questions weren't
his style.

"On and off since I was twelve." Those dark green
eyes flicked up to his. "Don't worry. I know what
I'm doing. Any work that's done in my shop is guar-
anteed."

"Your shop?"

"My shop."

She unearthed a calculator and began to figure the
total with long, elegantly shaped fingers that were still
grimy.

He was putting her back up. Maybe it was the
shoes, she thought. Or the tie. There was something
arrogant about a maroon tie. "That's the damage."
C.C. turned the invoice around and started down the
list point by point.

He wasn't paying any attention, which was totally
out of character. This was a man who read every word

of every paper that crossed his desk. But he was looking at her, frankly fascinated.

"Any questions?" She glanced up and found her
gaze locked with his. She could almost hear the click.

"You're C.C.?"

"That's right." She was forced to clear her throat.
Ridiculous, she told herself. He had ordinary eyes.
Maybe a little darker, a bit more intense than she had
noted at first, but still ordinary. There was no earthly
reason why she couldn't look away from them. But
she continued to stare. If she had been of a fanciful
state of mind—which she assured herself she was
not—she would have said the air thickened.

"You have grease on your cheek," he said quietly,
and smiled at her.

The change was astonishing. He went from being
an aloof, annoying man to a warm and approachable
one. His mouth softened as it curved, the impatience
in his eyes vanished. There was humor there now, an
easy, inviting humor that was irresistible. C.C. found
herself smiling back.

"It goes with the territory." Maybe she'd been a
tad abrupt, she thought, and made an effort to correct
it. "You're from Boston, right?"

"Yes. How did you know?"

Her lips remained curved as she shrugged. "Between the Massachusetts plates and your speech pattern, it wasn't hard. We get a lot of trade from Boston
on the island. Are you here on vacation?"

"Business." Trent tried to remember the last time
he'd taken a vacation, and couldn't quite pin it down.
Two years? he wondered. Three?

C.C. pulled a clipboard from under a pile of catalogues and scanned the next day's schedule. "If

you're going to be around for a while, we could fit that lube job in tomorrow.''

''I'll keep it in mind. You live on the island?''

''Yes. All my life.'' The chair creaked as she brought her long legs up to sit Indian-style. ''Have you been to Bar Harbor before?''

''When I was a boy, I spent a couple of weekends here with my mother.'' Lifetimes ago, he thought. ''Maybe you could recommend some restaurants or points of interest. I might squeeze in some free time.''

''You shouldn't miss the park.'' After unearthing a sheet of memo paper, she began to write. ''You really can't go wrong anywhere as far as seafood, and it's early enough in the season that you shouldn't have any problem with crowds and lines.'' She offered the paper, which he folded and slipped into his breast pocket.

''Thanks. If you're free tonight maybe you could help me sample some of the local seafood. We could discuss my carburetor.''

Flustered and flattered, she reached out to accept the credit card he offered. She was on the point of agreeing when she read the name imprinted there. ''Trenton St. James III.''

''Trent,'' he said easily, and smiled again.

It figured, C.C. thought. Oh, it absolutely figured. Fancy car, fancy suit, fancy manners. She should have spotted it right off. She should have *smelled* it. Seething, she imprinted the card on the credit card form. ''Sign here.''

Trent took out a slim gold pen and signed while she rose and stalked over to a pegboard to retrieve his keys. He glanced over just as she tossed them to him. *At* him was more accurate. He managed to snag them before they hit his face. He jingled them lightly in his hand as she stood, hands on hips, face dark with fury.

"A simple no would have done the job."

"Men like you don't understand a simple no." C.C. turned to the glass wall, then whirled back. "If I'd known who you were, I'd have drilled holes in your muffler."

Slowly Trent slipped the keys into his pocket. His temper was renowned. It wasn't hot—that would have been easier to dodge. It was ice. As he stood it slid through him, frosting his eyes, tightening his mouth, coating his voice. "Would you like to explain?"

She strode toward him until they were toe to toe and eye to eye. "I'm Catherine Colleen Calhoun. And I want you to keep your greedy hands off my house."

Trent said nothing for a moment as he adjusted his thoughts. Catherine Calhoun, one of the four sisters who owned The Towers—and one who apparently had strong feelings regarding the sale. Since he was going to have to maneuver around all four of them, he might as well start here. And now.

"A pleasure, Miss Calhoun."

"Not mine." She reached down and ripped off his copy of the credit card receipt. "Get your butt back in your big, bad BMW and head back to Boston."

"A fascinating alliteration." Still watching her, Trent folded the paper and put it into his pocket. "You, however, are not the only party involved."

"You're not going to turn my house into one of your glossy hotels for bored debutantes and phony Italian counts."

He nearly smiled at that. "You've stayed in one of the St. James hotels?"

"I don't have to, I know what they're like. Marble lobbies, glass elevators, twenty-foot chandeliers and fountains spurting everywhere."

"You have something against fountains?"

"I don't want one in my living room. Why don't you go foreclose on some widows and orphans and leave us alone?"

"Unfortunately, I don't have any foreclosures scheduled this week." He held up a hand when she snarled. "Miss Calhoun, I've come here at the request of your liaison. Whatever your personal feelings, there are three other owners of The Towers. I don't intend to leave until I've spoken with them."

"You can talk until your lungs collapse, but...what liaison?"

"Mrs. Cordelia Calhoun McPike."

C.C.'s color fluctuated a bit, but she didn't back down. "I don't believe you."

Without a word, Trent set his briefcase down onto the piles of paper on her desk and flipped the combination. From one of his neatly ordered files he withdrew a letter written on heavy ivory paper. C.C.'s heart dropped a little. She snatched it from him and read.

Dear Mr. St. James,

The Calhoun women have taken your offer to The Towers under consideration. As this is a complex situation, we feel it would be in everyone's best interest to discuss the terms in person, rather than communicating by letter.

As their representative, I would like to invite you to The Towers—(*C.C. gave a strangled groan*)—for a few days. I believe this more personal approach will be of mutual benefit. I'm sure you'll agree that having a closer, more informal look at the property that interests you will be an advantage.

Please feel free to contact me, at The Towers, if you are amenable to the arrangement.

Very truly yours,
Cordelia Calhoun McPike

C.C. read it through twice, grinding her teeth. She would have crumpled the letter into a ball if Trent hadn't rescued it and slipped it back into its file.

"I take it you weren't apprised of the arrangement?"

"Apprised? Damn straight I wasn't apprised. That meddlesome old... Oh, Aunt Coco, I'm going to murder you."

"I assume Mrs. McPike and Aunt Coco are one and the same person."

"Some days it's hard to tell." She turned back. "But either way, both of them are dead."

"I'll sidestep the family violence, if you don't mind."

C.C. stuck her hands into her coverall pockets and glared at him. "If you still intend to stay at The Towers, you're going to be neck deep in it."

He nodded, accepting. "Then I'll take my chances."

Chapter Two

Aunt Coco was busily arranging hothouse roses in two of the Dresden vases that had yet to be sold. She hummed a current rock hit as she worked, occasionally adding a quick bum-bum-bum or ta-te-da. Like the other Calhoun women, she was tall, and liked to think that her figure, which had thickened only a little in the past decade, was regal.

She had dressed and groomed carefully for the occasion. Her short, fluffy hair was tinted red this week and pleased her enormously. Vanity was not a sin or character flaw in Coco's estimation, but a woman's sacred duty. Her face, which was holding up nicely, thank you, from the lift she'd had six years before, was scrupulously made up. Her best pearls swung at her ears and encircled her neck. Coco decided, with a quick glance in the hall mirror, that the black jumpsuit was both dramatic and sleek. The backless heels she wore slapped satisfactorily against the chestnut floor and had her teetering at six foot.

An imposing and, yes, regal figure, she bustled from room to room, checking and rechecking every detail. Her girls might be just a tiny bit upset with her for inviting company without mentioning it. But she could always claim absentmindedness. Which she did whenever it suited her.

Coco was the younger sister of Judson Calhoun, who had married Deliah Brady and sired four girls. Judson and Deliah, whom Coco had loved dearly, had been killed fifteen years before when their private plane had gone down over the Atlantic.

Since then, she had done her best to be father and mother and friend to her beautiful little orphans. A widow for nearly twenty years, Coco was a striking woman with a devious mind and a heart the consistency of marshmallow cream. She wanted, was determined to have, the best for her girls. Whether they liked it or not. With Trenton St. James's interest in The Towers, she saw an opportunity.

She didn't care a bit whether he bought the rambling fortress of a house. Though God knows how much longer they could hold on to it in any case, what with taxes and repairs and heating bills. As far as she was concerned, Trenton St. James III could take it or leave it. But she had a plan.

Whether he took or left it, he was going to fall head over bank account with one of the girls. She didn't know which one. She'd tried her crystal ball but hadn't come up with a name.

But she knew. She had known the moment the first letter had come. The boy was going to sweep one of her darlings away into a life of love and luxury.

She'd be damned if any one of them would have one without the other.

With a sigh, she adjusted the taper in its Lalique holder. She had been able to give them love, but the luxury... If Judson and Deliah had lived, things would have been different. Surely Judson would have pulled himself out of the financial difficulty he'd been suffering. With his cleverness, and Deliah's drive, it would have been a very temporary thing.

But they hadn't lived, and money had become an increasing problem. How she hated to have to sell off the girls' inheritance piece by piece just to keep the sagging roof they all loved over their heads.

Trenton St. James III was going to change all that by falling madly in love with one of her darling babies.

Maybe it would be Suzanna, she thought, plumping the pillows on the parlor sofa. Poor little dear with her heart broken by the worthless cur she had married. Coco's lips tightened. To think he had fooled all of them. Even her! He had made her baby's life a misery, then had divorced her to marry that busty bimbo.

Coco let out a disgusted breath then cast a beady eye on the cracked plaster in the ceiling. She would have to make sure that Trenton would suit as a father to Suzanna's two children. And if he didn't...

There was Lilah, her own lovely free spirit. Her Lilah needed someone who would appreciate her lively mind and eccentric ways. Someone who would nurture and settle. Just a bit. Coco wouldn't tolerate anyone who would try to smother her darling girl's mystical bent.

Perhaps it would be Amanda. Coco twitched a drapery so that it covered a mouse hole. Hardheaded, practical-minded Amanda. Now that would be a match! The successful businessman and woman, wheeling and dealing. But he would have to have a softer side, one that recognized that Mandy needed to be cherished, as well as respected. Even if she didn't recognize it herself.

With a satisfied sigh, Coco moved from parlor to sitting room, from sitting room to library, library to study.

Then there was C.C. Shaking her head, Coco adjusted a picture so that it hid—almost—the watermarks on the aging silk wallpaper. That child had inherited the Calhoun stubbornness in spades. Imagine, a lovely girl wasting her life diddling with engines and fuel pumps. A grease monkey. Lord save us.

It was doubtful that a man like Trenton St. James III would be interested in a woman who spent all of her time under a car. Then again, C.C. was the baby of the family at twenty-three. Coco felt that she had more than enough time to find her little girl the perfect husband.

The stage was set, she decided. And soon, Mr. St. James would be walking into Act One.

The front door slammed. Coco winced, knowing that the vibration would have pictures jittering on the walls and crockery dancing on tables. She worked her way through the winding maze of rooms, tidying as she went.

"Aunt Coco!"

Coco's hand lifted automatically to pat her breast. She recognized C.C.'s voice, and the fury in it. Now what could have happened to fire the girl up? she wondered, and put on her best sympathetic smile.

"Just coming, dear. I didn't expect you home for hours yet. It's such a pleasant..." She trailed off as she saw her niece, stripped down to fighting weight in torn jeans and a T-shirt, traces of grease still on her face and the hands she had fisted and jammed at her hips. And the man behind her—the man Coco recognized as her prospective nephew-in-law. "Surprise," she finished, and pasted the smile back into place. "Why, Mr. St. James, how lovely." She stepped forward, hand extended. "I'm Mrs. McPike."

"How do you do?"

"It's so nice to meet you at last. I hope you had a pleasant trip."

"An...interesting one, all in all."

"Even better than pleasant." She patted his hand before releasing it, approving his level gaze and well-pitched voice. "Please, come in. I believe a person should begin as they mean to go on, so I want you to begin to make yourself at home right now. I'll just fix us all some tea."

"Aunt Coco," C.C. said in a low voice.

"Yes, dear, would you like something other than tea?"

"I want an explanation, and I want it now."

Coco's heart hammered a bit, but she gave her niece an open, slightly curious smile. "Explanation? For what?"

"I want to know what the hell he's doing here."

"Catherine, really!" Coco tsk-tsked. "Your manners, one of my very few failures. Come, Mr. St. James—or may I call you Trenton—you must be a bit frazzled after the drive. You did say you were driving? Why don't we just go in and sit in the parlor?" She was easing him along as she spoke. "Marvelous weather for a drive, isn't it?"

"Hold it." C.C. moved quickly and planted herself

in their path. "Hold it. Hold it. You're not tucking him up in the parlor with tea and small talk. I want to know why you invited him here."

"C.C." Coco gave a long-suffering sigh. "Business is more pleasant and more successful on all sides when it's conducted in person, and in a relaxed atmosphere. Wouldn't you agree, Trenton?"

"Yes." He was surprised that he had to hold back a grin. "Yes, I would."

"There."

"Not another step." C.C. flung out both hands. "We haven't agreed to sell."

"Of course not," Coco said patiently. "That's why Trenton is here. So we can discuss all the options and possibilities. You really should go up and wash before tea, C.C. You've engine grease or whatever on your face."

With the heel of her hand, C.C. rubbed at it. "Why wasn't I told he was coming?"

Coco blinked and tried to leave her eyes slightly unfocused. "Told? Why, of course, you were told. I would hardly have invited company without telling all of you."

Face mutinous, C.C. held her ground. "You didn't tell me."

"Now, C.C., I..." Coco pursed her lips, knowing—since she'd practiced in the mirror—that it made her look befuddled. "I didn't? Are you certain? I would have sworn I told you and the girls the minute I got Mr. St. James's acceptance."

"No," C.C. said flatly.

"Oh, my." Coco lifted her hands to her cheeks. "Oh, how awful, really. I must apologize. What a dreadful mix-up. And all my fault. C.C., I do beg your pardon. After all, this is your house, yours and your sisters'. I would never presume on your good nature and your hospitality by..."

Before Coco had trailed off again, the guilt was working away. "It's your house as much as ours, Aunt Coco. You know that. It's not as if you have to ask permission to invite anyone you like. It's simply that I think we should have—"

"No, no, it's inexcusable." Coco had blinked enough to have her eyes glistening nicely. "Really it was. I just don't know what to say. I feel terrible about the whole thing. I was only trying to help, you see, but—"

"It's nothing to worry about." C.C. reached out for her aunt's hand. "Nothing at all. It was just a little confusing at first. Look, why don't I make the tea, and you can sit with—him."

"That's so sweet of you, dear."

C.C. muttered something unintelligible as she walked down the hall.

"Congratulations," Trent murmured, sending Coco an amused glance. "That was one of the smoothest shuffles I've ever witnessed."

Coco beamed and tucked her arm through his. "Thank you. Now, why don't we go in and have that chat?" She steered him to a wing chair by the fireplace, knowing that the springs in the sofa were only a memory. "I must apologize for C.C. She has a very quick temper but a wonderful heart."

Trent inclined his head. "I'll have to take your word for it."

"Well, you're here and that's what matters." Pleased with herself, Coco sat across from him. "I know you'll find The Towers, and its history, fascinating.''

He smiled, thinking he'd already found its occupants a fascination.

"My grandfather," she said, gesturing to a portrait of a dour-faced thin-lipped man above the ornate cherrywood mantel. "He built this house in 1904."

Trent glanced up at the disapproving eyes and lowered brows. "He looks...formidable," he said politely.

Coco gave a gay laugh. "Oh, indeed. And ruthless in his prime, so I'm told. I only remember Fergus Calhoun as a doddering old man who argued with shadows. They finally put him away in 1945 after he tried to shoot the butler for serving bad port. He was quite insane—Grandfather," she explained. "Not the butler."

"I...see."

"He lived another twelve years in the asylum, which put him well into his eighties. The Calhouns either have long lives or die tragically young." She crossed her long, sturdy legs. "I knew your father."

"My father?"

"Yes, indeed. Not well. We attended some of the same parties in our youth. I remember dancing with him once at a cotillion in Newport. He was dashingly handsome, fatally charming. I was quite smitten." She smiled. "You resemble him closely."

"He must have fumbled to let you slip through his fingers."

Pure feminine delight glowed in her eyes. "You're quite right," she said with a laugh. "How is Trenton?"

"He's well. I think if he had realized the connection, he wouldn't have passed this business on to me.''

She lifted a brow. As a woman who followed the society and gossip pages religiously, she was well aware of the senior St. James's current messy divorce. ''The last marriage didn't take?''

It was hardly a secret, but it made Trent uncomfortable just the same. ''No. Should I give him your regards when I speak with him?''

''Please do.'' A sore point, she noted, and skimmed lightly over it. ''How is it you ran into C.C.?''

Fate, he thought, and nearly said so. ''I found myself in need of her services—or I should say my car needed them. I didn't immediately make the connection between C.C.'s Automovations and Catherine Calhoun.''

''Who could blame you?'' Coco said with a fluttering hand. ''I hope she wasn't too, ah, intense.''

''I'm still alive to talk about it. Obviously, your niece isn't convinced to sell.''

''That's right.'' C.C. wheeled in a tea cart, steering it across the floor like a go-cart and stopping it with a rattle between the two chairs. ''And it's going to take more than some slick operator from Boston to convince me.''

''Catherine, there is no excuse for rudeness.''

''That's all right.'' Trent merely settled back. ''I'm becoming used to it. Are all your nieces so... aggressive, Mrs. McPike?''

''Coco, please,'' she murmured. ''They're all lovely women.'' As she lifted the teapot, she sent C.C. a warning glance. ''Don't you have work, dear?''

''It can wait.''

"But you only brought out service for two."

"I don't want anything." She plopped down on the arm of the sofa and folded her arms over her chest.

"Well then. Cream or lemon, Trenton?"

"Lemon, please."

Swinging one long, booted leg, C.C. watched them sip tea and exchange small talk. Useless talk, she thought nastily. He was the kind of man who had been trained from diapers on the proper way to sit in a parlor and discuss nothing.

Squash, polo, perhaps a round of golf. He probably had hands like a baby's. Beneath that tailored suit, his body would be soft and slow. Men like him didn't work, didn't sweat, didn't feel. He sat behind his desk all day, buying and selling, never once thinking of the lives he affected. Of the dreams and hopes he created or destroyed.

He wasn't going to mess with hers. He wasn't going to cover the much-loved and much-cracked plaster walls with drywall and a coat of slick paint. He wasn't going to turn the drafty old ballroom into a nightclub. He wasn't going to touch one board foot of her wormy rafters.

She would see to it. She would see to him.

It was quite a situation, Trent decided. He parried Coco's tea talk while the Amazon Queen, as he'd begun to think of C.C., sat on a sagging sofa, swinging a scarred boot and glaring daggers at him. Normally he would have politely excused himself, headed back to Boston to turn the whole business over to agents. But he hadn't faced a true challenge in a long time. This one, he mused, might be just what he needed to put him on track.

The place itself was an amazement—a crumbling

one. From the outside it looked like a combination of English manor house and Dracula's castle. Towers and turrets of dour gray stone jutted into the sky. Gargoyles—one of which had been decapitated—grinned wickedly as they clung to parapets. All of this seemed to sit atop a proper two-story house of granite with neat porches and terraces. There was a pergola built along the seawall. The quick glimpse Trent had had of it had brought a Roman bathhouse to mind for reasons he couldn't fathom. As the lawns were uneven and multileveled, granite walls had been thrown up wherever they were terraced.

It should have been ugly. In fact, Trent thought it should have been hideous. Yet it wasn't. It was, in a baffling way, charming.

The way the window glass sparkled like lake water in the sun. Banks of spring flowers spread and nodded. Ivy rustled as it inched its patient way up those granite walls. It hadn't been difficult, even for a man with a pragmatic mind, to imagine the tea and garden parties. Women floating over the lawns in picture hats and organdy dresses, harp and violin music playing.

Then there was the view, which even on the short walk from his car to the front door had struck him breathless.

He could see why his father wanted it, and was willing to invest the hundreds of thousands of dollars it would take to renovate.

"More tea, Trenton?" Coco asked.

"No, thank you." He sent her a charming smile. "I wonder if I might have a tour of the house. What I've seen so far is fascinating."

C.C. gave a snort Coco pretended not to hear. "Of course, I'd be delighted to show you through." She rose and with her back to Trent wiggled her eyebrows at her niece. "C.C., shouldn't you be getting back?"

"No." She rose and, with an abrupt change of tactics, smiled. "I'll show Mr. St. James through, Aunt Coco. It's nearly time for the children to be home from school."

Coco glanced at the mantel clock, which had stopped weeks before at ten thirty-five. "Oh, well..."

"Don't worry about a thing." C.C. walked to the doorway and with an imperious gesture of her hand waved Trent along. "Mr. St. James?"

She started down the hall in front of him then up a floating staircase. "We'll start at the top, shall we?" Without glancing back, she continued on and up, certain Trent would start wheezing and panting by the third flight.

She was disappointed.

They climbed the final circular set that led to the highest tower. C.C. put her hand on the knob and her shoulder to the thick oak door. With a grunt and a hard shove, it creaked open.

"The haunted tower," she said grandly, and stepped inside amid the dust and echoes. The circular room was empty but for a few sturdy and fortunately empty mouse traps.

"Haunted?" Trent repeated, willing to play.

"My great-grandmother had her hideaway up here." As she spoke, C.C. moved over to the curved window. "It's said she would sit here, on this window seat, looking out to sea as she pined for her lover."

"Quite a view," Trent murmured. It was a dizzying drop down to the cliffs and the water that slapped and retreated. "Very dramatic."

"Oh, we're full of drama here. Great-Grandmama

apparently couldn't bear the deceit any longer and threw herself out this very window." C.C. smiled smugly. "Now, on quiet nights you can hear her pacing this floor and weeping for her lost lover."

"That should add something to the brochure."

C.C. jammed her hands into her pockets. "I wouldn't think ghosts would be good for business."

"On the contrary." His lips curved. "Shall we move on?"

Tight-lipped, C.C. strode out of the room. Using both hands, she tugged on the knob, then dug in a bit and prepared to put her back into it. When Trent's hand closed over hers, she jolted as though she'd been scalded.

It felt as though she had.

"I can do it," she muttered. Her eyes widened as she felt his body brush hers. He brought his other arm around, caging her, trapping her hands under his. C.C.'s heart bounded straight into her throat, then back-flipped.

"It looks like a two-man job." With this, Trent gave a hard tug that brought the door to and C.C. back smartly against him.

They stood there a moment, like lovers looking out at a sunset. He caught himself drawing in the scent of her hair while his hands remained cupped over hers. It passed through his mind that she was quite an armful—an amazingly sexy armful—then she jumped like a rabbit, slamming back against the wall.

"It's warped." She swallowed, hoping to smother the squeak in her voice. "Everything around here is warped or broken or about to disintegrate. I don't know why you'd even consider buying it."

Her face was pale as water, Trent noted, making

her eyes that much deeper. The panicked distress in them seemed more than a warped tower door warranted. "Doors can be repaired or replaced." Curious, he took a step toward her and watched her brace as if for a blow. "What's wrong with you?"

"Nothing." She knew if he touched her again she would go off like a rocket through what was left of the roof. "Nothing," she repeated. "If you want to see anything else, we'd better go down."

C.C. let out a long, slow breath as she followed him down the circular stairs. Her body was still throbbing oddly, as if she'd brushed a hand over a live wire. Not enough to get singed, she thought, just enough to let you know there was power.

She decided that gave her two reasons to get rid of Trenton St. James quickly.

She took him through the top floor, through the servants' wing, the storage rooms, making certain to point out any cracked plaster, dry rot, rodent damage. It pleased her that the air was chill, slightly damp and definitely musty. It was even more gratifying to see that his suit was sprinkled with dust and his shoes were rapidly losing their shine.

Trent peered into one room that was crowded with furniture boxes, broken crockery. "Has anyone gone through all this stuff?"

"Oh, we'll get around to it eventually." She watched a fat spider sneak away from the dim light. "Most of these rooms haven't been opened in fifty years—since my great-grandfather went insane."

"Fergus."

"Right. The family only uses the first two floors, and we patch things up as we have to." She ran her finger along an inch-wide crack in the wall. "I guess you could say if we don't see it, we don't worry about it. And the roof hasn't crashed down on our heads. Yet.''

He turned to study her. "Have you ever thought about turning in your socket wrench for a real estate license?''

She only smiled. "There's more down this way.'' She particularly wanted to show him the room where she had tacked up plastic to cover the broken windows.

He walked with her, gingerly across a spot where two-by-fours had been nailed over a hole in the floor. A high arched door caught his eyes, and before C.C. could stop him, he had his hand on the knob.

"Where does this lead to?''

"Oh, nowhere,'' she began, and swore when he pulled it open. Fresh spring air rushed in. Trent stepped out onto the narrow stone terrace and turned toward the pie-shaped granite steps.

"I don't know how safe they are.''

He flicked a glance over his shoulder. "A lot safer than the floor inside.''

With an oath, C.C. gave up and climbed after him.

"Fabulous,'' he murmured as he paused on the wide passageway between turrets. "Really fabulous.''

Which was exactly why C.C. hadn't wanted him to see it. She stood back with her hands in her pockets while he rested his palms on the waist-high stone wall and looked out.

He could see the deep blue waters of the bay with the boats gliding lightly over it. The valley, misty and mysterious, spread like a fairy tale. A gull, hardly more than a white blur, banked over the bay and soared out to sea.

"Incredible." The wind ruffled his hair as he followed the passage, down another flight, up one more. From here it was the Atlantic, wild and windy and wonderful. The sound of her ceaseless war on the rocks below echoed up like thunder.

He could see that there were doors leading back in at various intervals, but he wasn't interested in the interior just now. Someone, one of the family, he imagined, had set out chairs, tables, potted plants. Trent looked out over the roof of the pergola, to the tumbling rocks below.

"Spectacular." He turned to C.C. "Do you get used to it?"

She moved her shoulders. "No. You just get territorial."

"Understandable. I'm surprised any of you spend time inside."

With her hands still tucked in her pockets, she joined him at the wall. "It's not just the view. It's the fact that your family, generations of them, stood here. Just as the house has stood here, through time and wind and fire." Her face softened as she looked down. "The children are home."

Trent looked down to see two small figures race across the lawn toward the pergola. The sound of their laughter carried lightly on the wind.

"Alex and Jenny," she explained. "My sister Suzanna's children. They've stood here, too." She turned to him. "That means something."

"How does their mother feel about the sale?"

She looked away then as worry and guilt and frustration fought for control. "I'm sure you'll ask her yourself. But if you pressure her." Her head whipped around, hair flying. "If you pressure her in any way, you'll answer to me. I won't see her manipulated again.''

"I have no intention of manipulating anyone."

She gave a bark of bitter laughter. "Men like you make a career out of manipulation. If you think you've happened across four helpless women, Mr. St. James, think again. The Calhouns can take care of themselves, and take care of their own."

"Undoubtedly, particularly if your sisters are as obnoxious as you."

C.C.'s eyes narrowed, her hands fisted. She would have moved in then and there for the kill, but her name was murmured quietly behind her.

Trent saw a woman step through one of the doors. She was as tall as C.C., but willowy, with a fragile aura that kicked Trent's protective instincts into gear before he was aware of it. Her hair was a pale and lustrous blond that waved to her shoulders. Her eyes were the deep blue of a midsummer sky and seemed calm and serene until you looked closer and saw the heartbreak beneath.

Despite the difference in coloring, there was a resemblance—the shape of the face and eyes and mouth—that made Trent certain he was meeting one of C.C.'s sisters.

"Suzanna." C.C. moved between her sister and Trent, as if to shield. Suzanna's mouth curved, a look that was both amused and impatient.

"Aunt Coco asked me to come up." She laid a hand on C.C.'s arm, soothing her protector. "You must be Mr. St. James."

"Yes." He accepted her offered hand and was surprised to find it hard and callused and strong.

"I'm Suzanna Calhoun Dumont. You'll be staying with us for a few days?"

"Yes. Your aunt was kind enough to invite me."

"Shrewd enough," Suzanna corrected with a smile as she put an arm around her sister. "I take it C.C.'s given you a partial tour."

"A fascinating one."

"I'll be glad to continue it from here." Her fingers pressed lightly but with clear meaning into C.C.'s arm. "Aunt Coco could use some help downstairs."

"He doesn't need to see any more now," C.C. argued. "You look tired."

"Not a bit. But I will be if Aunt Coco sends me all over the house looking for the Wedgwood turkey platter."

"All right then." She sent Trent a last, fulminating glance. "We aren't finished."

"Not by a long shot," he agreed, and smiled to himself as she slammed back inside. "Your sister has quite an…outgoing personality."

"She's a fire-eater," Suzanna said. "We all are, given the right circumstances. The Calhoun curse." She glanced over at the sound of her children laughing. "This isn't an easy decision, Mr. St. James, one way or the other. Nor is it, for any of us, a business one."

"I've gathered that. For me it has to be a business one."

She knew too well that for some men business came first, and last. "Then I suppose we'd better take it one step at a time." She opened the door that C.C. had slammed shut. "Why don't I show you where you'll be staying?"

Chapter Three

"So, what's he like?" Lilah Calhoun crossed her long legs, anchoring her ankles on one arm of the couch and pillowing her head on the other. The half-dozen bracelets on her arm jingled as she gestured toward C.C. "Honey, I've told you, screwing your face up that way causes nothing but wrinkles and bad vibes."

"If you don't want me to screw my face up, don't ask me about him."

"Okay, I'll ask Suzanna." She shifted her sea-green eyes toward her older sister. "Let's have it."

"Attractive, well mannered and intelligent."

"So's a cocker spaniel," Lilah put in, and sighed. "And here I was hoping for a pit bull. How long do we get to keep him?"

"Aunt Coco's a little vague on the particulars." Suzanna sent both of her sisters an amused look. "Which means she's not saying."

"Mandy might be able to pry something out of

her." Lilah wiggled her bare toes and shut her eyes. She was the kind of woman who felt there was something intrinsically wrong with anyone who stretched out on a couch and didn't nap. "Suze, have the kids been through here today?"

"Only ten or fifteen times. Why?"

"I think I'm lying on a fire engine."

"I think we ought to get rid of him." C.C. rose and, to keep her restless hands busy, began to lay a fire.

"Suzanna said you already tried to throw him off the parapet."

"No," Suzanna corrected. "I said I stopped her before she thought to throw him off the parapet." She rose to hand C.C. the fireplace matches she'd forgotten. "And while I agree it's awkward to have him here while we're all so undecided, it's done. The least we can do is give him a chance to say his piece."

"Always the peacemaker," Lilah said sleepily, and missed Suzanna's quick wince. "Well, it might be a moot point now that he's gone through the place. My guess is that he'll be making some clever excuse and zooming back to Boston."

"The sooner the better," C.C. muttered, watching the flames begin to lick at the apple wood.

"I've been dismissed," Amanda announced. She hurried into the room as she hurried everywhere. Pushing a hand through her chin-length honey-brown hair, she perched on the arm of a chair. "She's not talking, either." Amanda's busy hands tugged at the hem of her trim business suit. "But I know she's up to something, something more than real estate transactions."

"Aunt Coco's always up to something." Suzanna

moved automatically to the old Belker cabinet to pour her sister a glass of mineral water. "She's happiest when she's scheming."

"That may be true. Thanks," she added, taking the glass. "But I get nervous when I can't get past her guard." Thoughtful, she sipped, then swept her gaze over her sisters. "She's using the Limoges china."

"The Limoges?" Lilah pushed up on her elbows. "We haven't used that since Suzanna's engagement party." And could have bitten her tongue. "Sorry."

"Don't be silly." Suzanna brushed the apology away. "She hasn't entertained much in the past couple of years. I'm sure she's missed it. She's probably just excited to have company."

"He's not company," C.C. put in. "He's nothing but a pain in the—"

"Mr. St. James." Suzanna rose quickly, cutting off the finale of her sister's opinion.

"Trent, please." He smiled at her, then with some wryness at C.C.

It was quite a tableau, he thought, and had enjoyed it for perhaps a minute before Suzanna had seen him in the doorway. The Calhoun women together, and separately, made a picture any man still breathing had to appreciate. Long, lean and leggy, they sat, stood or sprawled around the room.

Suzanna stood with her back to the window, so that the last lights of the spring evening haloed around her hair. He would have said she was relaxed but for that trace of sadness in her eyes.

The one on the sofa was definitely relaxed—and all but asleep. She wore a long, flowered skirt that reached almost to her bare feet and regarded him through dreamy amused eyes as she pushed back a curling mass of waist-length red hair.

Another sat perched on the arm of a chair as if he would spring up and into action at the sound of a bell only she could hear. Sleek, slick and professional, he thought at first glance. Her eyes weren't dreamy or sad, but simply calculating.

Then there was C.C. She'd been sitting on the stone hearth, chin on her hands, brooding like some modern-day Cinderella. But she had risen quickly, defensively, he noted, to stand poker straight with the fire behind her. This wasn't a woman who would sit patiently for a prince to fit a glass slipper on her foot.

He imagined she'd kick him smartly in the shins or somewhere more painful if he attempted it.

"Ladies," he said, but his eyes were on C.C. without him even being aware of it. He couldn't resist the slight nod in her direction. "Catherine."

"Let me introduce you," Suzanna said quickly. "Trenton St. James, my sisters, Amanda and Lilah. Why don't I fix you a drink while you—"

The rest of the offer was drowned out by a war whoop and storming feet. Like twin whirlwinds, Alex and Jenny barreled into the room. It was Trent's misfortune that he happened to be standing in the line of fire. They slammed into him like two missiles and sent him tumbling to the couch on top of Lilah.

She only laughed and said she was pleased to meet him.

"I'm so sorry." Suzanna collared each child and sent Trent a sympathetic glance. "Are you all right?"

"Yes." He untangled himself and rose.

"These are my children, Disaster and Calamity."

She kept a firm maternal arm around each. "Apologize."

"Sorry," they told him. Alex, a few inches taller than his sister looked up from under a mop of dark hair.

"We didn't see you."

"Didn't," Jenny agreed, and smiled winningly.

Suzanna decided to go into the lecture about storming into rooms later and steered them both toward the door. "Go ask Aunt Coco if dinner's ready. Walk!" she added firmly but without hope.

Before anyone could pick up the threads of a conversation, there was a loud, echoing boom.

"Oh, Lord," Amanda said into her glass. "She's dragged out the gong again."

"That means dinner." If there was one thing Lilah moved quickly for, it was food. She rose, tucked her arm through Trent's and beamed up at him. "I'll show you the way. Tell me, Trent, what are your views on astral projection?"

"Ah..." He sent a glance over his shoulder and saw C.C. grinning.

Aunt Coco had outdone herself. The china gleamed. What was left of the Georgian silver that had been a wedding present to Bianca and Fergus Calhoun glittered. Under the fantasy light of the Waterford chandelier the rack of lamb glistened. Before any of her nieces could comment, she dived cleanly into polite conversation.

"We're dining formal style, Trenton. So much more cozy. I hope your room is suitable."

"It's fine, thank you." It was, he thought, big as a barn, drafty, with a hole the size of a man's fist in the ceiling. But the bed was wide and soft as a cloud. And the view... "I can see some islands from my window."

"The Porcupine islands," Lilah put in, and passed him a silver basket of dinner rolls.

Coco watched them all like a hawk. She wanted to see some chemistry, some heat. Lilah was flirting with him, but she couldn't be too hopeful about that. Lilah flirted with men in general, and she wasn't paying any more attention to Trent than she did to the boy who bagged groceries in the market.

No, there was no spark there. On either side. One down, she thought philosophically, three to go.

"Trenton, did you know that Amanda is also in the hotel business? We're all so proud of our Mandy." She looked down the rosewood table at her niece. "She's quite a businesswoman."

"I'm assistant manager of the BayWatch, down in the village." Amanda's smile was both cool and friendly, the same she would give to any harried tourist at checkout time. "It's not on the scale of any of your hotels, but we do very well during the season. I heard you're adding an underground shopping complex to the St. James Atlanta."

Coco frowned into her wine as they discussed hotels. Not only was there not a spark, there wasn't even a weak glow. When Trent passed Amanda the mint jelly and their hands brushed, there was no breathless pause, no meeting of the eyes. Amanda had already turned to giggle with little Jenny and mop up spilled milk.

Ah, there! Coco thought triumphantly. Trent had grinned at Alex when the boy complained that brussels sprouts were disgusting. So, he had a weakness for children.

"You don't have to eat them," Suzanna told her suspicious son as he poked through his scalloped potatoes to make sure nothing green was hidden inside. "Personally, I've always thought they looked like shrunken heads."

"They do, kinda." The idea appealed to him, as his mother had known it would. He speared one, stuck it into his mouth and grinned. "I'm a cannibal. Uga bugga."

"Darling boy," Coco said faintly. "Suzanna's done such a marvelous job of mothering. She seems to have a green thumb with children as well as flowers. All the gardens are our Suzanna's work."

"Uga bugga," Alex said again as he popped another imaginary head into his mouth.

"Here you go, little creep." C.C. rolled her vegetables onto his plate. "There's a whole passel of missionaries."

"I want some, too," Jenny complained, then beamed at Trent when he passed her the bowl.

Coco put a hand to her breast. Who would have guessed it? she thought. Her Catherine. The baby of her babies. While the dinner conversation bounced around her, she sat back with a quiet sigh. She couldn't be mistaken. Why, when Trent had looked at her little girl—and she at him—there hadn't just been a spark. There had been a sizzle.

C.C. was scowling, it was true, but it was such a *passionate* scowl. And Trent had smirked, but it was such a *personal* smirk. Positively intimate, Coco decided.

Sitting there, watching them, as Alex devoured his

little decapitated heads, and Lilah and Amanda argued over the possibility of life on other planets, Coco could almost hear the loving thoughts C.C. and Trent sent out to each other.

Arrogant, self-important jerk.

Rude, bad-tempered brat.

Who the hell does he think he is, sitting at the table as if he already owned it?

A pity she doesn't have a personality to match her looks.

Coco smiled fondly at them while the "Wedding March" hummed through her head. Like a general plotting strategy, she waited until after coffee and dessert to spring her next offensive.

"C.C., why don't you show Trenton the gardens?"

"What?" She looked up from her friendly fight with Alex over the last bite of her Black Forest cake.

"The gardens," Coco repeated. "There's nothing like a little fresh air after a meal. And the flowers are exquisite in the moonlight."

"Let Suzanna take him."

"Sorry." Suzanna was already gathering a heavy-eyed Jenny into her arms. "I've got to get these two washed up and ready for bed."

"I don't see why—" C.C. broke off at the arched look from her aunt. "Oh, all right." She rose. "Come on then," she said to Trent and started out without him.

"It was a lovely meal, Coco. Thank you."

"My pleasure." She beamed, imagining whispered words and soft, secret kisses. "Enjoy the gardens."

Trent walked out of the terrace doors to find C.C. standing, tapping a booted foot on the stone. It was time, he thought, that someone taught the green-eyed witch a lesson in manners.

"I don't know anything about flowers," she told him.

"Or about simple courtesy."

Her chin angled. "Now listen, buddy."

"No, you listen, buddy." His hand snaked out and snagged her arm. "Let's walk. The children might still be within earshot, and I don't think they're ready to hear any of this."

He was stronger than she'd imagined. He pulled her along, ignoring the curses she tossed out under her breath. They were off the terrace and onto one of the meandering paths that wound around the side of the house. Daffodils and hyacinths nodded along the verge.

He stopped beneath an arbor where wisteria would bloom in another month. C.C. wasn't certain if the roar in her head was the sound of the sea or her own ragged temper.

"Don't you ever do that again." She lifted a hand to rub where his fingers had dug. "You may be able to push people around in Boston, but not here. Not with me or any of my family."

He paused, hoping and failing to get a grip on his own temper. "If you knew me, or what I do, you'd know I don't make a habit of pushing anyone around."

"I know exactly what you do."

"Foreclose on widows and orphans? Grow up, C.C."

She set her teeth. "You can see the gardens on your own. I'm going in."

He merely shifted to block her path. In the moonlight, her eyes glowed like a cat's. When she lifted her hands to shove him aside, he clamped his fingers onto her wrists. In the brief tug-of-war that followed, he noted—irrelevantly he assured himself—that her skin was the color of fresh cream and almost as soft.

"We're not finished." His voice had an edge that was no longer coated with a polite veneer. "You'll have to learn that when you're deliberately rude, and deliberately insulting, there's a price."

"You want an apology?" she all but spat at him. "Okay. I'm sorry I don't have anything to say to you that isn't rude or insulting."

He smiled, surprising both of them. "You're quite a piece of work, Catherine Colleen Calhoun. For the life of me I can't figure out why I'm trying to be reasonable with you."

"Reasonable?" She didn't spit the word this time, but growled it. "You call it reasonable to drag me around, manhandle me—"

"If you call this manhandling, you've led a very sheltered life."

Her complexion went from creamy white to bright pink. "My life is none of your concern."

"Thank God."

Her fingers flexed then balled into fists. She hated the fact, loathed it, that her pulse was hammering double time under his grip. "Will you let me go?"

"Only if you promise not to take off running." He could see himself chasing her, and the image was both embarrassing and appealing.

"I don't run from anyone."

"Spoken like a true Amazon," he murmured, and released her. Only quick reflexes had him dodging the fist she aimed at his nose. "I should have taken that into account, I suppose. Have you ever considered intelligent conversation?''

''I don't have anything to say to you.'' She was ashamed to have struck out at him and furious that she'd missed. ''If you want to talk, go suck up to Aunt Coco some more.'' In a huff, she plopped down on the small stone bench under the arbor. ''Better yet, go back to Boston and flog one of your underlings.''

''I can do that anytime.'' He shook his head and, certain he was taking his life in his hands, sat beside her.

There were azaleas and geraniums threatening to havebee nape acefu lplace .Buta sh esat,sm el ling

the tender fragrance of the earliest spring blooms mixed with the scent of the sea, listening to some night bird call its mate, he thought that no boardroom had ever been so tense or hostile.

''I wonder where you developed such a high opinion of me.'' And why, he added to himself, it seemed to matter.

''You come here—''

''By invitation.''

''Not mine.'' She tossed back her head. ''You come in your big car and your dignified suit, ready to sweep my home out from under me.''

''I came,'' he corrected, ''to get a firsthand look at a piece of property. No one, least of all me, can force you to sell.''

But he was wrong, she thought miserably. There were people who could force them to sell. The people who collected the taxes, the utility bills, the mortgage they'd been forced to take out. All of her frustration, and her fear, over every collection agency centered on the man beside her.

"I know your type," she muttered. "Born rich and above the common man. Your only goal in life is to make more money, regardless of who is affected or trampled over. You have big parties and summer houses and mistresses named Fawn."

Wisely he swallowed the chuckle. "I've never even known a woman named Fawn."

"Oh, what does it matter?" She rose to pace the path. "Kiki, Vanessa, Ava, it's all the same."

"If you say so." She looked, he was forced to admit, magnificent, striding up and down the path with the moonlight shooting around her like white fire. The tug of attraction annoyed him more than a little, but he continued to sit. There was a deal to be done, he reminded himself. And C. C. Calhoun was the foremost stumbling block.

So he would be patient, Trent told himself, and wily and find the hook. "Just how is it you know so much about my type?"

"Because my sister was married to one of you."

"Baxter Dumont."

"You know him?" Then she shook her head and jammed her hands into her pockets. "Stupid question. You probably play golf with him every Wednesday."

"No, actually our acquaintance is only slight. I do know of him, and his family. I'm also aware that he and your sister have been divorced for a year or so."

"He made her life hell, scraped away her self-esteem, then dumped her and his children for some little French pastry. And because he's a big-shot lawyer from a big-shot family, she's left with nothing but a miserly child-support check that comes late every month.''

"I'm sorry for what happened to your sister." He rose as well. His voice was no longer sharp but fatalistic. "Marriage is often the least pleasant of all business transactions. But Baxter Dumont's behavior doesn't mean that every member of every prominent Boston family is unethical or immoral."

"They all look the same from where I'm standing."

"Then maybe you should change positions. But you won't, because you're too hardheaded and opinionated."

"Just because I'm smart enough to see through you."

"You know nothing about me, and we both know that you took an uncanny dislike to me before you even knew my name."

"I didn't like your shoes?"

That stopped him. "I beg your pardon?"

"You heard me." She folded her arms and realized she was starting to enjoy herself. "I didn't like your shoes." She flicked a glance down at them. "I still don't."

"That explains everything."

"I didn't like your tie, either." She poked a finger on it, missing the quick flare in his eyes. "Or your fancy gold pen." She tapped a fist lightly at his breast pocket.

He studied her jeans, worn through at the knees, her T-shirt and scuffed boots. "This from an obvious fashion expert."

"You're the one out of place here, Mr. St. James III."

He took a step closer. C.C.'s lips curved in a challenging smile. "And I suppose you dress like a man because you haven't figured out how to act like a woman."

It was a bull's-eye, but the dart point only pricked her temper. "Just because I know how to stand up for myself instead of swooning at your feet doesn't make me less of a woman."

"Is that what you call this?" He wrapped his fingers around her forearms. "Standing up for yourself?"

"That's right. I—" She broke off when he tugged her closer. Their bodies bumped. Trent watched the temper in her eyes deepen to confusion.

"What do you think you're doing?"

"Testing the theory." He looked down at her mouth. Her lips were full, just parted. Very tempting. Why hadn't he noticed that before? he wondered vaguely. That big, insulting mouth of hers was incredibly tempting.

"Don't you dare." She meant it to come out as an order, but her voice shook.

His eyes came back to hers and held. "Afraid?"

The question was just the one to stiffen her spine. "Of course not. It's just that I'd rather be kissed by a rabid skunk."

She started to pull back, then found herself tight against him, eyes and mouth lined up, warm breath mingling. He hadn't intended to kiss her—certainly not—until she'd thrown that last insult in his face.

"You never know when to quit, Catherine. It's a flaw that's going to get you in trouble, starting now."

She hadn't expected his mouth to be so hot, so hard, so hungry. She had thought the kiss would be

sophisticated and bland. Easily resisted, easily forgotten. But she had been wrong. Dangerously wrong.
Kissing him was like sliding into molten silver. Even
as she gasped for air, he heightened the kiss, plunging
his tongue deep, taunting, tormenting, teasing hers.
She tried to shake her head but succeeded only in
changing the angle. The hands that had reached for
his shoulders in protest slid possessively around his
neck.

He'd thought to teach her a lesson—about what
he'd forgotten. But he learned. He learned that some
women—this woman—could be strong and soft, frus-
trating and delightful, all at once. As the waves
crashed far below, he felt himself battered by the unexpected. And the unwanted.

He thought, foolishly, that he could feel the star-
light on her skin, taste the moondust on her lips. The
groan he heard, vibrating low, was his own.

He lifted his head, shaking it, as if to clear the fog
that had settled over his brain. He could see her eyes,
staring up at his—dark, dazed.

"I beg your pardon." Stunned by his action, he
released her so quickly that she stumbled back even
as her hands slid away from him. "That was completely inexcusable."

She said nothing, could say nothing. Feelings, too
many of them, clogged in her throat. Instead she made
a helpless gesture with her hands that made him feel
like a lower form of life.

"Catherine...believe me, I don't make a habit
of—" He had to stop and clear his dry throat. Lord,
he wanted to do it again, he realized. He wanted to
kiss the breath from her as she stood there, looking

lost and helpless. And beautiful. "I'm terribly sorry. It won't happen again."

"I'd like you to leave me alone." Never in her life had she been more moved. Or more devastated. He had just opened up a door to some secret world, then slammed it again in her face.

"All right." He had to stop himself from reaching out to touch her hair. He started back down the path toward the house. When he looked back, she was still standing as he had left her, staring into the shadows, with moonlight showering her.

His name is Christian. I have found myself walking along the cliffs again and again, hoping for a few words with him. I tell myself it's because of my fascination with art, not the artist. It could be true. It must be true.

I am a married woman and mother of three. And though Fergus is not the romantic husband of my girlish dreams, he is a good provider, and sometimes kind. Perhaps there is some part of me, some small defiant part that wishes I had not bent to my parents' insistence that I make a good and proper marriage. But this is foolishness, for the deed has been done for more than four years.

It's disloyal to compare Fergus with a man I hardly know. Yet here, in my private journal, I must be allowed this indulgence. While Fergus thinks only of business, the next deal or dollar, Christian speaks of dreams and images and poetry.

How my heart has yearned for just a little poetry.

While Fergus, with his cool and careless generosity, gave me the emeralds on the day of Ethan's birth, Christian once offered me a wildflower. I have kept it, pressing it here between these pages. How much lovelier I would feel wearing it than those cold and heavy gems.

We have spoken of nothing intimate, nothing that could be considered improper. Yet I know it is. The way he looks at me, smiles, speaks, is gloriously improper. The way I look for him on these bright summer afternoons while my babies nap is not the action of a proper wife. The way my heart drums in my breast when I see him is disloyalty in itself.

Today I sat upon a rock and watched him wield his brush, bringing those pink and gray rocks, that blue, blue water to life on canvas. There was a boat gliding along, so free, so solitary. For a moment I pictured the two of us there, faces to the wind. I don't understand why I have these thoughts, but while they remained with me, clear as crystal, I asked his name.

"Christian," he said. "Christian Bradford. And you are Bianca."

The way he said my name—as if it had never been said before. I will never forget it. I toyed with the wild grass that pushed itself through the cracks in the rocks. With my eyes cast down, I asked him why his wife never came to watch him work.

"I have no wife," he told me. "And art is my only mistress."

It was wrong for my heart to swell so at his words. Wrong of me to smile, yet I smiled. And he in return. If fate had dealt differently with me, if time and place could have been altered in some way, I could have loved him.

I think I would have had no choice but to love him.

As if we both knew this, we began to talk of inconsequential matters. But when I rose, knowing my time here was at an end for the day, he bent over and plucked up a tiny spike of golden heather and slipped it into my hair. For a moment, his fingers hovered over my cheek and his eyes were on mine. Then he stepped away and bid me good day.

Now I sit with the lamp low as I write, listening to Fergus's voice rumble as he instructs his valet next door. He will not come to me tonight, and I find myself grateful. I have given him three children, two sons and a daughter. By providing him with an heir, I have done my duty, and he does not often find the need to come to my bed. I am, like the children, to exist to be well dressed and well mannered, and to be presented at the proper occasions—like a good claret—for his guests.

It is not much to ask, I suppose. It is a good life, one I should be content with. Perhaps I was content, until that day I first walked along the cliffs.

So tonight, I will sleep alone in my bed, and dream of a man who is not my husband.

Chapter Four

When you couldn't sleep, the best thing to do was get up. That's what C.C. told herself as she sat at the kitchen table, watching the sunrise and drinking her second cup of coffee.

She had a lot on her mind, that was all. Bills, the dyseptic Oldsmobile that was first on her schedule that morning, bills, an upcoming dentist appointment. More bills. Trenton St. James was far down on her list of concerns. Somewhere below a potential cavity and just ahead of a faulty exhaust system.

She certainly wasn't losing any sleep over him. And a kiss, that ridiculous—*accident* was the best term she could use to describe it—wasn't even worth a moment's thought.

Yet she had thought of little else throughout the long, sleepless night.

She was acting as though she'd never been kissed before, C.C. berated herself. And, of course, she had, starting with Denny Dinsmore, who had planted the first sloppy mouth-to-mouth on her after their eighth-grade Valentine's dance.

Naturally there had been no comparison between Denny's fumbling yet sincere attempt and the stunning expertise of Trent's. Which only proved, C.C. decided as she scowled into her coffee, that Trent had spent a large part of his life with his lips slapped up against some woman's. Lots of women's.

It had been a rotten thing to do, she thought now. Particularly in the middle of what had been becoming a very satisfactory argument. Men like Trent didn't know how to fight fair, with wit and words and good honest fury. They were taught how to dominate, by whatever manner worked.

Well, it had worked, she thought, running a fingertip over her lips. Damn him and the horse he rode in on. It had worked like a charm, because for one moment, one brief, trembling moment she had felt something fine and lovely—something more than the exciting press of his mouth on hers, more than the possessive grip of his hands.

It had been inside her, beneath the panic and the pleasure, beyond the whirl of sensation—a glow, warm and golden, like a lamp in the window on a stormy night.

Then he had turned off that lamp, with one quick, careless flick, leaving her in the dark again.

She could have hated him for that alone, C.C. thought miserably, if she hadn't already had enough to hate him for.

"Hey, kid." Lilah breezed through the doorway, tidy in her park service khakis. Her mass of hair was in a neat braid down her back. Swinging at each ear was a trio of amber crystal balls. "You're up early."

"Me?" C.C. forgot her own mood long enough to stare. "Are you my sister or some clever imposter?"

"You be the judge."

"Must be an imposter. Lilah Maeve Calhoun's never up before eight o'clock, which is exactly twenty minutes before she has to rush out of the house to be five minutes late for work."

"God, I hate to be so predictable. My horoscope," Lilah told her as she rooted through the refrigerator. "It said that I should rise early today and contemplate the sunrise."

"So how was it?" C.C. asked as her sister brought a cold can of soda and a wicked slice of the Black Forest cake to the table.

"Pretty spectacular as sunrises go." Lilah shoveled cake into her mouth. "What's your excuse?"

"Couldn't sleep."

"Anything to do with the stranger at the end of the hall?"

C.C. wrinkled her nose and filched a cherry from Lilah's plate. "Guys like that don't bother me."

"Guys like that were created to bother women, and thank God for it. So..." Lilah stretched her legs out to rest her feet on an empty chair. The kitchen faucet was leaking again, but she liked the sound of it. "What's the story?"

"I didn't say there was a story."

"You don't have to say, it's all over your face."

"I just don't like him being here, that's all." Evading, C.C. rose to take her cup to the sink. "It's like we're already being pushed out of our own home. I know we've discussed selling, but it was all so vague and down some long, dark road." She turned back to her sister. "Lilah, what are we going to do?"

"I don't know." Lilah's eyes clouded. It was one of the few things she couldn't prevent herself from worrying about. Home and family, they were her weaknesses. "I guess we could sell some more of the crystal, and there's the silver."

"It would break Aunt Coco's heart to sell the silver."

"I know. But we may have to go piece by piece—or make the big move." She scooped up some more cake. "As much as I hate to say it, we're going to have to think hard, and practically, and seriously."

"But, Lilah, a hotel?"

Lilah merely shrugged. "I don't have any deep, moral problem with that. The house was built by crazy old Fergus to entertain platoons of guests, with all kinds of people racing around to serve meals and tidy linens. It seems to me that a hotel just about suits its original purpose." She gave a long sigh at C.C.'s expression. "You know I love the place as much as you do."

"I know."

What Lilah didn't add was that it would break her heart to have to sell it but that she was prepared to do what was best for the family.

"We'll give the gorgeous Mr. St. James a couple more days, then have a family meeting." She offered C.C. a bolstering smile. "The four of us together can't go wrong."

"I hope you're right."

"Honey, I'm always right—that's my little cross to bear." She took a swig of the sugar-ladened soft drink. "Now, why don't you tell me what kept you up all night?"

"I just did."

"No." Head cocked, she waved her fork at C.C. "Don't forget Lilah knows all and sees all—and what she doesn't she finds out. So spill it."

"Aunt Coco made me take him out in the garden."

"Yeah." Lilah grinned. "She's a wily old devil. I figured she was plotting some romance. Moonlight, flowers, the distant lap of water on rocks. Did it work?"

"We had a fight."

Lilah nodded, giving a go-ahead signal with her hand as she sipped. "That's a good start. About the house?"

"That..." C.C. began to pluck dried leaves from a withered philodendron. "And things."

"Like?"

"Names of mistresses," C.C. muttered. "Prominent Boston families. His shoes."

"An eclectic argument. My favorite kind. And then?"

C.C. jammed her hands into her pockets. "He kissed me."

"Ah, the plot thickens." She had Coco's love of gossip and, leaning forward, cradled her chin on her hands. "So, how was it? He's got a terrific mouth—I noticed it right off."

"So kiss him yourself."

After thinking it over a moment, Lilah shook her head—not without some regret. "Nope, terrific mouth or not, he's not my type. Anyway, you've already locked lips with him, so tell me. Was he good?"

"Yeah," C.C. said grudgingly. "I guess you could say that."

"Like on a scale of one to ten?"

The chuckle escaped before C.C. realized she was

laughing. "I wasn't exactly thinking about a rating system at the time."

"Better and better." Lilah licked her fork clean. "So, he kissed you and it was pretty good. Then what?"

Humor vanished as C.C. blew out a long breath. "He apologized."

Lilah stared, then slowly, deliberately set down her fork. "He what?"

"Apologized—very properly for his inexcusable behavior, and promised it wouldn't happen again. The jerk." C.C. crumbled the dead leaves in her hand. "What kind of a man thinks a woman wants an apology after she's been kissed boneless?"

Lilah only shook her head. "Well, the way I see it, there are three choices. He *is* a jerk, he's been trained to be overly polite, or he was incapable of thinking rationally."

"I vote for jerk."

"Hmm. I'm going to have to think about this." She drummed her cerise-tipped fingers on the table. "Maybe I should do his chart."

"Whatever sign his moon is in, I still vote for jerk." C.C. walked over to kiss Lilah's cheek. "Thanks. Gotta go."

"C.C." She waited until her sister turned back. "He has nice eyes. When he smiles, he has very nice eyes."

Trent wasn't smiling when he finally managed to escape from The Towers that afternoon. Coco had insisted on giving him a tour of the cellars, every damp inch, then had trapped him with photo albums for two hours.

It had been amusing to look at baby pictures of C.C., to view, through snapshots, her growing up from toddler to woman. She had been incredibly cute in pigtails and a missing tooth.

During the second hour, his alarm bells had sounded. Coco had begun to pump him none too subtly about his views on marriage, children, relationships. It was then he'd realized that behind Coco's soft, misty eyes ticked a sharp, calculating brain.

She wasn't trying to sell the house but to auction off one of her nieces. And apparently C.C. was the front-runner, with him preselected as the highest bidder. Well, the Calhoun women were in for a rude awakening, Trent determined. They were going to have to look elsewhere on the marriage market for a suitable candidate—and good luck to him.

And the St. Jameses would have the house, Trent promised himself. By damn they would, with no strings or wedding veils attached.

He started down the steep, winding drive in a controlled fury. When he caught the sound of his own voice as he muttered to himself, Trent decided that he would take a long, calming drive. Perhaps to Acadia National Park where Lilah worked as a naturalist. Divide and conquer, he thought. He would seek out each of the women in their own work space and rattle their beautiful chains.

Lilah seemed to be receptive, he thought. Any one of them would be more so that C.C. Amanda appeared to be sensible. He was certain Suzanna was a reasonable woman.

What had gone wrong with sister number four?

But he found himself heading down to the village, past Suzanna's fledgling landscape and garden business, past the BayWatch Hotel. When he drove up to C.C.'s garage, he told himself that was what he'd meant to do all along.

He would start with her, the sharpest thorn in his side. And when he was done, she would have no illusions about trapping him into marriage.

Hank was climbing into the tow truck as Trent climbed out of the BMW. "'Lo." Grinning, Hank pulled on the brim of his gray cap. "Boss's inside. Got us a nice fender bender over at the visitor's center."

"Congratulations."

"Ayah, we've been needing a little bodywork 'round here. Now, once the season picks up, business'll boom." Hank slammed the door then leaned his head out of the window, disposed to chat.

For some reason, Trent found himself noticing the boy—really noticing him. He was young, probably about twenty, with a round, open face, a thick down-east accent and a shock of straw-colored hair that shot out in all directions.

"Have you worked for C.C. long?"

"Since she bought the place from old Pete. That'll be, ah, three years. Ayah. Three years, nearly. She wouldn't hire me till I finished high school. Funny that way."

"Is she?"

"Once she gets a bee in her bonnet ain't no shaking it loose." He nodded toward the garage. "She's a might touchy today."

"Is that unusual?"

Hank chuckled and switched the radio on high. "Can't say she's all bark and no bite, 'cause I've seen her bite a time or two. See ya."

"Sure."

When Trent walked in, C.C. was buried to the waist under the hood of a late-model sedan. She had the radio on again, but this time it was her hips rather than her boots keeping time.

"Excuse me," Trent began, then remembered they had been through that routine before. He walked up and tapped her smartly on the shoulder.

"If you'd just…" But she turned her head only enough to see the tie. It wasn't maroon today, but navy. Still, she was certain of its owner. "What do you want?"

"I believe it was a lube job."

"Oh." She went back to replacing spark plugs. "Well, leave it outside, put the key on the bench, and I'll get to it. It should be ready by six."

"Do you always do business so casually?"

"Yeah."

"If you don't mind, I think I'll hold on to my keys until you're less distracted."

"Suit yourself." Two minutes passed in humming silence broken only by the radio's prediction of thunderstorms that evening. "Look, if you're just going to stand around, why don't you do something useful? Get in and start her up."

"Start her up?"

"Yeah, you know. Turn the key, pump the gas." She cocked her head up and blew at her bangs. "Think you can handle it?"

"Probably." It wasn't exactly what he'd had in mind, but Trent walked around to the driver's side. He noted that there was a car seat strapped in the front, and something pink and gooey on the carpet. He slid in and turned the key. The engine turned over and purred, quite nicely, he thought. Apparently C.C. thought differently.

Taking up her timing light, she began to make adjustments.

"It sounds fine," Trent pointed out.

"No, there's a miss."

"How can you hear anything with the radio blasting?"

"How can you not hear it? Better," she murmured. "Better."

Curious, he got out to lean over her shoulder. "What are you doing?"

"My job." Her shoulders moved irritably, as if there were an itch between the blades. "Back off, will you?"

"I'm only expressing normal curiosity." Without thinking, he set a hand lightly on her back and leaned farther in. C.C. jolted, felt a flash of pain then swore like a sailor.

"Let me see." He grabbed the hand she was busy shaking.

"It's nothing. Take off, will you? If you hadn't been in my way, my hand wouldn't have slipped."

"Stop dancing around and let me see." He took a firm grip on her wrist and examined her scraped knuckles. The faint well of blood beneath the engine grease caused him a sharp and ridiculous sense of guilt. "You'll need something on this."

"It's just a scratch." God, why wouldn't he let go of her hand? "What I need to do is finish this job."

"Don't be a baby," he said mildly. "Where's the first-aid kit?"

"It's in the bathroom, and I can do it myself."

Ignoring her, he kept hold of her wrist as he walked

around to shut the engine off. "Where's the bath-room?"

She jerked her head toward the hallway that sepa-rated the garage from the office. "If you'd just leave your keys—"

"You said it was my fault you hurt your hand, so I'll take the responsibility."

"I wish you'd stop pulling me around," she said as he hauled her toward the hallway.

"Then keep up." He pushed open a door into a white-tiled bathroom the size of a broom closet. Ig-noring her protests, he held C.C.'s hand under a spray of cool water. The dimensions of the room had them standing hip to hip. They both did their level best to ignore that as he took the soap and, with surprising gentleness, began to clean her hand. "It isn't deep," he said, annoyed that his throat was dry.

"I told you, it's just a scratch."

"Scratches get infected."

"Yes, doctor."

With a retort on the tip of his tongue, he glanced up. She looked so cute, he thought, with grease on her nose and her mouth in a five-year-old's pout. "I'm sorry," he heard himself say, and the petulance faded from her eyes.

"It wasn't your fault." Wanting something to do, she opened the mirrored cabinet over the sink for the first-aid kit. "I can take care of it, really."

"I like to finish what I start." He took the kit from her and found the antiseptic. "I guess I should say this is going to sting."

"I already know it stings." C.C. let out a little hiss as he swabbed the cut. Automatically she leaned over to blow on the heat, just as he did the same. Their heads bumped smartly. Rubbing hers with her free hand, C.C. gave a half laugh. "We make a lousy team."

"It certainly looks that way." With his eyes on hers, Trent blew softly on her knuckles. Something flickered in those pretty green irises, he noted. Alarm, surprise, pleasure, he couldn't be sure, but he would have wagered half his stock options that C. C. Calhoun was totally ignorant of her aunt's romantic plotting.

He brought her hand to his lips—just a test, he assured himself—and watched what was definitely confusion darken her eyes. Her hand went limp in his. Her mouth opened and stayed that way, with no sound coming out.

"A kiss is supposed to make it better," he pointed out and, for purely selfish reasons, whispered his lips over her hand again.

"I think…it would be better if…" Lord, the room was small, she thought distractedly. And getting smaller all the time. "Thanks," she managed. "I'm sure it's fine now."

"It needs to be bandaged."

"Oh, well, I don't—"

"You'll only get it dirty." Enjoying himself enormously, he took a roll of gauze and began to wrap her hand.

Thinking it would put some distance between them, C.C. turned. As if following the moves of a dance, Trent turned as well. Now they were facing, rather than side-by-side. He shifted—there was room to do little else—and her back was against the wall.

"Hurt?"

She shook her head. She wasn't hurt, C.C. decided,

she was crazy. A woman had to be crazy to have her heart pounding like a jackhammer because a man was wrapping gauze around her skinned knuckles.

"C.C." He taped the gauze competently in place. "Can I ask you a personal question?"

"I…" She lifted her shoulders and swallowed.

"What exactly is a lube job?"

She caught the amusement in his eyes, and, charmed by it, smiled back. "Forty-seven-fifty."

"Oh." They were as close as they had been the night before, when they'd been arguing. This, Trent decided, was much more pleasant. "Are you going to flush my radiator?"

"Absolutely."

"Then I'm forgiven for last night?"

Her brows lifted. "I didn't say that."

"I wish you'd reconsider." With her hand held between them, he shifted slightly closer. "You see, if I'm going to be damned for it, it's harder to resist the urge to sin again."

Flustered, she pressed back against the wall. "I don't think you're the least bit sorry about what you did."

He considered her a moment, the wide eyes, the tempting mouth. "I'm afraid you're right."

As she stood, torn between delight and terror, the phone began to shrill. "I've got to get that." Nimble as a greyhound, she streaked by him and out of the room.

He followed more slowly, surprised at himself. There was no doubt in his mind that she was as much victim of her aunt's fantasies as he. Another woman, certainly one with matrimony on her mind, would have smiled—or pouted. Would have slid her arms seductively around him—or held him sulkily away. But another woman would not have stood with her back planted against the wall as if facing a firing squad. Another woman would not have looked at him with big, helpless eyes and stammered.

Or looked so alluring while she did so.

C.C. snatched up the phone in her office, but her mind was blank. She stood, staring through the glass wall with the phone at her ear for ten silent seconds before the voice through the receiver brought her back.

"What? Oh, yes, yes, this is C.C. Sorry. Is that you, Finney?" She let out a long, pent-up breath as she listened. "Did you leave the lights on again? Are you sure? Okay, okay. It might be the starter motor." She ran a distracted hand through her hair and started to ease a hip down on the desk when she spotted Trent. She popped back up like a spring. "What? I'm sorry, could you say that again? Uh-huh. Why don't I come take a look at it on my way home? About six-thirty." Her lips curved. "Sure. I always have a taste for lobster. You bet. Bye."

"A mechanic who makes house calls," Trent commented.

"We take care of our own." Relax, she ordered herself. Relax right now. "Besides it's easy when there's the offer of an Albert Finney lob-stah dinner on the other end."

There was a tug of annoyance he tried mightily to ignore. "How's the hand?"

She wriggled her fingers. "Fine. Why don't you hang your keys on the pegboard?"

He did so. "Do you realize you've never called me by name?"

"Of course I have."

"No, you've called me names, but never by my name." He lifted a hand to gesture the thought away. "In any case, I need to talk to you."

"Listen, if it's about the house, this really isn't the time or place."

"It isn't, precisely."

"Oh." She looked at him, feeling that odd little jolt in her heart. "I'm really getting backed up. Can it wait until you pick up your car?"

He wasn't used to waiting for anything. "It won't take long. I feel I should warn you, as I believe you're as unaware as I was, of your aunt's plans."

"Aunt Coco? What plans?"

"The white-lace-and-orange-blossom type of plans."

Her expression went from baffled to stunned to suspicion. "Marriage? That's absurd. Aunt Coco's not planning to be married. She doesn't even see anyone seriously."

"I don't think she's the candidate." He walked toward her, keeping his eyes on her. "You are."

Her laugh was quick and full of fun as she sat on the edge of the desk. "Me? Married? That's rich."

"Yes, and so am I.'

Her laughter dried up. Using the palms of her hands, she levered herself off the desk. When she spoke, her voice was very cool, with licks of temper beneath. "Exactly what are you implying?"

"That your aunt, for reasons of her own, invited me here not only to look over the house, but her four very attractive nieces."

Her face went dead pale, as he now knew it did when she was desperately angry. "That's insulting."

"That's a fact."

"Get out." She gave him one hard shove toward the door. "Get out. Get your keys, your car and your ridiculous accusations and get out."

"Hold on and shut up for one minute." He took her firmly by the shoulders. "Just one minute, and when I'm done if you still think I'm being ridiculous, I'll leave."

"I know you're ridiculous. And conceited, and arrogant. If you think for one minute that I have—have designs on you—"

"Not you," he corrected with a little shake. "Your well-meaning aunt. 'Why don't you show Trenton the garden, C.C.? The flowers are exquisite in the moonlight.'"

"She was just being polite."

"In a pig's eye. Do you know how I spent my morning?"

"I couldn't be less interested."

"Looking through photo albums." He saw the anger turn to distress and pressed on. "Dozens of them. You were quite the adorable child, Catherine."

"Oh, God."

"And bright, too, according to your doting aunt. Spelling bee champ in the third grade."

With a strangled groan, she lowered to the desk again.

"Not a single cavity in your mouth."

"She didn't," C.C. managed.

"Oh, that and more. Top honors in your auto mechanics class in high school. Using the bulk of your inheritance to buy this shop from your employer. I'm told you're a very sensible woman who knows how to keep her feet on the ground. Then again, you come from excellent stock and were well-bred.''

''Like a holstein,'' she muttered, firing up.

''As you like. Naturally, with your background, brains and beauty, you'd make the right man the most excellent of wives.''

She was no longer pale, but blushing furiously. ''Just because Aunt Coco's proud of me doesn't mean she's asking you to pick out a silver pattern.''

''After she finished relating your virtues and showing me the pictures—quite lovely ones—of you in your prom dress.''

''My—'' C.C. only shut her eyes.

''She began to ask me my views on marriage and children. Dropping rather large, heavy hints that a man in my position needs a stable relationship with a stable woman. Such as yourself.''

''All right, all right. Enough.'' She opened her eyes again. ''Aunt Coco often gets ideas in her head about what's best for my sisters and me. If she goes overboard.'' C.C. set her teeth. ''When she goes overboard, it's only because she loves us and feels responsible. I'm sorry she made you uncomfortable.''

''I didn't tell you this to embarrass you or to have you apologize.'' Suddenly awkward, he slipped his hands into his pockets. ''I thought it best if you knew the way her thoughts were headed before, well, something got out of hand.''

''Got out of hand?'' C.C. repeated.

''Or was misunderstood.'' Odd, he thought, it was usually so easy to lay the ground rules. He certainly couldn't remember fumbling before. ''That is, after last night... I realize you've been sheltered to a certain degree.''

The fingers of C.C.'s good hand began to drum on the knee of her coveralls.

Perhaps he should start again. "I believe in honesty, C.C., in both my business and my personal relationships. Last night, between temper and the moonlight, we—I suppose you could say we lost control for a moment." Why did that seem so pale and inadequate a description for what had happened? "I wouldn't want your lack of experience, and your aunt's fantasies to result in a misunderstanding."

"Let me see if I get this. You're concerned that because you kissed me last night, and my aunt brought up the subject of marriage along with my baby pictures this morning, that I might get some wild idea in my head that I might be the next Mrs. St. James."

Thrown off, he ran a hand over his hair. "More or less. I thought it would be better, certainly more fair, if I told you straight off so that you and I could handle it reasonably. That way you wouldn't—"

"Develop any delusions of grandeur?" she suggested.

"Don't put words in my mouth."

"How can I? There's no room with your foot in there."

"Damn it." He hated the fact that she was absolutely right. "I'm simply trying to be perfectly honest with you so that there won't be any misunderstanding when I tell you I'm very attracted to you."

She only lifted a brow, too furious to see that his own words had left him speechless. "Now, I take it, I'm supposed to be flattered."

"You're not supposed to be anything. I'm merely trying to lay out the facts."

"I'll give you some facts." She shoved a hand into his chest. "You're not attracted to me, you're attracted to the image of the perfect and enviable Trenton St. James III. My aunt's fantasies, as you call them, are a result of a wonderful loving heart. Something I'm sure you can't understand. And as far as I'm concerned, I wouldn't think about spending five minutes with you much less the rest of my life. You may end up with my home, but not with me, buster." She was revving up and feeling wonderful. "If you came crawling to me on your hands and knees with a diamond as big as my fist in your teeth, I'd laugh in your face. Those are the facts. I'm sure you can find your way out."

She turned and strode down the hall. Trent winced as the door slammed.

"Well," he murmured, pressing his fingers to his eyes. "We certainly cleared that up."

Chapter Five

Insufferable. It was the perfect word to describe him, C.C. decided, and hugged it to her throughout the rest of the day.

By the time she got home, the house was quiet and settled for the night. She could hear, faintly, the soft and haunting notes of the piano from the music room. Turning away from the stairs, she followed the music.

It was Suzanna, of course, who sat at the lovely old spinet. She had been the only one who had stuck with the lessons or shown any real talent. Amanda had been too impatient, Lilah too lazy. And C.C.... She looked down at her hands. Her fingers had been more at home smeared with motor oil than at the keys of a piano.

Still she loved to listen. There was nothing that soothed or charmed her more than music.

Suzanna, lost somewhere in her own heart, sighed a little as the last notes died.

"That was beautiful." C.C. walked over to kiss her sister's hair.

"I'm rusty."

"Not from where I'm standing."

Smiling, Suzanna reached back to pat her hand and felt the gauze. "Oh, C.C., what did you do?"

"Just scraped my knuckles."

"Did you clean it well? When was your last tetanus shot?"

"Slow down, Mommy. It's clean as a whistle and I had a tetanus shot six months ago." C.C. sat on the bench, facing out into the room. "Where is everyone?"

"The kids are fast asleep—I hope. Wiggle your fingers."

C.C. sighed and complied.

With a satisfied nod, Suzanna continued. "Lilah's out on a date. Mandy's looking over some ledger or other. Aunt Coco went up hours ago to have a bubble bath and put cucumber slices on her eyes."

"What about him?"

"In bed, I imagine. It's nearly midnight."

"Is it?" Then she smiled. "You were waiting up for me."

"I was not." Caught, Suzanna laughed. "Exactly. Did you fix Mr. Finney's truck?"

"He left his lights on again." She yawned hugely. "I think he does it on purpose just so I can come over and recharge his battery." She stretched her arms to the ceiling. "We had lobster and dandelion wine."

"If he wasn't old enough to be your grandfather, I'd say he has a crush on you."

"He does. And it's mutual. So, did I miss anything around here?"

"Aunt Coco wants to have a séance."

"Not again."

Suzanna ran her hands lightly over the keys, improvising. "Tomorrow night, right after dinner. She insists there's something Great-Grandmother Bianca wants us to know—Trent, too."

"What does he have to do with it?"

Suzanna brushed at C.C.'s bangs. "If we decide to sell him the house, he'll more or less inherit her."

"Is that what we're going to do, Suzanna?"

"It might be what we have to do."

C.C. rose to toy with the tassels of the floor lamp. "My business is doing pretty good. I could take out a loan against it."

"No."

"But—"

"No," Suzanna repeated. "You're not going to risk your future on the past."

"It's my future."

"And it's our past." She rose, as well. When that light came into Suzanna's eyes, even C.C. knew better than to argue. "I know how much the house means to you, to all of us. Coming back here after Bax—after things didn't work out," Suzanna said carefully, "helped keep me sane. Every time I watch Alex or Jenny slide down the banister, I remember doing it myself. I see Mama sitting here at the piano, hear Papa telling stories in front of the fire."

"Then how can you even think of selling?"

"Because I learned to face realities, however unpleasant." She lifted a hand to C.C.'s cheek. Only five years separated them. Sometimes Suzanna felt it was fifty. "Sometimes things happen to you, or around you, that you just can't control. When that happens, you gather up what's important in your life, and go on.''

"But the house is important."

"How much longer do you really think we can hang on?"

"We could sell the lithographs, the Limoges, a few other things."

"And drag out the unhappiness." She knew entirely too much about that. "If it's time to let go, I think we should let go with some dignity."

"Then you've already made up your mind."

"No." Suzanna sighed and sat again. "Every time I think I have, I change it. Before dinner, the children and I walked along the cliffs." Eyes dreamy, she stared through the darkened window. "When I stand there, looking out over the bay, I feel something, something so incredible, it breaks my heart. I don't know what's right, C.C. I don't know what's best. But I'm afraid I know what has to be done."

"It hurts."

"I know."

C.C. sat beside her, rested her head on Suzanna's shoulder. "Maybe there'll be a miracle."

Trent watched them from the darkened hallway. He wished he hadn't heard them. He wished he didn't care. But he had heard, and for reasons he didn't choose to explore, he did care. Quietly he went back up the stairs.

"Children," Coco said with what she was certain was the last of her sanity, "why don't you read a nice book?"

"I want to play war." Alex swished an imaginary saber through the air. "Death to the last man."

And the child was only six, Coco thought. What would he be in ten years' time? "Crayons," she said hopefully, cursing rainy Saturday afternoons. "Why don't you both draw beautiful pictures? We can hang them on the refrigerator, like an art show."

"Baby stuff," Jenny said, a cynic at five. She hefted an invisible laser rifle and fired. "Z-z-zap! You're zapped, Alex, and totally disengrated."

"Disintergrated, dummy, and I am not either. I threw up my force field."

"Nuh-uh."

They eyed each other with the mutual dislike only siblings can feel after being cooped up on a Saturday. By tacit agreement, they switched to hand-to-hand combat. As they wrestled over the faded Aubusson carpet, Coco cast her gaze to the ceiling.

At least the match was taking place in Alex's room, so little harm could be done. She was tempted to go out and close the door, leaving them to finish up themselves, but she was, after all, responsible.

"Someone's going to get hurt," she began, in the age-old refrain of adult to child. "Remember what happened last week when Jenny gave you a bloody nose, Alex?"

"She did not." Masculine pride rose to the fore-front as he struggled to pin his agile sister to the mat.

"Did too, did too," she chanted, hoping to do so again. She scissored her quick little legs over him.

"Excuse me," Trent said from the doorway. "I seem to be interrupting."

"Not at all." Coco fluffed her hair. "Just some youthful high spirits. Children, say hello to Mr. St. James."

"'Lo," Alex said as he struggled to get his sister into a headlock.

Trent's answering grin struck Coco with inspiration. "Trenton, might I ask you a favor?"

"Of course."

"All the girls are working today, as you know, and I have just one or two quick, little errands to run. Would you mind terribly keeping an eye on the children for a short time?"

"An eye on them?"

"Oh, they're no trouble at all." She beamed at him, then down at her grandniece and grandnephew. "Jenny, don't bite your brother. Calhouns fight fair." Unless they fight dirty, she thought. "I'll be back before you know I'm gone," she promised, easing past him.

"Coco, I'm not sure that I—"

"Oh, and don't forget about the séance tonight." She hurried down the steps and left him to fend for himself.

Jenny and Alex stopped wrestling to stare owlishly at him. They would fight tooth and nail but would unite without hesitation against an outside force.

"We don't like baby-sitters," Alex told him dangerously.

Trent rocked back on his heels. "I'm already sure I don't like being one."

Alex's arm was around his sister's shoulders now, rather than her neck. Hers slipped round his waist. "We don't like it more."

Trent nodded. If he could handle a staff of fifty, he could certainly handle two sulky children. "Okay."

"When we went back to Boston last summer for a

visit, we had a sitter." Jenny eyed him with suspicion. "We made everybody's life a living hell."

Trent turned the chuckle into a cough. "Is that so?"

"Our father said we did," Alex corroborated. "And he was glad to see the back of us."

The infant profanity was no longer amusing. Trent struggled to keep the burn of anger out of his eyes and merely nodded. Baxter Dumont was obviously a prince among men. "I once locked my nanny in the closet and climbed out the window."

Alex and Jenny exchanged interested glances. "That's pretty good," Alex decided.

"She screamed for two hours," Trent improvised.

"We put a snake in our baby-sitter's bed and she ran out of the house in her nightgown." Jenny smiled smugly and waited to see if he could top it.

"Nicely done." What now? he wondered. "Have you any dolls?"

"Dolls are gross," Jenny said, loyal to her brother.

"Off with their heads!" Alex shouted, sending her into giggles. He sprang up, flourishing his imaginary sword. "I'm the evil pirate, and you're my prisoners."

"Uh-uh, I had to be prisoner last time." Jenny scrambled to her feet. "It's my turn to be the evil pirate."

"I said it first."

She gave him a hefty shove. "Cheater, cheater, cheater."

"Baby, baby, baby," he jeered, and pushed her back.

"Hold it!" Trent shouted before they could dive for each other. The unfamiliar masculine tone had them stopping in their tracks. "*I'm* the evil pirate," he told them, "and you're both about to walk the plank."

He enjoyed it. Their children's imagination might have been a bit bloody-minded, but they played fair when the rules were set. There would have been any number of people he knew socially who would have been stunned to see Trenton St. James III crawling around on the floor or firing a water pistol, but he could remember being closed in on rainy days himself.

The play went from pirates to space marauders to Indian rampage. At the end of a particularly gruesome battle, the three of them were sprawled on the floor. Alex, rubber tomahawk in hand, played dead so long he fell asleep.

"I won," Jenny said, then with her feather headdress falling over her eyes, cuddled against Trent's side. She, too, in the enviable way of children, was asleep in moments.

C.C. found them like that. The rain was patting gently at the windows. In the bath down the hall, a drip fell musically into a bucket. Otherwise there was only the sound of gentle, even breathing.

Alex was sprawled on his face, his fingers still clutched over his weapon. In addition to bodies, the floor was scattered with miniature cars, defeated action figures and a few plastic dinosaurs. Avoiding the casualties, she stepped inside.

She wasn't exactly sure what her feelings were at finding Trent sleeping on the floor with her niece and nephew. What she was certain of was that if she hadn't seen it for herself, she wouldn't have believed it.

His tie and shoes were gone, his hair mussed, and there was a streak of damp down his linen shirt.

The tug on her heart was slow and tender and very real. Why, he looked…sweet, she thought, then immediately jammed her hands into her pockets. That was absurd. A man like Trent was never sweet.

Maybe the kids had knocked him unconscious, she mused, and leaned over him. He opened his eyes, stared up at her for a moment, then made some kind of sleepy noise deep in his throat.

"What are you doing?" she whispered.

"I'm not completely sure." He lifted his head and looked around. Jenny was tucked into the curve of his arm, and Alex was down for the count on the other side. "But I think I'm the only survivor."

"Where's Aunt Coco?"

"Running a few errands. I'm keeping my eye on the kids."

She lifted a brow. "Oh, I can see that."

"I'm afraid there was a major battle, and many lives were lost."

C.C.'s lips twitched as she went to Alex's bed for a blanket. "Who won?"

"Jenny claimed victory." Gently he slipped his arm out from under her head. "Though Alex will disagree."

"Undoubtedly."

"What should we do with them?"

"Oh, we'll keep them, I suppose."

He grinned back at her. "No, I meant should they be put in bed or something?"

"No." Expertly she flipped open the blanket and spread it over both of them where they lay. "They'll be fine." She had a ridiculous urge to slip an arm around his waist and lay her head on his shoulder. She squashed it ruthlessly. "It was nice of you to offer to look after them."

"I didn't offer precisely. I was dragooned."

"It was still nice of you."

He caught up with her at the door. "I could use a cup of coffee."

C.C. hesitated only a moment. "All right. I'll fix it. It looks like you've earned it." She flicked a glance over her shoulder as she started down the stairs. "How'd your shirt get wet?"

"Oh." He brushed a hand over it, faintly embarrassed. "A direct hit with a death ray disguised as a water pistol. So, how was your day?"

"Not nearly as adventurous as yours." She turned into the kitchen and went directly to the stove. "I only rebuilt an engine."

When the coffee was started, she moved over to light a fire in the kitchen hearth. She had rain in her hair, Trent noticed. He wasn't a lyrical man, but he found himself thinking that the droplets of water looked like a shower of diamonds against the glossy cap.

He'd always preferred women with long hair, he reminded himself. Feminine, soft, wavy. And yet... the style suited C.C., showing off her slender neck, perfectly framing that glorious white skin.

"What are you staring at?"

He blinked, shook his head. "Nothing. Sorry, I was just thinking. It's ah...there's something comforting about a fire in the kitchen."

"Hmm." He looked weird, she thought. Maybe it was the lack of a tie. "Do you want milk in your coffee?"

"No, black."

Her arm brushed his as she walked to the stove. This time it was he who stepped back. "Did Aunt Coco say where she was going?"

Maybe there was static electricity in the air, he thought. That would explain the jolt he'd felt when he'd touched her. "Not exactly. It doesn't matter, the kids were entertaining."

She studied his face as she handed him a mug. "I think you mean it."

"I do. Maybe I haven't been around children enough to become jaded. Those two are quite a pair."

"Suzanna's a terrific mother." Comfortable, she leaned back against the counter as she sipped. "She used to practice on me. So, how's the car running?"

"Better than it has in months." He toasted her with the mug. "I'm afraid I didn't notice anything was off until after you'd worked on it. I don't really know anything about engines."

"That's all right. I don't know how to plot a corporate takeover."

"I was sorry you weren't there when I came around to pick it up. Hank said you'd gone to dinner. I guess you had a good time—you didn't get in until late."

"I always have a good time with Finney." She turned around to raid the cookie jar, then offered him one as he tried to ignore the little nip of jealousy.

"An old friend?"

"I guess you could say so." C.C. took a deep breath and prepared to launch into the speech she had practiced all day. "I'd like to straighten out the business you brought up yesterday."

"It isn't necessary. I got the picture."

"I could have explained things without being so hard on you."

He tilted his head, studying her thoughtfully. "You could have?"

"I like to think so." Determined to wipe the slate clean, she set the coffee aside. "I was embarrassed, and being embarrassed makes me angry. This whole situation is difficult."

He could still hear, very clearly, the unhappiness in her voice as she had spoken with Suzanna the night before. "I think I'm beginning to understand that."

Her eyes came back to his, and she sighed. "Well, in any case, I can't help but resent the fact that you want to buy The Towers, or that we might have to let you—but that's a separate thing from Aunt Coco's maneuvers. I think I realized, after I stopped being mad, that you were just as embarrassed as I was. You were just so damned polite."

"It's a bad habit of mine."

"You're telling me." She waved half a cookie at him. "If you hadn't brought up the kiss—"

"I understand that was an error in judgment, but since I'd already apologized for it, I thought we could deal with it reasonably."

"I didn't want an apology," C.C. muttered. "Then or now."

"I see."

"No, you don't. You certainly don't. What I meant was that an apology was unnecessary. I may be inexperienced by your standards, and I may not be sophisticated like the women you're used to dealing with, but I'm not foolish enough to start weaving daydreams out of one stupid kiss." She was getting angry again and was determined not to. After one deep, cleansing breath, she tried again. "I'd simply like to put that, and our conversation yesterday behind us, completely and totally. If it turns out that we will have business dealings, it would be wiser all around if we can be civilized."

"I like you this way."

"What way?"

"When you're not taking potshots at me."

She finished off her cookie and grinned. "Don't get used to it. All Calhouns have hideous tempers."

"So I've been warned. Truce?"

"I suppose. Want another cookie?"

He was staring again, she noted, and her own eyes widened when he reached out to brush his fingertips down her hair. "What are you doing?"

"Your hair's wet." He stroked it again, fascinated. "It smells like wet flowers."

"Trent—"

He smiled. "Yes?"

"I don't think this is the best way to handle things."

"Probably not." But his fingers trailed down through her hair to the nape of her neck. He felt her quick shudder. "I can't quite get you out of my mind. And I keep having these uncontrollable urges to get my hands on you. I wonder why."

"Because—" she wet her lips "—I irritate you."

"Oh, you do that, without question." He pressed those fingers at the back of her neck and had her moving forward an inch. "But not simply in the way you mean. It's not simple at all. Though it should be." His other hand skimmed over the collar of her denim work shirt, then cupped her chin. "Otherwise, why would I feel this irresistible need to touch you every time I get near you?''

''I don't know.'' His fingers, light as a feather, trailed down to where her pulse thudded at the base of her throat. ''I wish you wouldn't.''

''Wouldn't what?''

''Touch me.''

He slid his hand down her sleeve to her bandaged hand, then lifted it to his lips. ''Why?''

''Because you make me nervous.''

Something lit in his eyes, turning them almost black. ''You don't even mean to be provocative, do you?''

''I wouldn't know how.'' Her eyes fluttered closed on a strangled moan when he brushed his lips over her jawline.

''Honeysuckle,'' he murmured, drawing her closer. He'd once thought it such a common flower. ''I can all but taste it on you. Wild and sweet.''

Her muscles turned to water as his mouth cruised over hers. So much lighter, so much gentler than the first time. It wasn't right that he could do this to her. The part of her mind that was still rational all but shouted it. But even that was drowned out by the flood of longing.

''Catherine.'' He had her face framed between his hands now as he nipped seductively at her lips. ''Kiss me back.''

She wanted to shake her head, to pull away and walk casually, even callously out of the room. Instead she flowed into his arms, her mouth lifting to his, meeting his.

His fingers tightened before he could prevent it, then slipped down to pull her more truly against him.

He could think of nothing, wanted to think of nothing—no consequences, no rules, no code of behavior. For the first time in his memory, he wanted only to feel. Those sharp and sweet sensations she had racing through him were more than enough for any man.

She was strong—had always been strong—but not enough to prevent time from standing still. It was this one moment, she realized, that she had been waiting for all of her life. As her hands slid up his back, she held the moment to her as completely as she held him.

The fire crackled in the grate. The rain pattered. There was the light, spicy scent of the potpourri Lilah set everywhere about the house. His arms were so strong and sure, yet with a gentleness she hadn't expected from him.

She would remember it all, every small detail, along with the dark excitement of his mouth and the sound of her name as he whispered it against hers.

He drew her away, slowly this time, more shaken than he cared to admit. As he watched, she ran her tongue over her lips as if to savor a last taste. That small, unconscious gesture nearly brought him to his knees.

"No apology this time," he told her, and his voice wasn't steady.

"No."

He touched his lips to hers again. "I want you. I want to make love with you."

"Yes." It was a glorious kind of release. Her lips curved against his. "Yes."

"When?" He buried his face in her hair. "Where?"

"I don't know." She shut her eyes on the wonder of it. "I can't think."

"Don't." He kissed her temple, her cheekbone, her mouth. "This isn't the time for thinking."

"It has to be perfect."

"It will be." He framed her face again. "Let me show you."

She believed him—the words and what she saw in his eyes. "I can't believe it's going to be you." Laughing, she threw her arms around him, holding him close. "That I've waited all my life to be with someone. And it's you."

His hand paused on its way to her hair. "All of your life?"

Dreamily in love, she hugged him tighter. "I thought I'd be afraid the first time, but I'm not. Not with you."

"The first time." He shut his eyes. *Her* first time. How could he have been so stupid? He'd recognized the inexperience, but he hadn't thought, hadn't believed she was completely innocent. And he'd all but seduced her in her own kitchen. "C.C."

"I'm thirsty," Alex complained from the doorway, and had them springing apart like guilty children. He eyed them suspiciously. "What are you doing that stuff for? It's disgusting." He sent Trent a pained look, man-to-man. "I don't get why anybody wants to go around kissing girls."

"It's an acquired taste," Trent told him. "Why don't we get you a drink, then I need to talk to your aunt a minute. Privately."

"More mush stuff."

"What mush stuff?" Amanda wanted to know as she breezed in.

"Nothing." C.C. reached for the coffeepot.

"Lord, did I have a day," Amanda began, and grabbed a cookie.

Suzanna walked in two seconds later, followed by Lilah. As the kitchen filled with feminine laughter and scent, Trent knew his moment was lost.

When C.C. smiled at him across the room, he was afraid his head would be lost with it.

Chapter Six

It was Trent's first séance. He sincerely hoped it would be his last. There was simply no gracious way to decline attending. When he suggested that perhaps this was a family evening, Coco merely laughed and patted his cheek.

"My dear, we wouldn't think of excluding you. Who knows, it may be you the restless spirits choose to speak through."

The possibility did very little to cheer him up.

Once the children were tucked into bed for the evening, the rest of the family, along with the reluctant Trent, gathered around the dining room table. The stage had been set.

A dozen candles flickered atop the buffet. Dimestore holders cheek by jowl with Meissen and Baccarat. Another trio of white tapers glowed in the center of the table. Even nature seemed to have gotten into the spirit of things—so to speak.

Outside, the rain had turned into a wet fitful snow,

blown about by a rising wind. As warm and cold air collided, thunder boomed and lightning flickered.

It was a dark and stormy night, Trent thought fatalistically as he took his seat.

Coco had not, as he'd secretly feared, worn a turban and a fringed shawl. As always, she was meticulously groomed. Around her neck, she did wear a large amethyst crystal, which she toyed with constantly.

"Now, children," she instructed. "Take hands and form the circle."

The wind knocked at the windows as C.C. slipped her hand into Trent's. Coco took his other. Directly across from him Amanda grinned, the amusement and sympathy obvious as she linked with her aunt and Suzanna.

"Don't worry, Trent," she told him. "The Calhoun ghosts are always well behaved around company."

"Concentration is essential," Lilah explained as she closed the gap between her eldest and youngest sister. "And very basic, really. All you have to do is clear your mind, particularly of any cynicism." She winked at Trent. "Astrologically, it's an excellent night for a séance."

C.C. gave his hand a quick, reassuring squeeze as Coco took over.

"We must all clear our minds and open our hearts." She spoke in a soothing monotone. "For some time I've felt that my grandmother, the unhappy Bianca, has wanted to contact me. This was her summer home for the last years of her young life. The place where she spent her most joyous and most tragic moments. The place where she met the man she loved, and lost."

She closed her eyes and took a deep breath. "We are here, Grandmama, waiting for you. We know your spirit is troubled."

"Does a spirit have a spirit?" Amanda wanted to know and earned a glare from her aunt. "It's a reasonable question."

"Behave," Suzanna murmured, and smothered a smile. "Go ahead, Aunt Coco."

They sat in silence, with only Coco's voice murmuring over the crackle of the fire and the moan of the wind. Trent's mind wasn't clear. It was filled with the way C.C. had fit in his arms, with the sweet and generous way her mouth had opened to his. The way she had looked at him, her eyes clouded and warm with emotions. Emotions he had recklessly stirred in her.

Guilt almost smothered him.

She wasn't like Marla or any of the women he had coolly romanced over the years. She was innocent and open and, despite a strong will and a sharp tongue, achingly vulnerable. He had taken advantage of that, inexcusably.

Not that it was entirely his fault, he reminded himself. She was, after all, a beautiful, desirable woman. And he was human. The fact that he wanted her—strictly on a physical plane—was only natural.

He glanced over just as she turned her head and smiled at him. Trent had to fight down a foolish urge to lift her hand to his lips and taste her skin.

She touched something in him, damn it. Something he was determined would remain untouched. When she smiled at him—even when she scowled at him—she made him feel more, want more, wish more, than any woman he'd ever known.

It was ridiculous. They were miles apart in every way. And yet, with her hand warm in his as it was now, he felt closer to her, more in tune with her, than he'd ever felt with anyone.

He could even see them sitting together on a sunny summer porch, watching children play on the grass. The sound of the sea was as soothing as a lullaby. The air smelled of roses climbing up the trellis. And of honeysuckle, growing wild where it chose.

He blinked, afraid his heart had stopped. The image had been so clear and so terrifying. It was the atmosphere, he assured himself. The candles flickering, the wind and lightning. It was playing games with his imagination.

He wasn't a man to sit on the porch with a woman and watch children. He had work, a business to run. The idea of him becoming involved with a bad-tempered auto mechanic was simply absurd.

Cold air seemed to slap him in the face. As he stiffened, he saw the flames of the candles lean dramatically to the left. A draft, he told himself, as the cold chilled him to the bone. The place was full of them.

He felt C.C.'s shudder. When he looked at her, her eyes were wide and dark. Her fingers curled tight around his.

"She's here!" There was both surprise and excitement in Coco's voice. "I'm sure of it."

In her delight, she nearly pulled her hands free and broke the chain. She had believed—well, had wanted to believe—but she had never actually felt a *presence* so distinctly.

She beamed down the table at Lilah, but her niece had her eyes closed and a faint smile on her lips.

"A window must have come open," Amanda said, and would have bolted up to check if Coco hadn't hissed at her.

"No such thing. Sit still, everyone. Sit still. She's here. Can't you feel it?"

C.C. did, and wasn't sure whether she should feel foolish or frightened. Something was different. She was certain that Trent sensed it, as well.

It was as though someone had gently closed a hand over her and Trent's joined ones. The cold vanished, replaced by a soothing, comforting warmth. So real was it that C.C. looked over her shoulder, certain she would see someone standing behind her.

Yet all she saw was the dance of fire and candlelight on the wall.

"She's so lost." C.C. let out a gasp when she realized it was she herself who had spoken. All eyes fixed on hers. Even Lilah's lazily opened.

"Do you see her?" Coco demanded in a whisper, squeezing C.C.'s fingers.

"No. No, of course not. It's just..." She couldn't explain. "It's so sad," she murmured, unaware that tears glistened in her eyes. "Can't you feel it?"

Trent could, and it left him speechless. Heartbreak, and a longing so deep it was immeasurable. Imagination, he told himself. The power of suggestion.

"Don't close it off." Coco searched desperately for the proper procedure. Now that something had actually happened, she hadn't a clue. A flash of lightning had her jolting. "Do you think she'll speak through you?"

At the opposite end of the table, Lilah smiled. "Just tell us what you see, honey."

"A necklace," C.C. heard herself say. "Two tiers

of emeralds flanked by diamonds. Beautiful, brilliant.'' The gleam hurt her eyes. ''She's wearing them, but I can't see her face. Oh, she's so unhappy.''

''The Calhoun necklace,'' Coco breathed. ''So, it's true.''

Then, as if a sigh passed through the air, the candles flickered again, then ran straight and true. A log fell in the grate.

''Weird,'' Amanda said when her aunt's hand fell limply from hers. ''I'll fix the fire.''

''Honey.'' Suzanna studied C.C. with as much concern as curiosity. ''Are you okay?''

''Yes.'' C.C. cleared her throat. ''Sure.'' She shot Trent a quick look. ''I guess the storm got to me.''

Coco lifted a hand to her breast and patted her speeding heart. ''I think we could all use a nice glass of brandy.'' She rose, more shaken than she wanted to admit, and walked to the buffet.

''Aunt Coco,'' C.C. began. ''What's the Calhoun necklace?''

''The emeralds.'' She passed the snifters. ''There was a legend that's been handed down through the family. You know part of it, how Bianca fell in love with another man, and died tragically. I suppose it's time I told you the rest of it.''

''You kept a secret?'' Amanda grinned as she swirled her drink. ''Aunt Coco, you amaze me.''

''I wanted to wait for the right time. It seems it's now.'' She took her seat again, warming the brandy between her hands. ''Rumor was that Bianca's lover was an artist, one of the many who came to the island in those days. She would go to meet him when Fergus was away from the house, which was often. Theirs was not precisely an arranged marriage, but the next thing to it. She was years younger than he, and apparently quite beautiful. Since Fergus destroyed all pictures of her after her death, there's no way of knowing for sure."

"Why?" Suzanna asked. "Why would he do that?"

"Grief perhaps." Coco shrugged.

"Rage, more likely," Lilah put in.

"In any case." Coco paused to sip. "He destroyed all reminders of her, and the emeralds were lost. He had given Bianca the necklace when she gave birth to Ethan, her eldest son." She glanced at Trent. "My father. He was just a child at the time of his mother's death, so the events were never very clear in his mind. But his nanny, who had been fiercely loyal to Bianca, would tell him stories about her. And those he remembered. She didn't care for the necklace, but wore it often."

"As a kind of punishment," Lilah put in. "And a kind of talisman." She smiled at her aunt. "Oh, I've known about the necklace for years. I've seen it—just as C.C. did tonight." She lifted the brandy to her lips. "There are earrings to match. Emerald teardrops, like the stone in the center of the bottom tier."

"You're making that up," Amanda accused her, and Lilah merely moved her shoulders.

"No, I'm not." She smiled at C.C. "Am I?"

"No." Uneasy, C.C. looked to her aunt. "What does all this mean?"

"I'm not altogether sure, but I think the necklace is still important to Bianca. It was never seen after she died. Some believed Fergus threw it into the sea."

"Not on your life," Lilah said. "The old man

wouldn't have thrown a nickel into the sea, much less an emerald necklace."

"Well…" Coco didn't like to speak ill of an ancestor, but she was forced to agree. "Actually, it would have been out of character. Grandpapa counted his pennies."

"He made Silas Marner look like a philanthropist," Amanda put in. "So, what happened to it?"

"That, my dear, is the mystery. My father's nanny told him that Bianca was going to leave Fergus, that she had packed a box, what the nanny called a treasure box. Bianca had secreted away what was most valuable to her."

"But she died instead," C.C. murmured.

"Yes. The legend is that the box, with its treasure, is hidden somewhere in the house."

"Our house?" Suzanna gaped at her aunt. "Do you really think there's some kind of treasure chest hidden around here for—what—eighty years, and no one's found it?"

"It's a very big house," Coco pointed out. "For all we know she might have buried it in the roses."

"If it existed in the first place," Amanda murmured.

"It existed." Lilah sent a nod toward C.C. "And I think Bianca's decided it's time to find it."

When everyone began to talk at once, arguments and suggestions bouncing around the table, Trent raised a hand. "Ladies. Ladies," he repeated, waiting for them to subside. "I realize that this is family business, but as I was invited to participate in this… experiment, I feel obligated to add a calming note. Legends are most often exaggerated and expanded over time. If there ever was a necklace, wouldn't it be more likely that Fergus sold it after the death of his wife?''

"He couldn't sell it," Lilah pointed out, "if he couldn't find it."

"Do any of you really think your great-grandfather buried treasure in the garden or hid it behind a loose stone?'' One glance around the table told him that was precisely how they were thinking. Trent shook his head. "That kind of fairy tale's more suited for Alex and Jenny than for grown women." He spread his hands. "You don't even know for certain if there was a necklace in the first place."

"But I saw it," C.C. said, though it made her feel foolish.

"You imagined it," he corrected. "Think about it. A few minutes ago six rational adults were sitting around this table holding hands and calling up ghosts. All right as an odd sort of parlor game, but for anyone to actually believe in messages from the other-world..." He certainly wasn't going to add that for a moment, he'd felt something himself.

"There's something appealing about a cynical, practical-minded man." Lilah rose to open one of the drawers of the buffet and unearthed a pad and pencil. After coming over to kneel by C.C.'s chair, she began to sketch. "I certainly respect your opinion, but the fact is not only did the necklace exist, I'm certain it still does."

"Because of a nanny's bedtime stories?"

She smiled at him. "No, because of Bianca." She slid the pad toward C.C. "Is that what you saw to-night?"

Lilah had always been a careless and clever artist. C.C. stared at the rough sketch of the necklace, two ornate and filigreed tiers studded with square-cut emeralds, sprinkled with diamond brilliants. From the bottom tier a large gem in the shape of a teardrop dripped.

"Yes." C.C. traced a fingertip over it. "Yes, this is it."

Trent studied the drawing. If indeed such a piece did exist, and Lilah's drawing was anywhere close to scale, it would undoubtedly be worth a fortune.

"Oh, my," Coco murmured as the pad was passed to her. "Oh, my."

"I think Trent has a point." Amanda gave the sketch a hard look before handing it to Suzanna. "We can hardly take the house apart stone by stone, even if we wanted to. Despite any sort of paranormal experience, the first order of business is to make certain—absolutely certain," she added when Lilah sighed, "that the necklace is a fact. Even eighty years ago, something like this had to cost an incredible amount of money. There has to be a record. If Lilah's famous vibes are wrong and it was sold again, there would be a record of that as well."

"Spoken like a true stick-in-the-mud," Lilah complained. "I guess this means we spend our Sunday pushing through a paper mountain."

C.C. didn't even try to sleep. She wrapped herself in her flannel robe and, with the house creaking around her, left her room for Trent's. She could hear the murmur of the late news from Amanda's room. Then the hum of sitars from Lilah's. It didn't occur to her to feel awkward or to hesitate. She simply knocked on Trent's door and waited for him to answer.

When he did, with his shirt open and his eyes a little sleepy, she felt her first frisson of nerves.

"C.C.?"

"I need to talk to you." She glanced toward the bed, then away. "Can I come in?"

How was a man to deal fairly when even flannel had become erotic? "Maybe it would be better if we waited until morning."

"I'm not sure I can."

The knots in his stomach tightened. "Okay. Sure." The sooner he explained himself to her, the better. He hoped. Trent let her in and closed the door. "Do you want to sit down?"

"Too much nervous energy." Hugging herself, she walked to the window. "It stopped snowing. I'm glad. I know Suzanna was worried about some of her flowers. Spring's so unpredictable on the island." She dragged a hand through her hair as she turned. "I'm making small talk, and I hate that." A deep breath settled her. "Trent, I need to know what you think about tonight. Really think about it."

"Tonight?" he said carefully.

"The séance." She rubbed her hands over her face. "Lord, I feel like an imbecile even saying it, but, Trent, something happened." Now she thrust those restless hands toward him, waiting for him to clasp them in his. "I'm very grounded, very literal minded. Lilah's the one who believes in all this stuff. But now…Trent, I need to know. Did feel anything?"

"I don't know what you mean. I certainly felt foolish several times."

"Please." She gave his hands an impatient shake. "Be honest with me. It's important."

Isn't that what he'd promised himself he would do? "All right, C.C. Tell me what you felt."

"The air got very cold. Then it was as if something—someone—was standing behind us. Behind and between the two of us. It wasn't something that frightened me. I was surprised, but not afraid. We were holding hands, like this. And then..."

She was waiting for him to say it, to admit it. Those big green eyes demanded it. When he did so, it was with great reluctance. "It felt as though someone put a hand over ours."

"Yes." Eyes closed, she brought his hands to her curved lips. "Yes, exactly."

"Shared hallucination," he began, but she cut him off with a laugh.

"I don't want to hear that. No rational explanations." She pressed his hand to her cheek. "I'm not a fanciful person, but I know it meant something, something important. I *know*."

"The necklace?"

"Only a part of it—and not this part. All the rest—the necklace, the legend, we'll figure it out sooner or later. I think we'll have to because it's meant. But this, this was like a blessing."

"C.C.—"

"I love you." Eyes dark and brilliant, she touched his cheek. "I love you, and nothing in my life has ever felt so right."

He was speechless. Part of him wanted to step back, smile kindly and tell her she was letting the moment run away with her. Love didn't happen in a matter of days. If it happened at all, which was rare, it took years.

Another part, buried deep, wanted to hold her close so that the moment would never end.

"Catherine—"

But she was already moving into his arms. They seemed to be waiting for her. As if he had no control over them, they wrapped around her. The warmth, her warmth, seeped into him like a drug.

"I think I knew the first time you kissed me." She pressed her cheek to his. "I didn't want it, didn't ask for it, but it's never been like that for me before. I don't think I ever expected it to be. There you were, so suddenly, so completely in my life. Kiss me again, Trent. Kiss me now."

He was helpless to do otherwise. His lips were already burning for hers. When they met, the fire only sparked hotter. She was molten in his arms, sending white licks of flame shooting through his system. When he couldn't prevent his demand from increasing, she didn't hesitate, but strained against him, offering everything.

She slid her hands under his shirt, delighted to feel his quick, involuntary tremor. His muscles bunched under her fingers with the kind of strength she wanted, needed.

The wind sighed outside the windows as she sighed in his arms.

He couldn't get enough. He found himself wanting to devour her as his lips raced crazily over her face, down her throat where his teeth scraped lightly over her skin. The scent of honeysuckle wheeled in his head. She arched back, her low whimpers of pleasure pounding in his blood.

He had to touch her. He would go mad if he didn't. Mad if he did. When he parted her robe, he groaned, discovering she was naked for him beneath. Desperate, he filled his hand with her.

Now she knew what it was to have the blood swim. She could all but feel it racing under her skin, beating hot wherever he touched. There was a weakness here, a glorious one, mixed with a kind of manic strength. She wanted to give him both somehow and found the way when his mouth came frantically back to hers.

She trembled even as she answered. She surrendered even as she heated. As her head fell back and her fingers dug hard into his shoulders, he felt something move through him that was more than desire, deeper than passion.

Happiness. Hope. Love. As he recognized the feelings, terror joined them.

Breath heaving, he pulled away.

Her robe had fallen off one shoulder, baring it. Already his mouth had supped there. Her eyes were as brilliant as the emeralds she had imagined. Smiling, she lifted a trembling hand to his cheek.

"Do you want me to stay tonight?"

"Yes—no." Holding her at arm's length was the hardest thing he'd ever done. "Catherine…" He did want her to stay, he realized. Not just tonight, and not simply because of that glorious body of hers. The fact that he did made it all the more important to set things right. "I don't—I haven't been fair with you, and this has gotten out of hand so quickly." A long, unsteady breath escaped him. "Lord, you're beautiful. No," he said quickly when she smiled and started to step forward. "We need to talk. Just talk."

"I thought we had."

If she continued to look at him that way, he'd stop giving a damn about fairness. Or his own survival. "I haven't made myself clear,'' he began slowly. "If I had known—if I had realized how completely innocent you are, I wouldn't—well, I hope I would have been more careful. Now I can only try to make up for it.''

"I don't understand.''

"No, that's the problem." Needing some distance, he walked away. "I said I was attracted to you, very attracted. And that's obviously true. But I would never have taken advantage of you if I had known.''

Suddenly cold, she drew the robe around her. "You're upset because I haven't been with a man before?''

"Not upset." Frustrated, he turned back. "'Upset' isn't the word. I can't seem to find one. There are rules, you see." But she only continued to stare at him. "Catherine, a woman like you expects—deserves—more than I can give you.''

She lowered her gaze to her hands as she carefully fastened the belt to her robe. "What is that?''

"Commitment. A future.''

"Marriage.''

"Yes.''

Her knuckles were turning white. "I suppose you think this—what I said—is part of Aunt Coco's plans.''

"No." He would have gone to her then if he'd dared. "No, of course I don't.''

"Well." She struggled to make her fingers relax. "That's something, I suppose.''

"I know your feelings are honest—exaggerated perhaps—but honest. And it's completely my fault. If this hadn't happened so quickly, I would have explained to you from the first that I have no intention of marrying, ever. I don't believe that two people can be loyal to each other, much less happy together for a lifetime.''

"Why?"

"Why?" He stared at her. "Because it simply doesn't work. I've watched my father go from marriage to divorce to marriage. It's like watching a tennis match. The last time I heard from my mother, she was on her third marriage. It simply isn't practical to make vows knowing they'll only be broken.''

"Practical," she repeated with a slow nod. "You won't let yourself feel anything for me because it would be impractical."

"The problem is I do feel something for you."

"Not enough." Only enough to cut out her heart. "Well, I'm glad we got that sorted out.'' Blindly she turned for the door. "Good night.''

"C.C." He laid a hand on her shoulder before she could find the knob.

"Don't apologize," she said, praying her control would hold a few more minutes. "It isn't necessary. You've explained it all perfectly."

"Damn it, why don't you yell at me? Call me a few of the names I'm sure I deserve." He'd have preferred that to the quiet desolation he'd seen in her eyes.

"Yell at you?" She made herself turn and face him. "For being fair and honest? Call you names? How can I call you names, Trent, when I feel so terribly sorry for you?"

His hand slipped away from her. She held her head up. Under the hurt, just under it, was pride.

"You're throwing away something—no, not throwing," she corrected. "You're politely handing back something you'll never have again. What you've turned out of your life, Trent, would have been the best part of it.''

She left him alone with the uneasy feeling that she was absolutely right.

There was a party tonight. I thought it would be good for me to fill the house with people and lights and flowers. I know that Fergus was pleased that I supervised all the details so carefully. I had wondered if he had noticed my distraction, or how often I walked along the cliffs these afternoons, or how many hours I have begun to spend in the tower, dreaming my dreams. But it does not seem so.

The Greenbaums were here, and the McAllisters and the Prentises. Everyone who summers on the island, that Fergus feels we should take note of, attended. The ballroom was banked with gardenias and red roses. Fergus had hired an orchestra from New York, and the music was both lovely and lively. I believe Sarah McAllister drank too much champagne, for her laugh began to grate on my nerves long before supper was served.

My new gold dress suited very well, I think, for it gathered many compliments. Yet when I danced with Ira Greenbaum, his eyes were on my emeralds. They hung like a shackle around my neck.

How unfair I am! They are beautiful, and mine only because Ethan is mine.

During the evening, I slipped up to the nursery to check on the children, though I know how doting Nanny is to all of them. Ethan woke and sleepily asked if I had brought him any cake.

He looks like an angel as he sleeps, he, and my

other sweet babies. My love for them is so rich, so deep, that I wonder why it is my heart cannot transfer any of that sweet feeling to the man who fathered them.

Perhaps the fault is in me. Surely that must be so. When I kissed them good-night and stepped out into the hall again, I wished so desperately that rather than go back to the ballroom to laugh and dance, I could run to the cliffs. To stand at the cliffs with the wind in my hair and the sound and smells of the sea everywhere.

Would he come to me then, if I dared such a thing? Would he come so that we would stand there together in the shadows, reaching out for something we have no business wanting, much less taking?

I did not go to the cliffs. My duty is my husband, and it was to him I went. Dancing with him, my heart felt as cold as the jewels around my neck. Yet I smiled when he complimented me on my skill as a hostess. His hand at my waist was so aloof, but so possessive. As we moved to the music, his eyes scanned the room, approving what was his, studying his guests to be certain they were impressed.

How well I know what status and opinion mean to the man I married. And how little it seems they have come to mean to me.

I wanted to shout at him. "Fergus, for God's sake, look at me. Look at me and see. Make me love you, for fear and respect cannot be enough for either of us. Make me love you so that I will never again turn my steps toward the cliffs and what waits for me there."

But I did not shout. When he told me impatiently

that it was necessary for me to dance with Cecil Barkley, I murmured my assent.

Now the music is done and the lamps are snuffed out. I wonder when I will see Christian again. I wonder what will become of me.

Chapter Seven

C.C. sat cross-legged in the center of an ocean of papers. Her assignment—whether or not she'd chosen to accept it—had been to go through all of the notes and receipts and scraps that had been stuffed into three cardboard boxes marked miscellaneous.

Nearby Amanda sat at a card table, with several more bulging boxes at her feet. With her hair clipped back and reading glasses sliding down her nose, she meticulously studied each paper before laying it on one of the various stacks she had started.

"This should have been done decades ago," she commented.

"You mean it should have been burned decades ago."

"No." Amanda shoved the glasses back into place. "Some of it's fascinating, and certainly deserves to be preserved. Stuffing papers into cardboard boxes is not my idea of preserving family history."

"Does a recipe for gooseberry jam rate as family history?"

"For Aunt Coco it does. That goes under kitchen, subheading menus."

C.C. shifted then waved away a cloud of dust. "How about a bill for six pair of white kid gloves and a blue silk parasol?"

"Clothing, by the date. Hmm, this is interesting. Aunt Coco's progress report from her fourth-grade teacher. And I quote, 'Cordelia is a delightfully gregarious child. However, she tends to daydream and has trouble finishing assigned projects.'"

"That's a news flash." Stiff, C.C. arched her back and rotated her head. Beside her, the sun was streaming through the smudges on the storeroom window. With a little sigh, she rested her elbows on her knees and studied it.

"Where the devil is Lilah?" Impatient as always, Amanda tapped her foot as she grumbled. "Suzanna had dispensation because she took the kids to the matinee, but Lilah's supposed to be on duty."

"She'll show up," C.C. murmured.

"Sure. When it's done." Digging into a new pile, Amanda sneezed twice. "This is some of the dirtiest stuff I've ever seen."

C.C. shrugged. "Everything gets dirty if it sits around long enough."

"No, I mean really dirty. It's a limerick written by Great-Uncle Sean. 'There was a young lady from Maine, whose large breasts drove the natives insane. They...' Never mind," Amanda decided. "We'll start a file on attempted pornography." When C.C. made no comment, she glanced over to see her sister still staring at a sunbeam. "You okay, sweetie?"

"Hmm? Oh, yeah. I'm fine."

"You don't look like you slept very well."

C.C. shrugged then busied herself with papers again. "I guess the séance threw me off."

"Not surprising." Her lips pursed as she sorted through more receipts. "I never put any stock in that business. Bianca's tower was one thing. I guess we've all felt something—well, something up there. But I always thought that it was because we knew Bianca had tossed herself out of the window. Then last night…" When the shiver caught her, she rubbed her chilled arms. "I know that you really saw something, really experienced something."

"I know the necklace is real," C.C. said.

"I'll agree it *was* real—especially when I have a receipt in my hand."

"Was and is. I don't think I would have seen it if it had been pawned or tossed into the sea. It might sound loony, but I know Bianca wants us to find it."

"It does sound loony." With a sigh, Amanda leaned back in the creaking chair. "And what's loonier is that I think so, too. I just hope nobody at the hotel finds out I'm spending my free time looking for a buried treasure because my long-dead ancestor told us to. Oh!"

"Did you find it?" C.C. was already scrambling up.

"No, no, it's an old date book. 1912. The ink's a bit faded, but the handwriting's lovely—definitely feminine. It must be Bianca's. Look. 'Send invitations.' And here's the guest list. Wow, some party. The Prentises." Amanda took off her glasses to gnaw on the earpiece. "I bet they were Prentise Hall—one of the cottages that burned in '47."

"'Speak to gardener about roses,'" C.C. read over her sister's shoulder. "'Final fitting on gold ball gown. Meet Christian, 3:00 p.m.' Christian?" She laid a tensed hand on Amanda's shoulder. "Could that have been her artist?"

"Your guess is as good as mine." Quickly Amanda pushed her glasses back on. "But look here. 'Have clasp on emeralds strengthened.' Those could be the ones."

"They have to be."

"We still haven't found any receipts."

C.C. gave a tired look at the papers littering the room. "What are our chances?"

Even Amanda's organizational skills quaked. "Well, they improve every time we eliminate a box."

"Mandy." C.C. sat on the floor beside her. "We're running out of time, aren't we?"

"We've only been at it for a few hours."

"That's not what I mean." She rested her cheek on Amanda's thigh. "You know it's not. Even if we find the receipt, we still have to find the necklace. It could take years. We don't have years. We're going to have to sell, aren't we?"

"We'll talk about it tomorrow night, at the family meeting." Troubled, she stroked C.C.'s hair. "Look, why don't you go take a nap? You really do look beat."

"No." She rose, pacing over the papers to the windows and back. "I'm better off keeping my mind and my hands busy. Otherwise, I might strangle someone."

"Trent, for instance?"

"An excellent place to start. No." With a sigh, she

stuck her hands into her pockets. "No, this mess isn't really his fault."

"Are we still talking about the house?"

"I don't know." Miserable, she sat on the floor again. At least she could be grateful she'd cried herself dry the night before. "I've decided that all men are stupid, selfish and totally unnecessary."

"You're in love with him."

A wry smile curved her lips. "Bingo. And to answer your next question, no, he doesn't love me back. He's not interested in me, a future, a family, and he's very sorry he didn't make that clear to me before I made the mistake of falling for him."

"I'm sorry, C.C." After taking off her glasses, Amanda got up to cross the room and sit on the floor beside her sister. "I know how it must hurt, but you've only known him for a few days. Infatuation—"

"It's not infatuation." Idly she folded the recipe for jam into a paper airplane. "I've found out that falling in love doesn't have anything to do with time. It can take a year or an instant. It happens when it's ready to happen."

Amanda put an arm around C.C.'s shoulders and squeezed. "Well, I don't know anything about that. Fortunately, I've never had to worry about it." The fact made her frown, but only for a moment. "I do know this. If he hurt you, we'll make him sorry he ever crossed a Calhoun."

C.C. laughed then sent the gooseberry plane flying. "It's tempting, but I think it's more a matter of me hurting myself." She gave herself a little shake. "Come on, let's get back to work."

They'd barely gotten started again when Trent

came in. He looked at C.C., met a solid wall of ice. When he turned to Amanda, he fared little better.

"I thought you might be able to use some help," he told them.

Amanda glanced at C.C., noted her sister was employing the silent treatment. A very effective weapon, in Amanda's estimation. "That's nice of you, Trent." Amanda gave him a smile that would have frosted molten lava. "But this is really a family problem."

"Let him help." C.C. didn't even bother to look up. "I imagine he's just terrific at pushing papers."

"All right then." With a shrug, Amanda indicated another folding chair. "You can use that if you like. I'm organizing according to content and year."

"Fine." He took the chair and sat across from her. They worked in frigid silence, with the crinkle of papers and the tap of Amanda's shoe.

"Here's a repair bill," he said—and was ignored. "For repairing a clasp."

"Let me see." Amanda had already snatched it out of his hand before C.C. made the dash across the room. "It doesn't say what kind of necklace," she muttered.

"But the dates are right." C.C. stabbed a finger on it. "July 16, 1912."

"Have I missed something?" Trent asked them.

Amanda waited a beat, saw that C.C. wasn't going to answer and glanced up herself. "We came across a date book of Bianca's. She had a note to take the emeralds to have the clasp repaired."

"This might be what you need." His eyes were on C.C., but it was Amanda who answered.

"It may be enough to satisfy all of us that the Calhoun necklace existed in 1912, but it's a long way from helping us find it." She set the receipt aside. "Let's see what else we can turn up."

In silence, C.C. went back to her papers.

A few moments later, Lilah called from the base of the stairs. "Amanda! Phone!"

"Tell them I'll call back."

"It's the hotel. They said it's important."

"Damn." She set down the glasses before sending Trent a narrowed look. "I'll be back in a few minutes."

He waited until the sound of her rapid footsteps had finished echoing. "She's very protective."

"We stick together," C.C. commented, and set a paper on a pile without a clue to its contents.

"I've noticed. Catherine..."

Braced, C.C. flicked him her coolest glance. "Yes?"

"I wanted to make certain you were all right."

"All right. In what way?"

She had dust on her cheek. He wanted, badly, to smile and tell her. To hear her laugh as she brushed it off. "After last night—I know how upset you were when you left my room."

"Yes, I was upset." She turned over another piece of paper. "I guess I made quite a scene."

"No, that's not what I meant."

"I did." She forced her lips to curve. "I guess I'm the one who should apologize this time. The séance, all that happened during it, went to my head." Not my head, she thought, but my heart. "I must have sounded like an idiot when I came to your room."

"No, of course not." She was so cool, he thought. So composed. And she baffled him. "You said you loved me."

"I know what I said." Her voice dropped another ten degrees, but her smile stayed in place. "Why don't we both chalk it up to the mood of the moment?"

That was reasonable, he realized. So why did he feel so lost. "Then you didn't mean it?"

"Trent, we've only known each other for a few days." Did he want to make her suffer? she wondered.

"But you looked so—devastated when you left."

She arched a brow. "Do I look devastated now?"

"No," he said slowly. "No, you don't."

"Well, then. Let's forget it." As she spoke, the sun lost itself behind the clouds. "That would be best for both of us, wouldn't it?"

"Yes." It was just what he'd wanted. Yet he felt empty when he stood up again. "I do want what's best for you, C.C."

"Fine." She studied the paper in her hand. "If you're going down, ask Lilah to bring up some coffee when she comes."

"All right."

She waited until she was sure he was gone before she covered her face with her hands. She'd been wrong, C.C. discovered. She hadn't nearly cried herself dry.

Trent went back to his room. His briefcase was there, stacked with work he had intended to do while away from his office. Taking a seat at the scarred kneehole desk, he opened a file.

Ten minutes later, he was staring out the window without having glanced at the first word.

He shook himself, picked up his pen and ordered

himself to concentrate. He succeeded in reading the first word, even the first paragraph. Three times. Disgusted, he tossed the pen aside and rose to pace.

It was ridiculous, he thought. He had worked in hotel suites all over the world. Why should this room be any different? It had walls and windows, a ceiling—so to speak. The desk was more than adequate. He could even, if he chose, light a fire to add some cheer. And some warmth. God knew he could use some warmth after the thirty icy minutes he'd spent in the storeroom. There was no reason why he shouldn't be able to sit down and take care of some business for an hour or two.

Except that he kept remembering—how lovely C.C. had looked when she'd come into the room in her gray flannel robe and bare feet. He could still see the way her eyes had glowed when she had stood almost where he was standing now, smiling at him. Frowning, he rubbed at a dull pain around his heart. He wasn't accustomed to aches there. Headaches certainly. Never heartaches.

But the memory of the way she'd slipped into his arms haunted him. And her taste—why was it that it still hovered just a breath from his own lips?

It was guilt, that was all, he assured himself. He had hurt her, the way he was certain he'd never hurt another woman. No matter how cool she had been today, no matter how composed, that was a guilt he would live with for a long time.

Maybe if he went up and talked to her again. His hand was on the knob before he stopped himself. That would only make things worse, if possible. Just because he wanted to assuage some guilt was no excuse to put her in an uncomfortable position again.

She was handling it, better than he by all accounts. She was strong, obviously resilient. Proud. Soft, his mind wandered. Warm. Incredibly beautiful.

On an oath he began to pace again. It would be wiser for him to concentrate on the house rather than any of its occupants. The few days he'd spent in it might have caused a personal upheaval, but it had given him time and opportunity to formulate plans. From the inside. It had given him a taste of the mood and tone and the history. And if he could settle down for a few moments, he could put some of those thoughts on paper.

But it was hopeless. The minute he took his pen in hand, his mind went blank. He was feeling closed in, Trent told himself. He just needed some air. Snatching up a jacket, he did something he hadn't given himself time to do in months.

He took a walk.

Following instinct, he headed toward the cliffs. Down the uneven lawn, around a crumbling stone wall. Toward the sea. The air had a bite. It seemed that spring had decided to pick up her pretty skirts and retreat. The sky was gray and moody, with a few hopeful patches of blue. Wildflowers that had been brave enough to shove their way through rock and soil blew fitfully in the wind.

Trent walked with his hands in his pockets, and his head down. Depression wasn't a familiar sensation, and he was determined to walk it off. When he glanced back, he could just see the peaks of towers above and behind. He turned away and faced the sea—unknowingly mirroring the stance of a man who had painted there decades before.

Breathtaking. It was the only word that came to his

mind. Rocks tumbled dizzily down, pink and gray where the wind buffeted them, black where the water struck and funneled. Bad-tempered whitecaps churned, slicing at the darker water. Smoky fog rolled and shredded, and the air held a fresh threat of rain.

It should have been gloomy. It was simply spectacular.

He wished she was with him. That she would be here, now, beside him before time passed or the wind changed. She would smile, he thought. Laugh, as she planted those long, gorgeous legs and lifted her face to the blow. If she had been there, the beauty of it wouldn't make him feel so lonely. So damned lonely.

The tingle at the base of his neck had him turning, nearly reaching out. He'd been so certain that he would look and see her walking toward him. There was nothing but the slope of rock, and the wind. Yet the feeling of another presence remained, very real, so that he almost called out.

He was a sensible man, Trent assured himself. He knew he was alone. Yet it seemed as though someone was there with him, waiting. Watching. For a moment, he was certain he caught the light, drifting scent of honeysuckle.

Imagination, he decided, but his hand wasn't quite steady as he lifted it to push the blowing hair out his eyes.

Then there was weeping. Trent froze as he listened to the sad, quiet sound that sobbed just under the wind. It ebbed and flowed, like the sea itself. Something clenched inside his stomach as he strained to hear—though common sense told him there could be nothing to hear.

A nervous breakdown? he wondered. But the sound

was real, damn it. Not a hallucination. Slowly, ears pricked, he climbed down a jumble of rocks.

"Who's there?" he shouted as the sound sighed and drifted on the wind. Chasing it, he hurried down, driven by an urgency that drummed through his blood. A shower of loose stones rattled into space, bringing him sharply back to reality.

What in God's name was he doing? Scrambling down a cliff wall after a ghost? He lifted his hands and saw that despite the brisk wind his palms were sweating. All he could hear now was the frantic pounding of his own heart. After forcing himself to stand still and take a few calming breaths, he looked around for the easiest form of assent.

He had just started back when the sound came again. Weeping. No, he realized. Whimpering. It was quite clear now and nearly under his feet. Crouching, Trent searched behind an outcrop of rock. It was a poor, pitiful sight, he thought. The little black puppy was hardly more than a ball of fur-covered bones. Relief poured through him, making him laugh out loud. He wasn't going crazy after all. As Trent studied it, the terrified pup tried to inch back, but there was nowhere to go. Its little frightened eyes fixed on Trent as it trembled. "Had a rough time, have you?" Cautiously Trent reached out, ready to snatch his hand back if the pup snapped. Instead it simply cowered and whined. "It's okay, fella. Relax. I won't hurt you." Gently he stroked the puppy between the ears with his fingertips. Still shivering, the pup licked Trent's hand. "Guess you're feeling pretty lonely." He sighed as he calmed the dog. "Me, too. Why don't we go back to the house?" He gathered the dog up, zipping it inside his jacket for the climb. When he was halfway to the top, Trent stopped then turned blindly around. It was at least fifty yards from where he had stood looking out to sea to where he had discovered the stray. His palms grew damp again when he realized it would have been impossible for him to have heard the puppy's whines from the ridge above. The distance and the wind would have smothered the whimpers. Yet he had heard…something. And, hearing it, had climbed down to find the lost dog. ''What the devil was it?'' Trent murmured, and cuddling the pup closer, headed for home. He was just beginning to feel foolish when he crossed the lawn. What was he supposed to say to his hostesses? Look what followed me home? How about—Guess what? I decided to take my life in my hands and climb back down the cliff. Look what I found. Neither opening seemed quite suitable. The sensible thing would be to get in the car and drive the dog down to the village. There was bound to be an animal shelter or vet. He could hardly march into the parlor and dump his find on the rug. But he couldn't, Trent discovered. He simply couldn't turn the shivering ball of fur over to strangers. The little guy trusted him and was even now curling softly under his heart. As he stood hesitating, C.C. came out of the house.

Trent shifted and tried to look natural. ''Hi.''

'Hi.'' She paused to button her denim jacket. ''We're out of milk. Do you need anything from the village?''

A can of dog food, he thought, and cleared his throat. ''No, thanks. I, ah…'' The pup wriggled against his shirt. ''Did you find anything?''

''Lots of things, but nothing that tells us where to look for the necklace.'' Her misery turned to curiosity as she watched the ripples run along his jacket. "Is everything all right?"

"Fine. Just fine." Trent cleared his throat, folded his arms. "I took a walk."

"Okay." It was awful, she thought, just awful. He could hardly meet her eyes. "Aunt Coco's making a light lunch if you're hungry."

"Oh—thanks."

She started to move by him when a high-pitched yip stopped her in her tracks. "What?"

"Nothing." He smothered an involuntary chuckle as the puppy wiggled along his ribs.

"Are you all right?"

"Yes, yes, I'm fine." He gave her a sheepish smile as the dog poked his nose above the zipper of the jacket.

"What have you got?" C.C. forgot her vow to keep her distance and stepped closer to tug the zipper down. "Oh! Trent, it's a puppy."

"I found him down in the rocks," he began quickly. "I wasn't sure just what to—"

"Oh, you poor little thing." She was already cooing as she gathered the puppy to her. "Are you lost?" She rubbed her cheek over its fur, nuzzled nose to nose. "There now, it's all right." The puppy wagged his tail so fast and hard he nearly fell out of her grip.

"Cute, isn't he?" Grinning, Trent moved closer to stroke. "Looks like he's been on his own for a while."

"He's just a baby." She crooned and cuddled. "Where did you say you found him?"

"Down on the rocks. I was walking." And thinking of you. Before he could stop himself, Trent reached out to touch her hair. "I couldn't just leave him there."

"Of course not." She looked up and saw that she was all but in his arms. His hand was in her hair, his eyes on hers.

"Catherine—"

The pup yipped again and had her jolting back. "I'll take him in. He must be cold, and hungry."

"All right." The only place left for his hands was his pockets. "Why don't I run down and get the milk?"

"Okay." Her smile was strained as she backed toward the steps. She turned and, murmuring to the puppy, dashed inside.

By the time Trent returned, the stray had a place of honor by the kitchen hearth and the undivided attention of four beautiful women.

"Wait until Suze and the kids get back," Amanda was saying. "They'll flip. He sure goes for your liver pâté, Aunt Coco."

"Obviously a gourmet among dogs." Lilah, already on her hands and knees, leaned her nose against his. "Aren't you, cutie?"

"I'm sure he should have something more bland." Coco was also on the floor, charmed. "With the proper care, he'll be very handsome."

The pup, amazed at his good fortune, raced in circles. Spotting Trent, he gamboled over, tripping over his own feet. The women scrambled up, all asking him questions at the same time.

"Hold on." Trent set the grocery bag on the table, then crouched down to scratch the pup's belly. "I don't know where he came from. I found him when

I was walking along the cliffs. He was hiding out. Weren't you, boy?''

"I suppose we should ask around, to see it anyone's lost him," Coco began, then held up a hand as her nieces voiced unanimous dissent. "It's only right. But it is up to Trent, since he found him."

"I think you should do what you think's best." He rose to pull the milk out of the bag. "He could probably use some of this."

Amanda already had a saucer and was arguing with Lilah on the proper amount to give their new guest.

"What else did you get?" C.C. poked at the bag.

"A few things." He moved his shoulders, then gave up. "I thought he should have a collar." Trent pulled out a bright red collar with silver studs.

C.C. couldn't hold back the grin. "Very fashionable."

"And a leash." Trent set that on the table, as well. "Puppy food."

"Uh-huh." C.C. began to go through the bag herself. "And puppy treats, rawhide bones."

"He'll want to gnaw," Trent told her.

"Sure, he will. A ball and a squeaky mouse." Laughing, she squeezed the rubber toy.

"He should have something to play with." He didn't want to add that he'd searched for a dog bed and cushion but hadn't come across them.

"I didn't know you were a softie."

He glanced down at the happily lapping puppy. "Neither did I."

"What's his name?" Lilah wanted to know.

"Well, I..."

"You found him, you get to name him."

"Do it quick," Amanda advised him. "Before Li-lah sticks him with something like Griswold."

"Fred," Trent said on impulse. "He looks like a Fred to me."

Unimpressed with his christening, Fred plopped down with one ear in the saucer of milk and went to sleep.

"Well, that's settled." Amanda gave the pup one last pat before she rose. "Come on, Lilah, it's your turn to take a shift."

"I'll give you a hand." Instincts humming, Coco hustled her two nieces out of the room and left C.C. alone with Trent.

"I'd better go, too." C.C. started for the door. Trent laid a hand on her arm to stop her.

"Wait."

"What for?"

"Just…wait."

She stood, battling back hurt. "I'm waiting."

"I—how's your hand?"

"It's fine."

"Good." He felt like an idiot. "That's good."

"If that's all…"

"No. I wanted to tell you…I noticed a rattle in the car when I drove down to the village."

"A rattle?" She pursed her lips. "What kind of rattle?"

An imaginary one, he thought, but shrugged. "Just a rattle. I was hoping you could take a look at it."

"All right. Bring it in tomorrow."

"Tomorrow?"

"My tools are at the shop. Is there anything else?"

"When I was walking, I kept wishing you were with me."

She looked away until she was sure she had rebuilt the chink he'd just knocked in her defensive wall. "We want different things, Trent. Let's just leave it at that." She turned toward the door. "Try to get your car in early," she added without looking around. "I've got an exhaust system to replace tomorrow."

Chapter Eight

C.C. fired up her torch, flipped down her faceplate and prepared to cut off the tail pipe on the rusted exhaust of a '62 Plymouth.

The day was not going well.

She wasn't able to get the scheduled family meeting off her mind. No other paperwork on the necklace had shown up, though they had gone through reams and reams of receipts and old ledgers. She knew, because of Amanda's refusal to talk, that the news wasn't good.

Added to that had been another restless night. She heard Fred's whimpering and had gone to check on him only to hear Trent's low murmuring soothing the puppy behind his bedroom door.

She'd stood there for a long time, listening.

The fact that he'd taken the stray into his room, cared enough to comfort and nurture only made C.C. love him more. And the more she loved, the more she hurt.

She knew she was hollow eyed this morning, because she'd made the mistake of looking at a mirror. That she could handle. Her looks had never been a major concern. The bills she had found in the morning mail were.

She'd been telling the truth when she'd told Suzanna the business was doing well. But there were still rough spots. Not all of her customers paid promptly, and her cash flow was too often merely a trickle. Six months, she thought as she cut through the old metal. She only needed six months. But that was too long, much too long to help keep The Towers.

Her life was changing, changing fast, and none of it seemed to be for the better.

Trent stood watching her. She had some battered hulk of a car up on the lift and stood under it, wielding a torch. While he watched, she shifted aside as a pipe clattered to the floor. She was wearing coveralls again, thick safety gloves and a helmet. The music she never seemed to be without jingled from the radio on the workbench.

Surely a man was over the edge when he thought how delightful it would be to make love on a concrete floor with a woman who was dressed like a welder.

C.C. changed positions, then saw him. Very carefully she shut off the torch before she lifted the shield of her helmet.

"I couldn't find anything wrong with your car. Keys are in the office. No charge." She flipped down the shield again.

"C.C."

"What?"

"How about dinner?"

She pushed back the shield and eyed him warily. "How about it?"

"I mean..." With a leery glance overhead, he stepped under the car with her. "I'd like you to have dinner with me tonight."

She shifted her weight. "I've had dinner with you every night for several nights." She flipped the shield down. Trent flipped it up again.

"No, I mean I want to take you out to dinner."

"Why?"

"Why not?"

She lifted a brow. "Well, that's very nice, but I'm a little pressed tonight. We're having a family meeting." She pulled down the shield again and prepared to relight the torch.

"Tomorrow then." Annoyed, Trent pushed the shield back up. "Do you mind? I like to see you when I talk to you."

"Yes, I mind because I've got work. And no, I won't have dinner with you tomorrow."

"Why?"

She blew out a long breath that ruffled her bangs. "Because I don't want to."

"You're still angry with me."

Her eyes, which had begun to heat, went flat. "We settled all that, so there's no reason to go out on a date."

"Just dinner," he said, finding he couldn't let go. "No one's calling it a date. One simple meal, as friends, before I go back to Boston."

"You're going back?" She felt her heart drop to her knees and turned away to rattle through some tools.

"Yes, I have meetings scheduled for the middle of

the week. I'm expected in the office Wednesday afternoon.''

Just like that, she thought as she picked up a pipe wrench and set it down again. I've got meetings scheduled, see you later. Sorry I broke your heart. ''Well, then, have a nice trip.''

''C.C.'' He laid a hand on her arm before she could hide behind the shield again. ''I'd like to spend a little time with you. I'd feel a lot better about everything if I was sure we parted on good terms.''

''You want to feel better about things,'' she muttered, then made herself relax her jaw. ''Sure, why not? Dinner tomorrow night is fine. You deserve a send-off.''

''I appreciate it. Really.'' He touched her cheek, started to lean toward her. C.C. pulled the shield down with a snap.

''Better stand back from the torch, Trent,'' she said sweetly. ''You might get burned.''

Family meetings with the Calhouns were traditionally noisy, argumentative and drenched with tears and laughter. This one was abnormally subdued. Amanda, in her capacity as adviser on finances, sat at the head of the table.

The room was silent.

Suzanna had already put the children to bed. It had been a little easier than usual as both of them had exhausted themselves with Fred—and vice versa.

Trent had excused himself discreetly, directly after dinner. It hardly mattered, C.C. thought. He would know the outcome soon enough.

She was afraid everyone knew it already.

''I guess we all know why we're here,'' Amanda

began. "Trent's going back to Boston on Wednesday, and it would be best all around it we gave him our decision about the house before he left."

"It would be better if we concentrated on finding the necklace." Lilah's stubborn look was offset by the nervous way she twisted the obsidian crystals around her neck.

"We're all still looking for the papers." Suzanna laid a hand on Lilah's arm. "But I think we have to face the reality that finding the necklace could take a long time. Longer than we have."

"Thirty days is longer than we have." All eyes turned to Amanda. "I got a notice from the lawyer last week."

"Last week!" Coco put in. "Stridley contacted you and you didn't mention it?"

"I was hoping I could get an extension without worrying everyone." Amanda laid her hand on the file she set on the table. "No deal. We've been chipping away at the back taxes, but the hard fact is that we haven't been making enough headway. The insurance premiums are due. We can make them all right, and the mortgage—for the time being. The utility bills over the winter were higher than usual, and the new furnace and repairs to the roof ate up a lot of our principal."

C.C. held up a hand. "How bad is it?"

"As bad as it gets." Amanda rubbed at an ache in her temple. "We could sell off a few more pieces, and keep our head above water. Just. But taxes are due again in a couple months, and we'll be back where we started."

"I can sell my pearls," Coco began, and Lilah cut her off.

"No. Absolutely not. We agreed a long time ago that there were some things that couldn't be sold. If we're going to face facts," she said grimly, "then let's face them."

"The plumbing's shot," Amanda continued, and had to clear her tightening throat. "If we don't get the rewiring done, we could end up burning the place down around our ears. Suzanna's lawyer's fees—"

"That's my problem," Suzanna interrupted.

"That's *our* problem," Amanda corrected, and got a unanimous note of assent. "We're a family," she continued. "We've been through the very worst together, and we handled it. Six or seven years ago, it looked as if everything was going to be fine. But... taxes have gone up, along with the insurance, the repairs, everything. It's not as though we're paupers, but the house eats up every cent of spare cash, and then some. If I thought we could weather this, hang in for another year or two, I'd say sell the Limoges, or a few antiques. But it's like trying to plug a hole in a dam and watching others spring out while your fingers are slipping."

"What are you saying, Mandy?" C.C. asked her.

"I'm saying." Amanda pressed her lips together. "I'm saying the only realistic choice I see is for us to sell the house. With the offer from St. James, we can pay off the debts, keep most of what's important to all of us and buy another. If we don't sell, it's going to be taken away from us in any case within a few months." A tear trickled down her cheek. "I'm sorry. I just can't find a way out."

"It's not your fault." Suzanna reached out for her hand. "We all knew it was coming."

Amanda sniffled and shook her head. "What buffer

we had, we lost in the stock market crash. We just haven't been able to recover. I know I made the investments—''

"*We* made the investments." Lilah leaned over to join hands, as well. "On the recommendation of a very reputable broker. If the bottom hadn't fallen through, if I'd won the lottery, if Bax hadn't been such a greedy bastard, maybe things would be different now. But they're not."

"We'll still be together." Coco added her hand. "That's what matters."

"That's what matters," C.C. agreed, and laid her hand on top. And that, if nothing else, felt right. "What do we do now?"

Struggling for composure, Amanda sat back. "I guess we ask Trent to come down and make sure the offer still stands."

"I'll get him." C.C. pushed away from the table to walk blindly from the room.

She couldn't believe it. Even as she walked through the huddle of rooms, into the hallway, up the steps with her hand trailing along the banister, she couldn't believe it. None of it would be hers much longer.

There would come a time very soon when she wouldn't be able to step from her room onto the high stone terrace and look out at the sea. She wouldn't be able to climb the steps to Bianca's tower and find Lilah curled on the window seat, dreaming out through the dusty glass. Or Suzanna working in the garden with the children racing on the lawn nearby. Amanda wouldn't come bolting down the stairs in a hurry to get somewhere, do something. Aunt Coco would no longer fuss over the stove in the kitchen.

In a matter of moments, the life she'd known was

over. The one to come had yet to begin. She was somewhere in a kind of limbo, too stunned from the loss to ache.

Trent crouched beside the fire where Fred snored on the bright red cushion in his new wicker dog bed. He was going to miss the little devil, Trent realized. Even if he had the time or inclination for a pet back in Boston, he didn't have the heart to take Fred away from the children, or from the women, if it came to that.

He'd seen C.C. tossing the ball for the pup in the side yard that afternoon when she'd come home from work. It had been so good to hear her laugh, to see her wrestle with the dog and Suzanna's children.

Oddly it reminded him of the image he'd had— daydream, he corrected. The daydream he'd had when his mind had wandered the night of the séance. Of him and C.C. sitting on a sunny porch, watching children play in the yard.

It was foolishness, of course, but something had tugged at him that afternoon when he'd stood at the door and looked at her tossing a ball to Fred. A good something, he remembered, until she'd turned and had seen him. Her laughter had died, and her eyes had gone cool.

He straightened, studying the flames in the fire. It was crazy, but he wished with his whole heart that she would flare up, just once more. Throw another punch at him. Call him names. The worst kind of punishment was her steady, passionless politeness.

The sound of the knock on the door had Fred yipping quietly in his sleep. When Trent answered, finding C.C. on the other side of the threshold, twin twinges of delight and distress danced through his system. He wouldn't be able to turn her away this time. It wouldn't be possible to tell her, or himself, that it couldn't be. He had to... Then he looked into her eyes.

"What's wrong? What's happened?" He reached out to comfort, but she stepped stiffly away.

"We'd like you to come downstairs, if you don't mind."

"Catherine—" But she was already walking away, her stride lengthening in her hurry for distance.

He found them all gathered around the dining room table, their faces composed. He was astute enough to understand that he was facing one combined will.

The Calhouns had closed ranks.

"Ladies?"

"Trent, sit down, please." Coco gestured to the chair beside her. "I hope we didn't disturb you?"

"Not at all." He looked at C.C., but she was staring fixedly at the wall above his head. "Are we having another séance?"

"Not this time." Lilah nodded toward Amanda. "Mandy?"

"All right." She took a deep breath and was relieved when Suzanna's hand gripped hers under the table. "Trent, we've discussed your offer for The Towers, and have decided to accept it."

He gave her a blank look. "Accept it?"

"Yes." Amanda pressed her free hand to her quivering stomach. "That is, if your offer still stands."

"Yes, of course it does." He scanned the room, his gaze lingering on C.C. "You're certain you want to sell?"

"Isn't that what you wanted?" C.C.'s voice was clipped. "Isn't that what you came for?"

"Yes." But he'd gotten a great deal more than he'd bargained for. "My firm will be delighted to purchase the property. But...I want to be certain that you're all agreed. That this is what you want. All of you."

"We're all agreed." C.C. went back to staring at the wall.

"The lawyers will handle the details," Amanda began again. "But before we hand things over them, I'd like to review the terms."

"Of course." He named the purchase price again. Hearing it had tears burning in C.C.'s eyes. "There's no reason why we can't be flexible on the timing," he went on. "I realize you'll want to do some kind of inventory before you—relocate."

It was what they wanted, he reminded himself. It was business. It shouldn't make him feel as if he'd just crawled out from under a rock.

"I think we'd like to make the move quickly." Suzanna glanced around the table for confirmation. "As soon as we can find another house."

"If there's anything I can do to help you—"

"You've done enough," C.C. interrupted coolly. "We can take care of ourselves."

"I'd like to add a condition." Lilah leaned forward. "You're purchasing the house, and the land. Not the contents."

"No. Naturally the furniture, heirlooms, personal possessions remain yours."

"Including the necklace." She inclined her head. "Whether it's found before we leave, or after, the Calhoun necklace belongs to the Calhouns. I want that in writing, Trent. If anytime during your renovations, the necklace is recovered, it belongs to us."

"All right." The little clause would drive the lawyers crazy, he thought. But that was their problem. "I'll see that it's put in the contract."

"Bianca's tower." She spoke slowly, afraid her voice would break. "Be careful what you do with it."

"How about some wine?" Coco rose, hands fluttering. "We should have some wine."

"Excuse me." C.C. made herself stand slowly, fighting the impulse to race from the room. "If we're all through, I think I'll go up. I'm tired."

Trent stared after her, but Suzanna stopped him. "I don't think she'd be receptive right now. I'll go."

C.C. went to the terrace to lean out over the wall and let the cold wind dry the tears. There should be a storm, she thought. She wished there was a storm, something as angry and as passionate as her own heart.

Pounding a fist on the wall, she cursed the day she'd ever met Trent. He wouldn't take her love, but he would take her home. Of course, if he had accepted the first and returned it, he could never have taken the house.

"C.C." Suzanna stepped out to slip an arm around her shoulders. "It's cold. Why don't we go inside?"

"It's not right."

"No." She gathered her sister closer. "It's not."

"He doesn't even know what it means." She dashed the angry tears away. "He can't understand. He wouldn't want to."

"Maybe he doesn't. Maybe no one can but us. But it's not his fault, C.C. We can't blame him because we couldn't hang on." She looked away from the gardens she loved, toward the cliffs that always drew her. "I left here once before—it seems like a lifetime ago, but it was only seven years. Nearly eight now."

She sighed. "I thought it was the happiest day of my life, leaving the island for my new home in Boston."

"You don't have to talk about that. I know it hurts you."

"Not as much as it once did. I was in love, C.C., a new bride with the future in the palm of my hand. And when I turned around and saw The Towers disappearing behind me, I cried like a baby. I thought it would be easier this time." As tears threatened, she closed her eyes. "I wish it were. What is it about this place that pulls us so?" she wondered.

"I know we can find another house." C.C. linked fingers with her sister. "I know we'll be all right, even happy. But it hurts. And you're right, it's not Trent's fault. But..."

"You have to blame someone." Suzanna smiled.

"He hurt me. I really hate to admit that, but he hurt me. I want to be able to say that he made me fall in love with him. Even that he let me fall in love with him. But I did it all by myself."

"And Trent?"

"He isn't interested."

"From the way he looks at you, I'd say you're wrong."

"Oh, he's interested," C.C. said grimly. "But love has nothing to do with it. He very politely refused to take advantage of my—my lack of experience, as he called it."

"Oh." Suzanna looked out toward the cliffs again. Rejection, she knew, was the sharpest blade of all. "It doesn't help much, but it might have been more difficult for you if he hadn't been—sensible."

"He's sensible, all right," C.C. said through her teeth. "And being a sensible and a civilized man, he'd like us to be friends. He's even taking me to dinner tomorrow so he can be certain I'm not pining away for him, and he can go back to Boston guilt free.''

"What are you going to do?''

"Oh, I'll go to dinner with him. I can be just as damned civilized as he can.'' She set her chin. "And when I'm finished, he's going to be sorry he ever set eyes on Catherine Calhoun.'' She whirled toward her sister. "Do you still have that red dress? The beaded one that's cut down to sin?''

Suzanna's grin spread. "You bet I do.''

"Let's go take a look at it.''

Well, well, well, C.C. thought. What a difference a day and a tight silk dress could make. Lips pursed, she turned in front of the cracked cheval glass in the corner of her room. The dress was just a smidgen too small for her—even with the frantic alterations Suzanna had made. It only made more of a statement.

Don't you wish you had me, it said quite clearly. C.C. ran her hands over her hips. And he could wish until his head exploded.

The dress was a form-fitting glitter of flame that licked down from its plunging neckline to the abbreviated hem. Suzanna had ruthlessly slashed it off so that it hit C.C. midthigh. The long sleeves ended in points over her wrists. And she'd added Coco's rhinestone ear clips, with their wicked sparkle.

The thirty minutes she'd spent on makeup seemed to have paid off. Her lips were as red as the dress, thanks to Amanda's contribution. Her eyes were shadowed with copper and emerald, thanks to Lilah. Her hair was as glossy as a raven's wing and slicked back a bit at the temples.

All in all, C.C. thought as she turned, Trenton St. James III was in for a surprise.

"Suzanna said you needed some shoes." Lilah walked in and stopped in midyawn. The shoes dangled from her fingertips as she stared. "I must have passed through a parallel universe."

C.C. grinned and spun a circle. "What do you think?"

"I think Trent's going to need oxygen." Approving, she passed C.C. a pair of spiked snakeskin heels. "Kiddo, you look dangerous."

"Good." She pulled on the shoes. "Now if I can just walk in these without falling on my face."

"Practice. I've got to get Mandy."

A few moments later, all three sisters supervised C.C.'s walk. "You'll be having dinner," Amanda put in, wincing at each wobble. "So you'll be sitting down most of the time."

"I'm getting it," C.C. muttered. "I'm just not used to heels. How do you work in these things all day?"

"Talent."

"Walk slower," Lilah suggested. "More deliberately. As if you have all the time in the world."

"Take if from her," Amanda agreed. "She's an expert at slow."

"In this case—" Lilah gave Amanda an arched look "—slow is sexy. See?"

Taking her sister's advice, C.C. walked with a cautious deliberation that came off as slinky. Amanda held out her hands. "I stand corrected. What coat are you wearing?"

"I haven't thought of it."

"You can wear my black silk cape," Amanda decided. "You'll freeze but you'll look great doing it. Perfume. Aunt Coco's got some of that smoldering French stuff left from Christmas."

"No." Suzanna shook her head. "She should stick with her usual scent." Tilting her head, she studied her sister and smiled. "The contrast will drive him crazy."

Unaware of what was in store for him, Trent sat in the parlor with Coco. His bags were packed. His calls were made. He wished he could come up with a reasonable excuse to stay another few days.

"We've enjoyed having you," Coco told him when he'd expressed his appreciation for her hospitality. "I'm sure we'll be seeing each other again soon."

Her crystal ball didn't lie, she reminded herself. It still linked Trent up with one of her nieces, and she wasn't ready to wave surrender.

"I certainly hope so. I have to say, Coco, how much I admire you for raising four such lovely women."

"Sometimes I think we raised each other." She smiled mistily around the room. "I'm going to miss this place. To be honest I didn't think it mattered to me until...well, until now. I didn't grow up here as the girls did. We traveled quite a bit, you see, and my father only came back sporadically. I always thought it was the fact that his mother had died here that put him off. Then, of course, I spent my married life and the first few years of my widowhood in Philadelphia. Then when Judson and Deliah were killed, I came here for the girls." She sent him a sad, apologetic smile. "I'm sorry to get sentimental on you, Trenton."

"Don't apologize." He sipped thoughtfully at his aperitif. "My family has never been close, and as a result, there was never a home like this in my life. I think that's why I've begun to understand what it could mean."

"You should settle down," she said, cagily, she thought. "Find a nice girl, make a home and family of your own. Why, I can't think of anything lonelier than not having anyone to go home to."

Wanting to avoid that line of thought, he reached down to throw the ball for Fred. They both watched as the dog bounded after it, tripped himself up and went sprawling.

"Not particularly graceful," Trent mused. He rose and went over to retrieve the ball himself. Scratching the dog's belly, he glanced over. The first thing he saw was a pair of very slim black heels. Slowly his gaze traveled up a long, shapely pair of legs. With the breath backing up in his lungs, he sat back on his heels.

There was a sparkle of scarlet, snug and sleek over a curvy feminine form.

"Lose something?" C.C. asked as his eyes fixed on her face.

Her lips were curved and red and slick. Trent ran his tongue over his teeth to be certain he hadn't swallowed it. On unsteady legs, he rose.

"C.C.?"

"We were having dinner tonight, weren't we?"

"We…yes. You look wonderful."

"Do you like it?" She turned a circle so that he could see the back of the dress dipped even lower than the front. "I think red's a cheerful color." And powerful, she thought, still smiling.

"It suits you. I've never seen you in a dress before."

"Impractical when it comes to changing fuel pumps. Are you ready to go?"

"Go where?"

Oh, she was going to enjoy this. "To dinner."

"Right. Yes."

She inclined her head the way Suzanna had showed her and handed him her cape. It was a service he'd performed hundreds of times for dozens of women. But his hands fumbled.

"Don't wait up, Aunt Coco."

"No, dear." Behind their retreating backs, she grinned and raised her fists in the air. The moment the front door shut, the three remaining Calhouns exchanged high fives.

Chapter Nine

"**I**'m glad you talked me into going out tonight." C.C. reached for the door handle before she remembered to let Trent open the car for her.

"I wasn't sure you'd still be willing to go." He closed his hand over hers.

"Because of the house?" As casually as possible, C.C. slid her hand from under his and lowered herself into the car. "That's done. I'd rather not talk about it tonight."

"All right." He closed the door, rounded the hood. "Amanda recommended the restaurant." He had his hands on the keys but continued to stare at her.

"Something wrong?"

"No." Unless you counted his nervous system. After starting the car, he tried again. "I thought you might like dining near the water."

"Sounds fine." His radio was on a classical station. Not her usual style, she thought. But it wasn't a usual night. C.C. settled back and prepared to enjoy the ride. "Have you heard that rattle again?"

"What rattle?"

"The one you asked me to fix yesterday."

"Oh, that rattle." He smiled to himself. "No. It must have been my imagination." When she crossed her legs, his fingers tightened on the wheel. "You never told me why you decided to be a mechanic."

"Because I'm good at it." She shifted in her seat to face him. He caught a drift of honeysuckle and nearly groaned. "When I was six, I took apart our lawn mower's engine, to see how it worked. I was hooked. Why did you go into hotels?"

"It was expected of me." He stopped, surprised that that had been the first answer out of his mouth. "And I suppose I got good at it."

"Do you like it?"

Had anyone ever asked him that before? he wondered. Had he ever asked himself? "Yes, I guess I do."

"Guess?" Her brows lifted into her bangs. "I thought you were sure of everything."

He glanced at her again and nearly ran off the road. "Apparently not."

When they arrived at the waterfront restaurant, he was used to the transformation. Or thought he was. Then he went around to open the car door for her. She slid out, rose up. They were eye to eye, barely a whisper apart. C.C. held her ground, wondering if he could hear the way her heart was pounding against her ribs.

"Are you sure nothing's wrong?"

"No, I'm not sure." No one, he was certain, this

impossibly sexy was meant to be resisted. He cupped a hand at the back of her neck. "Let me check."

She eased away the instant before his lips brushed hers. "This isn't a date, remember? Just a friendly dinner."

"I'd like to change the rules."

"Too late." She smiled and offered a hand. "I'm hungry."

"You're not the only one," he murmured, and took her inside.

He wasn't sure how to handle her. The smooth moves he'd always taken for granted seemed rusty. The setting was perfect, the little table beside the window with water lapping just outside. As the sun set away in the west, it deepened and tinted the bay. He ordered wine as she picked up her menu and smiled at him.

Under the table, C.C. gently eased out of her shoes. "I haven't been here before," she told him. "It's very nice."

"I can't guarantee the food will be as exceptional as your aunt's."

"No one cooks like Aunt Coco. She'll be sorry to see you go. She likes cooking for a man."

"Will you?"

"Will I what?"

"Be sorry to see me go."

C.C. looked down at the menu, trying to concentrate on her choices. The hard fact was, she had none. "Since you're still here, we'll have to see. I imagine you have a lot to catch up on in Boston."

"Yes, I do. I've been thinking that after I do, I may take a vacation. A real one. Bar Harbor might be a good choice."

She looked up, then away. "Thousands think so," she murmured, relieved when the waiter served the wine.

"If you could go anywhere you liked, where would it be?"

"That's a tough question, since I haven't been any-where." She sipped, found the wine as smooth as chilled silk on her tongue. "Somewhere where I could see the sun set on the water, I think. Someplace warm." She shrugged. "I suppose I should have said Paris or London."

"No." He laid a hand on hers. "Catherine—"

"Are you ready to order?"

C.C. glanced quickly at the waiter who hovered beside them. "Yes." She slid her hand from Trent's and picked arbitrarily from the menu. Cautious, she kept one hand in her lap as she lifted her wine. The moment they were alone again, she started to speak. "Have you ever seen a whale?"

"I...no."

"You'll be coming back occasionally while you're—while you're having The Towers converted. You should take a day and go out on one of the whale-watch boats. The last time I managed it, I saw three humpback. You need to dress warmly though. Even in high summer it's cold once you get out on the Atlantic. It can be a rough ride, but it's worth it. You might even think about offering some sort of package yourself. You know, a weekend rate with a whale-watch tour included. A lot of the hotels—"

"Catherine." He stopped her by closing a hand over her wrist before she could lift her glass again. He could feel the rapid, unsteady beat of her pulse. Not passion this time, he thought. But heartache.

"The papers haven't been signed yet," he said quietly. "There's still time to look for other options."

"There aren't any other options." He cared, she realized as she studied his face. It was in his eyes as they looked into hers. Concern, apology. It made it worse somehow, knowing he cared. "We sell to you now, or The Towers is sold later for taxes. The end result is the same, and there's a little more dignity doing it this way."

"I might be able to help. A loan."

She retreated instantly. "We can't take your money."

"If I buy the house from you, you're taking my money."

"That's different. That's business. Trent," she said before he could argue, "I appreciate the fact that you'd offer, especially since I know the only reason you're here is to buy The Towers."

It was, he thought. Or it had been. "The thing is, C.C., I feel like I'm foreclosing on those widows and orphans."

She managed a smile. "We're five strong, self-sufficient women. We don't blame you—or maybe I do, a little, but at least I know I'm being unfair when I do. My feelings for you don't make it easy to be fair.

"What are your feelings?"

She let out a little sigh as the waiter served the appetizers and lit the candle between them. "You're taking the house, you might as well take it all. I'm in love with you. But I'll get over it." With her head tilted slightly, she lifted her fork. "Is there anything else you want to know?"

When he took her hand again, she didn't pull back,

but waited. "I never wanted to hurt you," he said carefully. How well her hand fit into his, he thought, looking down at it. How comforting it was to link his fingers with hers. "I'm just not capable of giving you—of giving anyone—promises of love and fidelity."

"That's sad." She shook her head as his eyes came back to hers. "You see, I'm only losing a house. I can find another. You're losing the rest of your life, and you only have one." She forced her lips to curve as she drew away from him. "Unless, of course, you subscribe to Lilah's idea that we just keep coming back. This is nice wine," she commented. "What is it again?"

"Pouilly Fumé."

"I'll have to remember that." She began to talk cheerfully as she ate the meal without tasting a thing. By the time coffee was served, she was wound like a top. C.C. knew that she would rather take an engine apart with her fingernails than face another evening such as this.

To love him so desperately, yet to have to be strong enough, proud enough to pretend she was capable of living without him. To sit, greedily storing each gesture, each word, while pretending it was all so casual and easy.

She wanted to shout at him, to rage and damn him for stirring her emotions into a frenzy then calmly walking away from the storm. But she could only cling to the cold comfort of pride.

"Tell me about your home in Boston," she invited. That would be something, she thought, to be able to picture him in his own home.

He wasn't able to take his eyes off her. The way

the clusters at her ears shot fire. The way the candlelight flickered dreamily in her eyes. But all through
the evening, he had felt as though she had blocked
off a part of herself, the most important part of herself. And he might never see the whole woman again.

"My home?"

"Yes, where you live."

"It's just a house." It occurred to him quite suddenly that it didn't mean a thing to him. An excellent
investment, that was all. "It's only a few minutes
from the office."

"That's convenient. Have you lived there long?"

"About five years. Actually, I bought it from my
father when he and his third wife split. They decided
to liquidate some assets."

"I see." And she was very much afraid that she
did. "Does your mother live in Boston, too?"

"No. She travels. Being tied down to one place
doesn't agree with her."

"Sounds like Great-Aunt Colleen." C.C. smiled
over the rim of her cup. "That's my father's aunt, or
Bianca's oldest child."

"Bianca," he mused, and thought again of that moment when he'd felt that soft and soothing warmth
over his and C.C.'s joined hands.

"She lives on cruise ships. Every now and again
we get a postcard from some port of call. Aruba or
Madagascar. She's eighty-something, obsessively single and mean as a shark with a hangover. We all live
in fear that she might decide to visit."

"I didn't realize you had any relatives living other
than Coco and your sisters." His brows drew together. "She might know something about the necklace."

"Great-Aunt Colleen?" Considering it, C.C. pursed her lips. "I doubt it. She was a child when Bianca died, and spent most of her girlhood in boarding schools." Without thinking, she pulled off her earrings and massaged the tender lobes. Desire spread like brushfire through Trent's blood. "Anyway, if we could find her—which isn't likely—and mentioned the whole business, she'd probably come steaming back to hack away at the walls. She doesn't have any love for The Towers, but she has a great deal for money."

"She doesn't sound like a relative of yours."

"Oh, we have a number of oddities in our family closet." After dropping the earrings into her bag, she leaned an elbow on the table. "Great-Uncle Sean—he was Bianca's youngest—was shot climbing out of his married paramour's window. One of his paramours, I should say. He survived, then took off for the West Indies, never to be heard of again. That was sometime during the thirties. Ethan, my grandfather, lost the bulk of the family fortune on cards and horses. Gambling was his weakness, and that's what killed him. He had a wager that he could sail from Bar Harbor to Newport and back within six days. He made it to Newport, and was heading back ahead of schedule when he ran into a squall and was lost at sea. Which meant he lost his last bet as well."

"They sound like an adventurous pair."

"They were Calhouns," C.C. explained, as if that said it all.

"I'm sorry the St. Jameses don't have anything to compare with it."

"Ah, well. I've always wondered if Bianca would have stepped back from that tower window if she'd known how messed up her children would become." C.C. looked thoughtfully out to where lights played on the dark water. "She must have loved her artist very much."

"Or was very unhappy in her marriage."

C.C. looked back. "Yes, there is that. Maybe we should head back. It's getting late." She started to rise, remembered, then slid her bare foot around the floor beneath the table.

"What is it?"

"I've lost my shoes." So much, she thought, for the sophisticated image.

Trent bent down to look himself and got an eyeful of long, slim leg. "Ah..." He cleared his throat and trained his eyes on the floor. "Here you go." He took both, then straightening, smiled at her. "Put your foot out. I'll give you a hand." He watched her as he slipped the shoes onto her feet and remembered that he'd once thought she would never stand for being a Cinderella. He trailed his finger up her instep and caught the flicker in her eyes. The flicker of desire that, no matter what common sense told him, he very much wanted.

"Have I mentioned that you have truly incredible legs?"

"No." She had one hand balled in a fist at her side and struggled to concentrate on it rather than the sensations his touch had spurting through her. "It's nice of you to notice."

"It's difficult not to. They're the only ones I've known that look sexy in coveralls."

Ignoring the thud of her own heart, she leaned toward him. "That reminds me."

He could kiss her now, he thought. He had only to

shift a mere inch to have his mouth on hers, where he wanted it. "What?"

"I don't think your shocks have more than another couple thousand miles on them." With a smile, she rose. "I'd look into that when you get home." Pleased with herself, C.C. started out ahead of him.

When they settled in the car, she congratulated herself. A very successful evening all in all, she thought. Maybe he wasn't miserable, as she was, but she was damn sure she'd made him uncomfortable a time or two. He'd go back to Boston the next day.... She turned to stare out the window until she was certain she could deal with the pain. He'd go back, but he wouldn't forget her quickly or easily. His last impression of her would be one of a composed, self-contained woman in a sexy red dress. Better, C.C. decided, much better than the picture of a mechanic in coveralls with grease on her hands.

More importantly, she'd proven something to herself. She could love, and she could let go.

She looked up as the car started to climb. She could see the shadowy peaks of the two towers spearing into the night sky. Trent slowed the car as he looked, as well.

"The light's on in Bianca's tower."

"Lilah," C.C. murmured. "She often sits up there." She thought of her sister sitting by the window, looking out into the night. "You won't tear it down, will you?"

"No." Understanding more than she knew, he closed his hand over hers. "I promise you it won't be torn down."

The house disappeared as the road curved away, then all but filled the view. They could hear the beat and slap of the sea as they looked at it. Lights were sprinkled on throughout, glowing against the dull gray stone. A slender shadow moved in front of the tower window, stood for a moment, then slid away.

Inside, Lilah called down the stairs. "They're back."

Four women raced to the windows to peer out.

"We shouldn't spy on them," Suzanna murmured, but moved the curtain aside a bit more.

"We're not." Amanda strained her eyes. "We're just checking, that's all. Can you see anything?"

"They're still in the car," Coco complained. "How are we supposed to see what's going on if they're going to sit in the car?"

"We could use our imaginations." Lilah shook her hair back. "If that man isn't begging her to go to Boston with him, then he really is a jerk."

"To Boston?" Alarmed, Suzanna glanced over. "You don't think she'd go to Boston, do you?"

"She'd go to the Ukraine if he had the sense to ask her," Amanda commented. "Look, they're getting out."

"Maybe if we just cracked a window a little bit, we could hear—"

"Aunt Coco, that's ridiculous." Lilah clucked her tongue.

"You're right, of course." Color tinged Coco's cheek.

"Of course I'm right. They'd hear the windows creak if we tried." Grinning, she pressed her face against the glass. "We'll just have to read their lips."

"This was nice," C.C. said as she stepped out of the car. "I haven't been out to dinner in a while."

"You had dinner with Finney."

She gave him a blank look, then laughed. "Oh, Finney, sure." The breeze played with her bangs as she smiled. "You've got quite a memory."

"Some things seem to stick to it." The jealousy he felt was, unfortunately, no memory. "Doesn't he ever take you out?"

"Finney? No, I just go to his place."

Frustrated, Trent jammed his hands into his pockets. "He should take you out."

She smothered a chuckle as the image of old Albert Finney escorting her to a restaurant ran through her mind. "I'll be sure to mention it to him." She turned to start up the steps.

"Catherine, don't go in yet." He took her hands.

At the windows four pairs of eyes narrowed.

"It's late, Trent."

"I don't know if I'll see you again before I leave." It took all her strength to keep her eyes steady. "Then we'll say goodbye now."

"I need to see you again."

"The shop's open at eight-thirty. I'll be there."

"Damn it, C.C., you know what I mean." His hands were on her shoulders now.

"No, I don't."

"Come to Boston." He blurted it out, shocking himself while she stood calmly waiting.

"Why?"

To give himself a moment to find control again, he stepped back. "I could show you around." How much more inane could he get? Trent wondered. How much more beautiful could she look? "You said you'd never been. We could...have some time together."

Inside her wrap, she shivered, but her voice was

calm and smooth. "Are you asking me to come to Boston and have an affair with you?"

"No. Yes. Oh, Lord. Just wait." He turned to pace a few steps away and breathe.

Inside, Lilah smiled. "Why, he's in love with her after all, but he's too stupid to know it."

"Shh!" Coco waved a hand. "I can almost hear what they're saying." She had an ear at the base of the water glass she pressed up to the window.

At the bottom of the steps, Trent tried again. "Nothing I begin ends the way I expect it to when I'm with you." He turned back. She was still standing with the house behind her, the dress glimmering like liquid fire in the dark. "I know I have no business asking you, and I didn't intend to. I intended to say a very civil goodbye and let you go."

"And now?"

"Now I want to make love with you more than I want to go on breathing."

"To make love," C.C. repeated steadily. "But you don't love me."

"I don't know anything about love. I care for you." He walked back to touch a hand to her face. "Maybe that could be enough."

She studied him, realizing he didn't have any idea that he was breaking an already shattered heart. "It might be, for a day or a week or a month. But you were right about me, Trent. I expect more. I deserve more." Keeping her eyes on his, she slid her hands over his shoulders. "I offered myself to you once. That won't happen again. And neither will this."

She pressed her mouth against his, pouring every scrap of her tattered emotions into it. Her arms enfolded him even as her body swayed seductively toward his. With a sigh, her lips parted, inviting him to take.

Off balance, needy, he dragged her head back and plundered. Unsteady, his hands skimmed beneath her wrap, urgently seeking the warmth of her skin.

So many feelings, too many feelings, bombarded him. He wanted only to fill himself with the taste of her. But there was more. She wouldn't let him take only the kiss, but all the emotion that went with it. He felt he was drowning in it, but it was so strong and heady a flood, he couldn't fight.

Love me! Why can't you love me? Her mind seemed to scream it even as she was borne away on the tide of her own longings. Everything she wanted was here, inside the circle of her arms. Everything but his heart.

"Catherine." He couldn't get his breath. Dragging her closer, he pressed his mouth to her neck. "I can't get close enough."

She held him to her a moment longer, then slowly, painfully, pulled away. "Yes, you could. And that's what hurts the most." Turning, she dashed up the steps.

"Catherine."

She paused at the door. With her head high, she turned around. He was already coming after her when he saw the tears glittering in her eyes. Nothing else would have stopped him.

"Goodbye, Trent. I hope to God that keeps you up at night."

As he listened to the echo of the door slamming, he was certain it would.

It cannot go on. I can no longer pretend that I am disloyal to my husband only between the covers of this journal. My life, so calm and ordered during my twenty-four years, has become a lie this summer. One I must atone for.

As autumn approaches and we make our plans to return to New York, I thank God I will soon leave Mount Desert Island behind me. How close, how dangerously close I have come these past days to breaking my marriage vows.

And yet, I grieve.

In another week, we will be gone. I may never see Christian again. That is how it should be. How it must be. But in my heart I know that I would give my soul for one night, even one hour, in his arms. Imagining how it could be obsesses me. With him there would finally be passion, and love, even laughter. With him it would not simply be a duty, cold and silent and soon over.

I pray to be forgiven for the adultery I have committed in my heart.

My conscience has urged me to keep away from the cliffs. And I have tried. It has demanded that I be a more patient, loving and understanding wife to Fergus. I have done so. Whatever he has asked of me, I have done. At his request, I gave a tea for several of the ladies. We have gone to the theater, to countless dinner parties. I have listened until my head was throbbing to talk of business and fashion and the possibility of war. My smile never falters, for Fergus prefers that I look content at all times. Because it pleases him, I wear the emeralds when we go out in the evenings.

They are my penance now, a reminder that a sin is not always in the action, but in the heart.

I sit here in my tower now as I write. The cliffs are below, the cliffs where Christian paints. Where I go when I sneak from the house like a randy housemaid. It shames me. It sustains me. Even now I look down and see him. He faces the sea, and waits for me.

We have never touched, not once, though the ache is in both of us. I have learned how much passion there can be in silences, in long, troubled looks.

I will not go to him today, but only sit here and watch him. When I feel I have the strength, I will go to him only to say goodbye and wish him well.

While I live through the long winter that faces me, I will wonder if he will be here next summer.

Chapter Ten

"Here are the papers you asked for, Mr. St. James."

Oblivious to his secretary's presence, Trent continued to stand at the window, staring out. It was a habit he'd developed since returning to work three weeks before. Through the wide tinted glass, he could watch Boston bustling by below. Steel-and-glass towers glittered beside elegant brownstones in a architectural potpourri. Thick traffic weaved and charged on the streets. In sweats and colorful running shorts, joggers paced themselves along the path beside the river. Then there was the river itself, streaming with boats, sails puffed full of warm spring breezes.

"Mr. St. James?"

"Yes?" He glanced around at his secretary.

"I've brought you the papers you requested."

"Thank you, Angela." In an old habit, he looked at his watch. It occurred to him, painfully, that he had rarely thought of the time when he'd been with C.C. "It's after five. You should go home to your family."

Angela hesitated. She'd worked for Trenton for six years. It had only been during the past couple of weeks that he had begun calling her by her first name or inquiring about her family. The day before, he'd actually complimented her on her dress. The change in him had the entire staff baffled. As his secretary, she felt obligated to dig out the source of it.

"May I speak with you a minute?"

"All right. Would you like to sit down?"

"No, sir. I hope you won't consider this out of place, Mr. St. James, but I wanted to know if you're feeling well."

A ghost of a smile played around his mouth. "Don't I look well?"

"Oh, yes, of course. A little tired perhaps. It's just that since you returned from Bar Harbor, you seem distracted, and different somehow."

"You could say I am distracted. I am different, and to answer your original question, no, I don't think I am entirely well."

"Mr. St. James, if there's anything I can do…"

Studying her, he sat on the edge of his desk. He had hired her because she was efficient and quick. As he recalled, he had nearly passed her over because she'd had two small children. It had worried him that she wouldn't be able to balance her responsibilities, but he'd taken what he'd considered a chance. It had worked very well indeed.

"Angela, how long have you been married?"

"Married?" Thrown off, she blinked. "Ten years."

"Happily?"

"Yes, Joe and I are happy."

Joe, he mused. He hadn't even known her husband's name. Hadn't bothered to find it out. "Why?"

"Why, sir?"

"Why are you happy?"

"I...I suppose because we love each other."

He nodded, gesturing to prod her along. "And that's enough?"

"It certainly helps you get through the rough spots." She smiled a little, thinking of her Joe. "We've had some of them, but one of us always manages to pull the other through."

"You consider yourself a team then. So you have a great deal in common?"

"I don't know about that. Joe likes football and I hate it. He loves jazz, and I don't understand it." It wouldn't occur to her until later that this was the first time she'd felt completely at ease with Trent since she'd taken the job. "Sometimes I feel like wearing earplugs all weekend. Whenever I feel like shipping him out, I think about what my life would be without him. And I don't like what I see." Taking a chance, she stepped closer. "Mr. St. James, if this is about Marla Montblanc getting married last week, well, I'd just like to say that you're better off."

"Marla got married?"

Truly baffled, Angela shook her head. "Yes, sir. Last week, to that golf pro. It was in all the papers."

"I must have missed it." There had been other things in the papers that had captured his attention.

"I realize you'd been seeing her for quite a while."

Seeing her, Trent mused. Yes, that cool, passionless phrase described their relationship perfectly. "Yes, I had been."

"You're not—upset?"

"About Marla? No." The fact was he hadn't thought of her in weeks. Since he'd walked into a garage and spotted a pair of scarred boots.

Another woman, Angela realized. And if she'd had this kind of affect on the boss, she had all of Angela's support. "Sir, if someone—something else," she corrected cautiously, "is on your mind, you may be overanalyzing the situation."

The comment surprised him enough to make him smile again. "Do I overanalyze, Angela?"

"You're very meticulous, Mr. St. James, and analyze details finitely, which works very well in business. Personal matters can't always be dealt with logically."

"I've been coming to that same conclusion myself." He stood again. "I appreciate the time."

"My pleasure, Mr. St. James." And it certainly had been. "Is there anything else I can do for you?"

"No, thank you." He turned back to the window. "Good night, Angela."

"Good night." She was grinning when she closed the door at her back.

Trent stood where he was for some time. No, he hadn't noticed the announcement of Marla's wedding. The papers had also been full of the upcoming sale of The Towers. "Bar Harbor landmark to become newest St. James Hotel," he remembered. "Rumors of lost treasures sweeten the deal."

Trent wasn't certain where the leak had come from, though he wasn't surprised by it. As he'd expected, his lawyers had grumbled over the clause Lilah had insisted on. Whispers of emeralds had sneaked down the hallways. It was only natural that they would find their way onto the street and into print.

Newspapers and tabloids had been rife with speculation on the Calhoun emeralds for more than a week. They'd been termed priceless and tragic and legendary—all the right adjectives to ensure more newsprint.

Fergus Calhoun's business exploits had been rehashed, along with his wife's suicide. An enterprising reporter had even managed to track down Colleen Calhoun aboard a cruise ship in the Ionian Sea. The grande dame's pithy reply had been printed in italics. *"Humbug."*

He wondered if C.C. had seen the papers. Of course, she had, he thought. Just as she'd probably been hounded by the press.

How was she taking it? Was she hurt and miserable, forced to answer questions when some nosy reporter stuck a tape recorder in her face? He smiled a little. *Forced?* He imagined she'd throw a dozen reporters out of the garage if they had the nerve to try.

God, he missed her. And missing her was eating him alive. He woke up each morning wondering what she was doing. He went to bed each night to toss restlessly as thoughts of her invaded his brain. When he slept, she was in his dreams. She was his dream.

Three weeks, he thought. He should have adjusted by now. Yet every day that he was here and she was somewhere else, it got worse.

The revised contracts for the sale of The Towers were sitting on his desk. He should have signed them days ago. Yet he couldn't make himself take that final step. The last time he had looked at them, he had only been able to focus on three words.

Catherine Colleen Calhoun.

He'd read it over and over, remembering the first time she'd told him her name, tossing it at him as though it had been a weapon. She'd had grease on her face, Trenton remembered. And fire in her eyes.

Then he would think of other times, odd moments, careless words. The way she had scowled at him from her perch on the arm of the sofa while he'd had tea with Coco. The look on her face when they'd stood on the terrace together, watching the sea. How perfectly her mouth had fit to his when he had kissed her under an arbor of wisteria not yet in bloom.

It would be blooming now, he mused. Those first fragrant flowers would be opening. Would she think of him at all when she walked there?

If she did, he was very much afraid the thoughts wouldn't be kind.

She'd cursed him when she'd seen him last. She'd leveled those deep green eyes at him and had hoped that the kiss, the last kiss they'd shared, would keep him up at night.

He doubted even she could know how completely her wish had come true.

Rubbing his tired eyes, he walked back to his desk. It was, as always, in perfect order. As his business was—as his life had been.

Things had changed, he was forced to admit. He had changed, but perhaps he hadn't changed so completely. Once again, he picked up the contracts to study them. He was still a skilled and organized businessman, one who knew how to maneuver a deal and make it work to his advantage.

He picked up his pen and tapped it lightly on the papers. A germ of an idea had rooted in his mind a few days before. Now he sat quietly and let it form, shift, realign.

It was unusual, he considered. Maybe even mildly eccentric, but...but, he thought as a smile began to curve his mouth, if he played his cards right, it could work. It was his job to make it work. Slowly he let out a long breath. It might just be the most important deal of his life.

He picked up the phone and, employing all of the St. James clout, began to turn the first wheels.

Hank finished sanding the fender on the '69 Mustang, then stood back to admire his work. "Coming along just fine," he called to C.C.

She glanced over, but her hands were full with the brake shoes she was replacing above her head. "It's going to be a beauty. I'm glad we got the shot at reconditioning it."

"You want me to start on the primer?"

She swore as brake fluid dripped onto her cheek. "No. You told me three times today that you've got a hot date tonight. Get cleaned up and take off."

"Thanks." But he'd been too well trained to leave without replacing tools and material. "You found another house yet?"

"No." She ignored the sudden ache in her stomach and concentrated on her work. "We're all going out tomorrow to look."

"Won't be the same, not having Calhouns in The Towers. Sure is something about that necklace, though. Papers are full of stories about it."

"They'll die down." She hoped.

"Guess if you find it, you'd be millionaires. You could retire and move to Florida."

Despite her mood, she had to chuckle. "Well, we haven't found it yet." Just the receipt, she mused, which Lilah had unearthed during her one and only shift in the storeroom. "Florida'll have to wait. The brakes won't."

"Guess I'll be going. Want me to lock up the office?"

"Go ahead. Have a good time."

He went out whistling, and C.C. stopped a moment to rest her arms and neck. She wished she'd been able to keep Hank around a while longer, for company, for the distraction. Even if he rambled on about the house and the necklace, he helped keep her mind occupied.

No matter how loudly she played the radio, once she was alone, there was too much silence.

They would hear from the lawyer any day. Perhaps Aunt Coco had gotten a call from Stridley that afternoon, telling her that the contracts had been signed and a settlement date set.

Would Trent come to the settlement? she wondered. No, no, of course not. He would send a representative, and that was for the best.

Besides, she had too much to do to worry about it. House hunting, the search through old papers for a clue to the emeralds' whereabouts, the classic Mustang she intended to baby along to gleaming perfection. She barely had a moment to catch her breath much less brood about seeing Trent over the settlement table.

If only it would stop hurting, even for a few moments.

It would get better, she told herself as she returned to the brake job. It had to. After they'd found a new house and settled in. After the talk of the necklace had died away. Everything would get back to normal—or what she would have to accept as normal. If the ache never completely went away, then she would learn to live with it.

She had her family. Together, they could handle anything.

Her shoulders were stiff by the time she'd finished. Rolling them a little, she started to step out from under the car when she realized the radio had stopped playing. She glanced over. And saw Trent standing by the workbench. The wrench she was holding clattered to the floor.

"What are you doing here?"

"Waiting for you to finish." She looked fabulous, was all he could think. Absolutely fabulous. "How are you?"

"Busy." Rocked from the pain, she turned to hit a button on the wall. The lift groaned as it brought the car down. "You're here about the house, I guess."

"Yes, you could say that's a large part of it."

"We've been expecting to hear from the lawyer."

"I know."

When the car was settled, she took a rag and wiped her hands, keeping her eyes on them. "Amanda's handling the details. She's at the BayWatch if you need to discuss anything."

"What I need to discuss concerns you. Us."

She looked up, then took a quick step back when she realized he'd moved over to stand next to her. "I really don't have anything else to say to you."

"Okay, then I'll do the talking. In just a minute."

He moved fast. Still, she was certain if she'd been

expecting it, she could have evaded him. She wasn't certain she would have tried.

It felt so good, so right, to have his mouth covering hers, his hands framing her face. Her pride faltered long enough to have her reaching up to grasp his wrists, holding on as she let her needs flow into the kiss.

"I've thought about doing that for three and a half weeks," he murmured.

She squeezed her eyes tight. "Go away, Trent."

"Catherine—"

"Damn you, I said go away." She yanked free, then turned to brace her palms on the bench. "I hate you for coming here, for making a fool out of me again."

"You're not the fool. You never were."

When his hand brushed lightly over her shoulder, she snatched up a hammer and whirled. "If you touch me again, so help me, I'll break your nose."

He looked at her. The fire was in her eyes again. "Thank God. You're back." Delighted but cautious, he held up a hand. "Just listen, please. Business first."

"My business with you is settled."

"There's been a change in the plans." He plucked some change out of the can on the bench. "Can I buy you a drink?"

"No. Say what you have to say, then get out."

With a shrug, he strolled over to the soft drink machine and plugged in the change. It was then that C.C. noticed he was wearing scuffed high-tops.

"What are those?" she asked, staring at them.

"These?" Trent grinned as he popped the top on the can. "New shoes. What do you think?" When she simply gaped, he took a long drink. "I know, not quite the usual image, but things change. A number of things have changed. Would you mind putting down that hammer?"

"What? Oh. All right." She set it aside. "You said plans had changed. Does that mean you've decided not to buy The Towers?"

"Yes and no. Would you rather go into the office to discuss this?"

"Damn it, Trent, just tell me what's going on."

"All right. Here's the deal. We take one wing, the west, I think, so it doesn't involve Bianca's tower. We have it extensively remodeled. My preference is to salvage as much of the original material as possible and reconstruct, whenever possible, according with the original blueprints. It should maintain its turn-of-the-century feel. That will be part of the draw."

"The draw?" she repeated, lost.

"We can easily have ten suites without compromising the architecture. If memory serves, the billiard room would be excellent for dining, with the west tower remodeled for more intimate meals and private parties."

"Ten suites?"

"In the west wing," he agreed. "With an accent on aesthetics and intimacy. We'll have to put all the fireplaces back in working order. I think, with what we'll offer, we'll have year-round clientele rather than just seasonal."

"What are you going to do with the rest of the house?"

"That would be up to you, and your family." He set the drink aside and came toward her. "The way I see it, you could live very easily on the first two floors and the east wing. God knows there's plenty of room.''

Confused, she pressed her fingers to her temple. "We'd be, what—renting it from you?"

"That's not exactly what I had in mind. I was thinking more of a partnership." He took her hand, examining it closely. "Your knuckles have healed."

"What kind of partnership?"

"The St. James Corporation fronts the money for the renovations, advertising and so forth. Once the retreat—I like retreat better than hotel in this case— once it's in operation, we split the profits, fifty-fifty."

"I don't understand."

"It's really very simple, C.C." He lifted her hand, kissed one finger. "We compromise. We have our hotel, you have your home. Nobody loses."

Afraid to feel it, she banked down the little flicker of hope. "I don't see how it could work. Why would anyone want to pay to stay in someone else's home?"

"A landmark," he reminded her, and kissed another finger. "With a legend, a ghost and a mystery. They'll pay very well to stay here. And when they get a taste of Coco's bouillabaisse—"

"Aunt Coco?"

"I've already offered her the position of chef. She's delighted. There's still the matter of a manager, but I think Amanda will fit the slot, don't you?" His eyes smiled as he brushed a kiss over her third finger.

"Why are you doing this?"

"I'm a businessman. It makes good business sense. I've already begun the market research." He turned her hand over and pressed his lips to the palm. "That's what I've told my board of directors. I think you know differently."

"I don't know anything." She pulled her hand away to walk to the open garage doors. "All I know is that you come back here with some sort of wild scheme—"

"It's a very solid plan," he corrected. "I'm not a wild-scheme sort of person. At least I never have been." He went to her again, taking her shoulders. "I want you to keep your home, C.C."

With her lips pressed tight, she closed her eyes. "So, you're doing it for me."

"For you, your sisters, Coco, even Bianca." Hands firm, he turned her to face him. "And I'm doing it for me. You wanted to keep me up at night, and you did."

She managed a weak smile. "Guilt works miracles."

"It has nothing to do with guilt. It never did. It has to do with love. With being in love. Don't pull away," he said quietly when she jerked against his hold. "Business is closed for the day. Now it's just you and me. This is as personal as it gets."

At her sides, her hands clenched into fists. "It's all personal with me, don't you understand? You came here and changed everything in my life, then waltzed away again. Now you come back and tell me you've altered the plans."

"You weren't the only one things changed for. Nothing's been the same for me since I met you." Panic snaked through him. She wasn't going to give him another chance. "I didn't ask for this. I didn't want it."

"Oh, you made it abundantly clear what you didn't want." She shoved against him and got nowhere. "You have no right to start this up again."

"The hell with rights." He gave her a hard shake. "I'm trying to tell you that I love you. That's a first for me, and you're not going to turn it into an argument."

"I'll turn it into whatever I want," she tossed back, furious when her voice broke. "I'm not going to let you hurt me again. I'm not going to—" Then she went still, eyes widening. "Did you say you were in love with me?"

"Just shut up and listen. I've spent three and a half weeks feeling empty and miserable without you. I went away because I thought I could. Because I thought that was right and fair and best for both of us. Logically, it was. It still is. We're nothing alike. I couldn't see any percentage in risking both our futures when you'd certainly be better off with someone else. Someone like Finney."

"Finney?" A shout of laughter escaped. "Oh, that's rich." While her emotions whirled, she knocked a fist against his chest. "Tell you what, why don't you take your percentages back to Boston and draw a graph? Now leave me alone. I've got work to do."

"I'm not finished." When she opened her mouth to swear at him, he let instinct rule and kissed her until she quieted. As breathless as she, he rested his brow against hers. "That has nothing to do with logic or percentages." Still holding on, he took a step back so that he could see her. "Catherine, every time I reminded myself that I didn't believe in love or marriage or lifetimes, I remembered the way I felt with you."

"How? How did you feel with me?"

"Alive. Happy. And I knew I was never going to

feel that way again unless I came back." He let his hands slide away. "C.C., you told me once that what we had could be the best part of my life. You were right. I don't know if I can make it work, but I need to try. I need you."

He was afraid, she realized. Even more afraid than she was. With her eyes on his, she lifted a hand to his cheek. "I can give you a guarantee on a muffler, Trent. Not on this."

"I'd settle for you telling me you still love me, that you'll give me another chance."

"I still love you. But I can't give you another chance."

"Catherine—"

"Because you haven't taken the first one yet." She touched her lips to his once, then twice. "Why don't we take it together?" she asked, then laughed when he dragged her close. "Now you've done it. You'll have grease all over you."

"I'll have to get used to it." After one last spin, he drew away to study her face. Everything he needed was right there, in her eyes. "I love you, Catherine. Very much."

She brought his hand to her cheek. "I'll have to get used to it. Maybe if you said it a few hundred times."

He told her as he held her, as he traced kisses over her face, as he lingered over the taste of her mouth.

"I think it's working," she murmured. "Maybe we should close the garage doors."

"Leave them up." He stepped back again, struggling to clear his head. "I'm still St. James enough to want to do things in their proper order, but I'm running low on control."

"What order is that?" Smiling, she ran a finger up his shirt to toy with the top button.

"Wait." Churning, he put a hand over hers. "I thought about this all the way up from Boston. It played a lot of different ways—I'd take you out again. A little wine, a lot of candlelight. Or we'd walk in the garden again at dusk."

He glanced around the garage. Honeysuckle and motor oil, he thought. Perfect.

"But this seems like the right time, the right place." He reached in his pocket for a small box, then opening it, handed it to her. "You once said if I offered you a diamond, you'd laugh in my face. I thought I might have more luck with an emerald."

Tears backed up in her throat as she stared down at the deep green stone in its simple gold setting. It gleamed up at her, full of hope and promise. "If this is a proposal, you don't need any luck at all." Wet and brilliant, her eyes came back to his. "The answer was always yes."

He slid the ring onto her finger. "Let's go home."

"Yes." Her hand linked with his. "Let's go home."

*   *   *   *   *

A MAN FOR AMANDA

Prologue

Bar Harbor
June 8, 1913

In the afternoon, I walked to the cliffs. The day, our first day back in The Towers, was bright and warm. The rumble of the sea was as I had left it ten long months ago. There was a fishing boat chugging over the blue-green water, and a neat sloop gliding cheerfully along. So much was the same, and yet, one vital change dimmed the day for me.

He was not there.

It was wrong of me to wish to find him waiting where I had left him so many months ago. To find him painting as he always did, slicing the brush against canvas like a dueler in the heat of battle. It was wrong of me to wish to see him turn, look at me with those intense gray eyes—to see him smile, to hear him say my name.

Yet I did wish it.

My heart was dancing in my breast as I rushed from the house to race across the lawn, past the gardens and down the slope.

The cliffs were there, so high and proud, jutting up to the pure summer sky. The sea, almost calm today, mirrored the color so that it seemed I stood cupped in a lovely blue ball. The rocks tumbled down before me, down and down to where the waves slapped and hissed. Behind me, the towers of my summer home, my husband's home, speared up, arrogant and beautiful.

How strange that I should love the house when I have known such unhappiness inside it.

I reminded myself that I am Bianca Calhoun, wife of Fergus Calhoun, mother to Colleen and Ethan and Sean. I am a respected woman, a dutiful wife, a devoted mother. My marriage is not a warm one, but that does not alter the vows I took. There is no place in my life for romantic fancies and sinful dreams.

Still, I stood and I waited. But he did not come. Christian, the lover I have taken only with my heart, did not come. He may not even be on the island any longer. Perhaps he has packed up his canvases and brushes, moved from his cottage and gone on to paint some other sea, some other sky.

It would be best. I know it would be best. Since I met him last summer, I have hardly gone an hour without thinking of him. Yet I have a husband I respect, three children I love more than my life. It is to them I must be faithful, not to the memory of something that never was. And never could be.

The sun is setting as I sit and write by the window of my tower. In a short time I must go down and help

Nanny put my babies to bed. Little Sean has grown so, and is already beginning to toddle. Soon he will be as quick as Ethan. Colleen, quite the young lady at four, wants a new pink dress.

It is of them I must think, my children, my precious loves, and not of Christian.

It will be a quiet night, one of very few we will have during our summer on Mount Desert Island. Fergus has already talked of giving a dinner dance next week. I must...

He is there. Down below on the cliffs. He is hardly more than a shadow with the distance and the dimming light. Yet I know it is he. Just as I knew, as I stood and pressed my hand to the glass, that he was looking up, looking for me. However impossible it is, I would swear I could hear him call my name. So softly.

Bianca.

Chapter One

He was a solid wall of denim and muscle. Ramming into him knocked the wind out of her lungs and the packages out of her hands. In her rush to get from one place to the next, she didn't even bother to glance at him but dove to save the flying boxes.

If he'd been looking where he'd been going, she wouldn't have run into him. Amanda managed to bite her tongue before she snapped out the thought, and scowled instead at the run-down heels of his boots. In a hurry, as usual, she knelt on the sidewalk outside the boutique where she'd been shopping, to gather up her scattered packages.

"Let me give you a hand, honey."

The slow southwestern drawl grated on her nerves. She had a million things to do, and scrambling on the sidewalk with a tourist wasn't on her schedule. "I've got it," she muttered, leaning over so that her chin-length hair drifted down to curtain her face. Everything was grating on her nerves today, she thought as she hurried to restack bags and boxes. This little irritation was the last in a long line.

"It's an awful lot for one person to carry."

"I can manage, thanks." She reached for a box just as her persistent helper did the same. The brief tug-of-war had the top slipping off and the contents spilling onto the sidewalk.

"Now, that's mighty pretty." There was amused, masculine approval in the voice as he scooped up a scrap of thin red silk that pretended to be a nightie.

Amanda snatched it from him and stuffed it into one of the bags. "Do you mind?"

"No, ma'am. I sure don't."

Amanda pushed back her tumbled hair and took her first good look at him. So far, all she'd seen were a pair of cowboy boots and the line of faded denim from knee to ankle. There was a great deal more of him. Even crouched down beside her he looked big. Shoulders, hands. Mouth, she thought nastily. Right now he was using it to grin at her. It might, under different circumstances, have been an engaging enough grin. But at the moment it was stuck in the middle of a face she'd decided to dislike on sight.

Not that it wasn't a good one, with its slashing warrior's cheekbones, velvet green eyes and deep tan. The curl of his reddish-blond hair over the collar of his denim shirt might have been charming. If he hadn't been in her way.

"I'm in a hurry," she told him.

"I noticed." He flipped a long finger through her hair to tuck it behind her ear. "Looked like you were on the way to a fire when you plowed into me."

"If you'd moved," she began, then shook her head. Arguing would take time she simply didn't have. "Never mind." Grabbing at packages, she rose. "Excuse me."

"Hold on."

He unfolded himself as she tapped her foot and waited. Disconcerted, she frowned up at him. At five feet ten inches, she was accustomed to meeting most men almost eye to eye. With this one she had several extra inches to go. "What?"

"I can give you a ride to that fire if you need it."

Her brow arched in her frostiest look. "That won't be necessary."

Using a fingertip, he pushed a box back in place before it could slide out of her grip. "You look like you could use a little help."

"I'm perfectly capable of getting where I'm going, thank you."

He didn't doubt it for a minute. "Then maybe you can help me." He liked the way her hair kept falling into her eyes, and the impatient way she kept blowing it away again. "I just got into town this morning." His gaze lazily skimmed her face. "I thought maybe you could make some suggestions about...what I should do with myself."

At the moment, she had a pocketful of them. "Try the chamber of commerce." She started by him, then whirled when his hand came down on her arm. "Look, buster, I don't know how they do things back in Tucson—"

"Oklahoma City," he corrected.

"Wherever, but around here, cops take a dim view of men who hassle women on the streets."

"That so?"

"You bet it's so."

"Well then, I'll have to watch my step since I plan to be around awhile."

"I'll hang out a bulletin. Now, excuse me."

"Just one more thing." He held up a pair of brief black panties embroidered with red roses. "I think you forgot this."

She grabbed the bikinis, then stalked off as she balled them into her pocket.

"Nice meeting you," he called after her, and laughed when she doubled her already hurried pace.

Twenty minutes later, Amanda gathered up her packages from the back seat of her car. Balancing some under her chin, she kicked the door closed with her foot. She'd nearly forgotten about the encounter already. There was too much on her mind. Behind her, the house rose up into the sky, its gray stones staid, its towers and peaks fanciful and its porches sagging. Next to her family, there was nothing Amanda loved more than The Towers.

She raced up the steps, avoided a rotting board then struggled to free a hand enough to open the towering front door. "Aunt Coco!" The moment she stepped into the hall, an oversize black puppy raced down the stairs. On the third from the bottom, he tripped, rolled and went sprawling onto the gleaming chestnut floor. "Almost made it that time, Fred."

Pleased with himself, Fred danced around Amanda's legs as she continued to call for her aunt.

"Coming. I'm coming." Tall and stately, Cordelia Calhoun McPike hurried in from the rear of the house. She wore peach linen slacks under a splattered white apron. "I was in the kitchen. We're going to try my new recipe for cannelloni tonight."

"Is C.C. home?"

"Oh, no, dear." Coco patted the hair she'd tinted the day before to Moonlit Blonde. In an old habit, she peeked into the hall mirror to make certain the shade suited her—for the moment. "She's down at her garage. Something about rocker arms, I think—though what rocking chairs have to do with cars and engines, I can't say."

"Great. Come upstairs, I want to show you what I got."

"Looks like you bought out the shops. Here, let me help you." Coco managed to grab two bags before Amanda dashed up the stairs.

"I had the best time."

"But you hate to shop."

"For myself. This was different. Still, everything took longer than I thought it would, so I was afraid I wouldn't get back and be able to stash it all before C.C. got home." She rushed into her room to dump everything onto the big four-poster bed. "Then this stupid man got in my way and knocked everything all over the sidewalk." Amanda stripped off her jacket, folded it, then laid it neatly over the back of a chair. "Then he had the nerve to try to pick me up."

"Really?" Always interested in liaisons, romances and assignations, Coco tilted her head. "Was he attractive?"

"If you go for the Wild Bill Hickok type. Anyway, I made it—no thanks to him."

As Amanda sorted through the bags, Fred tried twice, unsuccessfully, to leap onto the bed. He ended by sitting on the rug to watch.

"I found some wonderful decorations for the bridal

shower.'' She began to pull out white-and-silver bells, crepe paper swans, balloons. "I love this frilly parasol," she went on. "Not C.C.'s style maybe, but I thought if we hung it up over…Aunt Coco." With a sigh, Amanda sat on the bed. "Don't start crying again."

"I can't help it." Already sniffling, Coco took an embroidered hankie from her apron pocket and dabbed carefully at her eyes. "She's the baby, after all. The youngest of my four little girls."

"There's not one of the Calhoun women who could be called little," Amanda pointed out.

"You're still my babies, and have been ever since your mother and father died." Coco used the hankie expertly. She didn't want to smear her mascara. "Every time I think of her being married—and in only a matter of days, really—I just fill up. I adore Trenton, you know." Thinking of her future nephew, she blew delicately into the hankie. "He's a wonderful man, and I knew they'd be perfect together right from the start, but it's all so fast."

"You're telling me." Amanda combed a hand through her sleek cap of hair. "I've barely had time to organize. How anyone expects to put on a wedding with barely three weeks notice—or why they'd want to try—is beyond me. They'd be better off eloping."

"Don't say that." Scandalized, Coco stuck her hankie back into her pocket. "Why, I'd be furious if they cheated me out of this wedding. And if you think you can when your time comes, think again."

"My time isn't going to come for years, if ever." Meticulously Amanda tidied the decorations again. "Men are as far down on my list of priorities as they can get."

"You and your lists." Coco clucked her tongue. "Let me tell you, Mandy, the one thing you can't plan in this life is falling in love. Your sister certainly didn't plan it, and look at her. Squeezing fittings for a wedding dress in between her carburetors and transmissions. Your time may come sooner than you think. Why just this morning when I was reading my tea leaves—"

"Oh, Aunt Coco, not the tea leaves."

Grandly Coco drew herself up to her considerable height. "I've read some very fascinating things in the tea leaves. After our last séance, I'd think you'd be a bit less cynical."

"Maybe something happened at the séance, but—"

"Maybe?"

"All right, something did happen." Letting out a deep breath, Amanda shrugged. "I know C.C. got an image—"

"A vision."

"Whatever—of Great-Grandmama Bianca's emerald necklace." And it had been spooky, she admitted to herself, the way C.C. had been able to describe it, though no one had seen the two tiers of emeralds and diamonds in decades. "And no one who's lived in this house could deny that they've felt some—some presence or something up in Bianca's tower."

"Aha!"

"But that doesn't mean I'm going to start gazing into crystal balls."

"You're just too literal minded, Mandy. I can't think where you get it from. Perhaps from my Aunt Colleen. Fred, we must not chew on the Irish lace," Coco cautioned as Fred began to gnaw on Amanda's bedspread. "In any case, we were speaking of tea leaves. When I took a reading this morning, I saw a man.''

Amanda rose to hide the decorations in her closet. "You saw a man in your teacup.''

"You know very well it doesn't work precisely like that. I saw a man, and I had the strongest feeling that he's very close.''

"Maybe it's the plumber. He's been underfoot for days.''

"No, it's not the plumber. This man—he's close, but he's not from the island.'' She let her eyes unfocus as she did when she practiced looking psychic. "In fact he's from some distance away. He's going to be an important part of our lives. And—I'm quite sure of this—he's going to be vitally important to one of you girls.''

"Lilah can have him,'' Amanda decided, thinking of her free-spirited older sister. "Where is she anyway?''

"Oh, she was meeting someone after work. Rod or Tod or Dominick.''

"Damn it.'' Amanda scooped up her jacket to hang it neatly in the closet. "We were supposed to go through more of the papers. She knew I was counting on her. We have to find some lead as to where the emeralds are hidden.''

"We'll find them, dear.'' Distracted, Coco poked through the other packages. "When the time is right. Bianca wants us to. I believe she'll show us the next step very soon.''

"We need more than blind faith and mystic visions. Bianca could have hidden them anywhere.'' Scowling, she plopped down onto the bed again.

She didn't care about the money—though the Calhoun emeralds were reputed to be worth a fortune. It was the publicity that had resulted when Trent, her sister's fiancé, had contracted to buy The Towers, and the old legend had become public knowledge. Amanda's idea of an ordered existence had been thrown into chaos since the first story had hit.

It certainly made good print, Amanda mused as her aunt oohed and aahed over the lingerie she had bought for her sister's shower.

Early in the second decade of the century, when the resort of Bar Harbor was in its elegant heyday, Fergus Calhoun had built The Towers as an opulent summer home. There on the cliffs overlooking Frenchman Bay, he and his wife, Bianca, and their three children had vacationed, giving elaborate parties for other members of the well-heeled society.

And there, Bianca had met a young artist. They had fallen in love. It was said that Bianca had been torn between duty and her heart. Her marriage, which had been firmly supported by her parents, had been a cold one. With her heart leading her, she had planned to leave her husband and had packed away a treasure box that had contained the emeralds Fergus had given her on the birth of their second child and first son. The whereabouts of the necklace was a mystery as, according to legend, she had thrown herself from the tower window, overwhelmed with guilt and despair.

Now, eighty years later, interest in the necklace had been revived. Even as the remaining Calhouns searched through decades of papers and ledgers for a clue, reporters and hopeful fortune hunters had become a daily nuisance.

Amanda took it personally. The legend, and the people in it, belonged to her family. The sooner the necklace was located, the better. Once a mystery was solved, interest faded quickly.

"When is Trent coming back?" she asked her aunt.

"Soon." Sighing, Coco stroked the silky red chemise. "As soon as he ties things up in Boston, he'll be on his way. He can't stand being away from C.C. There will barely be enough time to begin the renovations on the west wing before they'll be off on their honeymoon." Tears filled her eyes again. "Their honeymoon."

"Don't start, Aunt Coco. Think of what a fabulous job you'll do catering the reception. It's going to be great practice for you. This time next year you'll be starting your new career as chef for The Towers Retreat, the most intimate of the St. James hotels."

"Imagine it." Coco patted her hand at her breast.

At the knock on the front door, Fred was up and howling.

"You stay here and imagine it, Aunt Coco. I'll go answer the door."

In a race with Fred, she clattered down the steps. When the dog's four legs tangled, sending him somersaulting, she laughed and gathered him up. She was snuggling the dog against her cheek when she opened the door.

"You!"

The tone of her voice had Fred quaking. Not so the man who stood at the threshold, grinning at her. "Small world," he said in the same slow drawl he'd used when they'd knelt on the sidewalk. "I'm liking it better all the time."

"You followed me."

"No, ma'am. Though it would've been a damn good idea. The name's O'Riley. Sloan O'Riley."

"I don't care what your name is, you can turn around and start walking." She started to slam the door in his face, but he slapped a hand against it and held it wide.

"I don't think that's such a good idea. I've come a long way to get a look at the house."

Her dark blue eyes narrowed. "Oh, have you? Well, let me tell you something, this is a home, a private home. I don't care what you've read in the papers and how badly you want a shot at looking under loose stones for the emeralds. This isn't Treasure Island, and I've had my fill of people like you who think they can just come knocking at the door, or sneaking into the garden at night with a pick and shovel."

She looked just fine, Sloan thought as he waited out the tirade. Every furious inch of her. She was tall for a woman and lean with it—but not too lean. She curved out nicely in all the right places. She looked as though she could ride hard all day and still have the energy to kick up her heels at night. Stubborn chin, he decided, and approved. When she jutted it out, her warm brown hair swayed with the movement. Big blue eyes. Even while they spit fire they reminded him of cornflowers. When it wasn't scowling or swearing, he imagined her full, shapely mouth would be soft.

Soft and tasty.

"You run down yet?" he asked when she stopped to take a breath.

"No, and if you don't leave right now, I'm going to let my dog loose on you."

Taking his cue, Fred leaped out of her arms. With neck fur bristling, he bared his teeth in a growl.

"Looks pretty fierce," Sloan commented, then hunkered down to hold out the back of his hand. Fred sniffed it, then his tail began to wag joyously as Sloan scratched his ears. "Yep, pretty fierce animal you got here."

"That's it." Amanda set her hands on her hips. "I'm getting the gun."

Before she could turn inside to look for the fictitious weapon, Coco came downstairs.

"Who is it, Amanda?"

"Dead meat."

"I beg your pardon?" She stepped up to the door. The moment she spotted Sloan her ingrained vanity took over. In the blink of an eye she whipped her apron off. "Hello." Her smile was warm and feminine as she extended a hand. "I'm Cordelia McPike."

"A pleasure, ma'am." Sloan brought her fingertips to his mouth. "As I was just telling your sister here—"

"Oh, my." Coco let out a trill of delighted laughter. "Amanda's not my sister. She's my niece. The third daughter of my late brother—my much older brother."

"My mistake."

"Aunt Coco, this jerk knocked me down outside of the boutique, then followed me home. He just wants to wheedle his way into the house because of the necklace."

"Now, Mandy, you mustn't be so harsh."

"That's partially true, Mrs. McPike." Sloan gave Amanda a slow nod. "Your niece and I did have a run-in. Guess I didn't get out of her way in time. And I am trying to get into the house."

"I see." Torn between hope and doubt, Coco

sighed. "I'm terribly sorry, but I don't think it would be possible to let you in. You see we have so much to do with the wedding—"

Sloan's eyes whipped back to Amanda. "You getting married?"

"My sister," she said tightly. "Not that it's any of your business. Now if you'll excuse us?"

"I wouldn't want to intrude, so I'll just be on my way. If you'll tell Trent that O'Riley was by, I'd appreciate it."

"O'Riley?" Coco repeated, then fluttered her hands. "Goodness, are you Mr. O'Riley? Please come in. Oh, I do apologize."

"Aunt Coco—"

"This is Mr. O'Riley, Amanda."

"I realize that. Why the devil have you let him in the house?"

"*The* Mr. O'Riley," Coco continued. "The one Trenton called about this morning. Don't you remember—of course you don't remember, because I didn't tell you." She patted her hands to her cheeks. "I'm afraid I'm just so flustered after keeping you standing outside that way."

"Don't you worry about it," he said to Coco. "It's an honest mistake."

"Aunt Coco." Amanda stood with her hand on the doorknob, ready to pitch the intruder out bodily if necessary. "Who is this O'Riley and why did Trent tell you to expect him?"

"Mr. O'Riley's the architect," Coco said, beaming.

Eyes narrowing, Amanda studied him from the tip of his boots to his wavy, disordered hair. "This is an architect?"

"Our architect. Mr. O'Riley will be in charge of the renovations for the retreat, and our living quarters. We'll all be working with Mr. O'Riley—"

"Sloan," he said.

"Sloan." Coco fluttered her lashes. "For quite some time."

"Terrific." Amanda let the door slam.

Sloan hooked his thumbs in his jean pockets and gave her a slow smile. "My thoughts exactly."

Chapter Two

"Where are our manners?" Coco said. "Here we are keeping you standing in the hall. Please, come in and sit down. What can I offer you? Coffee, tea?"

"Beer in a long-necked bottle," Amanda muttered.

Sloan merely smiled at her. "There you go."

"Beer?" Coco ushered him into the parlor, wishing she'd had a moment to freshen the flowers in the vase and plump the pillows. "I have some very nice beer in the kitchen that I use for my spiced shrimp. Amanda, you'll entertain Sloan, won't you?"

"Sure. Why not?" Though she wasn't feeling particularly gracious, Amanda gestured to a chair, then took one across from him in front of the fireplace. "I suppose I should apologize."

Sloan reached down to pet Fred, who had followed them in. "What for?"

"I wouldn't have been so rude if I'd realized why you were here."

"Is that so?" As Fred settled down on the rug between them, Sloan eased back in his chair to study his unwilling hostess.

After a humming ten seconds, she struggled not to fidget. "It was a natural enough mistake."

"If you say so. What exactly are these emeralds you figured I was here to dig up?"

"The Calhoun emeralds." When he only lifted a brow, she shook her head. "My great-grandmother's emerald necklace. It's been in all the papers."

"I haven't had much time to read the papers. I've been in Budapest." He reached into his pocket and pulled out a long, slim cigar. "Mind?"

"Go ahead." Automatically she rose to fetch an ashtray from across the room. Sloan considered it a pleasure to watch that out-of-my-way walk of hers. "I'm surprised Trent didn't mention it."

Sloan struck a match and took his sweet time lighting the cigar. He took an appreciative drag, then blew out a lazy stream of smoke. All the while, he was taking stock of the room, with its sagging sofa, the glistening Baccarat, the elegant old wainscoting and the peeling paint.

"I got a cable from Trent telling me about the house and his plans, and asking me to take it on."

"You agreed to take a job like this without even seeing the property first?"

"Seemed like the thing to do at the time." She sure had pretty eyes, Sloan thought. Suspicious, but pretty. He wondered how they'd look if he ever managed to get a smile out of her. "Besides, Trent wouldn't have asked if he didn't think I'd get a kick out of it."

Her foot began to tap as it did when she had sat in one place too long. "You know Trent well then?"

"We go back a few years. We were at Harvard together."

"Harvard?" Her foot stopped tapping as she gaped at him. "You went to Harvard?"

Another man might have been insulted. Sloan was amused. "Why, shucks, ma'am," he murmured, exaggerating his drawl, then watching her cheeks flush.

"I didn't mean to...it's just that you don't really seem—"

"The Ivy League type?" he suggested before he took another pull on the cigar. "Guess appearances can be deceiving. Take the house here for instance."

"The house?"

"You take your first look at it from the outside and it's hard to figure if it's supposed to be a fortress, a castle or an architect's nightmare. But you take the time to look again, and you see it's not supposed to be anything but what it is. A timeless piece of work, on the arrogant side, strong, maybe stubborn enough to hold its own, but with just enough fancy to add some charm." He grinned at her. "Some people believe that a house reflects the personality of the people who live in it."

He rose when Coco came back in wheeling a tray. "Oh, sit down, please. It's such a treat to have a man in the house. Isn't it, Mandy?"

"I'm all aflutter."

"I hope the beer's all right." She lifted a brimming pilsner glass from the tray.

"I'm sure it's fine."

"Do try some of these canapés. Mandy, I've brought us some wine." Delighted with the chance to socialize, she smiled at Sloan over the rim of her glass. "Has Amanda been telling you about the house?"

"We were just getting to it." Sloan took a long swallow of beer. "Trent wrote that it's been in the family since the early part of the century."

"Oh, yes. With Suzanna's children—Suzanna's my eldest niece—we've had five generations of Calhouns at The Towers. Fergus—" she gestured to the portrait of a dour-faced man over the mantel "—my grandfather, built The Towers in 1904, as a summer home. He and his wife, Bianca, had three children before she threw herself out of the tower window." As always, the idea of dying for love had her sighing. "I don't believe Grandpapa was ever quite right after that. He went insane later in life, but we kept him in a very nice institution."

"Aunt Coco, I'm sure Mr. O'Riley isn't interested in the family history."

"Not interested," Sloan agreed as he tapped out his cigar. "Fascinated. Don't stop now, Mrs. Mc-Pike."

"Oh, call me Coco. Everyone does." She fluffed her hair. "The house passed along to my father, Ethan. He was their second child, but the first son. Grandpapa was very adamant about the Calhoun line. His—Ethan's—elder sister, Colleen, was miffed about the arrangement. She rarely speaks to any of us to this day."

"For which we're all eternally grateful," Amanda put in.

"Well, yes. She can be a bit—overwhelming. That left Uncle Sean, my father's younger brother. He had a spot of trouble with a woman and sailed off to the West Indies before I was born. When my father was killed, the house passed to my brother, Judson. After his marriage he and his wife decided to live here year-round. They adored the place.'' She glanced around the parlor with its cracked walls and faded curtains. ''Judson had wonderful plans for revamping the house, but tragically he and Deliah were killed before he could begin to implement them. Then I came here to care for Amanda and her three sisters. Have another canapé.''

''Thanks. Can I ask why you decided to convert part of your home into a hotel?''

''That was Trent's idea. We're all so grateful to him, aren't we, Amanda?''

Since she accepted the fact that there would be no winding down Aunt Coco, Amanda smiled. ''Yes, we are.''

Coco sipped delicately from her glass. ''To be frank, we were in some financial distress. Do you believe in fate, Sloan?''

''I'm Irish and Cherokee.'' He spread his long fingers. ''That doesn't give me any other choice.''

''Well then, you'll understand. It was fated that Trent's father would see The Towers while he was sailing in Frenchman Bay, and seeing it, develop a deep desire for it. When the St. James's corporation offered to buy the house and turn it into a resort hotel, we were torn. It was our home after all, the only home my girls have ever known, but the upkeep...''

''I understand.''

''Things happen for the best,'' Coco put in. ''And it was really very exciting and romantic. We were on the brink, the very brink, of being forced to sell, when Trent fell in love with C.C. Of course he understood how much the house meant to her, and came up with this marvelous plan of converting the west wing into hotel suites. That way we can keep the house, and overcome the financial difficulty of maintaining it.''

"Everyone gets what they want," Sloan agreed.

"Exactly." Coco leaned forward. "With your heritage, I imagine you also believe in spirits."

"Aunt Coco—"

"Now, Mandy, I know how practical minded you are. It baffles me," she said to Sloan. "All that Celtic blood and not a mystical bone in her body."

Amanda gestured with her glass. "I leave that for you and Lilah."

"Lilah's my other niece," Coco told Sloan. "She's very fey. But we were talking about the supernatural. Do you have an opinion?"

Sloan set his glass aside. "I don't think you could have a house like this without a ghost or two."

"There." Coco clapped her hands together. "I knew as soon as I saw you we'd be kindred spirits. Bianca's still here, you see. Why at our last séance I felt her so strongly." She ignored Amanda's groan. "C.C. did, too, and she's nearly as practical minded as Amanda. Bianca wants us to find the necklace."

"The Calhoun emeralds?" Sloan asked.

"Yes. We've been searching for clues, but the clutter of eight decades is daunting. And the publicity has been a bother."

"That's a mild word for it." Amanda scowled into her glass.

"It might turn up during the renovation," Sloan suggested.

"We're hoping." Coco tapped one carefully manicured finger against her lips. "I think another séance might be in order. I'm sure you're very sensitive."

Amanda choked on her wine. "Aunt Coco, Mr. O'Riley has come here to work, not to play ghosts and goblins."

"I like mixing business and pleasure." He toasted Amanda with his glass. "In fact, I make a habit of it."

A new thought jumped into Coco's mind. "You're not from the island, Sloan."

"No, Oklahoma."

"Really? That's quite a distance." She slid her gaze smugly toward Amanda. "As architect for the renovations, you'll be very important to all of us."

"I'd like to think so," he said, baffled by the arched look Coco sent her niece.

"Tea leaves," Coco murmured, then rose. "I must go check on dinner. You will join us, won't you?"

He'd planned on taking a quick look at the house then going back to the hotel to sleep for ten hours. The annoyed look on Amanda's face changed his mind. An evening with her might be a better cure for jet lag. "I'd be mighty pleased to."

"Wonderful. Mandy, why don't you show Sloan the west wing while I finish things up?"

"Tea leaves?" Sloan asked when Coco glided from the room.

"You're better off in the dark." Resigned, she rose and gestured to the doorway. "Shall we get started?"

"That's a fine idea." He followed her into the hall and up the curving staircase. "Which do you like, Amanda or Mandy?"

She shrugged. "I answer to either."

"Different images. Amanda's cool and composed. Mandy's...softer." She smelled cool, he thought. Like a quiet breeze on a hot, dusty day.

At the top of the stairs she stopped to face him. "What kind of image is Sloan?"

He stayed one step below her so that they were eye to eye. Instinct told him they'd both prefer it that way. "You tell me."

He had the cockiest grin she'd ever seen. Whenever he used it on her she felt a tremor that she was certain was annoyance. "Dodge City?" she said sweetly. "We don't get many cowboys this far east." She turned and was halfway down the hall when he took her arm.

"Are you always in such a hurry?"

"I don't like to waste time."

He kept his hand on her arm as they continued to walk. "I'll keep that in mind."

My God, the place was fabulous, Sloan thought as they started up a pie-shaped set of steps. Coffered ceilings, carved lintels, thick mahogany paneling. He stopped at an arched window to touch the wavy glass. It had to be original, he thought, like the chestnut floor and the fancy plaster work.

True, there were cracks in the walls—some of them big enough that he could slide his finger in to the first knuckle. Here and there the ceiling had given way to fist-sized holes, and portions of the molding were rotted.

It would be a challenge to bring it back to its former glory. And it would be a joy.

"We haven't used this part of the house in years." Amanda opened a carved oak door and brushed away a spider web. "It hasn't been practical to heat it during the winter."

Sloan stepped inside. The sloping floor creaked ominously as he walked across it. Somewhere along the line heavy furniture had been dragged in or out, scarring the floor with deep, jagged grooves. Two of the panes on the narrow terrace doors had been broken and replaced with plywood. Mice had had a field day with the baseboard. Above his head was a faded mural of chubby cherubs.

"This was the best guest room," Amanda explained. "Fergus kept it for people he wanted to impress. Supposedly some of the Rockefellers stayed here. It has its own bath and dressing room." She pushed open a broken door.

Ignoring her, Sloan walked to the black marble fireplace. The wall above it was papered in silk and stained from old smoke. The chip off the corner of the mantel broke his heart.

"You ought to be shot."

"I beg your pardon?"

"You ought to be shot for letting the place go like this." The look he aimed at her wasn't lazy and amused, but hot and quick as a bullet. "A mantelpiece like this is irreplaceable."

Flustered, she stared guiltily at the chipped Italian marble. "Well, I certainly didn't break it."

"And look at these walls. Plasterwork of this caliber is an art, the same way a Rembrandt is art. You'd take care of a Rembrandt, wouldn't you?"

"Of course, but—"

"At least you had the sense not to paint the molding." Moving past her, he peered into the adjoining bath. And began to swear. "These are handmade tiles, for God's sake. Look at these chips. They haven't been grouted since World War I."

"I don't see what that's—"

"No, you don't see." He turned back to her. "You

haven't got a clue to what you've got here. This place is a monument to early-twentieth-century craftsmanship, and you're letting it fall apart around your ears. Those are authentic gaslight fixtures.''

"I know very well what they are,'' Amanda snapped back. "This may be a monument to you, but to me it's home. We've done everything we could to keep the roof on. If the plaster's cracked it's because we've had to concentrate on keeping the furnace running. And if we didn't worry about regrouting tiles in a room no one uses, it's because we had to repair the plumbing in another one. You've been hired to renovate, not to philosophize.''

"You get both for the same price.'' When he reached out toward her, she rammed back into the wall.

"What are you doing?''

"Take it easy, honey. You've got cobwebs in your hair.''

"I can do it,'' she said, then stiffened when he combed his fingers through her hair. "And don't call me 'honey.'''

"You sure fire up quick. I had a mustang filly once that did the same thing.''

She knocked his hand aside. "I'm not a horse.''

"No, ma'am.'' In an abrupt change of mood, he smiled again. "You sure aren't. Why don't you show me what else you've got?''

Wary, she eased to the side until she felt safe again. "I don't see the point. You haven't got a notebook.''

"Some things stick in your mind.'' His gaze lowered to her mouth, lingered, then returned to her eyes. "I like to get the lay of the land first before I start worrying about…details.''

"Why don't I draw you a map?"

He grinned then. "You always so prickly?"

"No." She inclined her head. It was true, she wasn't. She could hardly have made a success in her career as assistant manager in one of the resort's better hotels if she was. "Obviously you don't bring out the best in me."

"I'll settle for what I've got." He curled a hand around her arm. "Let's keep going."

She took him through the wing, doing her best to keep her distance. But he had a tendency to close in, blocking her in a doorway, maneuvering her into a corner, shifting unexpectedly to put them face-to-face. He had a slow and economical way of moving, wasting no gestures that would tip her off as to which way he was going to turn.

They were in the west tower the third time Amanda bumped into him. Every nerve was on edge when she stepped back. "I wish you wouldn't do that."

"Do what?"

"Be there." Annoyed, she shoved aside a cardboard box. "In my way."

"It seems to me you're in too much of a hurry to get someplace else to watch where you are."

"More homespun philosophy," she muttered, and paced to the curved window that overlooked the gardens. He bothered her, she was forced to admit, on some deep, elemental level. Maybe it was his size—those broad shoulders and wide-palmed hands. His sheer height. She was accustomed to being on a more even level with most men.

Maybe it was that drawl of his, slow and lazy and every bit as cocky as his grin. Or the way his eyes lingered on her face, persistent, with a half-amused gleam. Whatever it was, Amanda thought with a little shake, she would have to learn how to handle it.

"This is the last stop," she told him. "Trent's idea is to convert this tower into a dining room, more intimate than the one he wants on the lower level. It should fit five tables for two comfortably, with views of the garden or the bay."

She turned as she spoke, and an early evening sunbeam shot through the window to halo her hair and pool lustrously around her. Her hands gestured with her words, a graceful flow of movement underlined by nerves. She lifted one hand to her hair to push it back. The light streamed through the honey-brown tresses, tipping them with gold. In the single shaft of light, dust motes danced around her like minute flakes of silver.

His mind wiped clean as new glass, Sloan stood and stared.

"Is something wrong?"

"No." He took a step closer. "You sure are easy on the eyes, Amanda."

She took a step back. There wasn't amusement in his eyes now, or the quick flaring anger she had seen briefly earlier. What was there was a great deal more dangerous. "If you, ah, have any questions about the tower, or the rest of the wing—"

"That was a compliment. Maybe not as smooth as you're used to, but a compliment just the same."

"Thank you." Her eyes darted around the room for a means of dignified escape as she retreated another step. "I think we could—" She ended on a gasp as his arm snaked around her waist to draw her tight against him. "What the hell do you think you're doing?"

"Keeping you from taking the same jump as your great-grandma." He nodded toward the window at her back. "If you'd kept dancing backward, you might have gone right through the glass. Those panes don't look very strong."

"I wasn't dancing anywhere." But her heart was pounding as if she had just finished a fast rumba. "Let go."

"You're a real nice armful." He leaned closer to take a sniff of her hair. "Even with all those thorns." Enjoying himself, he kept his arm where it was. "You could've said thanks, Calhoun. I probably just saved your life."

Her pulse might have been jumping, but she refused to let herself be intimidated by some slow-talking cowboy with an attitude. "If you don't let me go, now, someone's going to have to save yours."

He laughed, delighted with her, and was tempted to scoop her up there and then. The next thing he knew, he was landing on his butt five feet away. With a smug smile, Amanda inclined her head.

"That concludes our tour for this evening. Now, if you'll excuse me." When she started by him, his hand snaked out and snagged her ankle. Amanda barely had time to shriek before she landed on the floor beside him. "Why, you—oaf," she decided, and tossed the hair out of her eyes.

"What's good for the goose is good for the gander." He tipped a fingertip under her chin. "More homespun philosophy. You've got quick moves, Calhoun, but you've got to remember to keep your eye on the target."

"If I were a man—"

"This wouldn't be half as much fun." Chuckling,

he gave her a quick, hard kiss, then tilted his head back to stare at her while she gaped. "Well, now," he said softly while lightning bolts went off inside his chest. "I think we'd better try that again."

She would have shoved him away. She knew she would have. Despite the heat trembling along her spine. Regardless of the thick syrupy longing that seemed to have replaced the blood churning in her veins. She would have shoved him away, had even lifted a hand to do so—certainly not to bring him closer—when footsteps clattered on the iron steps that led to the tower.

Sloan glanced up to see a tall, curvy woman in the doorway. She wore jeans that were ripped through at the knee with a plain white T-shirt tucked in the waist. Her hair was short and straight, offset by a fringe of sassy bangs. Below them her eyes registered surprise, then amusement.

"Hi." She looked at Amanda, grinning as she noted her sister's flushed face and tousled hair. The one place you didn't expect to see business-first Amanda Calhoun was on the floor with a strange and very attractive man. "What's going on?"

"We were going for the best two out of three," Sloan told her. He rose, then hauled Amanda up by the arm. With what sounded like a snarl, Amanda jerked out of his hold, then busied herself brushing the dust from her slacks.

"This is my sister, C.C."

"And you must be Sloan." C.C. walked in, offering her hand. "Trent's told me about you." Green eyes dancing, she flicked a glance at her sister, then back again. "I guess he didn't exaggerate."

Sloan held the offered hand a moment. C. C. Calhoun was exactly the opposite of the kind of woman he'd expected his old friend to be involved with. And because Trent was his friend, Sloan couldn't have been more delighted. "I can see why Trent's got himself roped and corralled."

"That's one of Sloan's whimsical compliments," Amanda pointed out.

With a laugh, C.C. threw an arm around Amanda's shoulders. "I think I figured that out. I'm glad to meet you, Sloan. Really glad. When I went up to Boston with Trent a couple of weeks ago, everyone I met was so…"

"Stuffy?" He grinned.

"Well." A little embarrassed, she moved her shoulders. "I guess it's hard for some of them to accept that Trent's going to marry a mechanic who knows more about engines than opera."

"Looks to me like Trent's getting one hell of a deal."

"We'll see." She knew with the least encouragement she would get mushy and embarrass herself. "Aunt Coco said you were staying for dinner. I was hoping you'd take one of the guest rooms here while you're on the island."

Sloan couldn't see it, but he'd have bet the pot that Amanda bit her tongue. The idea of ruffling her feathers made it tempting to change his plans. "Thanks, but I'm all taken care of. Besides…" Now he grinned at Amanda. "I'm going to be underfoot enough as it is."

"However you're most comfortable," C.C. told him. "Just so that you know you're welcome here at The Towers."

"I'll go down and see if Aunt Coco needs any

help." Amanda sent Sloan a cool nod. "C.C. will show you down when you're ready."

He winked at her. "Thanks for the tour, honey."

He could almost hear her grinding her teeth as she walked away.

"That's some sister you've got there."

"Yes, she is." C.C.'s smile was warm, and warning. "Trent tells me you're quite the ladies' man."

"He's still mad because I stole a woman out from under his nose when we were both still young and foolish." Sloan took C.C.'s hand as they walked through the doorway. "You sure you're stuck on him?"

She had to laugh. "Now I see why he told me to lock up my sisters."

"If they're anything like that one, I expect they can take care of themselves."

"Oh, they can. The Calhoun women are as tough as they come." She paused at the top of the iron circular stairs. "I'd better warn you. Aunt Coco claims she saw you in the tea leaves this morning."

"In the...aah."

She gave a half apologetic, half amused shrug. "It's kind of a hobby of hers. Anyway, she might start to try to manipulate, especially if she decides the fates have linked you with one of my sisters. She means well, but..."

"O'Rileys are pretty good at handling themselves, too."

It only took one long look at him to have her believing it. C.C. tapped his shoulder. "Okay then. You're on your own."

Sloan started down behind her. "C.C., are there

any men Amanda's involved with who I'm going to
have to hoist out of the way?"

C.C. stopped, studying him through the opposite
side of the open stairs. "No," she said after a moment. "Amanda's done all the hoisting herself."

"That's fine." He was smiling to himself as he
descended the winding stairs. When they reached the
second floor, he heard an echo of high-pitched
screams and the frantic yapping of the dog.

"My sister Suzanna's kids," C.C. explained before
he could ask. "Alex and Jenny are your typical quiet,
retiring children."

"I can hear that."

A sturdy pale-haired missile zoomed up the steps.
In reflex, Sloan caught it and found himself staring
into a curious little face with a pouty mouth and big
blue eyes.

"You're big," Jenny said.

"Nah. You're just short."

At five, she was just beginning to learn the wiles
of womanhood and sent him a beaming smile. "Can
I have a piggyback ride?"

"Got a quarter?" Giggling, she shook her head.
"Okay," he said, "the first one's free then." When
she squirmed around to his back, he started down
again. At the base of the steps, Amanda had a dark-
haired little boy in a headlock.

"Suzanna?" C.C. asked.

"In the kitchen. I was drafted to watch these two."
She narrowed her eyes at Jenny. "The little pig-nosed
one got away from me."

"Oink, oink." From the tower of Sloan's back,
Jenny giggled and snorted.

"Who's he?" Alex wanted to know.

"Sloan O'Riley." Sloan offered a hand, man to man, which Alex eyed dubiously before accepting it.

"You talk funny. Are you from Texas?"

"Oklahoma."

After a moment's consideration, Alex nodded. "That's almost as good. Did you ever shoot anybody dead?"

"Not lately."

"That's enough, you ghoul." C.C. took charge. "Come on, let's go get cleaned up for dinner." She swung Jenny from Sloan's back.

"Cute kids," Sloan commented when C.C. hauled them up the stairs.

"We like them." Amanda offered him a genuine smile. Seeing him with Jenny riding his back had softened her. "They'll be in school most of the day, so they shouldn't bother you while you're working."

"I don't figure they'd be a bother one way or the other. I've got a nephew of my own back home. He's a pistol."

"Those two can be shotguns, I'm afraid." But the affection came through. "It's nice for them to be around a man now and again."

"Your sister's husband?"

The smile faded. "They're divorced. You might know him. Baxter Dumont?"

A shutter seemed to come down over Sloan's eyes. "I've heard of him."

"Well, that's history. Dinner's nearly ready. Why don't I show you where to wash up?"

"Thanks." Distracted, Sloan followed her. He was thinking that there were some points of history that had an unfortunate habit of overlapping.

Chapter Three

Anticipating the shock, Amanda dove into the cold water of the pool. She surfaced with a delicious shiver then began the first of her usual fifty laps.

There was nothing she liked better than beginning a day with a vigorous workout. It ate away the old tension to make room for the new that would develop before the workday was done.

Not that she didn't enjoy her job as assistant manager of the BayWatch Hotel. Particularly since it gave her the privilege of using the hotel pool before the guests began to crowd in. It was the end of May and the season had begun to swing. Of course it was nothing compared to what it would be by midsummer, but most of the rooms in the hotel were occupied, which meant she had her hands full. This hour, which she gave herself whenever weather permitted, was prized.

As she approached one end of the pool, she curled, tucked and pushed off.

In another year, she thought as she sent beads of

water flying, she would be manager of The Towers Retreat. A St. James hotel. The goal that she had worked and struggled for since she'd taken her first part-time job as a desk clerk at sixteen was about to be realized.

It nagged at her from time to time that she would have the job only because Trent was marrying her sister. Whenever it did, she became only more determined to prove that she deserved it, that she had earned it.

She would be managing an exclusive hotel for one of the top chains in the country. And not just any hotel, she thought, cutting cleanly through the water, but The Towers. A part of her own heritage, her own history, her own family.

The ten luxurious suites Trent intended to create out of the crumbling west wing would be her responsibility. If he was right, the St. James name and the legend of The Towers would keep those suites filled year-round.

She would do a good job. An exceptional one. Every guest who traveled home from The Towers would remember the excellent service, the soothing ambience, the silky smooth organization.

It was going to happen. There would be no more slaving for a demanding and unappreciative supervisor, no more frustration at doing the work and handing over the credit. At last the credit, and the failure, would be hers alone.

It was only a matter of waiting until the remodeling was done.

And that brought her thoughts ramming headfirst into Sloan O'Riley.

She certainly hoped Trent knew what he was doing.

What baffled her most was how such a smooth and polished man such as Trenton St. James III had ever become friends with a throwback like O'Riley. The man had actually knocked her down. Of course, she'd knocked him down first, but that was entirely beside the point.

Amanda kicked off again. Her leanly muscled arms sliced through the water, her long legs scissored. She didn't regret, not for a minute, that she'd had the wit and the strength to get the best of him first. He'd been pushy and overfamiliar and too full of himself from the moment she'd met him. And he'd kissed her.

She turned her head up for air then slid her face into the water again.

She hadn't given him the least bit of encouragement. In fact, just the opposite. But he'd sat there, grinning like a fool, and had kissed her. The memory of it had her gasping for air again.

Not that she'd liked it, Amanda assured herself. If C.C. hadn't walked in, she would have given the arrogant Mr. O'Riley a piece of her mind. Except that she hadn't had one left.

Because she'd been angry, that's all. She wasn't a bit attracted to the rough, outdoorsy type with callused hands and dusty boots. She wasn't fool enough to fall for a pair of dark green eyes that crinkled at the corners when they smiled. Her image of the ideal man included a certain sophistication, smooth manners, culture, a quiet aura of success. If and when she became interested in a relationship, those would be her requirements. Slow-talking cowboys need not apply.

Maybe there had been something sweet about him

when he'd talked to the children, but it wasn't enough to overcome the rest of the deficits in his personality.

She remembered the way he'd flirted and charmed Aunt Coco at dinner. He'd kept C.C. amused with stories of Trent's college days and had been tolerant and easy with Alex's and Jenny's questions about horses and Indians and six-shooters.

But he'd watched Suzanna a little too closely, a little too carefully for Amanda's liking. A woman chaser, Amanda decided. If Lilah had been at dinner, he probably would have flirted with her, as well. But Lilah could take care of herself where men were concerned.

Suzanna was different. She was beautiful, sensitive and vulnerable. Her ex-husband had hurt her deeply, and no one, not even the cocky Sloan O'Riley was going to get the chance to hurt Suzanna again. Amanda would make sure of it.

When she reached the edge of the pool this time, she gripped the coping and dipped her head back into the water to slick her hair out of her eyes. Surfacing, she found herself staring up into a watery image that was entirely too familiar.

"Morning." Sloan grinned down at her. The sun was at his back, bringing out the reddish tones in his untidy hair. "You got a nice form there, Calhoun."

She blinked her eyes clear. "What the hell are you doing here?"

"Here?" He glanced over his shoulder at the whitewashed hotel. "You could say I'm hanging my hat here." Watching her, he jerked a thumb up and back. "Room 320."

"You're a guest at the BayWatch?" Amanda propped her elbows on the coping. "It figures."

Agreeable, Sloan crouched down. She had the clear creamy Calhoun skin, he noted, particularly striking, and vulnerable, now washed clean of any cosmetics. "Nice way to start the day."

Her full damp mouth turned down in a frown. "It was."

"Since we're asking, what are you doing here?"

"I work here."

Things were becoming more and more interesting, he thought. "No fooling?"

"No fooling," she said dryly. "I'm assistant manager."

"Well, now." He dipped an experimental finger into the water. "Checking out the water temperature for the guests? That's dedication."

"The pool doesn't open until ten."

"Don't worry." He hooked his thumbs in the front pockets of his jeans. "I wasn't planning on taking a dip just yet." What he had been planning was to take a walk, a long solitary one. But that was before he'd spotted her doing laps. "So, I guess if I have any questions about the place, you're the one I talk to."

"That's right." Amanda moved over to the steps to climb out. The one-piece sapphire-colored suit clung like a second skin as water slid from her. "Is your room satisfactory?"

"Hmm?" She had legs designed to make a man sweat, he thought, slim and shapely and a yard long.

"Your room," she repeated as she reached for her towel. "It suits you?"

"It suits me fine. Just fine." He skimmed his gaze up those damp calves and thighs, over the slim hips on a lazy journey to her face. "The view's worth the price of admission."

Amanda hooked the towel around her neck. "The view of the bay's free—like the continental breakfast now being served in The Galley. You'll want to take advantage of it."

"I've found that a couple of croissants and a cup of coffee don't do much to stanch the appetite." Because he wasn't ready for her to walk away, he reached out to take both ends of the towel in a light grip. "Why don't you join me for a real breakfast?"

"Sorry." Her heart was beginning to thud uncomfortably. "Employees are discouraged from socializing with the guests."

"I reckon we could make an exception in this case, seeing as we're...old friends."

"We're not even new friends."

There was that smile again, slow, insistent and all too knowing. And then he said, "That's something we can fix over breakfast."

"Sorry. Not interested." She started to turn away, but he tightened his grip on the towel and held her in place.

"Where I come from people are a mite more friendly."

Since he wasn't giving her a choice, she held her ground. "Where I come from people are a great deal more polite. If you have any problems with the service during your stay at the BayWatch, I'll be more than happy to accommodate you. If you have any questions about The Towers, I'll make myself available to answer them. Other than that, we have nothing to discuss."

He watched her patiently, admiring the way she could coat her husky voice with frost even while her eyes glinted. This was a woman with plenty of control. And, though he was certain she'd snarl at the term, plenty of spunk.

"What time do you go on the clock here?"

She let out a hiss of breath. Obviously the man's head was as thick as his accent. "Nine o'clock, so if you'll excuse me, I'd like to go get dressed."

Sloan squinted up at the sun. "Looks to me like you've got about an hour before you punch in. The way you move, it won't take you half that to get yourself together."

Amanda shut her eyes briefly on a prayer for patience. "Sloan, are you trying to irritate me?"

"Don't figure I have to. It seems to come natural." Casually he wound the ends of the towel around his fists and had her jerking closer. He grinned as her chin shot up. "See?"

She resented bitterly the way her pulse was dancing, and the tight, clutching sensation deep in her stomach. "What's the matter with you, O'Riley?" she demanded. "I've made it absolutely plain that I'm not interested."

"I'll tell you how it is, Calhoun." He flipped his wrists again, shortening the towel farther. The humor she was used to seeing in his eyes changed into something else in the space of a heartbeat. And that something else was dark and dangerous. And exciting. "You're one long, cool drink of water," he murmured. "Every time I'm around you I get this powerful thirst." With a last jerk, he had her tumbling against him, her hands trapped tight between their bodies. "That little sip I had yesterday wasn't nearly enough." Bending down, he nipped at her bottom lip.

He felt her tremor, but as he kept his eyes on hers, he could see it wasn't from fear. A trace of panic maybe, but not fear. Still he waited to see if she would give him a flat-out no. That was something he would have to respect, however much the need churned through him.

But she said nothing, only stared at him with those wide wary eyes. Softly he brushed his lips over hers and watched the thick lashes flutter down. "I want more," he murmured. And took.

Her hands curled into fists between them, but she didn't use them to push him away. The struggle was all inside her, a wild and violent combat that jolted her system even as he bombarded her senses. Caught in the crossfire, her mind simply shut down.

His mouth wasn't lazy now. Nor were his hands slow. Hard and hot, his lips took from hers while his fingers pressed against her damp back. The scrape of his teeth had her gasping, then moaning when his tongue slid seductively over hers.

Her fingers uncurled to clutch at his shirt, then to claw their way up to his shoulder, into his hair. The desperation was new, terrifying, wonderful. It drove her to strain against him while her mouth burned with an urgency that matched his.

The change rocked him. He was used to having his senses clouded by a woman, to having his body throb and his blood burn. But not like this. In the instant she went from dazed surrender to fevered urgency, he knew a need so sharp, so jagged that it seemed to slice through his soul.

Then all he knew was her. All he could feel was the cool slick silk of her skin. All he could taste was the honeyed heat of her mouth. All he could want was more.

She was certain her heart would pound its way out

of her breast. It seemed the heat from his body turned the water on her skin to steam, and the vapors floated through her brain. Nor did they clear when he eased her gently away.

"Amanda." He drew in a deep gulp of air but wasn't sure he'd ever get his breath back again. One look at her as she stood heavy eyed, her swollen lips parted, had the edgy desire cutting through him again. "Come up to my room."

"Your room?" She touched unsteady fingers to her lips, then her temple. "Your room?"

Lord, that throaty voice and those dazed eyes were going to have him on his knees. One thing he'd yet to do was beg for a woman. With her, he was afraid begging was inevitable.

"Come with me." Possessively he ran his hands over her shoulders. Somewhere along the line the towel had slid to the concrete. "We need to finish this in private."

"Finish this?"

On a groan, he brought his lips back to hers again in a last, long, greedy kiss. "Woman, I think you're going to be late for work."

He had her arm and had pulled her toward the gate before she shook her head clear. His room? she thought fussily. Finish this? Oh, Lord, what had she done? What was she about to do? "No." She jerked away and took a deep, cleansing breath that did nothing to stop the tremors. "I'm not going anywhere."

He tried to steady himself and failed. "It's a little late to play games." His hand snaked out to cup the back of her neck. "I want you. And there's no way in hell you're going to convince me you don't want me right back. Not after that."

"I don't play games," she said evenly, and wondered if he could hear her over the riot of her heartbeat. She was cold, so terribly cold. "I don't intend to start now." She was the sensible one, she reminded herself. She wasn't the kind of woman who raced into a hotel room to make love with a man she barely knew. "I want you to leave me alone."

"Not a chance." He struggled to keep his fingers light as temper and need warred inside him. "I always finish what I start."

"You can consider this finished. It had no business starting."

"Why?"

She turned away to snatch up her wrap. The thin terry cloth wasn't nearly enough to warm her again. "I know your type, O'Riley."

He reached deep for calm and rocked back on his heels. "Do you?"

Clumsy with temper, she fought to push her arms through the sleeves. "You swagger from town to town and fill a few free hours with an available woman having a quick roll between the sheets." She pulled the tie on the wrap tight. "Well, I'm not available."

"You figure you got me pegged, huh?" He didn't touch her, but the look in his eyes was enough to have her bracing. He didn't bother to explain that it was different with her. He hadn't yet explained it to himself. "You can take this as a warning, Calhoun. This isn't finished between us. I'm going to have you."

"Have me? *Have* me." Propelled by pride and fury, she took one long stride toward him. "Why you conceited self-absorbed sonofabitch—"

"You can save the flattery for later," he interrupted. "There will be a later, Amanda, when it's just you and me. And I promise you, it won't be quick." Because the idea appealed to him, he smiled. "No sir, when I make love with you, I'm going to take my time." He ran a finger down the collar of her wrap. "And I'm going to drive you crazy."

She slapped his hand away. "You already are."

"Thanks." He gave her a friendly nod. "I think I'll go see about that breakfast. You have a good day."

She would, she thought as he walked off whistling. She'd have a fine day if he was out of it.

It was bad enough that she had to work late, Amanda thought, without having to listen to one of Mr. Stenerson's droning lectures on efficiency. As manager of the BayWatch, Stenerson ruled his staff with fussy hands and whines. His preferred method of supervision was to delegate. In that way he could dole out blame when things went wrong, and gather in credit when things went right.

Amanda stood in his airy pastel office, staring at the top of his balding head as he ran through his weekly list of complaints.

"Housekeeping has been running behind by twenty minutes. In my spot check of the third floor, I discovered this cellophane wrapper under the bed of 302." He waved the tiny clear paper like a flag. "I expect you to have a better handle on things, Miss Calhoun."

"Yes, sir." *You officious little wienie.* "I'll speak to the housekeeping staff personally."

"See that you do." He lifted his ever-present clipboard. "Room service speed is off by eight percent.

At this rate of deterioriation, it will lower to twelve percent by the height of the season.''

Unlike Stenerson, Amanda had done time in the kitchen during the breakfast and dinner rush. ''Perhaps if we hired another waiter or two,'' she began.

''The solution is not in adding more staff, but in culling more efficiency from those we have.'' He tapped a finger on the clipboard. ''I expect to see room service up to maximum by the end of next week.''

''Yes, sir.'' *You supercilious windbag.*

''I'll expect you to roll up your sleeves and pitch in whenever necessary, Miss Calhoun.'' He folded his soft white hands and leaned back. Before he'd opened his mouth again, Amanda knew what was coming. She could have recited the speech by rote.

''Twenty-five years ago, I was delivering trays to guests in this very hotel. It was through sheer determination and a positive outlook that I worked my way up to the position I hold today. If you expect to succeed, perhaps even take over in this office after my retirement, you must eat, sleep and drink the Bay-Watch. The efficiency of the staff directly reflects your efficiency, Miss Calhoun.''

''Yes, sir.'' She wanted to tell him that in another year she would have her own staff, her own office and he could kiss his whipping boy goodbye. But she didn't tell him. Until that time, she needed the job and the weekly paycheck. ''I'll have a meeting with the kitchen staff right away.''

''Good, good. Now, I'll want you on call this evening, as I'll be incommunicado.''

As always, she thought but murmured her agreement.

"Oh, and check the August reservations. I want a report on the ratio of Escape Weekends to Seven-Day Indulgences. Oh, and speak with the pool boy about missing towels. We're five short already this month."

"Yes, sir." Anything else? she wondered. Shine your shoes, wash your car?

"That'll be all."

Amanda opened the door and struggled to keep her unflappable professional mask in place. All she really wanted to do was knock her head against the wall for a few indulgent minutes. Before she could retreat to some private, quiet place to do so, she was called to the front desk.

Sloan took a seat in the lobby just to watch her. He was surprised to see that she was still working. He'd put in a full day at The Towers, and the scarred briefcase beside the chair was bulging with notes, measurements and sketches. He was ready for a tall beer and a rare steak.

But here she was, soothing guests, instructing desk clerks, signing papers. And looking just as cool and fresh as spring water. He watched her pull off an earring, jiggling it in her palm as she took a phone call.

It was one of life's small pleasures to watch her, he decided. All that drive and energy, the effortless control. Almost effortless, he thought with a grin. There was a line between her brows—frustration, he thought. Annoyance. Or just plain stubbornness. He had a powerful urge to go up to her and smooth it away. Instead, he gestured to a bellman.

"Yes, sir."

"Is there a florist around here?"

"Yes, sir, just down the street."

Still watching Amanda, Sloan dug out his wallet

and pulled out a twenty. "Would you run down there and get me a red rose? A long-stemmed one that's still closed. And keep the change."

"Yes, *sir.* Thank you, sir."

While he waited, Sloan ordered a beer from the lobby bar and lighted a cigar. Stretching out his booted feet, he settled back to enjoy.

Amanda clipped on her earring then pressed a hand to her stomach. At least when she went down to give the kitchen staff a pep talk she could grab something to eat. A glance at her watch told her that she wouldn't have time to take her evening shift going through the paperwork, looking for a clue to the necklace. If there was any bright side to the enforced overtime, it was that Sloan wouldn't be at The Towers when she returned.

"Excuse me."

Amanda glanced up to see a trim, attractive man in a bone-colored suit. His dark hair was brushed back from a high forehead. Pale blue eyes smiled pleasantly as they looked into hers. The faint British accent added charm to his voice.

"Yes, sir. May I help you?"

"I'd like to speak with the manager."

Amanda felt her heart sink a little. "I'm sorry, Mr. Stenerson is unavailable. If there's a problem, I'll be glad to handle it for you."

"No problem, Miss—" his eyes flicked down to her name tag "—Calhoun. I'll be checking in for a few weeks. I believe I have the Island Suite."

"Of course. Mr. Livingston. We're expecting you." Quick and competent, she tapped the information into the computer herself. "Have you stayed with us before?"

"No." He smiled again. "Regrettably."

"I'm sure you'll find the suite very comfortable." She passed him a registration form as she spoke. "If there's anything we can do to make your stay more pleasant, don't hesitate to ask."

"I'm already certain it will be pleasant." He gave her another lingering look as he filled out the form. "Unfortunately, it must also be productive. I wanted to inquire about the possibility of renting a fax machine during my stay."

"We offer fax service for our guests' convenience," she said.

"I'll require my own." The diamond on his pinky winked as he slid the form across the counter. "I'm afraid I wasn't able to clear up all my business, as I had hoped. It simply wouldn't be practical for me to run down here every time I need to send or receive a document. Naturally, I'll be willing to pay whatever necessary for the convenience. If renting isn't feasible, perhaps I can purchase one."

"I'll see what I can arrange."

"I'd appreciate that." He offered her his credit card for an imprint. "Also, I'll be using the parlor in the suite as an office. I'd prefer if housekeeping left my papers and disarray undisturbed."

"Of course."

"Might I ask if you're familiar with the island?" Smiling, she handed him his card and his keys. "I'm a native."

"Wonderful." His eyes on hers, he held her hand lightly. "Then I'll know to come to you if I have any questions. You've been very helpful, Miss Calhoun." He glanced at her name tag again. "Amanda. Thank you."

"You're quite welcome." Her pulse gave a quick jitter as she slid her hand from his to signal a bellman. "Enjoy your stay, Mr. Livingston."

"I already am."

As he walked away, the young desk clerk beside Amanda gave a low feminine sigh. "Who was that?"

"William Livingston." Amanda caught herself staring after him and pulled herself back to file the imprint.

"Gorgeous. If he had looked at me the way he looked at you, I'd have melted on the spot."

"Melting's not part of the job description, Karen."

"No." Dreamy eyed, Karen put her hand on a ringing phone. "But it sure is part of being a woman. Front desk, Karen speaking. May I help you?"

William Livingston, Amanda thought, tapping his registration form against her palm. New York, New York. If he could afford a couple of weeks in the Island Suite, that meant he had money as well as charm, good looks and impeccable taste in clothes. If she'd been looking for a man, he would have fit the bill nicely.

Opening up the phone book, Amanda reminded herself she was looking for a fax machine, not a man.

"Hey, Calhoun."

With her finger on Office Supplies in the business section, she glanced up. Sloan, his chambray shirt rolled up to the elbows, his hair curling untidily over its collar, leaned on the counter.

"I'm busy," she said dismissively.

"Working late?"

"Good guess."

"You sure look pretty in that little suit." He reached over the counter to rub a thumb and finger down the crisp red lapel of her jacket. "Kinda prim and proper."

Unlike the little bounce her pulse had given when William Livingstone had taken her hand, it went haywire at Sloan's touch. Annoyed, she brushed it away. "Do you have a problem with your room?"

"Nope. It's pretty as a picture."

"With the service?"

"Slick as a wet rock."

"Then if you'll excuse me, I've got work to do."

"Oh, I figured that. I've been watching you tow the mark here for the last half hour."

The line appeared between her brows. "You've been watching me?"

His gaze lingered on her mouth as he remembered just how it tasted. "It made the beer go down easy."

"It must be nice to have so much free time. Now—"

"It's not how much, it's what you do with it. Since you were…tied up for breakfast, why don't we have dinner?"

Well aware that her co-workers had their ears pricked, Amanda leaned closer and kept her voice low. "Can't you get it through your head that I'm not interested?"

"No." He grinned, then sent a wink toward Karen, who was hovering as close as discretion allowed. "You said you didn't like to waste time. So I figured we could have a little supper and pick up where we left off this morning."

In his arms, she thought, lost for a moment. With her mind fuddled and her blood racing. She was staring at his mouth when it curved and snapped her back to reality. "I'm busy, and I have no desire—"

"You've got plenty of that, Amanda."

She set her teeth, wishing with all her heart she could call him a liar and mean it. "I don't want to have dinner with you. Clear?"

"As glass." He flicked a finger down her nose. "I'll be upstairs if you get hungry. Three-twenty, remember?" He lifted the rose from behind the counter and put it into her hand. "Don't work too hard."

"Two winners in one night," Karen murmured, and watched Sloan walk away. "Lord, he sure knows how to wear jeans, doesn't he?"

Indeed he did, Amanda thought, then cursed herself. "He's crude, annoying and intolerable." But she brushed the rosebud against her cheek.

"Okay, I'll take bachelor number two. You can concentrate on Mister Beautiful from New York."

Damn it, why was she so breathless? "I'm going to concentrate on my job," Amanda corrected. "And so are you. Stenerson's on the warpath, and the last thing I need is some cowboy stud interrupting my routine."

"I wish he'd offer to interrupt mine," Karen murmured, then bent over her terminal.

She wasn't going to think about him, Amanda promised herself. She set the rose aside, then picked it up again. It wasn't the flower's fault, after all. It deserved to be put in water and appreciated for what it was. Softening a bit, she sniffed at it and smiled. And it had been sweet of him to give it to her. No matter how annoying he might be, she should have thanked him.

Absently she lifted the phone as it rang. "Front desk, Amanda speaking. May I help you?"

"I just wanted to hear you say that." Sloan chuckled into the phone. "Good night, Calhoun."

Biting back an oath, Amanda banged down the receiver. For the life of her she couldn't understand why she was laughing when she took the rose back into her office to find a vase.

I ran to him. It was as if another woman burst out into the twilight to race over the lawn, down the slope, over the rocks. In that moment there was no right or wrong, no duty but to my own heart. Indeed, it was my heart that guided my legs, my eyes, my voice.

He had turned back to the sea. The first time I had seen him he had been facing the sea, fighting his own personal war with paint and canvas. Now he only stared out at the water.

When I called to him, he spun around. In his face I could see the mirror of my own joy. There was laughter, mine and his, as he rushed toward me.

His arms went around me, so tightly. My dreams had known what it would be like to finally be held by them. His mouth fitted truly to mine, so sweet, so urgent.

Time does not stop. As I sit here and write this, I know that. But then, oh then, it did. There was only the wind and the sound of the sea and the sheer and simple glory of being in his arms. It was as if I had waited my entire life, sleeping, eating, breathing, all for the purpose of that single precious window of time. If I have another hundred years left to me, I will never forget an instant of it.

He drew away, his hands sliding down my arms to

grip mine, then to bring them to his lips. His eyes
were so dark, like gray smoke.

"I'd packed," he said. "I'd made arrangements to
sail to England. Staying here without you was hell.
Thinking you would come back, and that I'd never be
able to touch you nearly drove me mad. Every day,
every night, Bianca, I've ached for you."

My hands moved over his face, tracing it as I'd
often longed to. "I thought I'd never see you again.
I tried to pray that I wouldn't." As shame crept
through my joy, I tried to turn away. "Oh, what you
must think of me. I'm another man's wife, the mother
of his children."

"Not here." His voice was rough, even as his
hands were gentle. "Here you belong to me. Here,
where I first saw you a year ago. Don't think of him."

He kissed me again, and I could not think, could
not care.

"I've waited for you, Bianca, through the chill of
winter, the warmth of spring. When I tried to paint,
it was your image that haunted me. I could see you
standing here, with the wind in your hair, the sunlight
turning it copper, then gold, then flame. I tried to
forget you." His hands were on my shoulders, holding me back while his eyes seemed to devour my face.
"I tried to tell myself it was wrong, that for your sake
if not my own, I should leave here. I would think of
you, with him, dancing at a ball, attending the theater, taking him into your bed." His fingers tightened
on my shoulders. "She is his wife, I would tell myself.
You have no right to want her, to wish that she would
come to you. That she could belong to you."

I lifted my fingers to his lips. His pain was my pain.

I think it will always be so. "I have come to you," I told him. "I do belong to you."

He turned away from me, the struggle between conscience and love as strong in him as it was in me. "I have nothing to offer you."

"Your love. There is nothing else I want."

"It's already yours, has been yours from the first moment I looked at you." He came back to me to touch my cheek. I could see the regret, and the longing, in those beautiful eyes. "Bianca, there is no future for us. I cannot and will not ask you to give up what you have."

"Christian—"

"No. Whatever wrongs I do, I will not do that. I know you would give me what I ask, what I have no right to ask, then come to hate me for it."

"No." Tears came to my eyes then, bitter in the cooling wind. "I could never hate you."

"Then I would hate myself." He crushed my fingers against his lips again. "But I'll ask you for the summer, for a few hours when you can come here and we can pretend winter will never be." He smiled and kissed me softly. "Come here and meet me, Bianca, in the sunlight. Let me paint you. I'll be content with that."

And so tomorrow, and every day during this sweet, endless summer I will go to him. On the cliffs above the sea we will take what happiness we can.

Chapter Four

"Well, hello."

At the husky greeting, Sloan looked up from his notes on the billiard room to see a willowy gypsy in a flowing flowered robe. Long cables of red hair streamed down her shoulders and back. Dreamy green eyes assessed him before she glided into the room like a woman who had all the time in the world and was willing to spend it generously.

"Hi." Sloan caught the elusive scent—like crushed wildflowers—before she offered a hand.

"I'm Lilah." Her voice was as lazily flirtatious as her eyes. "We've missed each other the past couple of days."

If there was a man who didn't get a jolt from this one, Sloan thought, he was dead and buried. "I'm real sorry about that."

She laughed then gave his hand a companionable squeeze. First impressions ranked high with Lilah, and she'd already decided to like him. "Me, too. Especially now. What have you been up to?"

"Getting a feel for the place, and the people in it. How about you?"

"I've been busy trying to figure out if I was in love."

"And?"

"Nope." She moved her shoulders gently, but he caught the wistful look in her eyes before she turned to move around the room. "So, what's the plan here, Sloan O'Riley?"

"Elegant dining in a turn-of-the-century atmosphere." He kicked back in the Windsor armchair he'd been using and gestured toward the papers spread over the library table. "We take out part of that wall there, open up into the adjoining study, add a couple of glass pocket doors, and we've got a lounge."

"Just like that?"

"Just like that—after we deal with the structural hassles. I'll have some preliminary sketches for your family and Trent to look over in a couple of days."

"It seems strange," she murmured, running a finger along the old, dusty chair rail. "Thinking about this place being fresh and new again, having people in it." But if she closed her eyes, she could see it perfectly, the way it had once been. "They used to give huge parties, very elaborate, very chic. I can imagine my great-grandfather standing here beside a billiard table sipping Scotch, and wheeling and dealing." She turned back to Sloan. "Do you think about those things when you make your sketches and calculate stress and space?"

"As a matter of fact, I do. There's a burn mark on

the floor right over there.'' He tipped his pencil toward the spot. ''I imagine some fat guy in a dinner suit dropped his cigar while he was discussing the war in Europe. A couple of others were standing by the window, stripped down to their shirtsleeves and swirling brandy while they talked about the stock market.''

Laughing, Lilah crossed back to him. ''And the ladies were down in the parlor.''

''Listening to piano music and gossiping about the latest fashions from Paris.''

Lilah tilted her head. ''Or discussing the possibility of being given the vote.''

''There you go.''

''I think you're just what The Towers needs,'' she decided. ''Can I take a look at your drawings, or are you temperamental?''

''I make it a policy never to turn down a beautiful woman.''

''Astute and clever.'' She went to lean over his shoulder and push through his papers. ''Why, it's the Emperor's Room.''

''The what?''

''The Emperor's Room, that's what I call the best guest room. Must be the harps and cherubs on the ceiling.'' Sliding her hair behind her shoulder, she leaned closer. ''This is great.''

The dressing room would be a cozy parlor, she noted, complete with a wet bar and an entertainment center that would be hidden behind the original paneling. The bath would remain almost as it was, with the addition of a private whirlpool tucked away in what had been an old storage closet.

''Both ends of one century,'' Lilah murmured. ''You've hardly changed any of the original layout.''

"Trent indicated he wanted to keep the luxury and convenience without altering the mood. We'll save most of the original materials, duplicate what's beyond hope."

"You're going to do it." And because she could see that as well, quite clearly, her eyes filled as she laid a hand on his shoulder. "My father wanted to. My mother and he used to talk about it all the time. I wish they could have seen this."

Touched, Sloan laid his hand over hers. Their fingers had linked when Amanda came to the door. Her first reaction was shock at seeing her sister with her cheek all but brushing Sloan's. Then came the spear of jealousy. There was no denying there was something private, even intimate passing between them. On the heels of that sharp green shaft, pride stepped in.

Hadn't she told herself he was a woman chaser?

"Excuse me." Her voice was a thin sheet of ice as she stepped into the room. "I've been looking for you, Lilah."

"You found me." She blinked back the tears but didn't bother to straighten. "I thought I'd come by and meet Sloan."

"I see you have." Determined to be casual if it killed her, Amanda jammed her hands into the pockets of her sweats. "It's your turn for a shift in the storeroom."

"That's what I get for having the day off." She wrinkled her nose, then sent Sloan a smile. "The Calhouns have become detectives, searching for clues to the hiding place of the elusive emeralds."

"So I've heard."

"Maybe you'll take a hack at one of the walls, and

they'll fall out, looking as fabulous and glittery as the day Bianca hid them.'' With a sigh, she drew away. ''Well, since duty calls, I'd better get dressed for it. Mandy, you ought to take a look at some of Sloan's sketches. They're great.''

''I'll bet.''

The tone would have been a direct tip-off, even if Lilah hadn't known her sister so well. So, Lilah thought with a lifted brow. That's the way it was. Since she'd never been able to resist teasing her sister, she leaned down to kiss Sloan's cheek. ''Welcome to The Towers.''

He didn't have a doubt as to what she was up to. The eyes might be dreamy, he thought, but there was a shrewd and devilish brain behind them. ''Thanks. I'm feeling more at home every day.''

''I'll meet you in the sweatshop in fifteen minutes,'' she said to Amanda, then grinned to herself as she went out.

''Is that your new uniform?'' he asked Amanda as she stood scowling in the center of the room, her hands still fisted in the pockets of baggy gray sweats.

''I don't go in until two today.''

''That's nice.'' He crossed his outstretched legs at the ankles. ''I like your sister.''

''That was obvious.''

He only grinned. ''What does she do, anyway?''

''If you mean professionally, she's a naturalist at Acadia National Park.''

''Wildflowers and stuff. It suits.''

As if the admiration in his voice didn't bother her in the least, she shrugged and walked to the terrace doors. ''I thought you'd be taking measurements or something." Glancing over her shoulder, she shot him a narrow look. "Of the rooms, that is."

This time he laughed outright. "You're mighty cute when you're jealous, Calhoun."

Now she turned to look deliberately down her nose. "I don't know what you're talking about."

"Sure you do, but you can relax. I've already set my sights on you."

Did he expect her to be flattered? she wondered. The hell of it was that, in a odd way, she was. "Do I look like a target?"

"I'd say more like the grand prize." In a gesture of peace, he held up a hand as she sucked in her breath to swear at him. "Before you get more fired up, why don't we deal with business?"

"I am not fired up," she lied. "And I don't see what business we could have."

"Trent said you were the one I should...collaborate with, until he got back. Seeing as you're the one who handles most of the family business, and you've got a firsthand knowledge of hotels."

Because it was logical, she calmed enough to consider it. "What do you want to know?"

How long it's going to take me to knock down that wall around you, he thought. "I figured you'd want to take a look at what I've started. I'd like to get to the drawing board soon."

Actually she was dying to see, but kept her agreement grudgingly cool. "All right, but I only have a few minutes."

"I'll take what I can get."

He waited as she crossed the room. She didn't trust him worth spit, Sloan decided. And that was just fine for now.

"I've got two of the suites mapped out," he told her, shuffling papers. "Plus the tower and most of the dining room here."

She leaned closer, squinting a bit to focus without her reading glasses. As Lilah had been, she was impressed with the sketches. Not only were they competent, but they showed a quick understanding of mood, tone and the practicality necessary for smooth service.

"You work fast," she said, surprised.

"When it's called for." He enjoyed watching the way she lifted a hand to tuck back the swing of hair, not with the sinuous movements of her redheaded sister, but with a quick, absent flick. She smelled of soap and some cool sprinkle of scent.

"What's this?"

"What's what?" He was too busy with the way the sunlight showered on her hair to pay attention to anything else.

"This." She tapped a finger on a sketch.

"Hmm. That's an old servants' stairway. We bring this wall out here, to box it in." He took her finger to slide it along the sketch, the rough side of his palm fitting over the smooth skin of her hand. "It makes this suite two levels, the sitting room and bath down here, two bedrooms and a master bath up here. Since the stairs are already open, it gives us a separation of functions without closing off the flow of space."

"It's nice." Vaguely uneasy with the contact, she flexed her hand but only succeeded in tangling her fingers with his. "I suppose you're going to get estimates and bids."

"I've made some calls."

Something seemed to be happening to her legs

from the knees down. They'd gone weak on her, as if she'd run a very long, very fast race. "Well, you..." She braced and turned her head to face him. His eyes were very close, very quiet, very calm. "Obviously you know what you're doing."

"Yeah, I do."

Oh, yeah, he did, she thought as she felt herself pulled toward him—not by his hand, but by something soft and warm and needy inside her. She had only to give in to it, to lean a little closer. Her mouth could be on his, and she would know, as she had known the day before, a kind of whippy excitement and dazzling pleasure. He was waiting, watching her, with those dark green eyes going from calm to intense, willing her to make that slight and significant move. As she began to slide toward him, she heard herself sigh.

Then she remembered.

He had been in almost this same position with Lilah just moments before. Faces close, fingers linked. Only a fool let herself be manipulated by a man who was that casual with a woman's feelings. And Amanda Kelly Calhoun was no fool.

She jerked back, tugging her hand from under his. Sloan felt the knots already winding through his stomach yank tighter.

"Did I miss something?" he asked with a casualness that cost him dearly.

"I don't know what you mean."

"The hell you don't. You were a hair's breadth away from kissing me, Mandy. Your eyes were full of it. Now you've got them frosted up again."

She wished it was as easy to put the ice back into her blood. "You're letting your ego get the best of you. But then, that's probably typical. If you want to take time out to flirt and snuggle with a woman, try Lilah again.''

He was used to holding on to his temper. When a man had a dangerous one, he learned early to keep it chained down. But it wasn't easy, not with her, not with the way she so consistently racked his system. ''Are you telling me that Lilah's available to any man who asks?''

She went from frost to fire so quickly he could only stare in amazed appreciation. ''You don't know anything about my sister, O'Riley. Watch what you say or you'll find yourself on your butt again.''

''I was asking what you said,'' he reminded her.

''I can say what I like, you can't. Lilah has a warm, generous heart. If you do anything to hurt her, I'll——''

''Hold on.'' Chuckling, he threw up both hands, palms out. ''I don't mind you taking a chunk out of me, Calhoun, but I'd rather it be for something I did—or was at least planning to do. First, I'm not quite the tomcat you seem to think I am. And second, I'm not interested in—what was it—snuggling with Lilah.''

Amanda's chin lifted a fraction higher. ''What's the matter with her?''

Exasperated, he let his hands fall again. ''Not a damn thing. Tell me, has your great-grandaddy's insanity trickled down or are you just being plain obstinate?''

''Take your pick.'' Now she was as embarrassed as she was angry and stalked over to the window to stare out. Whether he was a tomcat—as he'd put it—or not, it was no concerns of hers. It was her problem that she had overreacted to his meeting with Lilah. She was getting herself wound up over nothing, Amanda told herself. If she kept snapping at him every time they spent five minutes together, their business relationship would suffer. And business was, after all, her strongest suit. She gave herself another moment to be sure she'd regained some balance, then turned back.

"We seem to have gotten offtrack. Let's put this back on a professional level, and keep it there."

"You do that real well," he observed.

"What?"

"Pull yourself in. It can't be easy if being around me churns you up half as much as I get being around you." Then he grinned and recrossed his ankles. "Go ahead, be professional. I got real admiration for that side of you."

She wasn't sure whether to scream or laugh or just throw her hands up in defeat. Instead she shook her head and tried again. "I like your work."

"Thanks."

"Trent and I have discussed the budget for the project. He and C.C. may still be on their honeymoon when the bids start coming in. If that's the case, you and I will have to go over them. As far as the hotel section goes, you have a free hand. As to the other part of the house, the family part, we're only interested in essential repairs."

"Why? The place deserves a decent face-lift."

"Because the hotel is a business, and the Calhouns and St. Jameses will be partners. We have the property, he has the funds. We've all agreed that we won't take advantage of his generosity, or the fact that he's marrying C.C."

Sloan considered a moment. "Trent seems to have

other ideas. And I've never known him to let anyone take advantage.''

The smile softened her face. "I know, and we, all of us, appreciate that he's willing to help, but we feel strongly about this. The Towers, our part of it, is a Calhoun problem. Our position is that we'll accept the needed repairs to the plumbing, the wiring and other immediate necessities, then we'll pay him back from our share of the retreat. If business is good, we'll be able to take care of the rest ourselves within the next few years.''

There was pride at stake here, he noted. And more, integrity. He nodded. "You work things out with Trent. Meanwhile, I'll concentrate on the west wing.''

"Fine. If your schedule allows, you can take a look at the rest. It would be helpful if we had an idea what the budget will be on the family areas.''

He started to point out that he was an architect not a contractor, then shrugged. It wouldn't hurt him to take a look. "Sure. I'll work up an estimate.''

"I'd appreciate it. Once you do, I'd prefer if you gave it to me. Just me.''

"You're the boss.''

She lifted a brow. Odd, but she hadn't thought about it quite that way before. Her lips curved as she digested it. "Then we understand each other. One more thing.''

He linked his hands behind his head. "We can have as many things as you want.''

"Only one," she said, though her lips quivered. "When I was finalizing some of the wedding plans, I realized you were down as best man. I left your list with Aunt Coco.''

"My list?''

"Yes, of the timetable, the duties you're responsible for, that sort of thing. There's also a copy of the necessary information—the name and phone number of the photographer, the contact for the musicians, the bartender we hired…oh, and I jotted down the names of three shops where you can rent a tux." Once again she took in the sheer size of him. "You really should get in for a fitting right away."

"I've got it covered." Impressed, he shook his head. "You're damn efficient, Calhoun."

"Yes, I am. Well then, I'll let you get back to work. I'll be in the third-floor storeroom in the other wing until about one. After that you can reach me at the BayWatch if you have any questions."

"Oh, I know where to find you, Calhoun. Good hunting."

He watched her walk away, and thought of her sitting in the storeroom, surrounded by dusty boxes and mounds of yellowing papers. She'd probably already found a way to put things in their tidy place, he thought with a grin. He wondered if she realized what a sweet contrast it was. She would stack and catalogue and file in the most practical way possible, while she searched through pieces of the past for an old dream.

Amanda found no dreams that morning. By the time she arrived at the BayWatch, she had already put in a five-hour day. When she had started the quest for the necklace weeks before, she had promised herself she wouldn't become discouraged, no matter how long it took or how little she found.

Thus far, they had come across the original receipt for the emeralds, and a date book where Bianca had mentioned them. It was enough, Amanda had decided, to prove the necklace had indeed existed, and to keep hope alive that it would be found again.

She often wondered about it, about what it had meant to Bianca Calhoun and why she had secreted it away. If indeed she had. Another old rumor was that Fergus had tossed the necklace into the sea. After all the stories Amanda had heard about Fergus Calhoun's abiding love of a dollar, it was hard to believe that he had willfully thrown away a quarter of a million in jewels.

Besides, she didn't want to believe it, Amanda admitted as she pinned on her name tag. Though she wouldn't have cared for anyone to know it, she had a strong streak of the romantic, and that part of her held tight to the notion that Bianca had hidden away the emeralds, like a gift or promise, waiting for the time they would be needed again.

It embarrassed her a little to know she felt that way. Amanda preferred the outward, and the logical, routine of sorting through papers and organizing them in the practical pursuit of a valuable heirloom.

Bianca herself remained as much a mystery to Amanda as the necklace. Her ingrained pragmatism made it impossible to understand a woman who had risked everything for, and ultimately had died for, love. Feelings that intense and that desperate seemed unlikely to her, unless they were in the pages of a book.

What would it be like to love that strongly? she wondered. To feel as though your life were so completely bound to another's that it was impossible to survive without him. Inconvenient, she decided. Uncomfortable and unwise. She could only be grateful that she hadn't inherited that dangerous kind of passion. Feeling smug about her own unbattered heart, she settled down to work.

"Amanda?"

She was halfway through the August reservations and held up a hand. "Minute," she murmured, and totaled her calculations to that point. "What is it, Karen? Wow." She pushed her glasses back up her nose and studied the luxurious spray of roses in the desk clerk's arms. "What did you do, win a beauty pageant?"

"They're not mine." Karen buried her face in them. "Don't I wish. They just came in, for you."

"Me?"

"You're still Amanda Calhoun," Karen pointed out as she offered the florist's card. "Though if you want to trade places until these three dozen long-stemmed beauties fade, I'm game."

"Three dozen?"

"I counted." Grinning, Karen laid them on the desk. "Three dozen and one," she added, nodded toward the single rose that stood beside them.

Sloan, Amanda thought, and felt her heart give a quick, catchy sigh. How was she supposed to get a handle on a man who did sweet, unexpected things every time she thought she'd made up her mind about him? How could he have known about her secret weakness for red roses? She hadn't even thanked him for the first one.

"Aren't you going to read the card?" Karen demanded. "If I have to go back to the desk without knowing who sent them, I'll be distracted and my work will suffer. The evil Albert Stenerson'll fire me, and it'll be your fault."

"I already know who they're from," she began, unaware of the softness in her eyes. "It was really so sweet of him to—oh." Baffled, she studied the name on the card. Not Sloan, she realized, with a cutting edge of disappointment that surprised her. They weren't from Sloan.

"Well? Do you want me to beg?"

Still puzzled, Amanda handed the card over.

"*With my appreciation. William Livingston.* Whew." Karen tossed back her long, dark hair. "What did you have to do to deserve this kind of gratitude?"

"I got him a fax machine."

"You got him a fax machine," Karen repeated, handing the card back to Amanda. "Last Sunday I cooked a pot roast with all the trimmings and all I got was a bottle of cheap wine."

Amanda continued to frown and tapped the card on the edge of her desk. "I guess I'd better thank him."

"I guess you'd better." Karen picked up one of the roses and sniffed. "Unless you'd rather delegate. I'd be glad to go up and express your appreciation to Mr. Eyes-To-Die-For Livingston."

"Thanks, but I'll handle it." She picked up the phone, then sent Karen an arched look. "Scram."

"Spoilsport." Laughing, she went out, discreetly shutting the door at her back as Amanda dialed the extension for the Island Suite.

"Livingston."

"Mr. Livingston, this is Amanda Calhoun."

"Ah, the efficient Miss Calhoun." There was a laugh in his voice, a pleasant and flattering one. "What can I do for you?"

"I wanted to thank you for the flowers. They're beautiful. It was very thoughtful of you."

"Just a small way of showing you that I appreciate your help, and the quick work."

"That's my job. Please let me know if I can be of any further assistance during your stay."

"As a matter of fact, there is something you could help me with."

"Of course." Automatically she picked up a pen and prepared to write.

"I'd like you to have dinner with me."

"Excuse me?"

"I'd like to take you to dinner. Eating alone is unappetizing."

"I'm sorry, Mr. Livingston, it's against hotel policy for the staff to socialize with the guests. It's kind of you to ask."

"Kindness has nothing to do with it. Can I ask if you'd consider it if hotel policy could be...bent?"

There was no chance of that, Amanda thought. Not with Stenerson. "I'd be happy to consider it," she said tactfully. "Unfortunately, as long as you're a guest at the BayWatch—"

"Yes, yes. I'll get back to you shortly."

Amanda blinked at the dead receiver, shrugged, then replaced it to get back to work. Ten minutes later, Stenerson was opening her door.

"Miss Calhoun, Mr. Livingston would like to have dinner with you." His mouth primed up even more than usual. "You're free to go. Naturally, I'll expect you to conduct yourself in a manner that will reflect properly on the hotel."

"But—"

"Don't make a habit of it."

"I—" But he was already shutting the door. Amanda was still staring at it when her phone rang. "Miss Calhoun."

"Shall we say eight o'clock?"

On a long breath, she sat back in her chair. She was on the point of refusing when she caught herself stroking the single rosebud Sloan had given her. Amanda snatched back her hand and balled it in her lap.

"I'm sorry, I'm on until ten tonight."

"Tomorrow then. Where shall I pick you up?"

"Tomorrow's fine," she said on impulse. "Let me give you directions."

Chapter Five

Sloan knew the minute Trent returned to The Towers. Even in the library at the end of a long corridor he could hear the high happy yaps of the dog, the shouts of children and the mix of laughter. Setting aside his notebook, he strolled out to see his old friend.

Trent had gotten no further than the foyer. Jenny was hanging on his legs as Fred circled and danced. Alex was jumping up and down in a bid for attention while Coco, Suzanna and Lilah all fired questions at once. C.C. only stood beaming, held snug against Trent's side. At a shout from above, Sloan looked up to see Amanda bolting down the stairs. Her laughter glowed in her face as he'd never seen it before. Squeezing through her sisters, she took her turn at a hug.

"If you hadn't come back today, I was sending out a team of mercenaries," she told Trent. "Four days before the wedding and you're down in Boston."

"I knew you could handle the details."

"She has miles of lists," Coco put in. "It's frightening."

"There, you see?" Trent gave Amanda a quick kiss.

"What did you bring me? What did you bring me?" Jenny demanded.

"Talk about mercenary." Laughing, Suzanna scooped her daughter up. When she spotted Sloan in the hallway, her easy smile faded. She tried to tell herself that it was her imagination that his eyes changed whenever he looked at her. It had to be. What possible reason would he have for disliking her on sight?

Sloan studied her another moment, a tall, slender woman with pale blond hair pulled back in a ponytail, a face blessed with classical beauty and sad blue eyes. Dismissing her, he looked back at Trent. His smile came naturally again.

"I hate to interrupt when you're surrounded by beautiful women, but time's wasting."

"Sloan." His arm still around C.C., Trent stepped forward to grip Sloan's hand. In all of his varied groups of acquaintances, associates and colleagues, this was the only man he considered a genuine friend. "On the job already?"

"Getting started."

"You look like you've just gotten back from a long vacation in the tropics instead of six weeks in Budapest. It's good to see you."

"Same here." Sloan sent a quick wink at C.C. "It's really good to see that you're finally developing some taste."

"I like him," C.C. said.

"Women tend to," Trent said. "How's your family?"

Sloan's gaze flicked to Suzanna again. "They're fine."

"You two must have a lot to catch up on." Feeling awkward, Suzanna took her son's hand. "We're going to take a walk before dinner."

Amanda waited until Coco had urged everyone along toward the parlor before she put a hand on Sloan's arm. "Wait."

He grinned at her. "I've been waiting, Calhoun."

She wasn't even tempted to rise to the bait. "I want to know why you look at Suzanna that way."

The humor faded from his eyes. "What way is that?"

"Like you detest her."

It annoyed him that those particular and very private feelings showed so clearly. "You've got more imagination than I gave you credit for."

"It's not my imagination." Baffled, she shook her head. "What could you possibly have against Suzanna? She's the kindest, most good-hearted person I know."

It was difficult not to sneer, but he kept his face bland. "I didn't say I had anything against her. You did."

"You didn't have to say it. Obviously I can't make you talk about it, but—"

"Maybe that's because I'd rather talk about us." Casually he set both hands on the banister behind her, caging her between.

"There is no us."

"Sure there is. There's you and there's me. That makes us. That's real basic grammar."

"If you're trying to change the subject—"

"You're getting that line between your eyebrows again." He lifted a thumb to rub at it. "That Calhoun line. How come you never smile at me the way you smiled at Trent?"

"Because I like Trent."

"It's funny, most people figure I'm an amiable sort of guy."

"Not from where I'm standing."

"Why don't you stand a little closer?"

She had to laugh. If there had been a contest for persistence, Sloan O'Riley would have won hands down. "This is close enough, thanks." More than close enough, she added silently when she had to fight back an urge to run her fingers through that untidy mane of reddish-blond hair. "*Amiable* isn't the word I would use. Now, *cocky, annoying, tenacious,* those might suit."

"I kind of like tenacious." He leaned closer to breathe in her scent. "A man doesn't get very far if he caves in every time he runs into a wall. You climb over, tunnel under, or just knock the whole damn thing down."

She put a hand to his chest before he could close that last inch of distance. "Or he keeps beating his head against it until he has a concussion."

"That's a calculated risk, and worth it if there's a woman behind the wall looking at him the way you look at me."

"I don't look at you any particular way."

"When you forget that you want to be professional, you look at me with those big blue eyes of yours all soft, and a little scared. A lot curious. Makes me want

to scoop you up right there and carry you off to someplace real quiet so I can satisfy that curiosity.''

She could imagine it all too clearly, feel it all too
sharply. There was only one solution. Escape. "Well,
this has been fun, but I've got to go change."

"Are you going back to work?"

"No." Agile, she swooped under his arm and
swung up the steps. "I've got a date."

"A date?" he repeated, but she was already racing
across the second floor.

He told himself he wasn't waiting for her, though
he'd been pacing the foyer for a good twenty minutes.
He wasn't going to hang around like an idiot and
watch her go strolling off with some other man—after
she'd tied him into knots by just standing there and
looking at him. There was plenty for him to do, including enjoying the dinner Coco had invited him to,
talking over old times and new plans with Trent, even
sitting down at his drawing board. He wasn't about
to spend the evening mooning over the fact that some
obstinate woman preferred someone else's company
to his.

After all, Sloan reminded himself as he paced the
foyer, she was free to come and go as she pleased.
The same as he was. Neither one of them was
branded. Just because he had a hankering for her
didn't mean he was going to get riled up when she
spent a couple of hours with another man.

The hell it didn't.

Turning, he took the steps two at a time.

"Calhoun?" He strode down the corridor, banging
on doors. "Damn it, Calhoun, I want to talk to you."

He was at the far end of the hall and starting back when Amanda opened her door.

"What's going on?" she demanded.

He stared a moment as she stood in the stream of light that spilled out of the room behind her. She'd done something fancy to her hair, he noted, so that it looked sexily rumpled. Played with her face, too, in that damnably sultry way some women have a talent for. Her dress was a pale icy blue, full at the skirt, nipped at the waist with two skinny straps slinking over her shoulders. Chunky stones in a deeper blue glittered at her ears and throat.

She didn't look efficient, he thought furiously. She didn't look competent. She looked as delectable as a pretty white cake on a fancy tray. And he was damned if any other man was going to take even one small nibble.

Her foot was already tapping when he started toward her.

Amiable? she thought, and had to resist the urge to bolt back into her room and lock the door. No one would call him amiable now. He looked as though he'd just finished chewing a mountain of glass and was raring for the second course.

"What kind of date?" he snapped at her, and found himself further incensed by the fact that her skin smelled like glory.

Amanda inclined her head slowly. The hands she had fisted on her hips slid carefully to her sides. When you were facing a raging bull you didn't wave a red flag but tried to ease yourself over the fence. "The usual kind."

"Is that the way you dress for the usual kind?"

Irked, she glanced down and smoothed her skirts. "What's wrong with the way I'm dressed?"

For an answer, he took her arm and swung her around. He'd been right, he thought as his stomach clutched up. Those two little straps were all that were covering her back. Right down to the waist. "Where's the rest of it?"

"Rest of what?"

"The dress."

She turned back, still cautious, and examined his face. "Sloan, I think you've gone around the bend."

She didn't know how right she was, he thought. "I've got as much sense as any man can hang on to after ten minutes with you. Cancel."

"Cancel?" she repeated.

"The date, damn it." He nudged her none too gently toward her bedroom. "Go in and call him up and tell him you can't make it. Ever."

"You really are crazy." She forgot about bulls and red flags and cut loose. "I go where I please and with whom I please. If you think I'm going to break a date with an attractive, charming and intelligent man because some overbearing baboon tells me to, then think again."

"It's the date," he warned, "or that pretty stiff neck of yours."

Her eyes narrowed down to two slits of righteous blue fire. "Don't you threaten me, you pinhead. I have a dinner date with your antithesis. A gentleman." She elbowed him aside. "Now get out of my way."

"I'll get out of your way," he promised. "After I give you something to think about."

He had her back against the wall with his mouth

covering hers before she could blink. She could taste the anger. That, she would have fought against to the last breath. But she could also taste the need, and that, she surrendered to. It was such a perfect echo of her own.

He didn't care if it was unreasonable. He didn't care if it was wrong or stupid or any of the other terms that could so easily apply to his actions. He wanted to curse her for making him behave like some reckless teenager. But he could only taste her, drowning in the flavor that he was coming to understand he would always crave. He could only pull her closer against him so that he could feel the instant heat that pumped from her body into his.

He could sense each change as it flowed through her.

First the anger that kept her rigid and aloof. Then the surrender, reluctant then melting so that her bones seemed to dissolve. And the passion overlapping so quickly it stole his breath. It was that he understood he couldn't live without.

Her arms went around him as if they belonged there. Strained against his, her body throbbed until it was one sweet ache. This was an ache that once felt could never be forgotten, would always be craved. Eager, she nipped at his mouth, knowing in another moment delirium could overtake her. Wanting it, wanting that liberating mindless whirl of desire only he could ignite inside her.

Only he.

In one long possessive stroke his hands ran from her shoulders to her wrists, holding there a moment while her pulse scrambled under his palms. When he lifted his head, she leaned back limply against the wall, watching him while she struggled to catch her breath. While she fought to break through the torrent of sensations and understand the feelings beneath them.

The thought of another man touching her, of looking into her face and seeing it flushed with passion as it was now, of seeing her eyes clouded with it, terrified him. Because he preferred good clean anger to fear, he gripped her shoulders again, all but lifting her off her feet.

"Think about that," he told her in a low dangerous voice. "You think about that good and hard."

What had he done to her to make her need so terribly? He had to know, just by looking at her, that he had only to pull her inside her room to take everything he claimed to want. He had only to touch her again to have her desperate to give. He wouldn't even have to ask. It shamed her to realize it, destroyed her to understand that anyone would have such complete power over her pride and her will.

"You made your point," she said unsteadily, infuriated that tears were stinging the back of her eyes and throat. "Do you want to hear me say that you can make me want you? Fine. You can."

The sparkle of tears in her eyes did what her fury couldn't. It beat him soundly. There was regret in his voice when he lifted a hand to her face. "Amanda—"

She stiffened and shut her eyes. If he was gentle—she knew if he showed her even a scrap of tenderness, she would crumble. "You've got your conquest, Sloan. Now I'd appreciate it if you'd let me go."

He let his hand slide to his side before he stepped back. "I'm not going to tell you I'm sorry." But the way she looked at him made him feel as though he had just shattered something small and fragile.

"That's all right. I'm sorry enough for both of us."

"Amanda." Lilah stood at the top of the stairs, watching them both with her sleepy-eyed curiosity. "Your date's here."

"Thanks." Frantic for escape, she turned into her room to grab her jacket and purse. Being careful not to look at Sloan, she hurried out again to rush downstairs. Lilah glanced after her, then walked down the hall to rest her hands on Sloan's shoulders.

"You know, big guy, you look like you could use a friend."

He couldn't begin to put a name to any of the emotions currently running riot through him. "Maybe I'll just go downstairs and throw him out a window."

"You could," Lilah agreed after a moment, "but Mandy's always been a sucker for the underdog."

Sloan swore then decided to work off some of the frustration by pacing the corridor. "So, who is he anyway?"

"I've never met him before. His name's William Livingston."

"And?"

Lilah gave a gentle shrug. "Tall, dark and handsome as the saying goes. Very faint, very charming British accent, Italian suit, upper-class manners. That patina of wealth and breeding without being ostentatious."

Sloan swore and considered punching a hole in the wall. "He sounds just dandy."

"Sounds," she agreed, but her look was troubled. "What is it?"

"Bad vibes." Absently she ran a hand up and down her arm. "And he had a very muddy aura."

"Give me a break, Lilah."

With a little smile, she glanced back at him. "Don't knock it, Sloan. Remember, I'm on your side. I happen to think you're just what my take-it-all-too-seriously sister needs." In her easy way, she hooked a friendly arm through his. "Relax, Mr. William Livingston doesn't have a chance. Not her type." She laughed as she walked with him to the steps. "She thinks he is, but he's not. So let's go eat. There's nothing like Aunt Coco's Trout Amandine to put you in a good mood."

Pretending she had an appetite, Amanda studied her menu. The restaurant William had chosen was a lovely little place overlooking Frenchman Bay. Since the night was warm, they could enjoy the terrace service with candlelight flickering in the gentle sea breeze, and the fragile scent of spring flowers.

Amanda left the choice of wine up to him and tried to convince herself that she was about to have a delightful evening.

"Are you enjoying Bar Harbor?" she asked.

"Very much. I'm hoping to get some sailing in soon, but in the meantime, I've been content to enjoy the scenery."

"Have you been to the park?"

"Not yet." He glanced over at the bottle the waiter offered, perused the label, then nodded.

"You shouldn't miss it. The view from Cadillac Mountain is stupendous."

"So I'm told." He tasted the wine, approved, then

waited for Amanda's to be poured. "Perhaps you'll find some time and act as my guide."

"I don't think—"

"Hotel policy's already been bent," he interrupted, and touched his glass lightly to hers.

"I wanted to ask you how you managed it."

"Very simply. I gave your Mr. Stenerson a choice. Either he could make an exception to his policy, or I could move to another hotel where it wouldn't be an issue."

"I see." She took a thoughtful sip of wine. "That seems a bit drastic just for a dinner."

"A very delightful dinner. I wanted to get to know you better. I hope you don't mind."

What woman could? she asked herself, and only smiled.

It was impossible not to relax, not to be charmed by his stories, flattered by his attentiveness. He did not, as so many successful men did, talk constantly of his business. As an antique dealer he'd traveled all over the world and, throughout the meal, gave Amanda glimpses of Paris and Rome, London and Rio.

When her thoughts drifted now and again to another man, she doubled her determination to enjoy herself where she was, and with whom.

"The rosewood chiffonier in your foyer," he commented as they lingered over coffee and dessert. "It's a beautiful piece."

"Thank you. It's Regency period—I think."

He smiled. "You think correctly. If I had run into it at an auction, I would have considered myself very fortunate."

"My great-grandfather had it shipped over from England when he built the house."

"Ah, the house." William's lips curved as he lifted his cup. "Very imposing. I half expected to see medieval maidens drifting about on the lawn."

"Or bats swooping out of the tower."

On a delighted laugh, he squeezed her hand. "No, but perhaps Rapunzel letting down her hair."

The image appealed and made her smile. "We love it, and always have. Maybe the next time you visit the island you'll stay at The Towers Retreat."

"The Towers Retreat," he murmured, tapping a finger thoughtfully against his lips. "Where have I heard that before?"

"A projected St. James hotel?"

His eyes cleared. "Of course. I read something a few weeks ago. You don't mean to say that your home is The Towers?"

"Yes, it is. We hope to have the retreat ready for occupancy in about a year."

"That is fascinating. But wasn't there some legend attached to the place? Something about ghosts and missing jewelry?"

"The Calhoun emeralds. They were my great-grandmother's."

With a half smile, he tilted his head. "They're real? I thought it was just a clever publicity gimmick. Stay in a haunted house and search for missing treasure. That sort of thing."

"No, in fact we're not at all pleased that the whole business leaked out." Even thinking about it annoyed her so that she began to drum her fingers on the table. "The necklace is real—was real in any event. We don't know where it might have been hidden. In the meantime we're forever bothered by reporters or having to chase erstwhile treasure hunters off the grounds.''

"I'm sorry. That's very intrusive.''

"We hope to find it soon, and put an end to all the nonsense. Once renovations start, it might turn up under a floorboard.''

"Or behind the ubiquitous secret panel,'' he offered with a smile and made her laugh.

"We don't have any of those—at least that I know of.''

"Then your ancestor was remiss. A place like that deserves at least one secret panel.'' He laid a hand over hers again. "Perhaps you'll let me help you look for it...or at least let me use it as an excuse to see you again.''

"I'm sorry, but at least for the next few days I'm tied up. My sister's getting married on Saturday.''

He smiled over their joined hands. "There's always Sunday. I would like to see you again, Amanda. Very much.'' He let the subject, and her hand slip gently away.

On the drive home he kept the topics general. No pressure, Amanda thought, grateful. No arrogant assumptions or cocky grins. This was the kind of man who knew how to treat a woman with the proper respect and attention. William wouldn't knock her to the ground and laugh in her face. He wouldn't stalk her down like a gunslinger and fire out demands.

So why was she so let down when they stopped in front of the house and Sloan's car was nowhere in sight? Shaking off the mood, she waited for William to come around and open her door.

"Thank you for tonight," she told him. "It was lovely."

"Yes, it was. And so are you." Very gently he placed his hands on her shoulders before touching his lips to hers. The kiss was very warm, very soft—an expert caress of lips and hands. And to her disappointment, it left her completely unmoved.

"Are you really going to make me wait until Sunday to see you again?"

His eyes told her that he had not been unmoved. Amanda waited for the banked desire in them to strike some chord. But there was nothing.

"William, I—"

"Lunch," he said, adding a charming smile. "Something very casual at the hotel. You can tell me more about the house."

"All right. If I can swing it." She eased away before he could kiss her again. "Thanks again."

"My pleasure, Amanda." He waited, as was proper, for her to go inside. As the door shut behind her, his smile changed ever so slightly, hardened, cooled. "Believe me, it will be my pleasure."

He walked back to his car. He would drive it well out of sight of The Towers. And then he would come back to do a quick and quiet tour of the grounds, to note down the most practical entrances.

If Amanda Calhoun could be his entryway into The Towers, that was all well and good—with the side benefit of romancing a beautiful woman. If she didn't provide him with a way in, he would simply find a different route.

One way or the other, he didn't intend to leave Mount Desert Island without the Calhoun emeralds.

* * *

"Did you have a good time?" Suzanna asked when Amanda came in the front door.

"Suze." Amused but not surprised, Amanda shook her head. "You waited up again."

"No, I didn't." To prove it, Suzanna gestured with the mug in her hand. "I just came down to make myself some tea."

Amanda laughed as she walked over to rest her hands on her sister's shoulders. "Why is it that we Irish-as-Paddy's-pig Calhouns can't tell a decent lie?"

Suzanna gave up. "I don't know. We should practice more."

"Honey, you look tired."

"Mmm." Exhausted was the word, but she didn't care for it. Suzanna sipped the tea as they started up the stairs together. "Springtime. Everybody wants their flowers done yesterday. I'm not complaining. It looks like the business is finally going to turn a real profit."

"I still think you should hire on some more help. Between the business and the kids you run yourself ragged."

"Now who's playing mama? Anyway, Island Gardens needs one more good season before I can afford anything but one part-time helper. Plus I like to be busy." Even though fatigue was dragging at her, she paused outside of Amanda's door. "Mandy, can I talk to you for a minute before you go to bed?"

"Sure. Come on in." Amanda left the door slightly ajar as she slipped out of her shoes. "Is something wrong?"

"No. At least nothing I can put my finger on. Can I ask you what you think of Sloan?"

"Think of him?" Stalling, Amanda set her shoes neatly in the closet.

"Impressions, I guess. He seems like a very nice man. Both kids are already crazy about him, and that's an almost foolproof barometer for me."

"He's good with them." Amanda took off her earrings to replace them in her jewelry box.

"I know." Troubled, she wandered the room. "Aunt Coco's set to adopt him. He's slipped right into an easy relationship with Lilah. C.C.'s already fond of him, and not just because he's a friend of Trent's."

Pouting a little, Amanda unclasped her necklace. "His type always gets along beautifully with women."

Distracted, Suzanna merely shook her head. "No, it's not a man-woman kind of thing at all. Just a kind of innate relaxation."

Amanda had no comment for that as she recalled the fevered tension in him a few hours earlier.

"He seems like an easygoing, friendly man."

"But?"

"It's probably my imagination, but whenever he looks at me, I get this wave of hostility." With a half laugh, she shrugged. "Now I sound like Lilah."

Amanda's eyes met her sister's in the mirror. "No, I sensed something myself. I can't explain it. I even called him on it."

"Did he say anything? I don't expect everyone to like me, but when I feel a dislike this strong, at least I want to know why."

"He denied it. I don't know what to say, Suzanna, except that I don't think he's the kind of man who would react that way to someone he doesn't even know.'' She made a helpless gesture with her hands. ''He can certainly be annoying, but I don't think he's a man to be deliberately unfair. Maybe we're both being oversensitive.''

''Maybe.'' Suzanna pushed the uncomfortable feelings away. ''We're all a little crazed with C.C.'s wedding, and the renovations. Well, I won't lose any sleep over him.'' She kissed Amanda's cheek. ''Good night.''

''Night.'' As she eased down onto the bed, Amanda let out a long sigh. It was unfortunate, she thought. It was infuriating. But she already knew she'd be losing sleep over him.

Chapter Six

She was right on schedule. If there was one thing you could count on about Amanda Calhoun, Sloan thought, it was that she'd be on time. She was moving fast—typically—so he lengthened his stride and crossed the hotel patio to waylay her by the gate leading to the pool. His hand covered hers on the latch.

She jerked away, which was no less than he'd expected. "Don't you have anything better to do?" she asked.

"I want to talk to you."

"This is my time." She shoved open the gate, strode through then whirled around. "My personal time. I don't have to talk to you." To prove it, she slammed the gate smartly in his face.

Sloan took a long, slow breath, then opened the gate. "Okay, you can just listen." He caught up with her as she heaved her towel onto a deck chair.

"I'm not going to talk, and I'm not going to listen. There's absolutely nothing you have to say that could interest me.'' She stripped off her terry wrap, tossed it aside, then dove into the pool.

Sloan watched her through the first lap. She was mad enough to spit, he thought, then moved his shoulders. So, they'd do it the hard way.

With each kick and stroke, Amanda cursed him. She'd spent half the night replaying their last scene together over and over in her mind. It had made her miserable. It had made her furious. When she'd awakened that morning, she'd promised herself that he would never get the chance to touch her again. Certainly he would never get the chance to make her feel helpless and needy again.

Her life was just beginning to move along as she wanted. There was no way, no way in hell that Sloan O'Riley or anyone else was going to block her path.

She ran straight into him, a dud torpedo into a battleship. Sputtering, she surfaced to see him standing chest high in the water. Bare-chest high.

''What are you doing?''

''I figured I'd have a better chance of getting you to listen in here than I would if I stood on the side and yelled at you.''

Eyes narrowed, she slicked the hair back from her face. There was a laugh bubbling in her throat that she refused to acknowledge. ''The pool isn't open to guests until ten.''

''Yeah, I think you mentioned that. What you didn't mention is that this water is freezing.''

''Yeah.'' Now she did smile, and there was as much humor as smugness in the curve of her lips. ''I know. That's why I like to keep moving.''

She started off, slicing cleanly through the water. Less than a foot away, he was matching her stroke for stroke. He'd stripped off more than his shirt, she noted. The only thing covering that very long body was a pair of brief navy briefs. Each time her face went into the water, her eyes slid over to take another look.

His broad shoulders and chest tapered down to a narrow waist and hips. The skin was stretched taut over the bones there, without an ounce of excess flesh. His stomach was board flat, and...oh my. When she nearly sucked in water instead of air, Amanda forced her gaze to skip down several strategic inches to the hard, muscled thighs and calves.

The tough, weathered tan was over every inch of exposed flesh. His skin gleamed like wet copper. And what would it feel like to run her hands over it now? To feel those sleek, smooth muscles under her fingers? How could their bodies fit together now, if slick as otters, they slid against each other through the chill water?

Chill? she thought. The pool was beginning to feel like a sauna. Deliberately she pushed off hard and increased her pace. If she could outrace him, maybe she could outrace her own wayward thoughts.

He was still beside her, matching speed and stroke so that they crossed the pool in a kind of unstudied and effortless harmony. It was lovely, almost sensuous, the way their arms lifted and pulled at the same moment, the way their legs scissored and their bodies stretched...like making love, she thought dreamily, then shook herself to knock that hot image from her brain.

Amanda kicked in and put all that frustrated passion into speed. Still, their hands slapped the wall in unison. She began to enjoy it for what it was, an unstated competition between two people who were evenly matched. She'd lost track of the laps and didn't care. When her lungs were straining and her muscles weak, she gripped the edge of the pool to surface, laughing.

He knew she'd never looked more beautiful, with her hair and face drenched with water and her eyes filled with delight. More than anything he'd ever wanted, he wanted to pull her against him then, just to hold her while her laughter danced on the morning air. But he'd made a promise to himself sometime during his own sleepless night. He intended to keep it.

He sent her a friendly grin. "That warmed things up."

"You're pretty good. For an Okie."

"You're not bad yourself, for a female."

She laughed again and rested her head on the side of the pool to look at him. His hair was dark with water, curling over his brow and neck in a way that had her fingers itching to play with it. "I like to race."

"Race? Is that what we were doing? I thought we were just taking a nice, leisurely swim."

She tossed water into his eyes, then stood. "I have to get in."

"Are you going to let me talk to you now?"

The laughter faded from her eyes. "Let's just leave it," she suggested, and hitched herself up on the side of the pool.

He laid a hand on her leg. "Mandy—"

"I don't want to argue with you again. Since we've actually managed to get along for five minutes, why can't we just leave it at that?"

"Because I want to apologize."

"If you'd just—" She broke off to stare at him. "You what?"

"I want to apologize." He stood to put his hands lightly on her arms just beneath her shoulders. "I was out of line last night, way out, and I'm sorry."

"Oh." Disconcerted, she looked down and began to rub at the beads of water on her thigh.

"Now you're supposed to say, all right, Sloan, I accept your apology."

She looked up through wet, spiky lashes, then smiled. Things were suddenly too comfortable to cling to anger. "I guess I do. You acted like such a jerk."

He grimaced. "Thanks a lot."

"You did. Spouting off threats and orders. Then there was all that steam coming out of your ears."

"Want to know why?"

She shook her head and started to rise, but he held her in place. "You brought it up," he pointed out. "I couldn't stand the idea of you being with someone else. Look at me." Gently he cupped her chin, turning her face back to his. "You triggered something in me right off. I can't shake it. I don't much want to."

"I don't think—"

"Thinking has nothing to do with it. I know how I feel when I look at you."

She was losing fast. The quick skip of panic couldn't compete with the flood of pleasure. "I have to think," she murmured. "I'm made that way."

"Okay, well here's something new for you to think about. I'm falling in love with you."

Panic was more than a skip now, but a hard slap.

It darted into her eyes as she stared at him. "You don't mean that."

"Yes, I do. And you know it or you wouldn't be sitting there looking like a rabbit caught in the high beams."

"I don't—"

"I'm not asking how you feel," he cut in. "I'm giving you my side of it, so you can get used to it."

She didn't think she would, ever, any more than she would get used to him. Certainly it would be impossible to get used to the feelings shooting off inside her. Is this what love was? she wondered. This edgy and bright sensation that could turn warm and soft without warning? "I don't—I'm not sure how..." She let out a huff of breath. "Did you do this just to make me crazy?"

It helped to be able to smile. "Yep. Give me a kiss, Calhoun."

She twisted and slid wetly out of his hold. "I'm not kissing you again, because it erases every intelligent thought from my head."

Now he grinned. "Honey, that's the nicest thing you've ever said to me." When he rose smoothly from the pool, Amanda snatched up her towel. She snapped it once, hard enough to make the air crack.

"Keep back. I mean it. You either give me time to figure all this out or I aim and fire. And I aim below the belt." There was both amusement and challenge in her eyes when she tilted her chin. "You don't have a lot of protection at the moment."

He ran his tongue around his teeth. "You've got me there. How about a drive after you get off work?"

It would be nice, she thought, to go driving with

him up into the hills, with the windows open and the air streaming. But, regretfully, duty came first.

"I can't. C.C.'s shower's tonight. We're surprising her when she gets home from work." She frowned a little. "It's on your list."

"Guess it slipped my mind. Tomorrow then."

"I have the final meeting with the photographer, then I have to help Suzanna with the flowers. Not the next night, either," she said before he could ask. "Most of the out-of-town guests will be arriving, plus we've got the rehearsal dinner."

"Then the wedding," he said with a nod. "After the wedding, Calhoun."

"After the wedding, I'll..." She smiled, realizing she was enjoying herself. "I'll let you know." Grabbing her wrap, she headed for the gate.

"Hey. I haven't got a towel."

She tossed a laugh over her shoulder. "I know."

Late that afternoon, Sloan stood out on the lower terrace, making sketches of the exterior of The Towers. He wanted to add another outside stairway without disturbing the integrity of the building. He stopped when Suzanna came out carrying two wicker baskets pregnant with spring flowers.

"I'm sorry." She hesitated, then tried a smile. "I didn't know you were out here. I'm going to set things up for the shower."

"I'll be out of your way in a minute."

"That's all right." She set the basket down and went back inside.

Over the next few minutes, she went back and forth, carrying out chairs and paper decorations. They passed the time in nerve-racking silence until she finally set aside one of Amanda's swans and looked at him.

"Mr. O'Riley, have we met before?"

He kept right on sketching. "No."

"I wondered because you seemed to know me, and have a poor opinion of me."

His gaze lifted coldly to hers. "I don't know you—Mrs. Dumont."

"Then why—" She broke off. She hated confrontations, the way they tightened up her stomach muscles. Turning away, she started back inside. She could feel his eyes on her, icy and resentful. After bracing a hand on the jamb, she forced herself to turn back. "No, I'm not going to do this. You're in my home, Mr. O'Riley, and I refuse to walk on eggshells in my own home ever again. Now I want to know what your problem is."

He tossed his sketch pad onto a small glass-topped table. "The name doesn't ring any bells with you, Mrs. Dumont? O'Riley doesn't strike a chord?"

"No, why should it?"

His mouth tightened. "Maybe if I add a name to it. Megan. Megan O'Riley. Hear any bells now?"

"No." Frustrated, she pushed a hand through her hair. "Will you get to the point?"

"I guess it's easy for someone like you to forget. She wasn't anyone to you but a slight inconvenience."

"Who?"

"Megan. My sister, Megan."

Completely lost, Suzanna shook her head. "I don't know your sister."

The fact that the name meant nothing to her only infuriated him. Sloan stepped toward her, ignoring the quick fear in her eyes. "No, you never met her face-to-face. Why bother? You managed to see that she was pushed aside easily enough. Not that you ended up with any prize. Baxter Dumont was always a bastard, but she loved him."

"Your sister?" Suzanna lifted an unsteady hand to rub at her temple. "Your sister and Bax."

"Starting to get through?" When she started to turn away, he grabbed her arm and whirled her back. "Was it for love or money?" he demanded. "Either way, you could have shown some compassion. Damn it, she was seventeen and pregnant. Couldn't you have stood back far enough to let the spineless sonofabitch see his son?"

She'd gone a translucent shade of white. Under his hand, her arm seemed to turn to water. "Son," she whispered.

"She was just a kid, a terrified kid who'd believed every lie he'd told her. I wanted to kill him, but it would only have made it worse for Meg. But you, you couldn't even find it in your heart to give her the scraps from the table. You went right ahead with your fancy life as if she and the boy didn't exist. And when she called and begged you just to let him see the boy once or twice a year, you called her a whore and threatened to have her son taken away if she ever contacted your precious husband again."

She couldn't get her breath. Not since her last hideous argument with Bax had she found it so difficult to breathe. Weakly she batted at the hand that held her arm. "Please. Please, I need to sit down."

But he was staring at her. As the impetus of his own rage ebbed he could see that it wasn't shame in her eyes, it wasn't derision or even anger. It was pure shock. "My God," he said quietly, "you didn't know."

All she could do was shake her head. When his grip loosened, she turned and bolted into the house. Sloan stood for a moment, pressing his fingers against his eyes. All the disgust he had felt for Suzanna turned sharply on himself. He started after her and ran into a furious Amanda in the doorway.

"What did you do to her?" With both hands she shoved him back. "What the hell did you say to her to make her cry like that?"

The fist in his stomach squeezed tighter. "Where did she go?"

"You're not getting near her again. When I think that I'd begun to believe I could—damn you, O'Riley."

"There's nothing you can say to me that's worse than what I'm already thinking about myself. Now where is she?"

"You go to hell." She slammed the terrace door and flipped the lock.

Sloan gave brief thought to kicking it in then, swearing, went around to the stone steps on the side of the house. He found Suzanna standing on the second-floor balcony, looking out at the cliffs. He'd taken his first step toward her when Amanda burst out of the doors.

"You keep away from her." She already had a protective arm around her sister. "Just turn around and start walking. Don't stop until you get back to Oklahoma."

"This isn't any of your concern," Sloan told her, and Suzanna had to grab hold before Amanda sprang at him.

"It's all right." Suzanna squeezed Amanda's hand. "I need to talk to him, Mandy. Alone."

"But—"

"Please. It's important. Go down and finish setting up, will you?"

Reluctant, Amanda stepped back. "If it's what you want." She aimed a killing look at Sloan. "Watch your step."

When they were alone, Sloan struggled for the right words. "Mrs. Dumont. Suzanna—"

"What's his name?" she asked.

"What?"

"The boy. What's his name?"

"I don't—"

"Damn it, what's his name?" She whirled away from the wall. Shock had been replaced by angry tears. "He's half brother to my children. I want to know his name."

"Kevin. Kevin O'Riley."

"How old is he?"

"Seven."

Turning back to the sea, she shut her eyes. Seven years before she had been a new bride, full of hope and dreams and blind love. "And Baxter knew? He knew that she'd had his child?"

"Yes, he knew. Megan wouldn't tell anyone at first who the father was. But after she'd called and spoken to you...but she didn't speak to you, did she?"

"No." Suzanna continued to stare straight ahead. "Baxter's mother perhaps."

"I want to apologize."

"There's no need. If it had been one of my sisters, I would have struck out with more than a few hard words.'' To warm herself she cupped her elbows with her hands. "Go on."

She was tougher than she looked, Sloan thought, but it didn't ease his conscience. "After she'd called, she fell apart. That's when she finally told me everything. How she'd met Dumont when she'd gone to New York to visit some friends. He was there on some business and he started showing her around. She'd never been to New York before, and it—and he dazzled her. She was just a kid."

"Seventeen," Suzanna murmured.

"And naive with it. Well, she got over that quick enough." The bitterness came though. "He gave her all the usual bull about getting married, about how he'd come out to Oklahoma and meet her family. Once she got home, he never contacted her. She got through to him on the phone once or twice. He made excuses and more promises. Then she found out she was pregnant."

He steadied himself, trying not to remember how angry and frightened he'd been when he'd learned his baby sister was going to have a baby of her own.

"When she told him, he changed tactics fast. He said some pretty awful things to her, and she grew up fast. Too fast."

Suzanna understood that, more than he could know. "It must have been terribly difficult for her, having the child without having the father."

"She handled herself. I have a very supportive family. Well, you'd know about that."

"Yes."

"Luckily, money wasn't a problem, either, so she could get all the care she and the baby needed. She never wanted his money, Suzanna."

"No, I understand that, too."

He nodded slowly, seeing that she did. "And when Kevin was born...well, Meg was great. It was for his sake that she tried to contact Dumont again, and eventually decided to appeal to his wife. All she wanted was for her son to have some contact with his father."

"I understand." Steadier, she turned around to look at him. "Sloan, if I had any influence with Bax I'd use it." She lifted her hands and let them fall. "But I don't, not even when it concerns the children he's chosen to acknowledge."

"I figure Kevin's better off the way things are. Suzanna—" he dragged a hand through his disordered hair "—how the hell did a woman like you end up with Dumont?"

She smiled a little. "Once I was a young, naive girl who believed in happy ever after."

He wanted to take her hand but wasn't certain she'd accept it. "I know you said you didn't want an apology, but I'd feel a hell of a lot better if you'd take it just the same."

It was she who offered her hand. "It's easy to do when it's family. I guess in an odd way, that's what we are." She pressed her free hand to their joined ones. Later, she promised herself, she would find a few minutes alone to let the grief come. And to let it go. "I want to ask you a favor. I'd like for my children to know about Kevin, and unless it would upset your sister, for them to have a chance to meet each other."

"When I take a wrong turn, I take it big. It would mean a lot to her."

"Jenny and Alex are going to be thrilled." She looked at her watch. "Speaking of which, they're probably already home from school and driving Aunt Coco crazy. I'd better go.''

He looked down the steps toward the terrace. And thought of Amanda. ''Me, too. I've got other fences to mend.''

Suzanna lifted a brow. ''Good luck.''

He had a feeling he was going to need it. By the time he'd reached the terrace, he was sure of it. Amanda was there, fastening streamers while Lilah leisurely tied balloons to the back of chairs. A long table was already covered with a frilly white cloth.

Amanda heard the scrape of boot heels on stone and turned to aim one deadly glare. Lilah didn't need another hint.

''Well.'' She flicked a balloon with a fingertip to send it dancing. ''I think I'll go see if Aunt Coco's got any of those chocolate pastries ready.'' As she walked by Sloan, she paused. Unlike Amanda's, her eyes were cool, but the meaning was clear. ''I'd hate to think I was wrong about you.'' She walked through the terrace doors and, after a brief hesitation, shut them to give her sister privacy.

Amanda didn't wait to pounce. ''You've got a nerve, or maybe you're just plain stupid, showing your face here after what you did.''

''You don't know anything about it. Suzanna and I worked it out.''

''Oh, you think so?'' Ready to joust, she slammed down a package of pretty pink-and-silver plates. ''Not by a long shot. When I think that just a few hours ago you'd nearly convinced me you were the kind of man I could care about, then I come home and find my sister running away from you looking devastated. I want to know what you did.''

"I ran with the wrong information. And I'm sorry about it."

"That's not good enough."

His own emotions were a bit too raw for reason. "Well, it's going to have to be. If you want to know more, you're just going to have to ask Suzanna."

"I'm asking you."

"And I'm telling you that what happened was between her and me. It doesn't have anything to do with you."

"That's where you're wrong." She crossed the terrace until they were toe to toe. "You mess with one Calhoun, you mess with them all. I may have to put up with you until after the wedding, since you're supposed to be best man. But when it's over, I'm going to do whatever I have to do to see to it that you go back where you came from."

Pushed to the end of his chain, he took her by the lapels. "I told you before, I finish what I start."

"You are finished, O'Riley. The Towers doesn't need you, and neither do I."

He was just about to prove her wrong when Trent opened the terrace doors. Trent took one look at his friend and future sister-in-law glaring daggers at each other and cleared his throat.

"Looks like I'm going to have to work on my timing."

"Your timing's perfect." Amanda rammed an elbow into Sloan's stomach before she pulled away. "We've got no time for men around here tonight. Why don't you take this jerk you've sicced on us and go do something manly." She shoved by Trent and stalked into the house.

"Well." Trent let out a long breath. "I don't think

I mentioned the Calhoun temperament when I asked you to take on the job."

"No, you didn't." Scowling at the empty doorway, Sloan rubbed his stomach. "Is there a dark, noisy bar anywhere in this town?"

"I guess we could find one."

"Good. Let's go get drunk."

He found the bar, and he found the bottle. Sloan slumped in the corner booth and hissed through his teeth as the whiskey stung his throat. Over the first drink, and the second, he told Trent about his altercation with Suzanna.

"Baxter Dumont is Kevin's father? You never told me."

"I gave Meg my word I wouldn't tell anybody. Even our folks don't know."

Trent was silent a moment, sipping thoughtfully at his club soda. "It's hard to figure out how such a selfish bastard managed to father three terrific kids."

"It's a puzzle, all right." Sloan signaled for another round. "Then I go off and unload both barrels on Suzanna." He broke off and swore. "Damn it, Trent, I'm never going to forget the way she looked when I cut loose on her."

"She'll handle it. From what C.C.'s told me, she's dealt with worse."

"Yeah, maybe. Maybe. But I don't care much for slapping down women. I was already feeling like something you scrape off your shoe when Amanda lit into me."

"These women stick together."

"Yeah." Scowling, Sloan drank again. "Like a dirt clod."

"Why didn't you explain things to her?"

Sloan shrugged and knocked back more whiskey. He had his own share of pride. "It wasn't any of her business."

"You just explained it to me."

"That's different."

"Okay. Do you want some pretzels to go with that?"

"No."

They sat for a moment, nursing drinks, two dynamically different men, one in battered jeans, the other in tailored slacks; one slumped comfortably, the other comfortably alert. They'd both come from money— Trent from real estate, Sloan from oil, but their backgrounds and family lives had been opposites. Trent's first experience with real family ties had come through the Calhouns, and Sloan had known them always. They had almost nothing in common, and yet in their first semester in college they had become friends and had remained so for more than ten years.

Because he was feeling sorry for himself, Sloan enjoyed the sensation of getting steadily drunk. Because he recognized the symptoms, Trent stayed meticulously sober.

Over yet another drink, Sloan eyed his friend. "When'd you start wearing basketball shoes?"

Trent glanced down at his own feet and grinned to himself. They were a symbol of sorts of the way one hot-tempered brunette had changed his life. "They're not basketball shoes, they're running shoes."

"What's the difference?" Sloan narrowed his eyes. "And you're not wearing a tie. How come you're not wearing a tie?"

"Because I'm in love."

"Yeah." With a short oath, Sloan sat back. "See what it's doing to you? It makes you nuts."

"You hate ties."

"Exactly. Damn woman's been driving me crazy since the first time I saw her."

"C.C.?"

"No, damn it. We were talking about Amanda."

"Right." Settling back in the seat, Trent smiled. "Well, some woman's always driving you crazy. I've never seen anyone with a more...admirable affection for the gentler sex."

"Gentler my ass. First she runs into me, then she knocks me on my butt. I can hardly say two words without having her claw at me." After calling for another drink, he leaned across the table. "You've known me for over ten years. Wouldn't y'say that I was a kind of even-tempered, affable sort of man?"

"Absolutely." Trent grinned. "Except when you're not."

Sloan slapped a hand on the table. "There you go." Nodding agreement, he pulled out a cigar. "So what the hell's wrong with her?"

"You tell me."

"I'll tell you." He jabbed the cigar toward Trent's face. "She's got the devil's own temper and a mule's stubbornness to go with it. If a man can keep his eyes off her legs, it's plain enough to see." He picked up his fresh whiskey and scowled into it. "She sure enough has first-class legs."

"I've noticed. They run in the family." As Sloan downed the liquor, Trent winced. "Am I going to have to carry you home?"

"More'n likely." He settled back to let the whiskey spin in his head. "What you want to go and get yourself married for, Trent? We'd both be better off hightailing it outta here.''

"Because I love her."

"Yeah." On a sigh, Sloan let out a lazy stream of smoke. "That's how they get you. They get you all tangled up so you can't think straight. Used to be I thought women were God's own pleasure, but I know better now. They've only got one reason for being here, and that's to make a man's life misery." He squinted over at Trent. "Have you seen the way her skirt jiggles when she walks—especially when she's in a hurry, like she always is."

On a chuckle, Trent lifted his glass again. "I take the Fifth on that one."

"And the sassy way her hair moves when she's yelling at you. Her eyes get all snappy. Then you grab ahold of her to shut her up, and God Almighty." He took another quick slug of whiskey, but it did nothing to put out the fire. "You ever missed your step and gone down on an electric fence?"

"Can't say I have."

"It burns," Sloan murmured. "Burns like fire and knocks you senseless for a minute. When you get your senses back, you're kind of numb and shaky."

Carefully Trent set down his drink and leaned closer to study his friend. "Sloan, is this leading where I think it's leading, or are you just drunk?"

"Not drunk enough." Annoyed, he shoved the glass aside. "I haven't had a decent night's sleep since I set eyes on her. And since I set eyes on her it's like there was never anyone else. Like there's never going to be anyone else." With his elbows propped on the table, he rubbed his hands over his face. "I'm crazy in love with her, Trent, and if I could get my hands on her right now, I'd strangle her."

"Calhoun women have a talent for that." He grinned at Sloan. "Welcome to the club."

It rained all day so I could not go down to the cliffs to see Christian. For most of the morning I played games with the children to keep them from becoming fussy about being kept indoors. They squabbled, of course, but Nanny distracted them with cookies. Even the boys enjoyed the tea party we had with Colleen's little china dishes. For me, it was one of those sweet, insular days that a mother always remembers—the way her children laugh, the funny questions they ask, the way they lay their heads on your lap when nap time approaches.

The memory of this single day is as precious to me as any I have had, or will have. They will not be my babies very long. Already Colleen is talking about balls and dresses.

It makes me wonder what my life would be like if it could be Christian who would stroll into the parlor. He would not nod absently as he opened the brandy decanter. He would not forget to ask about his children.

No, my Christian would come to me first, his hands outstretched to meet mine as I rose to kiss him. He would laugh, as I hear him laugh during our stolen hours at the cliff.

And I would be happy. Without this bittersweet pain in my heart. Without this guilt. There would be no need then for me to seek the quiet and solitude of my tower, or to sit alone watching the gray rain as I write my dreams in this book.

I would be living my dreams.

But it is all just a fancy, like one of the stories I tell the children at bedtime. A happy-ever-after story with handsome princes and beautiful maidens. My life is not a fairy tale. But perhaps, someday someone will open these pages and read my story. I hope they will have a kind and generous heart, condemn me not for my disloyalty to a husband I have never loved, but rejoice for me in my joy in those few short hours with a man I will love even after death.

Chapter Seven

Sloan's head was filled with tiny little men wielding pick axes. To quiet them, he tried rolling over. A definite mistake, he realized, as the slight movement sent a signal to the army-navy band waiting in the wings to punch up the percussions. Gingerly he pulled a pillow over his face, hoping to smother the sound or—if that didn't work—himself.

But the noise kept booming until his abused system told him it was the door, not just the hangover. Giving up, he stumbled out of bed, grateful there was no one around to hear him whimper. With the road gang working away inside his temples, he turned the air between the bedroom and the parlor door a ribald shade of blue.

When he wrenched it open, Amanda took one look, noting the bloodshot eyes, night stubble and curled lip. He was wearing the jeans, unclasped, that he'd fallen asleep in, and nothing else.

"Well," she said primly, "you look like you had a delightful time last night."

And she looked as neat and crisp as a freshly starched shirt. It was, he was sure, reason enough for homicide. "If you came up here to ruin my day, you're too late." He started to swing the door shut, but she held it open and stepped inside.

"I have something to say to you."

"You've said it." Instantly he regretted turning sharply away. As his head throbbed nastily, he vowed to hold on to what was left of his dignity. He would not crawl away, but walk.

Because he looked so pitiful, she decided to help him out. "I guess you feel pretty lousy."

"Lousy?" He narrowed his eyes to keep them from dropping out of his head. "No, I feel dandy. Just dandy. I live for hangovers."

"What you need is a cold shower, a couple of aspirin and a decent breakfast."

After making an inarticulate sound in his throat, he groped his way toward the bedroom. "Calhoun, you're on dangerous ground."

"I won't be in your way long." Determined to accomplish her mission, she followed him. "I just want to talk to you about—" She broke off when he slammed the bathroom door in her face. "Well." Blowing out a huffy breath, she set her hands on her hips.

Inside, Sloan stripped off his jeans then stepped into the shower. With one hand braced on the tile, he turned the water on full cold. His single vicious curse bounced along the walls then slammed right back into his head. Still, he was a little steadier when he stepped out again, fought with the cap on the aspirin bottle and downed three.

His hangover hadn't gone away, he thought, but at least he was now fully awake to enjoy it. Wrapping a towel around his waist, he walked back into the parlor.

He'd thought she would have gotten the message, but there she was, hunched over his drawing board with glasses perched on her nose. She'd tidied up, too, he noted, emptying ashtrays, piling cups on the room service tray, picking up discarded clothes. In fact, she had her hands full of his clothes while she studied his drawings.

"What the hell are you doing?"

She glanced up and, determined to be cheerful, smiled. "Oh, you're back." The sight of him in nothing but a damp towel had her careful to keep her eyes strictly on his face. "I was just taking a look at your work."

"I don't mean that, I mean what are you doing picking up after me? It's not part of your job to play Sally Domestic."

"I didn't see how you could work in a sty," she shot back, "so I straightened up a little while I was waiting for you."

"I like working in a sty. If I didn't, I would've picked the damn stuff up myself."

"Fine." Incensed, she hurled his clothes into the air so that they scattered over the room. "Better?"

Slowly he pulled off the T-shirt that had landed on his head. "Calhoun, do you know what's more dangerous than a man with a hangover?"

"No."

"Nothing." He took one measured step toward her when there was another knock at the door.

"That's your breakfast." Amanda's voice was clipped as she strode toward the door. "I had them put a rush on it."

Defeated, Sloan sank onto the couch and put his head in his hands so that he could catch it easily when it fell off. "I don't want any damn breakfast."

"Well, you'll eat it and stop feeling sorry for yourself." She signed the check, then took the tray herself to place it on the table in front of him. "Whole wheat toast, black coffee and a Virgin Mary, heavy on the hot sauce. It'll take the edge off."

"An electric planer couldn't take the edge off." But he reached for the coffee.

Satisfied that she had made a good start, Amanda took off her glasses and slipped them into her pocket. He really did look pathetic, she thought. His wet hair was dripping down his face. She had a strong urge to kneel down beside him and stroke those damp curls back. But he'd probably have snapped her hand off at the wrist, and she had an equally strong urge to survive.

"Trent mentioned that you did quite a bit of drinking last night."

After trying the spiced-up tomato juice, he eyed her narrowly. "So you came by to see the morning-after in person."

"Not exactly." Her fingers toyed with her name tag, then the top button on her jacket. "I thought since it was my fault you got into this condition, I should—"

"Hold it. If I get drunk, it's because my hand reaches for the bottle."

"Yes, but—"

"I don't want your sympathy, Calhoun, or your guilt any more than I want your maid service."

"Fine." Pride and temper went to war. Pride won. "I merely came by this morning to apologize."

He bit off another piece of toast. It did soothing things to the rocky sea of his belly. "What for?"

"For what I said, and the way I acted yesterday." Unable to stand still, she walked over to the window and pulled the shades open, ignoring Sloan's quick hiss of pain. "Although I still think I was perfectly justified. After all, I only knew that you'd said something to hurt Suzanna badly." But there was regret in her eyes when she turned back. "When she told me about your sister—about Bax—I realized how you must have been feeling. Damn it, Sloan, you could have told me yourself."

"Maybe. Maybe you could have trusted me."

She took her glasses out again, playing with the earpieces to keep her hands busy. "It wasn't really a matter of trust, but of automatic reflex. You don't know what Suzanna went through, how deeply she was hurt. Or if you do, because of your own sister, then you should understand why I couldn't bear to see her look like that again." She shoved the glasses away. When she looked at him, her eyes were damp. "And it was worse, because I have feelings for you."

If there was one thing he had no defense against, it was tears. Wanting to ward them off as much as he wanted to make peace, he rose to take her hands. "I made my share of mistakes yesterday." Smiling, he rubbed her knuckles over his cheek. It felt good— damn good. "I guess it's as hard for you to apologize as it is for me."

"If you mean it's like swallowing a lump of coal, then you're right."

"Why don't we call it even, all around?" But when he lowered his head to kiss her, she stepped back.

"I really need to think straight for a while."

He caught her hand again. "I really need to make love with you."

Her heart took a quick leap into her throat. For someone who moved so slowly, how did he get from one point to the next so fast? "I'm, ah, on duty. I'm already over my break, and Stenerson—"

"Why don't I give him a call?" Still smiling, he began to kiss her fingers. The hangover was down to a dull ache, not nearly as noticeable as another, more pleasant one in the pit of his stomach. "Tell him I need the assistant manager for a couple hours."

"I think—"

"There you go again," he murmured, brushing his lips lightly over hers.

"No, really, I have to..." Her mind clouded as he trailed those lips down her throat. "I really have to get back to my desk. And I—" She took a big, shuddering gasp of air. "I need to be sure." Scrambling for survival, she pulled away. "I have to know what I'm doing."

Sloan pressed a hand to the familiar burn that spread inside his gut. He had a feeling he was just going to have to live with it for a while longer. "Tell you what, Calhoun. You think about it, and think hard, until after the wedding. Like we said before." Before she could relax, he had her chin cupped firmly in his hand. "And after the wedding, if you don't come to me, you'd better run fast."

The line appeared between her brows. "That sounds like an ultimatum."

"No, that's a fact. If I were you, I'd get out that door now, while I still had the chance."

All dignity, she marched to it before turning back with a smile that should have tipped him off. "Enjoy your breakfast," she told him, then slammed the door with a vengeance. She could almost see him holding his battered head.

"I didn't think I'd be nervous." C.C. stared at the wedding dress of snowy silk and lace that hung on the back of her closet door. "Maybe it'd be better if I just wore regular clothes."

"Don't be ridiculous. And stop fidgeting." Amanda bent close to her sister to add a bit more blusher to her cheeks. "You're supposed to be nervous."

"Why?" Annoyed with herself, C.C. pressed a hand to her fluttery stomach. "I love Trent and want to get married. Why should I be nervous now that it's going to happen?" She looked back at the dress and swallowed. "Less than an hour from now."

Amanda grinned. "Maybe I should call Aunt Coco and have her give you a booster-shot course on the birds and the bees."

"Very funny." But the idea did amuse her enough to make her smile. "When's Suzanna coming back?"

"I told you, as soon as she has the kids dressed. Jenny might love the idea of being flower girl, but Alex is a most reluctant ring bearer. He'd rather be carrying a machine gun down the aisle than a satin pillow. And before you ask, again, Lilah is supposed to be downstairs making sure all the last-minute details go off properly. Though why we think we can trust her is beyond me.''

"She'll be fine. She always handles things when it's important.'' C.C. laid a hand on Amanda's. "And it is important, Mandy.''

"I know, honey. It's the most important day of your life.'' Misty-eyed, she laid her cheek against C.C.'s. "Oh, I feel as though I should say something profound, but I can only say be happy.''

"I will be, and it's not as if I'll be really going away. We'll be living here most of the time, except when...when we're in Boston.'' Her throat filled up.

"Don't start,'' Amanda warned. "I mean it. After all the work I put in making you beautiful, you're not going out in the garden with red eyes and a runny nose.'' Blowing her own, she stepped back. "Now, let me help you get dressed.''

When Suzanna came in a short time later, a child's hand in each of hers, she had to struggle with her own tears. "Oh, C.C., you look wonderful.''

"Are you sure?'' Fretting, she plucked at the lace at her throat. The dress was a slim column, elegantly simple with only that whisper of lace at the neck, and another whisper at the hem to adorn it. "Maybe I should have gone for something less formal.''

"No, it's perfect.'' Suzanna bent down to her son, her own dress rustling with the movement. "Alex, stand still for five minutes, please.''

He tried out the sneer he'd been practicing in the mirror. "I hate cummerbunds.''

"I know, but if you don't want me to strap it around your mouth, you'll stand still.'' Tweeking his nose, she straightened. "I have something for you.''

She offered C.C. a small box. Inside was a single teardrop sapphire on a braided gold chain.

"Mama's necklace," C.C. whispered.

"Aunt Coco gave it to me when I—on my wedding day." She took it out to fasten around her sister's neck. "I want you to have it and wear it on yours."

C.C. lifted a hand to it, closing her fingers around the stone. "I'm not nervous anymore."

"Then that's my cue to panic." Afraid to say more, Amanda gave her a quick kiss. "I'll run downstairs and make sure everything's on schedule."

"Mandy—"

Amanda smiled over her shoulder. "Yes, I'll send Lilah up." She went out, hurrying downstairs while she ticked off duties in her mind. Taking a moment, she stopped by the hall mirror to adjust the spray of baby's breath over her ear.

"You look great." She glanced over and saw Sloan. "Just great."

"Thanks." They stood awkwardly a moment, a man in a tuxedo and a woman in a tea-length gown the color of ripe peaches. "I, uh, where's Trent?"

"He needed a couple of minutes to himself. His father came by with some advice." Relaxing slowly, Sloan grinned. "When a man's been married as many times as Mr. S.J., he comes up with some interesting viewpoints." He had to laugh at the expression on Amanda's face. "Don't worry, I nudged him along outside with a glass of champagne and Coco. Seems like they're old friends."

"I think she met him a long time ago." When Sloan took a step toward her, she began to talk rapidly. "You look terrific. I didn't expect you to look good in a tuxedo." Before he'd finished laughing, she was rambling on. "What I mean is I didn't expect it to suit you. I mean—"

"You're cute when you're flustered."

She ended up smiling at him. As far as she could recall, he was the only person who had ever accused her of being cute. "I really have to go." Before she gave in to the urge to fuss with his tie or something equally mushy. "We'll be starting in a few minutes. Guests need to be seen to."

"Most everybody's already in the garden."

"The photographer."

"All set up."

"The champagne."

"On ice." He took the last step toward her and tilted up her chin with a fingertip. "Weddings make you nervous, Calhoun?"

"This one does."

"Going to save a dance for me?"

"Of course."

He toyed with the flowers in her hair. "And later?"

"I…"

"C.C.'s ready!" Alex bellowed from the top of the stairs. "Can we get this dumb thing over with."

With a laugh, Sloan kissed her fingers. "Don't worry, I'll make sure the groom's in place."

"All right, and—damn!" She swore, then snatched up the ringing phone. "Hello? Oh, William, I really can't talk. We're about to start the wedding…. Tomorrow?" She lifted a distracted hand to her hair. "No, of course. Umm…yes, that's fine. Late afternoon would be best. Three o'clock? I'll see you then." Still off balance, she turned to find Sloan watching her with very cool, measuring green eyes.

"You take big chances, Calhoun."

"That wasn't what it sounded like." She caught herself trying to explain and frowned. "What do you mean, 'chances'?"

"That's something we'd better discuss later. We've got a wedding to get to."

"You're absolutely right." They strode off in opposite directions.

Moments later, the Calhoun women took their turns walking down the garden path. First Suzanna, then Lilah, then Amanda, followed by a beaming Jenny and a thoroughly embarrassed Alex. They took their places with Amanda doing her best not to glance in Sloan's direction. Then she forgot everything as she watched C.C. come forward, a wispy veil over her hair. Beside her, prepared to give her youngest niece away, Coco held her arm and wept.

She watched her sister marry under an arbor of delicately fragrant wisteria. Through a mist of tears she looked on as the man who was now her brother-in-law slipped the circle of emeralds onto C.C.'s finger. The look that passed between them spoke more eloquently of promises than any of the vows exchanged. With her hands clasped with her sisters', she saw C.C.'s face lift to Trent's as they shared their first kiss as husband and wife.

"Is it finally over?" Alex wanted to know.

"No," Amanda heard herself say as her gaze drifted to Sloan's. "It's just beginning."

"Beautiful wedding." After Amanda was thoroughly kissed by Trent's father, she managed to nod in agreement. "Trent tells me you put most of it together."

"I'm good with details," she said, and offered him a plate for the buffet.

"So I hear." Trim, tanned and expansive, St. James smiled at her. "I've also heard that all of the Calhoun sisters are lovely. I can now corroborate that myself."

He was quite the elegant old flirt, Amanda mused but smiled back as he arranged food on his plate. "We're delighted to welcome you to the family."

"It's odd the way things have worked out," he said. "A year ago I looked up from my boat in the bay and saw this house. I simply had to have it. Now, not only is part of it a portion of my business, but it's a part of my family." He glanced over to see Trent and C.C. dancing on the terrace. "She's made him happy," he said quietly. "I never quite had the knack for that myself." With a vague movement of his shoulders, he brushed the thought aside. "Would you care to dance?"

"I'd love to."

They'd hardly taken three steps on the dance floor, when Sloan swung Coco around and smoothly switched partners.

"You might have asked," Amanda muttered as his arms slid around her.

"I did, before. Anyway, she'll flirt with him the way he wants instead of treating him like a distant relation."

"He is a distant relation." But she glanced over and saw that Coco already had St. James laughing. "Everything's going well, I think."

"Smooth as glass." Just as smoothly, he noted, as she fit into his arms. "You did a good job."

"Thanks, but I hope it's the last wedding I have to plan for quite a while."

"Don't you think about getting married yourself?"

She missed a step and nearly stumbled over his feet. "No—that is, yes, but not really."

"That's a definitive answer."

"What I mean is it's not in my short-range plans." No matter what longings had tugged at her when her gaze had locked with Sloan's under the arbor. "I'm going to be busy over the next few years with the retreat. I've always wanted to manage a first-class hotel, to make policy instead of just carrying it out. It's what I've been working for, and now that Trent's giving me the chance, I can't afford to divide my loyalties."

"An interesting way of seeing it. With me it's always been a matter of getting tied down with one person in one place, then finding out I made a mistake."

"There's that, too." Relieved that they weren't arguing, she smiled. "I never asked, but I guess you do a lot of traveling."

"Here and there. A drawing board's portable. You might like to do some traveling yourself, check out the hotel competition. Why don't we go somewhere quiet and talk about it?"

"Sorry, I'm on call. And if you want to be helpful, you'll play best man and go get a few more bottles of champagne from the kitchen." She tucked her arm through his. "I've got to run up and get the streamers anyway."

"Streamers?"

"To decorate the car. They're up in my room."

"Tell you what," Sloan began when they reached

the kitchen. "Why don't I come up to your room and help you get the streamers?"

"Because I want to decorate the car before they get back from their honeymoon." With a laugh, she dashed away. Amanda was halfway down the hall on the second floor when the creak of a board overhead had her stopping. Tuned to the moans and groans of the old house, she frowned. Footsteps, she realized. Definitely footsteps. Wondering if one of the wedding guests had decided to take an impromptu tour, she started back toward the stairway. On the third-floor landing, she spotted Fred, curled up and sleeping.

"Fine watchdog," she muttered, bending down to shake him. He only rolled over with a groggy snore. "Fred?" Alarmed, she shook him again, but instead of bouncing up, ready to play, he lay still. When she picked him up, his head lolled onto her hand. Even as she gathered him up, someone shoved her from behind and sent her headfirst into the wall.

Stunned and sprawled on the dog, she struggled up to her knees. Someone was running down the stairs. With the wrath of the Calhouns filling her, she jumped up, Fred tucked under her arm like a furry football, and gave chase. She turned sharply on the second-floor landing, ears straining. On an oath she headed down to the main floor, heels clattering on wood. Sloan caught her as she stumbled on the last step.

"Whoa. What's the hurry?" Grinning, he scanned her tumbled hair and the spray of baby's breath now hanging to her shoulder. "What did you do, Calhoun, trip over the dog?"

"Did you see him?" she demanded, and broke out of Sloan's hold to rush to the door.

"See who?"

"There was somebody upstairs." Her heart was pumping fast and hard. She hadn't noticed it before. Or the fact that her legs were shaky. "Someone was sneaking around on the third floor. I don't know what they did to Fred."

"Hold on." Gently now, he guided her back to the stairs and eased her down. "Let's have a look." He took the dog, then pulling up an eyelid, swore. When he looked back at Amanda, there was a flat grimness in his eyes she'd never seen before. "Somebody drugged him."

"Drugged him?" Amanda gathered Fred back to her breast. "Who would drug a poor little dog?"

"Someone who didn't want him to bark, I imagine. Tell me what happened."

"I heard someone on the third floor and went up to see. I found Fred, just lying there." She nuzzled the puppy. "When I started to pick him up, someone pushed me into the wall."

"Are you hurt?" His hands were instantly on her face.

"No." She let out a disgusted breath. "If it hadn't stunned me for a minute, I would have caught him."

Eyes narrowed, Sloan sat back on his heels. "Didn't it occur to you to call for help?"

"No." The baby's breath was tickling her shoulder, so she pulled it away.

"Idiot."

"Look, O'Riley, nobody's going to poke around in my house, and hurt my dog and get away with it. If he hadn't had a start on me, I'd have caught him."

"And then what?" he demanded. "God Almighty,

Amanda, don't you realize he would have given you more than a push."

Actually she hadn't thought of it. But that didn't change the bottom line. "I can take care of myself. It's bad enough when people come to the door, or sneak around the grounds, but when they start breaking into the house, they're going to answer for it." She gave a nod of satisfaction as she rose. "I scared him good, anyway. The way he was running, he's halfway to the village by now. I don't think he'll be coming back. What about Fred?"

"I'll take care of him." He took the sleeping puppy from her. "He just needs to sleep it off. And you need to call the police."

"After the wedding." She shook her head before he could object. "I'm not spoiling this for C.C. and Trent just because some jerk decided to do some treasure hunting. What I will do is check the third floor and see if anything's missing. Then I'm going to go back out and make sure everything runs smoothly until it's time to throw rice at the bride and groom. After that, I'll call the police."

"Got it all figured out, nice and tidy, as usual." The hot edge of his temper seeped into his voice. "Things don't always work that way."

"I'll make it work."

"Sure you will. Can't have something like attempted robbery and a little assault mess up all your short-term plans. Just like you can't have someone like me messing up your long-term ones."

"I don't see what you're so upset about."

"You wouldn't," he said tightly. "You hear somebody in the house where they shouldn't be, get hit in the head, but you don't even think about calling for me. You don't think about asking somebody for help, not even when that somebody's in love with you."

The tightness in her chest returned, making her voice clipped. "I was just doing what I had to do."

"Yeah," he agreed with a slow nod. "You go ahead and do what you have to do now. I'll get out of your way."

Chapter Eight

And he'd stay out of her way, Sloan promised himself. The woman had fuddled his brain long enough.

He stood out on the terrace off his bedroom, trying to enjoy the balmy May evening. He'd left The Towers as soon as it had been possible. Oh, he'd done his duty, he thought. Amanda wasn't the only one who could do what was expected of her. With the help of Suzanna and the children, he'd decorated the newlyweds' car. A smile plastered on his face, he'd tossed the rice. He'd even given Coco his handkerchief when her own proved inadequate for her happy tears. He'd waited with a worried Lilah until Fred had given his first groggy bark.

Then he'd gotten the hell out of there.

She didn't need him. The fact that he hadn't realized until now just how much he needed her to need him didn't make it any easier. Here he was, waiting to sweep her off her feet, and she was chasing after thieves or making dates with guys named William.

Well, he was through making a fool of himself over her.

She had a job to do, and so did he. She had a life to live, and so did he. It was time he put things back in perspective. A man had to be crazy to think about saddling himself with an ornery, my-way-or-nothing female. A sane man wanted a nice, calm woman who'd give him some peace after a long day, not one who riled him up every time he took a breath.

So, he'd put Amanda Calhoun out of his mind and be a happier man for it.

"Sloan."

With one hand still braced on the railing, he turned. She was in the doorway, her fingers linked tight together. She'd changed the silk dress for a crisp cotton blouse and slacks. Very streamlined, very simple and certainly not sexy enough to make his heart start jumping as it was now.

"I knocked," she began, then with an uneasy movement of her shoulders, stepped onto the terrace. "I was afraid you wouldn't let me in, so I got a pass key."

"Isn't that against the rules?"

"Yes. I'm sorry, but I couldn't talk to you at home. I didn't even think I wanted to. Then after the police came and went, and everything was as close to normal as it gets, I couldn't settle down." She let out a long breath. Obviously he wasn't going to say anything to make it easier. He was just going to stand there, his white dress shirt unbuttoned and pulled out of the tuxedo pants, his feet bare and his eyes watchful. "I guess I'm not comfortable with unfinished business."

"All right." After lighting a cigar, he leaned back on the railing. "Finish it."

"It isn't as simple as that." A wayward breeze fluttered her hair. She shook it back impatiently. "I was upset and angry before—about there being someone in the house. My house. I know you were concerned and I was very abrupt with you. And after I'd calmed down some I realized you were hurt that I hadn't asked you to help."

He blew out smoke. "I'll get over it."

"It's just that—" She broke off to pace the narrow width of the balcony. No, he wasn't going to make it easier. "I'm used to handling things myself. I've always been the one who's been able to find the logical solution, or the straightest route. It's part of my make-up. When something needs to be done, I do it. I have to, I guess. It's not as though I don't ever want help. It's just...it's just that I'm more used to being asked for it, than asking for it myself."

"One of the things I admire about you, Amanda, is the way you get things done." His eyes stayed on hers as he took a long, contemplative drag. "Why don't you tell me what you're going to do about me?"

"I don't know what to do." When her voice rose, she struggled to calm it and started moving again. "I don't like that. I always know what to do if I reason it out long enough. But no matter how much I think it all through, I can't find an answer."

"Maybe that's because two and two don't always make four."

"But they should," she insisted. "They always have for me. All I know is that you make me feel... different than I've ever felt before. It scares me." When she whirled back, her eyes were wide and dark with anger. "I know it's easy for you, but not for me."

"Easy for me?" he repeated. "You think this is easy for me?" In two furious motions, he tossed the cigar onto the terrace and ground it out. "I've been on slow burn since the minute I laid eyes on you. That isn't easy on a man, Amanda, believe me."

Because she found it hard to breathe, her voice came out in a whisper. "No one's ever wanted me the way you do. That frightens me." She pressed her lips together. "I've never wanted anyone the way I want you. That terrifies me."

He reached out to snag her hand by the wrist. "Don't expect to say that to me, or look at me the way you look right now, then ask me to let you go."

While panic and excitement warred inside her, she shook her head. "That's not what I'm asking."

"Then spell it out."

"Damn it, Sloan, I don't want you to be reasonable. I don't want to think. I want you to make me stop thinking, right now." On a moan, she threw her arms around him, pressed her lips to his and took exactly what she wanted.

There was fear. She was afraid she was taking a giant step off the edge of a very steep cliff.

There was exhilaration. She was taking that step with her eyes wide open.

And he was with her, all the way. His body was free-falling with hers, caught in the crosswinds, soaring on the current.

"Sloan—"

"Don't say a word." His arms locked tight around her as he pressed his mouth to her throat. The pulse hammering there matched exactly the rhythm of his own. That was what he wanted. That unity. He realized he'd never found it with another woman. "Not a word. Just come inside."

He led her from the balcony to the bedroom, leaving the door open to let in the sunset and the scent of water and flowers. He touched her hair first, watching his own fingers tangle and stroke. Then softly, a whispering touch, his lips on hers. No, he didn't want words from her, because he wasn't certain he could ever find the right ones to tell her what was in his heart. But he could show her.

Unsteady, she braced her hands on his chest. She didn't want to be weak now, but strong. Yet as those lips roamed over her face, she trembled.

Very slowly, barely touching her, he unbuttoned her blouse and slid it from her shoulders. Beneath was a white cotton chemise that made him smile. He should have known that beneath her practical clothes his Amanda would have more practicality. Watching her, he unhooked her slacks so that they slipped to the floor. When she reached out, he took her hands.

"No, just let me touch you. Let me see what it does to you."

Helpless, she closed her eyes as his fingers skimmed, lightly tracing the curve of her breasts. As if she were fashioned of the most delicate glass, he swept those fingertips over her. Elegantly erotic, the fragile caress had the blood rushing under skin, heating it, sensitizing it until she thought she might die from sheer pleasure.

Her head fell back, a shuddering moan escaped as he continued those lazy explorations with patient, gentle hands. He saw the dark delight flicker over her face, felt it shivering through her body. As excitement rioted through him, he circled his thumbs in a whispering touch over the nipples that strained against the cotton. Then his tongue replaced his hands and she gripped frantically at his shoulders for balance.

"Please...I can't..."

Now she was falling fast and hard, but he was there to catch her. When her knees gave way, he lifted her, cradling her in his arms, covering her mouth with his before laying her on the bed.

"Nobody," she murmured against his lips. "Nobody's ever made love to me like this."

"I'm just getting started."

He was true to his word. With a leisurely pace he took her places she had never been, had her lingering there before gently urging her on. With each touch he opened doors always firmly locked, then left them wide so that light and wind tunneled through. Each time she arched against him, shuddering, he soothed her until she floated down again.

Her taste was enough. Honey here, whiskey there, then as delicate as spun sugar. He filled himself with it, nibbling her skin. Down her arms, her throat, those long, lovely legs. Whenever he was tempted to hurry, to take his own release, he found himself greedy for one more taste.

He skimmed his hands up her ribs, pushing her shirt up, then over her head. At last, at long last, he sampled the smooth skin of her breast. Her hands were in his hair, pressing him closer as colors seemed to shatter behind her eyes.

Slow burn. Is that what he'd said? she wondered frantically as his clever mouth inched lower, still lower. She understood now, now when her body was on fire from the inside, heating degree by degree. The sparks were shooting through her, little pinpoints of unspeakable pleasure as ancient as the first stars that winked to life in the sky beyond the window.

He was tugging the last barrier aside, and she could do nothing but writhe under his hands, the breath sobbing in her lungs.

When he flicked his tongue over her, she arched against him, her hands grabbing at the bedspread in taut fists. Sensations hammered her, too fast, too sharp. She struggled to separate them, but they were one wild maze without beginning or end.

Did she know she was calling out his name over and over? he wondered. Did she know that her body was moving in that slow, sinuous rhythm, as if he were already inside her? He slid up her gradually, savoring each instant, absorbing each ache, each need, each longing. Her eyes fluttered open, dark and dazed.

She could only see his face, so close to hers—his eyes so intense. Gracefully her arms lifted to brush his shirt aside, to touch as thoroughly as she had been touched. She rose to him, to press her lips to his chest, to glide them up to his throat.

The light grew dimmer, softer. The breeze quieted. In an easy dance she moved over him, undressing him, needing to show him what he had done to her heart as well as her body. Her lips curved against his flesh as she felt him tremble as she had trembled. The glory flowed through her like water, clear and bright, so that when her arms came around him, when her mouth opened willingly beneath his, she let it pour into the kiss.

With a murmuring sigh, he slid into her. Her breath caught, then released gently. They moved together, the pace deliberately slow, deliciously easy. The sweetness brought tears to her eyes that he kissed away.

Gradually sweetness became heat, and heat a fresh burning. As passion misted her vision, she felt his fingers link with hers, holding tight as she rode to the top of the crest. His name tumbled from her lips as he swept to the peak with her.

He lay with his lips pressed against her throat, still haunted by the taste of her. Beneath him she was quiet, her breathing deep and steady. He wondered if she slept, and started to ease his weight aside. But her arms slid up and around him again.

"Don't." Her voice was a husky whisper that sent his blood singing again. "I don't want it to end yet."

To satisfy them both, he rolled, reversing positions. Her hair brushed his cheek, a small thing that gave him tremendous happiness. "How's that?"

"Nice." She nuzzled her cheek against his. "It was all really, really nice."

"Is that the best you can do?"

"Umm. For right now. I don't think I've ever been this relaxed in my life."

"Good." Taking her hair in his hand, he pulled her head back to study her face. "It's getting too dark to see." Reaching over, he switched on the light.

Amanda brought up a hand to shield her eyes. "Why'd you do that?"

"Because I want to see you when we make love again."

"Again?" Chuckling, she dropped her head onto his shoulder. "You've got to be kidding."

"No, ma'am. I figure I might just get my fill of you by sunup."

Feeling deliciously lazy, she snuggled against him. "I can't stay the night."

"Wanna bet?"

"No, really." She arched like a cat when he stroked her back. "I wish I could, but I've got a whole list of things to do in the morning. Oh…" She shivered under his touch. "You've got such wonderful hands. Wonderful," she murmured as she lost herself in a long, dreamy kiss.

"Stay."

Her body shuddered as she felt him harden inside her. "Maybe for just a little while longer."

Drifting awake, she shifted. On a contented sigh, she reached out. Reluctantly she opened her eyes. Bright sunlight flooded the room, and she was alone in bed. Pushing her tumbled hair back, she sat up.

He'd gotten his way, she thought with a half smile. She had stayed the night, and he hadn't gotten enough of her—or she of him—until sunup.

It had been, she admitted freely, the most magnificent night of her life.

And where the hell was Sloan?

On cue, he walked in, pushing a room service cart. "Morning."

"Good morning." She smiled, though she felt awkward with him dressed and her still naked and in bed.

"I ordered us some breakfast." Sensing her dilemma, he plucked up a white terry-cloth robe from a chair. "Compliments of the BayWatch," he said as he handed it to her, then leaned over a bit farther to give her a leisurely kiss. "Why don't we eat on the terrace?"

"That'd be nice. Give me a minute."

When she joined him outside, there were plates set on the pale azure cloth, and a single rose in a clear vase. It touched her deeply that he would take as much care with the morning as he had with the night.

"You think of everything."

"Just of you." He grinned as he sat across from her. "We can look at this like a first date, since I never could convince you to have a meal with me before."

"No." Her gaze lowered as she poured coffee for both of them. "I guess you couldn't." Picking up her napkin, she began to pleat it with her fingers. They were having breakfast, she thought, after a long night of feasting. And they'd never even ridden in the same car, shared a pizza, talked on the phone.

It was idiotic, she told herself. It was scary.

"Sloan, I realize this might sound stupid at this stage, but I...I don't make a habit of spending the night with men in hotel rooms. I'm not usually intimate with someone I've known such a short time."

"You don't have to tell me that." He closed a hand over hers until she looked at him. "It's been a fast trip for both of us. Maybe it's because what happened between us is special. I'm in love with you, Amanda. No, don't pull away." He tightened his grip. "Normally I'm a patient man, but I have to work hard on it with you. I'm going to do my best to give you time."

"If I said I was in love with you—" she let out a cleansing breath "—what would happen next?"

In his eyes, something flickered and sent her already unsteady pulse jumping. "Sometimes you can't work out the answers first. You've got to be willing to gamble.''

"I've never been much of a gambler." She bit her lip, determined to get over that last skip of fear. "I wouldn't have come here last night if I hadn't been in love with you."

He lifted her hand to press his lips to the palm. Over it, he smiled at her. "I know."

The laugh was as much from relief as amusement. "You knew, but you just had to hear me say it."

"That's right." His eyes were suddenly very sober. "I had to hear you say it. Women aren't the only ones who need words, Amanda."

No, she thought, they weren't. "I love you, but I'm still a little scared of it. I'd like to take it slow, one step at a time."

"Fair enough. We can start by having our first date before the eggs get cold."

At ease, she buttered a piece of toast and split it with him. "You know, as long as I've worked here, I've never sat on one of those terraces and looked out at the bay."

"Never snuck into an empty room and played guest?" He laughed. "No, you wouldn't. You wouldn't even think about it. So, how does it feel, seeing it from the other side of the desk?"

"Well, the bed's comfortable, the hotel robes are roomy and the view's wonderful." There was laughter in her eyes, contented, easy laughter. "However, at The Towers Retreat, we'll offer all that and more. Private spas, romantic fireplaces, complimentary champagne with each reservation—I have to run that by Trent—*cordon bleu* meals prepared by Coco, world-renowned chef, all in a turn-of-the-century setting, complete with ghosts and a legendary hidden treasure." She rested her chin on her hand. "Unless we manage to get our hands on the emeralds before we open."

"Do you really believe they still exist?"

"Yes. Oh, not with any of the mystic business Aunt Coco or Lilah subscribe to. It's simple logic. They did exist. If anyone in the family had sold them, it would have come out. Therefore, they still exist. A quarter of a million in jewels doesn't just disappear."

His brow lifted. "They're that valuable?"

"Oh, probably more so by now—that's not even counting the aesthetic or intrigue value."

It changed the complexion of things for him entirely. "So what we've got is five women and two kids, who've been living alone in a house loaded with antiques, plus a fortune in jewels. And no security system."

She frowned a little. "It's not exactly loaded with antiques since we've had to sell off a lot over the years. And there's never been a problem. It's not as though any of us are helpless."

"I know. Calhoun women can take care of themselves. I'm beginning to think that besides being tough, they're stupid."

"Now, wait a minute—"

"No, you wait." To emphasize the point, he poked his fork at her. "First thing in the morning, we're going to see about an alarm system."

She'd already decided the same thing herself after yesterday's incident. But that didn't mean he could tell her to. "You're not going to start taking over my life."

"So, to be stubborn, you'll ignore the obvious, because I brought it up, and take a chance that someone might break in and hurt one of the kids.''

"Don't put words in my mouth," she tossed back. "I've been checking into alarms for the past two weeks."

"Why didn't you just say so?"

"Because you were too busy handing out orders." She might have said more, but the horn on one of the tourist boats distracted her. "What time is it?"

"About one."

"One?" Her eyes went huge. "In the afternoon? That's not possible, we just got up."

"It's real possible when you don't get to sleep until morning."

"I've got a million things to do." She was already pushing back from the table. "All that mess from the wedding has to be cleaned up. Trent's father was coming for brunch two hours ago, and William's coming by at three."

"Hold it." That brought him out of his chair. "You're not still going to see him?"

"Mr. St. James? He'll be gone by now. I can't believe I was so rude."

"William," he corrected, snagging her arm. "The attractive, intelligent man you had dinner with the other night."

"William? Well, of course I'm going to see him."

"No." He tugged her closer. "You're not."

The dangerous light in his eyes set off one in her own. "I just told you you weren't going to take over my life."

"I don't give a damn what you told me. There's no way in hell I'm going to let you waltz out of my bed and on to a date with another man."

With a little huff, she pulled her arm free. "You don't *let* me do anything. Get that straight. Next, it isn't a date. William Livingston is an antique dealer and I promised him I would show him through The Towers. He gets a busman's holiday, and I get a free assessment. Now move." She shoved past and headed for the shower. Muttering all the way, she slipped off the robe. She'd just finished adjusting the water temperature, stepping in and shutting the curtain when it was yanked open again.

"Damn it, Sloan!" She slicked the wet hair out of her eyes and glared.

"He's an antique dealer?"

"That's what I said."

"And he wants to look at furniture?"

"Exactly."

He hooked his thumbs in his belt loops. "I'm going with you."

"Fine." With a careless shrug, she picked up the soap and began to lather her shoulders. "Be a possessive bubblehead."

"Okay."

Telling herself she wasn't amused, she glanced over to see him pulling off his shirt. "What are you doing?"

Grinning, he tossed it aside. "I'll give you three guesses. A sharp lady like you should get it in one."

She bit back a chuckle as he unsnapped his jeans. "I don't have time for water games right now."

"Oh, I think we can sneak it in just under the wire."

"Maybe." She squeezed the wet soap between her hands and shot it at him, nodding approval when he caught it, chest high. "If you wash my back first."

* * *

Before stepping from his car, Livingston checked his microrecorder and the tiny camera in his pocket. He was very fond of technology and felt that the sophisticated equipment lent an air of elegance to the job. Since the moment he'd read about the Calhoun emeralds, he'd been obsessed by them, more than any other jewels he'd stolen in his long career. He was considered by Interpol, and indeed by himself, to be one of the most clever and elusive thieves on two continents.

The emeralds presented a challenge he couldn't resist. They weren't tucked in a vault or displayed in a museum. They weren't adoring some rich matron's neck. They were lying in wait somewhere in the odd old house, daring someone to find them. He intended to be that someone.

Though he wasn't opposed to employing violence in his work, he used it sparingly. He was sorry he'd had to use it on Amanda the day before, but he was much sorrier that she'd interrupted his search.

His own fault, he chided himself as he walked to the front door of The Towers. He'd been impatient and had decided that the wedding would be the perfect diversion, giving him the time and the privacy he required to case the interior of the house. Today, however, he would wander those rooms as a guest.

He might have been a thief from the South Side of Chicago, but when he put on a two-thousand-dollar suit, a trace of a British accent and polished manners, even the most discriminating invited him into their parlors.

He knocked and waited. The barking of the dog answered first, and Livingston's eyes hardened. He detested dogs, and the little bugger inside had nearly nipped him before he'd managed to give it a dose of phenobarbital.

When Coco answered the door, Livingston's eyes were clear and his charming smile already in place.

"Mr. Livingston, how nice to see you again." Coco started to offer a hand, then found it more judicious to grasp Fred's collar before the dog could leap at the man's calf. "Fred, stop that now. Mind your manners." Holding the snarling dog at bay, Coco offered a weak smile. "He really is a very gentle animal. He never acts like this, but he had an incident yesterday and isn't himself." After gathering Fred into her arms, she called for Lilah. "Let's go into the parlor, shall we?"

"I hope I'm not intruding on your Sunday, Mrs. McPike. I couldn't resist persuading Amanda to show me through your fascinating house."

"We're delighted to have you." Though she was becoming more disconcerted by the moment as Fred continued to snarl and snap. "Amanda's not here yet, though I can't think what's keeping her. She's always so prompt."

Lilah gave a half laugh as she came down the steps. "I can think exactly what's keeping her." There was no humor in her eyes as she studied their guest. "Hello again, Mr. Livingston."

"Miss Calhoun." He didn't care for the way she looked at him, as though she could see straight through the slick outer trappings to the ruthlessness inside.

"Fred's a bit high-strung today." With a quick pleading look, Coco passed the growling pup to Lilah. "Why don't you take him in the kitchen?" Her hands fluttered before she patted her hair. "Perhaps some herbal tea would soothe him."

"I'll take care of him." Lilah started down the hall, murmuring to the puppy, "I don't like him, either, Fred. Why do you suppose that is?"

"Well then." Relieved, Coco smiled again. "How about some sherry? You can enjoy it while I show you a particularly nice japanned cabinet. It's Charles II, I believe."

"I'd be delighted." He was also delighted to note that she was wearing an excellent set of pearls with matching earrings.

When Amanda arrived twenty minutes later, with Sloan stubbornly at her side, she found her aunt telling Livingston the family history while they admired an eighteenth-century credenza.

"William, I'm so sorry I'm late."

"Don't be." Livingston took one look at Sloan and concluded his entryway to The Towers wouldn't be Amanda after all. "Your aunt has been the most charming and informative of hostesses."

"Aunt Coco knows more about the furnishings than any of us," she told him. "This is Sloan O'Riley. Sloan is the architect who's designing the renovations."

"Mr. O'Riley." The handshake was brief. Sloan had already taken a dislike to the three-piece-suited, sherry-sipping antique dealer. "The work here must present quite a challenge."

"Oh, I'm getting by."

"I was just telling William how slow and tedious the job of sifting through all those old papers is. Not at all the exciting treasure the press makes it out to be." Coco beamed. "But I've decided to hold another séance. Tomorrow night, the first night of the new moon.''

Amanda struggled not to groan. ''Aunt Coco, I'm sure William isn't interested.''

''On the contrary.'' He turned all his charm on Coco while a plan formed in his mind. ''I'd love to attend myself, if I didn't have pressing business.''

''The next time then. Perhaps you'd like to go upstairs—''

Before she could finish, Alex burst through the terrace doors, followed by a speeding Jenny and a laughing Suzanna. All three had dirt streaked on their hands and jeans. Eyes narrowed, Alex skidded to a halt in front of Livingston.

''Who's that?'' he demanded.

''Alex, don't be a brat.'' Suzanna snagged his hand before he could spread any of his dirt over the buff-colored tailored pants. ''I'm sorry,'' she began. ''We've been in the garden. I made the mistake of mentioning ice cream.''

''Don't apologize.'' Livingston forced his lips to curve. If he disliked anything more than dogs, it was small, grubby children. ''They're...lovely.''

Suzanna squeezed her son's hand before he could resort to violence at the term. ''No, they're not,'' she said cheerfully. ''But we're stuck with them. We'll just get out of your way.'' As she dragged them off to the kitchen, Alex shot a last look over his shoulder.

''He has mean eyes,'' he told his mother.

''Don't be silly.'' She tousled his hair. ''He was just annoyed because you almost ran into him.''

But Alex looked solemnly at Jenny, who nodded. ''Like the snake on Rikki-Tikki-Tavi.''

"You move, I strike," Alex said in a fair imitation of the evil cartoon voice.

"Okay, guys, you're giving me the creeps." She laughed off the quick shiver. "The last one in the kitchen has to wash the bowls." She gave them a head start while she rubbed the chill from her arms.

Chapter Nine

"There, you see." Amanda gave Sloan a quick kiss on the cheek. "That wasn't so bad."

He wasn't quite ready to be placated. "He hung around for five hours. I don't see why Coco had to invite him for dinner."

"Because he's a charming, and single man." She laughed and slipped her arms around his neck. "Remember the tea leaves."

They stood at the seawall, inside an ornate pergola. Sloan decided it was as good a time as any to nibble on her neck. "What tea leaves?"

"The ones that...mmm. The ones that told Aunt Coco that there would be a man coming along who'd be important to us."

He switched to her ear. "I thought that was me."

"Maybe." She gave a surprised yip when he bit her. "Savage."

"Sometimes the Cherokee in me takes over."

She leaned back to study his face. In the bleeding

lights of sunset, his skin was almost copper, his eyes so dark a green they were nearly black. Yes, she could see both sides of his heritage, the Celtic and the Cherokee, both warriors, in those knife-edged cheekbones, the sculpted mouth, the wild reddish hair.

"I really don't know anything about you." Yet it hadn't been like making love to a stranger. When he had touched her, she'd known everything. "Just that you're an architect from Oklahoma who went to Harvard."

"You know I like beer and long-legged women."

"There's that."

Because he could see it was important to her, he sat on the wall, his back to the sea. "Okay, Calhoun, what do you want to know?"

"I don't want to interrogate you." The old nerves resurfaced, making it impossible for her to settle. "It's just that you know everything about me, really. My family, my background, my ambitions."

Because he enjoyed watching her move, he took out a cigar, lighted it, then began to speak. "My great-great-grandfather left Ireland for the New World, and headed west to trap beaver. A genuine mountain man. He married a Cherokee woman, and hung around long enough to get three sons. One day he went off trapping and never came back. The sons started a trading post, did pretty well. One of them sent for a mail-order bride, a nice Irish girl. They had a passel of kids, including my grandfather. He was, and is, a wily old devil who bought up land while it was cheap enough, then hung on until he could sell it at a profit. Keeping up family tradition, he married Irish, a redheaded spitfire who supposedly drove him crazy. He must have loved her a lot, because he named the first oil well after her.''

Amanda, who had been charmed thus far, blinked. ''Oil well?''

''He called it Maggie,'' Sloan said with a grin as he blew out smoke. ''She got such a kick out of it, he gave names to the rest of them, too.''

''The rest of them,'' Amanda said faintly.

''My father took over the company in the sixties, but the old man hasn't stopped putting his two cents in. He's still ticked that I didn't go into the company, but I wanted to build, and I figured Sun Industries didn't need me.''

''Sun Industries?'' She nearly choked. It was one of the biggest conglomerates in the country. ''You—I had no idea that you had money.''

''My family does, anyway. Problem?''

''No. I just wouldn't want you to think that I...'' She trailed off helplessly.

''That you were after the family fortune?'' He let out a hoot of laughter. ''Honey, I know you were after my body.''

He had the uncanny ability to make her want to swear and laugh at the same time. ''You really are a conceited jerk.''

He tossed the cigar aside before making a grab for her. ''But you love me.''

''Maybe I do.'' With pretended reluctance, she slipped her arms around him. ''A little.'' On a laugh, she lifted her lips to his. His mouth started off teasing, then heated with demands. His hands were light, then impatient, until she was wrapped tight around him, pouring herself mindlessly into the kiss.

"How do you do that to me?" she murmured as he nipped at her moist, parted lips.

"Do what?"

"Make me want you until it hurts."

On an unsteady moan, he pressed his lips to her throat. "Let's go inside. You can show me my room."

She tilted her head to give his busy mouth more freedom. "What room?"

"The room where we'll pretend I'm going to sleep when I'm sleeping with you."

"What are you talking about?"

"I'm talking about making love with you until we both need oxygen." Because he knew he was on the point of dragging her down on the hard, cold tiles, he set her away from him. "And I'm talking about the fact that I'm staying here until the alarm system's operational."

"But you don't need—"

"Oh, I need." He crushed his mouth to hers again to show her how much.

She waited for him, chiding herself for being as nervous as a new bride on her wedding night. Perhaps the waiting was more intense because she knew what they would bring to each other.

She slipped on a thin blue chemise, an impulsive extravagance that had been folded away for months. Unable to settle, she turned down the bed. There were candles she'd kept at the bedside and on the bureau for emergencies. But when she lighted them now, their glow was soft, romantic, and anything but practical. Suzanna had placed flowers in the room, as she always did. This time they were fragile lilies of the valley that added a haunting fragrance. Though there was no moonlight, she opened the terrace doors to let in the steady roar of the water on rocks.

Then he came to her, as she stood in the open doorway with the black night at her back.

The quick joke he'd meant to make melted from his mind. He could only stare, his hand growing damp on the knob, his heart bounding up to block his throat. To have her waiting for him, looking so desirable in the flicker of candlelight, to see that smile of welcome, was everything he'd ever wanted.

He wanted to be gentle with her, as he'd been so carefully gentle the night before. But when he crossed to her, the slow burn had already turned to fire. There was challenge instead of nerves in her eyes as she lifted her arms to take him in.

"I thought you'd never get here," she said, and, led by her own needs, crushed her mouth to his.

How could there be gentleness when there was such heat? How could there be patience when there was such urgency? Her body was already vibrating—Lord, he could feel each wild beat—as it fit itself to his. The flimsy material of her chemise teased the bare flesh of his chest, daring him to rip it aside and plunder. Her scent had wrapped itself around his system, taunting with dark secrets, seducing with fevered promises.

In that moment he was so full of her, he couldn't find himself.

Breathless, disoriented, he lifted his head. He knew his hands were big and could be rough if his heart didn't guide them. He knew his needs were huge and could be ruthless if he didn't retain control.

"Wait." He needed a moment to get back his breath and his sanity, but she was shaking her head.

"No." Her hands clutched in his hair, and she pulled him back to her.

She didn't know when the recklessness had burst through her, but it held sway now, as she fell with him onto the bed. Aggressive and desperate, her hands streaked over him. No weakness this time. No submission. She wanted the power, the power of knowing she could make him careless, make him as mindless and vulnerable as he made her.

In a tangle of arms and legs they rolled over the bed. Each time he tried to pull back, she was there, her mouth greedy, her low, sultry laughter pounding in his blood.

Her busy fingers rushed to unsnap his jeans, then tugged the denim over his hips. His muscles jumped and quivered when she danced those fingertips across his stomach. He swore, snatching her hands before she could drag him over that last jagged edge.

Breath heaving, he stared down at her, her wrists trapped in his hand. Her eyes were like cobalt, glistening dark in the shifting light. He could hear, over his own ragged breaths, the steady ticking of the bedside clock.

Then she smiled, a slow, lazy smile full of knowledge. And he heard nothing but the roar of his own needs.

Hot with hunger, his mouth fused with hers. Reckless with passion, his hands sought and took. She answered, demand for demand, pleasure for pleasure. Control snapped—he could almost hear the chain break as he sated himself with her. This was liberation, a world without reason. Desperate to feel her, he tore the chemise aside. Her quick gasp of surprise only fueled the fires.

Tossed in the whirlwind, she gave herself over to the speed, surrendered herself to the fury. No thought. No question. Only hot, damp flesh, ravenous, searching lips, quick, greedy hands.

His eyes open, fixed on hers, he drove himself into her, letting the shock of pleasure fill them both. Then she was rising up to meet him so that they drove each other into the dark.

"Yes, Mr. Stenerson." Amanda hummed a tune in her head as her supervisor droned on. And on. Ten more minutes, and she was off duty. Even the upcoming séance didn't dim her pleasure.

She would be with Sloan soon. Maybe there would be time for a walk before dinner.

"You don't seem to have your mind on your work, Miss Calhoun."

That brought her back with a jolt of guilt. "You were concerned about Mr. and Mrs. Wicken's complaint."

Glaring, he tapped his pencil on the desk. "I'm very concerned that one of our waiters spilled an entire tray of drinks in Mrs. Wicken's lap."

"Yes, sir. I arranged to have her slacks cleaned, and for a complimentary dinner for them any evening during their stay. They were satisfied."

"And you've fired the waiter?"

"No, sir."

His eyebrows rose up, wiggling like worms. "May I ask why not, when I specifically requested you do so?"

"Because Tim has been with us for three years,

and could hardly be blamed for spilling the tray when the little Wicken boy stuck out his foot and tripped him. Several other waiters, and several of the guests saw it happen."

"Be that as it may, I gave you a specific order."

"Yes, sir." The cheerful little tune in her head became a throbbing headache. She'd meant to go over all of this with Stenerson before. "And after a closer review of the circumstances, I chose to handle it differently."

"Need I remind you who is in charge of this hotel, Miss Calhoun?"

"No, sir, but I would think after all the years I've worked at the BayWatch, you would trust my judgment." She took a deep breath, and a big risk. "If you don't, it might be best if I turned in my resignation."

He blinked three times, then cleared his throat. "Don't you feel that's a bit rash?"

"No, sir. If you don't feel I'm competent to make certain decisions, it undermines the system."

"It isn't your competence, but your lack of experience. However," he added, holding up a hand, "I'm sure you did what you felt was best in this case."

"Yes, sir."

By the time she left his office, her jaw was clenched. Amanda forced it to relax when William stopped her in the lobby.

"I just wanted to tell you again how much I enjoyed the tour of your home, and the wonderful meal."

"It was our pleasure."

"I have the feeling if I asked you to dinner again,

you would have a different reason than hotel policy for saying no."

"William, I—"

"No, no." He patted her hand. "I understand. I'm disappointed, but I understand. I suppose Mr. O'Riley will attend the séance tonight?"

She laughed. "Whether he wants to or not."

"I really am sorry I'll miss it." He gave her hand a final squeeze. "It's at eight, did you say?"

"No, nine, sharp. Aunt Coco will have us all gathered around the dining table holding hands and sending out alpha waves or whatever."

"I hope you'll let me know if you receive any messages from…the other side."

"It's a deal. Good night."

"Good night." He glanced at his watch as she left. He had more than enough time to get ready.

"I thought I'd find you here." Amanda stepped into the large circular room the family called Bianca's tower. Lilah was curled on the window seat, as she often was, looking out to the cliffs.

"Yeah, just me and fierce Fred." Coming out of a private dream, she ruffled the dozing dog's fur. "We're getting in tune for tonight's séance."

"Spare me." Amanda plopped onto the seat beside her.

"Well, what's wiped off that satisfied smile you had on your face this morning? Did you fight with Sloan?"

"No."

"Then it must be the dastardly Stenerson." At Amanda's brief oath, Lilah grinned. "Right the second time. Why do you put up with him, Mandy? The man's a weasel."

"Because I work for him."

"So quit."

"Easy for you to say." She shot Lilah an impatient look. "We can't all drift around from day to day like dreamy forest sprites." She cut herself off, letting out a disgusted breath. "Sorry."

Lilah only shrugged. "It sounds like you've got more needling you than Stenerson."

"He started it. He said I didn't have my mind on my work, and he was right."

"So your mind was wandering. Big deal."

"It is a big deal. Damn it, I like my job, and I'm good at it. But I haven't been concentrating, not on that or the necklace, or anything, since…"

"Since the big gun swaggered in from the West."

"It's not funny."

"Sure it is." Lilah wrapped her arms around her knees and rested her chin on them. "So you lose a little concentration, misplace one of your lists or miss an appointment by five minutes. So what?"

"I'll tell you so what. He's changing me and I don't know what to do about it. I have responsibilities, obligations. Damn it, I have goals. I have to think about tomorrow, and five years from tomorrow." The trouble was, when she did, she thought of Sloan. "What if he's just a glitch? A wonderful, exciting glitch that throws off everything I've planned out? A few weeks from now, he finishes up here and heads back to Oklahoma, and my life's a mess."

"What if he asks you to go with him?"

"That's worse." Flustered, Amanda rose to wander in distracted circles. "What am I supposed to do?

Throw away everything I've worked for, everything I've hoped for just because he says saddle up?''

"Would you?"

Amanda shut her eyes. "I'm afraid I would."

"Then why don't you talk to him?"

"I can't." She sat again. "We haven't talked about the future. I guess neither of us wants to think about it. It was just that today, I started thinking—"

"You would get back to it."

"I started thinking," Amanda repeated, "that a month ago I didn't even know him. It's crazy to start planning my life around someone I've only known such a short time."

"And you've always been the sensible one," Lilah put in.

"Well, yes."

"Then relax." For encouragement she patted Amanda's shoulder. "When the time comes, you're bound to do the sensible thing."

"I hope you're right," Amanda murmured, then forced herself to add a decisive nod. "Of course, you're right. I'm going to work in the storeroom until dinner."

"See you're back on track already." Lilah chuckled to herself when Amanda strode out. "Come on, Fred." She nuzzled his nose. "Let's go see if we can derail her."

Sloan walked into the storeroom, armed with a bottle of champagne, a wicker basket and some of Lilah's sisterly advice. *Keep her off balance, big guy. The one thing you can't let her do is get logical on you.*

Though he wasn't exactly sure what had prompted

Lilah's visit, he approved the spirit of it. Just as he approved the way Amanda looked, hunched over a desk in the storeroom, glasses on her nose, hair clipped back. There were neatly labeled file boxes stacked behind her, dozens of dusty cardboard boxes scattered alongside her and several fat piles of paper in front of her.

"Hey, Calhoun, ready for a break?"

"What?" Her head came up quickly, but it took a moment for her eyes to focus. "Oh, hi. I didn't hear you come in."

"Where were you?"

She lifted a ledger. "Back in 1929. It seems my illustrious great-grandpapa made a little pin money running liquor in from Canada during Prohibition."

"Good old Fergus."

"Greedy old Fergus," she corrected. "But a businessman through and through. If he kept such meticulous books of his illegal activities, he certainly would have a record of sale if he sold the emeralds."

"I thought Bianca hid them."

"That's the legend." She leaned back to rub her tired eyes. "I'd rather have the facts. I had this thought that maybe he put them in a safe-deposit box he didn't tell anyone about. But I can't find any record of that, either."

"Maybe you're looking in the wrong place." He set the bottle and basket down as he stood behind her. Gently he began to massage her neck muscles. "Maybe you should concentrate on Bianca. It was her necklace after all."

"We don't have a lot of information about Bianca." When her eyes started to drift closed, she popped them open again. "Great-Grandpapa destroyed all of her pictures, her letters, just about everything concerning her. We've only come across one of her date books so far."

"He must have been crazy mad."

"Crazy, anyway. Grieving, I'd think."

"No." Bending, he kissed the top of her head. "If he'd been grieving, he would have kept everything."

"Maybe it hurt to remember."

"If he'd loved her, he would have wanted to remember. He would have needed to. When you love someone, everything about them's precious." He felt her muscles knot under his fingers. "What's the problem, Amanda? You're all tied up."

"I've been sitting too long, that's all."

"Then my timing's perfect." He stepped back to pick up the champagne."

"What's that for?"

"Most people drink it." Sloan released the cork. After the pop came the seductive hiss. "I don't know about you, but I worked my butt off today. I thought we'd take a first-class coffee break."

She didn't need champagne to cloud her brain. He did that all by himself. And that, she reminded herself as she rose, was exactly what she needed to avoid. "It's a nice thought, but I should go help Aunt Coco with dinner."

"Lilah's helping her."

"Lilah?" Amanda's brows shot up. "You've got to be kidding."

"Nope." He opened the basket to take out two fluted glasses. "Suzanna's doing homework with the kids, and you and I are having dinner alone."

"Sloan, I'm really not dressed to go out."

"I like you in sweats." He poured the wine and,

setting the bottle aside, lifted both glasses. "And we're not going anywhere."

"You just said—"

"I said we were having dinner alone, and we are. Right here."

"Here?" She gestured. "In the storeroom?"

"Yep. I got some of your aunt's pâté, some cold chicken and asparagus, and fresh strawberries." He tapped his glass against hers before drinking. "I've been thinking about you all day."

He didn't even have to try to make her knees weak. When he did sweet things, said sweet things, she dissolved into a puddle of love. "Sloan, we have to talk."

"Sure." But he bent down to rub his lips lazily over hers. "Why don't we get comfortable first?"

"What?" Already dizzy, she stared at him as he took out a blanket and spread it over the floor.

"Come on."

"I really think it would be better if we..." But he was already pulling her down to the blanket.

He took the glass from her hand, setting it on the floor before nuzzling her mouth. "This is better," he murmured. "Much better."

"The children are home," she managed as his hands slid under her shirt. "If someone came in—"

"I locked the door." Gently he skimmed the rough pad of his thumb over her nipples. "Pay attention, Calhoun, I'm going to show you how to relax."

She was so relaxed, she didn't think she could move. Heavy, her eyes fluttered partway open when Sloan lay a smidgen of pâté on her tongue.

"It's good," he told her, then spread a dab on her

bare shoulder so he could lick it off. "Here." He lifted her, cradling her against his chest before he handed her the glass of champagne. "We were supposed to drink this first, but I got distracted."

It tasted like sin on her tongue. She sipped again, then opened her mouth obediently when he fed her more pâté, this time on a conventional cracker.

"More?"

She sighed her assent. They began to feed each other tidbits from the basket between kisses. Replete, she watched him pour the last of the champagne. "We're going to be late for the séance."

"Nope." He drew her back more comfortably against his chest. "Coco decided that the vibes weren't right. Something about interference from a dark presence."

"Sounds just like my levelheaded aunt."

"Now she wants to wait until the last night of the new moon." He nuzzled her neck. "We can stay in here all night."

She was beginning to believe that with him, anything was possible. "That would make it my first all-night picnic."

"After we're married, we'll make it a regular event."

Champagne slopped over her hand and onto his leg as she jolted straight.

"Easy, Calhoun, don't waste it."

She struggled around to face him. "What do you mean, married?"

"You know, like man and wife, that kind of thing."

With deliberate care, she set the glass down. Just like that, she thought, both panicked and angry. Just as she'd expected. With him it was *saddle up, Calhoun. We're getting hitched.* "What gave you the idea that we were getting married?"

He didn't like the fact that the line was back between her brows. "I love you, you love me. You're the logical one, Amanda. The next step's marriage from my point of view."

"It may be a step from your point of view, but it's a big leap from mine. You can't just assume I'm going to take it."

"Why not?"

"Because you can't. In the first place, I'm not planning on marriage for years yet. I've got my career to think about."

"What's one got to do with the other?"

"Everything. You've already messed up my concentration, had me shuffling around my priorities." Knowing it sounded foolish, she stopped to drag a hand through her hair. "Look at me," she demanded. "Just look at me. I'm sitting on the storeroom floor, naked, and arguing with a man I've only known for two weeks. This isn't me."

With deceptive laziness, he skimmed his gaze down, then up again. "Then who the hell is it?"

"I don't know." Frantic, she snatched up her sweats and began to pull them on. "I don't know who I am anymore, and it's your fault. Nothing's made sense since you ran into me on the sidewalk."

"You ran into me."

"That's beside the point." Shaken to the core, she yanked the sweatshirt over her head. "I'm daydreaming when I'm supposed to be working. I'm making love with you when I should be keeping appointments. I'm having naked picnics when I should be filing papers. It's got to stop.''

''Maybe I should've just hit you over the head with the bottle of champagne instead of letting you drink it.'' Baffled, he scratched his head. ''Why don't you sit down, Calhoun, and we'll talk this thing out?''

''No, I will not sit down. You'll start on me again, and I won't be able to think. You're not going to make plans for the rest of my life without consulting me, without even having the courtesy to ask. I'm taking back control of my life.''

He rose then, naked and furious. ''You're mad because I want you to marry me.''

The breath hissed out between her clenched teeth. ''You're just stupid.'' She grabbed the closest thing handy and ended up hurling her glasses at him. ''Too stupid for words.'' With this she strode to the door, fought with and cursed the lock until she managed to open it. ''You can take your incredibly romantic proposal and stuff it.''

The hot and hazy afternoon was perfect for pleasure. Christian surprised me with a little basket of wine and cold ham. Together we sat in the wild grass beyond the rock and watched the boats glide by below. The light was so golden, like something poured out of a gilded pitcher. But it is always so when I'm with him. In this lovely fantasy of afternoons, there is nothing but sunlight and warm, fragrant air.

We talked of everything and nothing as he sketched me. He has already done two paintings of me since the summer began. Without risking modesty I can say he made me look beautiful. What woman is not when she is in love? And it was his eyes that studied me, his hands that drew my face, my hair. His feelings that guided his brush.

If I had not believed before how deep and true his love is for me, I would have seen it in the portraits he painted.

Will someone buy my portrait from him? It saddens me to think of it. Yet it makes me proud. That would be one way I could at last declare my feelings. Hanging on some pretty wall, the portrait of a woman whose eyes are filled with love for the man who painted her.

I say we talked of everything and nothing. We do not mention how quickly the days fly into weeks. There are so little of those weeks left before I must leave the island, and Christian. I think something in me will die this time.

Fergus and I attended a dinner dance tonight. He was very jolly, though there was much talk of war. He said that clever men know that there will always be war, and money to be made from it. I was stunned to hear him speak so, but he only brushed aside my concern.

"It's for you to think of how to spend the money, and for me to make it," he told me.

It upset me because it was not for money I married him, nor is it for money I stay with him. Both were for duty. Yet I have lived under his roof, eaten his food, taken his gifts without a thought.

It scrapes at my conscience to know that I appreciated the little picnic Christian brought to me so much more than I have ever appreciated all the sumptuous dinners Fergus's money has paid for.

Because it always pleases him, I wore the emeralds, and I have not yet put them away. They lie in the

*shadowed light, glinting at me, reminding me of both
my grief and my joy.*

*If it were not for the children...but I can't think of
it. There are the children. Whatever sins I commit, I
will never desert them. They have needs that neither
Christian nor I have a right to ignore. I know, in the
loneliness ahead of me, they will be solace. Being
blessed with them, it is not right to grieve for the child
Christian and I must never conceive.*

Yet, I do.

*Tonight when I turn off the lamp I'll try to sleep
quickly. For then it will be morning, and morning will
become the golden afternoon, when I can see Christian again.*

Chapter Ten

The only thing that prevented Amanda from slamming the door was the fact that Suzanna would have already put the children to bed. But she did kick it.

Limping and muttering and occasionally sending a furious look over her shoulder, she started down the hallway. At that point, she wasn't certain if she was more angry with Sloan for taking her assent for granted, or with herself for wanting to give it to him. Marriage hadn't been in her plans, but damn it, she was good at taking the unexpected and making it work. But if he thought she would give him the satisfaction of just hopping on board because he said so, then he didn't know Amanda Kelly Calhoun.

When we get married, she fumed. Not if, not will you or would you. And the problem, the big problem was that under the instant panic and anger had been a thrill. She paused outside of her bedroom door as her own soft sigh caught up with her. Oh, Lord, she did want to marry him. Despite all the good, solid,

sensible reasons against it, marrying him was exactly
what she wanted. Living with him would mean living
with the constant threat of upheaval. She smiled to
herself. And what more satisfying life could there be
for a woman so skilled at putting things back in
place?

With her hand on the doorknob, she hesitated, de-
bating whether she would go back, give in to the urge
to throw herself laughing into his arms and say…yes!

No. Resolute, Amanda pushed open the door. She
wasn't about to make it that easy for him. If he
wanted her, really wanted her, then he was going to
have to work a little harder. When he got it right—if
he got it right—she corrected as she shut the door
behind her, she would smile, slide her arms around
him and say—

An arm whipped around her throat and cut off her
breath. Instinctively she struggled, throwing both
hands up to the barrier to yank and scratch as she
fought to drag in the air to scream. Until the hard,
cold barrel of a gun pressed against her temple.

"Don't." The voice was only a harsh whisper at
her ear. "Be very still, and very quiet, and I won't
have to hurt you."

Obediently she let her arms fall limply to her sides,
but her mind was speeding. The children were just
down the hall. Their safety came first. And Sloan…
Sloan could come along at any moment, furiously demanding a showdown.

"That's better." The pressure on her windpipe
eased slightly. "If you scream, people are going to
get hurt—starting with you. I don't think you want
that." She shook her head. "Good. Now—" He

swore and tightened his grip again as Sloan bellowed in the corridor.

"Calhoun. I'm not finished with you."

"Be absolutely quiet," the man warned as he dragged her back. "Or I'll kill him."

Amanda shut her eyes and prayed.

Sloan shoved open the door of her room, but it was pitch-dark and silent inside. While he stood in the doorway, swearing, Amanda was pressed back into the corner, knowing the gun was now aimed in Sloan's direction. Her stomach seemed to be packed with ice as she stood, not even daring to breathe, willing him to turn and go. And when he did, when she heard his boots clanging on the stairs, she wondered if she would ever see him again.

"Now that we have a little privacy, we can talk." But the arm stayed around her throat and the gun at her temple. "About the emeralds."

"I don't know where they are."

"Yes. Initially I had trouble believing that, but now I'm sure you don't. So we'll play this a different way. We'll have to move quickly. First the storeroom. I'll take the papers you've yet to sort through. Then, to add a little flare to the trip, we'll fetch Coco's pearls, and a few of the smaller, more portable items."

"You'll never get out of the house."

"You just leave that up to me." There was a faint lilt of pleasure in the voice now, as if he would enjoy the challenge. "Now we're going to move quietly, and very quickly to the storeroom. If you try anything heroic, I'll regret shooting you."

She didn't dare, not with the children so close. But the storeroom, she thought, as she started out with him directly behind her. That was a different matter.

Sloan had left the lights on. The remnants of their picnic were spread over the floor. The air smelled, ever so lightly, of strawberries and champagne.

"Very sweet," Livingston murmured, then shut the door behind them. "It would have been more convenient for me if you had had the séance instead of a tryst." He loosened his hold so that she could step away, but kept his gun level.

Amanda stared at the man she knew as William Livingston. He was all in black with a soft leather pouch worn crosswise over his chest. On his hands were thin surgical gloves. The gun he carried was small, but she didn't doubt it was lethal, not when she looked into his eyes.

"No recriminations, Amanda?" His brow lifted when she said nothing. "I'd hoped you and I could enjoy each other while I was conducting business, but…let's not waste time." From his pouch he pulled out a denim duffel bag. "Just the papers from those boxes there. I'm sure you're too efficient to have filed away anything useful."

She bent to pick up the bag he'd tossed at her. "You've lost your accent."

"It's lost its purpose. Be quick, Amanda." His eyes narrowed as he gestured with the gun. "Very quick."

She began to stuff papers into the bag. He was stealing her history, she thought furiously. Her family. "These won't do you any good."

"I doubt you believe that, or you wouldn't be wasting your time with them." His posture seemed almost relaxed now as he stood between Amanda and the door. "You're much too practical. In my profession, it pays to do your homework. I know your family quite well.'' To hurry her along, he waved the gun. ''Which is why I chose to concentrate on you, the most efficient and straightforward of the Calhoun women.''

If his ego was the only thing she could strike at, she'd take her best shot. ''I hope you weren't expecting me to fall for you.'' She flicked a coolly dismissive glance over him. ''You're not my type—then or now.''

It hit the mark. His vanity was as huge as his ambition. ''It's a pity that the lack of time prevents me from testing that. Perhaps when I come back, we'll pick up where we left off.''

''Even if you get away tonight, you'll never get back in this house again.''

He only smiled. ''We'll see. Running into you like this complicates my plans, but it doesn't alter the final goal. The necklace. I want it very badly. Some jewels have power, and I have a feeling about this necklace. A strong feeling.''

The air in the room was suddenly cold, bone-chilling cold. The expression in Livingston's eyes changed. ''Drafts,'' he muttered uneasily. ''The place is full of drafts.''

But Amanda felt it, too, and was Calhoun enough to recognize it.

''It's Bianca,'' she said, and despite the gun, despite the odds, felt completely safe. ''If you've done your homework, then you'll know she's still here.'' The darting nerves in his eyes made her smile. ''I don't think she wants you to have the papers, or the necklace.''

''Ghosts?'' he laughed, but the sound was strained. Though he could see with his own eyes that nothing had changed, he was no longer sure he was alone in the room with Amanda. "That's unworthy of you."

"Then why are you frightened?"

"I'm not frightened, I'm in a hurry. That's enough." He found himself desperate to get out of the room, out of the house. Despite the eerie chill, a line of sweat dribbled down his back. "You carry the bag. Since this has taken longer than expected, we'll have to forgo Coco's pearls, for now." Impatient, he waved the gun at her. "Out the terrace doors."

Amanda debated heaving the duffel bag at him and running. But then he would have the papers. Instead, she struggled with it, then fumbled at the door. "It's stuck."

She was braced when he came up behind her to fight with the old latch. The minute the door opened, she stuck a foot behind him, threw her weight against him, then ran.

Wanting to lead him away from her family, she headed toward the west wing. As she hit the first set of stone stairs, she shouted for Sloan. The heavy bag bumped each step as she dragged it with her. She could hear him behind her, closing in, and zigged around a corner as the first bullet pinged off granite.

She didn't stop to catch her breath, though her lungs were beginning to burn. The May night was warm, oppressively warm after the cold of the storeroom. The air was heavy with the threat of rain.

The sensation of safety she had felt in the storeroom had vanished. There was no protection now, except for her knowledge of the complex layout of the terraces and stairs. But she was straining, fighting her way through the dark and through the sudden certainty that she could not handle this alone.

Then she saw Sloan, heading toward her from the opposite direction. The relief lasted only an instant before she heard another shot.

Lights were flashing everywhere inside the house. Sloan shouted at her before he came forward like a charging bull. Unarmed, Amanda realized, blind with fury, and straight into a loaded gun.

Without hesitation, she whirled away from Sloan and heaved the bag of papers at Livingston. As he snatched it up, she could hear raised voices from inside, Jenny's crying, the dog's frantic barks. Wanting to protect as much as be protected, Amanda raced toward Sloan. When she reached him, arms outstretched, he shoved her aside.

"Get in the house."

"He's got a gun," she said, desperately clinging to his arm. "Just let him go."

"I said get inside." He shook her off, then before her astonished eyes, leaped over the wall.

With her heart in her throat, she raced to it, to see him scrambling up from the terrace below. Even as Lilah burst through a door, Amanda was giving chase.

"What the hell's going on?" Lilah shouted after her.

"Call the police." After the single order, Amanda saved her breath for running, following the sound of stampeding feet and Fred's furious barks.

There was no moonlight to guide her, but she plunged heedlessly into the dark, screaming for Sloan when she heard the explosion of gunfire. She flew down the steps, tearing around the house in a dead run. Over her own ragged gasps, she heard a shouted curse, then the sound of tires squealing on asphalt.

In her hurry, she stumbled once, scrambling back

up from the driveway with gravel stinging her palms. Then for an instant, a terrifying instant, there was only the sound of the sea and the wind and her own thundering pulse.

Her legs trembled as she dashed down the slope, so blind with fear that she didn't see Sloan until she rammed into him.

"Oh, God." Her hands were instantly on his face. "I thought he'd killed you."

He was too infuriated at having lost his quarry to appreciate her concern. "Not for lack of trying. Are you all right?"

"Yes, yes, I'm fine. It was—"

"You're bleeding." Every other thought in his head vanished. "There's blood on your hands."

"I fell." She dropped her head onto his shoulder. "It was so dark, and I couldn't see." Fighting tears, she held on to him as Fred whined at their feet. In an abrupt change of mood, she pulled back, pushing at his chest with her sore hands. Her damp eyes sizzled. "Are you crazy, chasing after him that way? I told you he had a gun. He could have shot you."

"He damn near shot you," Sloan retorted. "And didn't I tell you to stay inside?"

"I don't take orders from you," she began.

"You're both alive," Lilah commented. Flashlight in hand, she strolled toward them. "I could hear you arguing from the end of the driveway." The light shot across papers scattered in the road. "What's all this?"

"Oh, God, he must have dropped some." Amanda was already down on her hands and knees, gathering them up.

"Must've been when Fred bit his leg." Far from

pacified, Sloan bent to snatch up a paper before it blew away.

"Fred bit him?" Amanda and Lilah said in unison.

"Good and hard from the sound of it." It was a small but sweet satisfaction. "We might have had him, too, but he had a car stashed down the road."

"And he might have shot both of you," Amanda retorted.

"Excuse me." Lilah felt she was doing her part by shining the light so they could see to find papers. "Who is he?"

"Livingston," Sloan told her, then added a string of curses. "You'll have to get the details from your sister."

"Inside," Lilah suggested. "The rest of the family is in an uproar."

"You called the police?"

"Yes." Right before she'd rushed out of the house, barefoot, to chase her sister down the graveled driveway. When Fred stopped to perk his ears then give a long, ululant howl, she laughed. "And I'd say they're on the way. Fred already hears the sirens."

Because her arms were full, Amanda pushed the papers into Lilah's arms, then began to pick up more as they started back. "He didn't get everything," she muttered, then thought of that moment in the storeroom when the air had changed. "I knew he wouldn't."

At the door of the house Suzanna stood, a slim gladiator, armed with a fireplace poker. "Is everyone all right?"

"Fine." Amanda let out an exhausted breath. "The kids?"

"In the parlor with Aunt Coco. Oh, honey, your hands."

"I just scraped them."

"I'll get some antiseptic."

"And some brandy," Lilah added, before laying the papers on a table in the hallway.

Twenty minutes later, the story had been related to the police, and the family was left alone to absorb it. Sloan paced behind the sofa while the Calhoun women huddled together.

"We had that—that thief to dinner." Coco glared into her brandy. "I baked a chocolate soufflé. And all the time he was plotting to steal from us."

"The police will shoot him," Alex piped up. "Bang! Between the eyes."

"I think we've had enough excitement for one night." Suzanna kissed the top of his head. Less sure of himself than he wanted to be, Alex slipped a hand into hers and held tight.

"He got most of the papers." With a sigh, Amanda reached for the pile she'd tossed onto the coffee table. "I hope Fred took a good chunk out of him."

"Good boy, Fred." Lilah cuddled the dog in her lap. "I don't think they'll do Livingston—or whoever he is—any good. He's not meant to find the emeralds. We are."

"He won't get the chance," Sloan said grimly. "Not with the security system I'm putting in." He shot a look at Amanda, daring her to argue, but she was staring at one of the papers.

"It's a letter," she murmured. "A letter from Bianca to Christian."

"Oh, my dear." Coco leaned forward. "What does it say?"

Amanda read,

"My love,
I'm writing this as the rain continues to fall and keeps me from you. I wonder what you are doing, if you paint today in the gloomy light and think of me. When I'm alone like this in my tower, separated from the reality of my duties, I let the memories sweep over me. Of the first time I saw you, standing on the cliffs. Of the last time I touched you. I'm praying for the sun, Christian, so that we can make more memories. I cannot tell you how you have changed me, how much more my eyes see, now that they see with my heart. I can't imagine how empty my life would have been without this time we had together. I know now that love is very rare, very precious. It is something to be cherished and held on to tightly while too often it is smothered, or brushed carelessly away. Remember, even when our time together ends, I will hold your love. It will live in my heart long after that heart stops beating.

Bianca."

Coco let out a long, dreamy sigh. "Oh, how much they must have loved each other."

"Yucky," Alex said sleepily, and rested his head on his mother's breast.

Amanda smoothed the letter out, hating the fact that it had become crumpled. "I guess she never got the chance to send it to him. All these years it's been mixed up with receipts and account sheets."

"And tonight *we* found it, not Livingston," Lilah reminded her.

"Luck," Amanda murmured.

"Fate," her sister insisted.

When the phone rang, Amanda was the first up to answer. "It's the police," she said, then settled back to listen. "I see. Yes, thank you for letting us know." She hung up, blowing out a disgusted breath. "Looks like he got away. He didn't go back to the BayWatch for any of his things, or he slipped in and took what he wanted and left the rest."

"Do they think he'll come back?" Alarmed, Coco patted her chest.

"No, but they're going to keep an eye on the house until they're sure he's left the island."

"I imagine he's halfway to New York by now." Suzanna shifted the drowsy children on her lap. "And if he comes back, we'll be ready for him."

"More than ready," Amanda agreed. "They have an APB out, but...I guess that's all that can be done for tonight."

"No." Sloan crossed the room to her. "There's a little more that has to be done." He nodded to the rest of the room as he pulled her toward the doorway. "You'll excuse us."

"They might, but I don't," Amanda told him. "Let go of my arm."

"Okay." He did, then nipping her by the waist, hauled her over his shoulder. "It's always the hard way with you."

"I will not be slung around like a sack of potatoes." As he climbed the stairs, she wriggled, trying for one clear shot with her foot.

"We left some loose ends before you stormed off

to go tangle with an armed robber. Now we're damn well going to tie them up. You like straight talk, Calhoun, and you're about to get some.''

"You don't know what I like.'' She slammed a fist into his back. "You don't know anything.''

"Then it's time I found out.'' He kicked open the door of her room, stalked over and dumped her onto the bed. When she scrambled up, fists raised, he shoved her down again. "You sit where I put you. So help me, we're going to have this out once and for all.''

Amanda stunned them both by covering her face with her hands and bursting into tears. She couldn't stop them. Everything that had happened in the past few hours reared up to set off an emotional jag that knocked her flat. On an oath, Sloan stepped toward her, then away, then dragged a helpless hand through his hair.

"Don't do that, Mandy.''

She only shook her head and continued to sob.

"Come on now, please.'' His voice gentled as he crouched in front of her. "I didn't mean to make you cry.'' Lost, he stroked her hair, patted her shoulder. "I'm sorry, honey. I know you've been through hell tonight. I should have waited to start on this.'' Cursing himself, he rubbed her arm. "Look, you can hit me if it'd make you feel better.''

She sniffled, drew in a hitching breath, then clipped him hard enough to send him sprawling. Through a veil of tears, she studied him as he dabbed at his mouth with the back of his hand.

"I forgot how literal minded you were.'' He sat where he was as they watched each other. "You finished crying?''

"I think so." Sniffling again, she dug into her pocket for a tissue. "Your lip's bleeding."

"Yeah." He started to reach for the tissue, but she was wiping her face with it. Laughing, he sat back again. "God Almighty, you're a piece of work."

"I'm glad you think this whole thing is a big joke. Men breaking into the house, waving guns around. You're lucky I didn't find you facedown in the road with a hole in your head."

He saw the tears welling again and took her hands. "Is that what this is about?" He pressed a kiss to her freshly bandaged palms. "You're upset because I went after him?"

"I told you not to."

"Hey." His gaze fixed on hers, he raised a hand to cup her chin. "Do you think I could stand around after he'd taken a potshot at you? The only thing I regret is that I didn't catch up with him, so I could rearrange that pretty face of his."

"That's just stupid machismo," she said, but turned her cheek into his hand.

"That's the second time tonight you've called me stupid. I'd like to get back to the first time."

Instantly she pulled back and pokered up. "I don't want to talk about it."

"Too bad. That little chase was quite a diversion, but it's done now. We're not. How come you jumped all over me when I mentioned marriage?"

"Mentioned it? You ordered it."

"I just said that—"

"You just assumed," she interrupted, then pushed by him to stand up. "Just because I love you, just because I've made love with you, doesn't give you

any right to take me for granted. I told you before
that I make my own plans."

"I've had it with your plans, Calhoun." He took
her arm to hold her still. "I've got plans, too, and
needs. It so happens they all include you. I love you,
damn it." He emphasized the point with a quick, frustrated shake. "You're the only woman I've ever
needed, really needed. The only woman I've ever
wanted to spend my life with, have children with,
make a home with. God knows why when you're as
ornery as a mule with two heads, but that's the way
it is."

"Then why didn't you just ask?"

Baffled, he shook his head. "Ask what?"

She made a strangled sound and began to pace
again. "It's not like I'm asking for Byron or Shelley.
I don't expect you to get down on your knees with a
hand over your heart. Maybe a little violin music
wouldn't have hurt," she muttered. "Or some candlelight."

"Violin music?"

"Forget it." She stopped, hands on her hips, to
face him down. "Do you think just because I'm sensible and organized that I don't need any trappings,
any romance? You come here, change my entire life,
make me love you so much I can't see straight, then
you don't even have the good sense to do it right."

"Hold on." He held up a hand before she could
stride by him again. "Are you saying you're mad
because I didn't ask you fancy enough?"

The sound came again, louder this time. Her face
was flushed with temper, her eyes glowing with it.
"You didn't ask at all, but why should you? You
already know the answer."

Trying to figure women, he thought while he rubbed his hands over his face, was like...trying to figure women. "You wait here," he told her, and strode out.

"Typical," Amanda called after him, then plopped down onto the bed. She was still stewing, her chin on her hand, when he came back in. "Now what?" she demanded.

"Just shut up a minute." He set the tape recorder he'd borrowed on her dresser, then pulled out a pack of matches. Systematically he began to light candles, moving from one part of the room to another while she scowled at him. When he was satisfied, he turned off the lights.

"What are you doing?"

"I'm getting things ready so I can ask you to marry me without having you throw something at me again."

Chin up, she jumped out of bed. "Now you're making fun of me."

"No, I'm not. Damn it, woman, are you going to argue with me all night or let me try to do this right?"

There was enough exasperation in his voice to make her stop and consider him. He didn't look terribly comfortable, she noted. And because he didn't, she wanted to smile. He was doing it for her, she realized. Because he loved her.

"I guess I'll let you try. What's that?" he asked, gesturing to the tape recorder.

"It's Lilah's." He punched the Play button. The soft, weeping sound of violins flowed into the room. Now she did smile, though her heart was beginning to thud.

"It's lovely."

"So are you, I should have made a point of telling you that more often." Stepping toward her, he held out a hand.

"Now's a good time to start." She placed her hand in his.

"I love you, Amanda." Very gently, he touched his lips to hers. "I love everything about you. The woman who makes lists and lines up her shoes in the closet. The woman who goes swimming in freezing water, just so she can be alone for a while. I love the incredibly sexy woman I found in bed, and the tough one, who knows her own mind. It's all the things you are I don't want to live without."

"I love you, too." She lifted a hand to his face. "I meant it when I said you'd changed my life. Tonight, when I read Bianca's letter, I understood how she felt. I'll never feel about anyone the way I feel about you. I'll never want to."

Smiling, he caught her wrist, turning it so that he could brush a kiss over her hand. "Then you're going to marry me?"

She laughed as she threw her arms around him. "I thought you'd never ask."

* * * * *

The Calhoun Saga
continued in March with

THE CALHOUN WOMEN
Lilah and Suzanna

containing FOR THE LOVE OF LILAH
and SUZANNA'S SURRENDER

Here's a sneak preview of
FOR THE LOVE OF LILAH

Chapter One

A storm was waiting to happen. From the high curving window of the tower, Lilah could see the silver tongue of lightning licking at the black sky to the east. Thunder bellowed, bursting through the gathering clouds to send its drumbeat along the teeth of rock. An answering shudder coursed through her—not of fear, but of excitement.

Something was coming. She could feel it, not just in the thickening of the air but in the primitive beating of her own blood.

When she pressed her hand to the glass, she almost expected her fingers to sizzle, snapped with the power of the electricity building. But the glass was cool and smooth, and as black as the sky.

She smiled a little at the distant rumble of thunder and thought of her great-grandmother. Had Bianca ever stood here, watching a storm build, waiting for it to crash over the house and fill the tower with eerie light? Had she wished that her lover had stood beside her to share the power and the unleashed passion? Of course she had, Lilah thought. What woman wouldn't?

But Bianca had stood here alone, Lilah knew, just as she herself was standing alone now. Perhaps it had been the loneliness, the sheer ache of it, that had driven Bianca to throw herself out of that very window and onto the unforgiving rocks below.

Shaking her head, Lilah took her hand from the glass. She was letting herself get moody again, and it had to stop. Depression and dark thoughts were out of character for a woman who preferred to take life as it came—and who made it a policy to avoid its more strenuous burdens.

Lilah wasn't ashamed of the fact that she would rather sit than stand, would certainly rather walk than run and saw the value of long naps as opposed to exercise for keeping the body and mind in tune.

Not that she wasn't ambitious. It was simply that her ambitions ran to the notion that physical comfort had priority over physical accomplishments.

She didn't care for brooding and was annoyed with herself for falling into the habit over the past few weeks. If anything she should be happy. Her life was moving along at a steady if unhurried pace. Her home and her family, equally important as her own comfort, were safe and whole. In fact, both were expanding along very satisfactory lines.

Her youngest sister, C.C., was back from her honeymoon and glowing like a rose. Amanda, the most practical of the Calhoun sisters, was madly in love and planning her own wedding.

The two men in her sisters' lives met with Lilah's complete approval. Trenton St. James, her new brother-in-law, was a crafty businessman with a soft heart under a meticulously tailored suit. Sloan O'Riley, with his cowboy boots and Oklahoma drawl, had her admiration for digging beneath Amanda's prickly exterior.

Of course, having two of her beloved nieces attached to wonderful men made Aunt Coco delirious with happiness. Lilah laughed a little, thinking how her aunt was certain she'd all but arranged the love affairs herself. Now, naturally, the Calhoun sisters' long-time guardian was itching to provide the same service for Lilah and her older sister Suzanna.

Good luck, Lilah wished her aunt. After a traumatic divorce, and with two young children to care for—not to mention a business to run—Suzanna wasn't likely to cooperate. She'd been badly burned once, and a smart woman didn't let herself get pushed into the fire.

For herself, Lilah had been doing her best to fall in love, to hear that vibrant inner click that came when you knew you'd found the one person in the world who was fated for you. So far, that particular chamber of her heart had been stubbornly silent.

There was time for that, she reminded herself. She was twenty-seven, happy enough in her work, surrounded by family. A few months before, they had nearly lost The Towers, the Calhoun's crumbling and eccentric home that stood on the cliffs overlooking the sea. If it hadn't been for Trent, Lilah might not have been able to stand in the tower room she loved so much and look out at the gathering storm.

So she had her home, her family, a job that interested her and, she reminded herself, a mystery to solve. Great-Grandmama Bianca's emeralds, she thought. Though she had never seen them, she was able to visualize them perfectly just by closing her eyes.

Two dramatic tiers of grass-green stones accented with icy diamonds. The glint of gold in the fancy filigree work. And dripping from the bottom strand, that rich and glowing teardrop emerald. More than its financial or even aesthetic value, it represented to Lilah a direct link with an ancestor who fascinated her, and the hope of eternal love.

The legend said that Bianca, determined to end a loveless marriage, had packed a few of her treasured belongings, including the necklace, into a box. Hoping to find a way to join her lover, she had hidden it. Before she had been able to take it out and start a life with Christian, she had despaired and leaped from the tower window to her death.

A tragic end to a romance, Lilah thought, yet she didn't always feel sad when she thought of it. Bianca's spirit remained in The Towers, and in that high room where Bianca had spent so many hours longing for her lover, Lilah felt close to her.

They would find the emeralds, she promised herself. They were meant to.

It was true enough that the necklace had already caused its problems. The press had learned of its existence and had played endlessly on the hidden-treasure angle. So successfully, Lilah thought now, that the annoyance had gone beyond curious tourists and amateur treasure hunters, and had brought a ruthless thief into their home.

When she thought of how Amanda might have been killed protecting the family's papers, the risk she had taken trying to keep any clue to the emeralds out of the wrong hands, Lilah shuddered. Despite Amanda's heroics, the man who had called himself William Livingston had gotten away with a sackful. Lilah sincerely hoped he found nothing but old recipes and unpaid bills.

William Livingston, alias Peter Mitchell, alias a dozen other names wasn't going to get his greedy hands on the emeralds. Not if the Calhoun women had anything to do about it. As far as Lilah was concerned, that included Bianca, who was as much a part of The Towers as the cracked plaster and creaky boards.

Restless, she moved away from the window. She couldn't say why the emeralds and the woman who had owned them preyed so heavily on her mind tonight. But Lilah was a woman who believed in instinct, in premonition, as naturally as she believed the sun rose in the east.

Tonight, something was coming.

She glanced back toward the window. The storm was rolling closer, gathering force. She felt a driving need to be outside to meet it.

DIANA PALMER
ANN MAJOR
SUSAN MALLERY

RETURN TO WHITEHORN

In **April 1998** get ready to catch the bouquet. Join in the excitement as these bestselling authors lead us down the aisle with three heartwarming tales of love and matrimony in Big Sky country.

A very engaged lady is having second thoughts about her intended; a pregnant librarian is wooed by the town bad boy; a cowgirl meets up with her first love. Which Maverick will be the next one to get hitched?

Available in **April 1998**.

Silhouette's beloved **MONTANA MAVERICKS** returns in Special Edition and Harlequin Historicals starting in February 1998, with brand-new stories from your favorite authors.

Round up these great new stories at your favorite retail outlet.

Take 4 bestselling love stories FREE

a FREE surprise gift!

Available in February 1998

ANN MAJOR

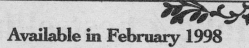

CHILDREN OF DESTINY
When Passion and Fate Intertwine...

SECRET CHILD

Although everyone told Jack West that his wife,
Chantal—the woman who'd betrayed him and sent
him to prison for a crime he didn't commit—had
died, Jack knew she'd merely transformed herself
into supermodel Mischief Jones. But when he
finally captured the woman he'd been hunting,
she denied everything. Who was she really—
an angel or a cunningly brilliant counterfeit?"

"Want it all? Read Ann Major."
—Nora Roberts, *New York Times*
bestselling author

Don't miss this compelling story
available at your favorite retail outlet.
Only from Silhouette books.

SUSAN MALLERY

Continues the twelve-book
series—36 HOURS—in
January 1998 with
Book Seven

THE RANCHER AND THE RUNAWAY BRIDE

When Randi Howell fled the altar, she'd been running for her
life! And she'd kept on running—straight into the arms of
rugged rancher Brady Jones. She knew he had his suspicions,
but how could she tell him the truth about her identity? Then
again, if she ever wanted to approach the altar in earnest, how
could she not?

For Brady and Randi and *all* the residents of Grand Springs,
Colorado, the storm-induced blackout was just the beginning
of 36 Hours that changed *everything!* You won't want to
miss a single book.

Available at your favorite retail outlet.

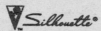